Praise for *The*

"*The Second Mother* is a gothic unraveling of a novel, as moody and atmospheric as the isolated island on which it's set."

—Jodi Picoult, *New York Times* bestselling author
of *Small Great Things* and *A Spark of Light*

"Rich in atmosphere, expertly plotted, and populated by characters that live and breathe, *The Second Mother* is as much a portrait of survival and redemption as it is a harrowing deep dive into the secrets and troubles of an isolated island in Maine. Jenny Milchman writes with insight and compassion, creating a vivid sense of place, and masterfully ratcheting up the tension page by gripping page."

—Lisa Unger, *New York Times* bestselling author
of *The Stranger Inside*

"*The Second Mother* is a tense, riveting story about a woman who flees to a remote island off the coast of Maine to escape a tragic past. Starkly beautiful, the island holds the hope of a new life and a new love, but schoolteacher Julie Weathers finds herself facing dangers she never imagined. Told with Milchman's stunning prose, *The Second Mother* is a gripping tale of obsession, secrets held close, and the dark side of island life. Harrowing and addictive, I dare you to put this book down once you've started."

—Heather Gudenkauf, *New York Times* bestselling author
of *The Weight of Silence* and *This Is How I Lied*

"When Julie arrives on a beautiful, rustic island off the coast of Maine—with a one-room schoolhouse, where people embrace a simple life—she is hoping for a chance to start over. Slowly and expertly, Milchman peels back the layers to reveal what lies beneath the idyllic surface. *The Second*

Mother is an atmospheric thriller resonating with the weight and power of secrets. Settle in someplace comfortable, lock the doors, and turn on the lights—you're not going to want to put this one down!"

—Jennifer McMahon, author of *The Winter People* and *The Invited*

"With her ever-masterful sense of place and astute psychological insight, Jenny Milchman takes us on a journey from the Adirondack Mountains to a remote island off the coast of Maine, and from the dark depths of grief into the light. This is a harrowing and heartrending story that earns its place in the sun."

—Carol Goodman, *New York Times* bestselling author of *The Lake of Dead Languages* and *The Sea of Lost Girls*

"Milchman owns a Highsmith mastery of emotional depth and psychological tension for all her rich, finely detailed settings. She is a true American regionalist artist. *The Second Mother* sweeps us away to an eerie island of complex villains, refreshingly women, that will chill your blood while it breaks your heart."

—Kalisha Buckhanon, author of *Speaking of Summer* and *Solemn*

"Jenny Milchman is one of the best suspense writers at work today, and *The Second Mother* is a page-turner extraordinaire. Milchman takes the nostalgic daydream of teaching in a one-room schoolhouse and turns it ever so slowly into an urgent nightmare. That the story is set on a remote island off the coast of Maine—one of the most claustrophobic places a stranger can ever set foot—is an added bonus."

—Paul Doiron, author of the Edgar Award–nominated Mike Bowditch series

Praise for *Wicked River*

"Milchman is the Swiss Army knife of thriller writers—*Wicked River* is partly a who-is-my-husband-really story, partly a horror-in-the-wilderness story, and partly a Manhattan-family drama, all rolled up in elegantly propulsive prose, and shot through with sinister suspense. The real mystery about Milchman is why she isn't already huge."

—Lee Child, *New York Times*
bestselling author of the Jack Reacher series

"On a honeymoon gone terribly awry, two newlyweds battle for their lives in a powerful story of survival told by one of the richest and most riveting voices in today's thriller fiction. From start to finish, *Wicked River* twists and tumbles and roars, carrying readers along for one hell of a thrill ride."

—William Kent Krueger, *New York Times*
bestselling author of *Ordinary Grace*

"*Wicked River* is an intriguing mix of hopes and fears. A tale fraught with danger, but loaded with place and character. It's spicy, smart, and entertaining."

—Steve Berry, *New York Times*
bestselling author of the Cotton Malone series

"A contemporary *Deliverance*, and a terrifying thrill ride into the darkest side of human nature. With a breakneck pace and shocking twists and turns around every bend, *Wicked River* will keep you up late at night—and haunt your dreams long after you're finished."

—Chevy Stevens, *New York Times*
bestselling author of *Still Missing* and *Those Girls*

"Riveting. A hybrid between John Fowles's classic *The Collector* and Erica Ferencik's *The River at Night*, this novel will appeal to fans of psychological suspense as well as those who enjoy trips to the backcountry."

—*Library Journal*

"Suspense oozes like blood from a wound on every page of Jenny Milchman's *Wicked River*. As scary and tense a book as I've read this year."

—John Lescroart, *New York Times* bestselling author of the Dismas Hardy series

"From time to time, I come across an action manuscript that shares my high regard for the [action] genre and the intensity it can achieve. One such book is Jenny Milchman's *Wicked River*, which I urge you to experience. It thoroughly gripped me, not only because of the excitement it creates and the inventiveness with which it does so, but also because of the subtext about a honeymoon in which the various stages of a marriage are condensed in a wilderness that's both physical and psychological. *Wicked River* is a wild ride."

—David Morrell, *New York Times* bestselling author of *First Blood*

"Jenny Milchman's characters jump off the page… *Wicked River* is compulsive reading—I kept holding my breath and turning the pages faster and faster. It's a book that should cement Jenny's place as a must-read thriller writer for fans hungry for domestic suspense in the style of Gillian Flynn."

—M. J. Rose, *New York Times* bestselling author

"Chock-full of suspense and danger, *Wicked River* by Jenny Milchman takes you on the journey of a lifetime, canoeing fast-moving rivers and hiking through tangled forests where humans have seldom trod. This is the story of Natalie and Doug's honeymoon. They wanted natural beauty and adventure; they get both, in abundance. You'll be glad you joined them. *Wicked River* is wicked thrilling!"

—Gayle Lynds, bestselling author
of *Masquerade* and *The Book of Spies*

"*Deliverance*, meet *Into the Wild*. Jenny Milchman knows how to construct a tautly wound, raw-boned thriller that will keep you up like the howl of wolves outside your tent."

—Andrew Gross, international bestselling author
of *The Blue Zone* and *The Dark Tide*

"A story about passion and betrayal on the high stakes stage, *Wicked River* is intensely gripping and perfectly paced—a real standout that pushes the domestic thriller category to its very edge. With her usual mastery of setting and character, Jenny Milchman has outdone herself."

—Carla Buckley, international bestselling
author of *The Good Goodbye*

the Second Mother

A NOVEL

Jenny Milchman

This one is for my brother and sister, Ezra and Kari, and for our parents, Alan and Madelyn, who made sure all our summers in Maine were times of beauty, peace, and togetherness.

Published by Sourcebooks Landmark, an imprint of Sourcebooks
P.O. Box 4410, Naperville, Illinois 60567-4410
(630) 961-3900
sourcebooks.com

Library of Congress Cataloging-in-Publication Data

Names: Milchman, Jenny, author.
Title: Second mother / Jenny Milchman.
Description: Naperville, IL : Sourcebooks Landmark, [2020]
Identifiers: LCCN 2019055787 | (trade paperback)
Classification: LCC PS3613.I47555 S43 2020 | DDC 813/.6--dc23
LC record available at https://lccn.loc.gov/2019055787

Printed and bound in the United States of America.
MA 10 9 8 7 6 5 4 3 2 1

PART I

FINDING MERCY

CHAPTER ONE

J ulie Mason found the ad on Opportunity.com, the site she frequented the most, in part because of its optimistic name. It seemed the essence of simplicity: clear and unambiguous in meaning. May as well have been called NewLife.com, although that might've sounded a little religious.

Looking to start all over again? the site's marketing message beckoned. *We can help.* Julie just lurked, had never taken an actual step forward with any of the opportunities that were posted. So far it was enough to read the listings, imagine other lives.

This latest post fit her qualifications, though, and its old-fashioned wording drew her eye. Like a classified ad from days of old, all those small, perfect squares lined up in columns above and below a newspaper fold. So many people searching for a second chance, and so many chances on offer.

Julie wasn't the only one with something to leave behind.

This particular *opportunity* seemed to come from a world that time forgot, one that had vanished in the crush of modern-day life, which had also crushed Julie.

Opportunity: Teacher needed for one-room schoolhouse on remote island in Maine. Certification in grades K-8 a must.

Julie read the post a second time, then a third, before glancing down at the clock in the corner of the screen. Nearly noon. Four whole hours gone since she'd sat down at the computer. This was how time passed for her these days, not in a fluid, comprehensible stream, or even streaking by, falling-star fast. Instead, it was as if time had a beast lapping at its heels, taking great, gobbling bites.

David wouldn't be home for hours still. And if she was going to give some thought to a real, actual *opportunity*, then she should eat lunch. That was what normal people who inhabited normal lives—lives where things moved, and changed, and were accomplished—did around noon.

The only problem was that she wasn't hungry, and she didn't think there was likely to be much food in the house anyway. Over the past year, they'd been subsisting on supermarket salads and sandwiches, pizza for a diversion. David had never really gotten the hang of grocery shopping. That had always been Julie's task, along with housecleaning, which explained why the floors were gritty underfoot, and the furniture languished beneath an opaque veil of dust like discards from Miss Havisham's attic.

Their finances were probably in tip-top order, however. And the yard looked shipshape, green and blooming at this height of summer, while never overgrown. Ole didn't-miss-a-step David saw to that.

Julie pushed the chair back from the desk she and her husband shared, its wheels grinding bits of dirt into the floorboards. David did the aforementioned finances here, and once, a long, long time ago, eons to her mind, Julie had used the laptop to communicate with the parents of her fifth-grade students and keep up with work on the school portal.

One year.

As of five days ago, it had been exactly a year, which meant that Julie had already lived this date, another July 28, without Hedley. Each day in which her daughter didn't take part was a new ordeal to be gotten through, a fresh cut in Julie's skin.

She stood up, legs wobbly from inactivity, or perhaps from the prospect of leaving the house. But maybe if she went out to a place where she could see and smell food, it would trigger her appetite. Her shorts slid downward alarmingly on her hips; Julie couldn't recall the last full meal she'd eaten.

Nowadays she nibbled. Bites here and there. Partial plates.

She patted her empty pockets. Cash and keys. That was the first step.

In Wedeskyull, New York, a town almost as remote as the island Julie had just read about, you didn't have to worry about locking doors. Julie skipped the step of locating her purse; how would she possibly find it in the unkempt clutter of the house? A quick peek in her closet, where her bag usually hung, revealed a tangle of clothes and the teetering stack of her old CD and DVD collection—soundtracks, shows, and musicals sequestered away now that she no longer played them for Hedley.

Julie settled for taking the Ford's extra keyless remote along with money from David's neat stack of emergency bills.

Her husband's punctilious ways kept their lives in order, and had probably enabled them to survive this past year. Without heat, you could die during an Adirondack winter. Every log in David's woodshed lay like a soldier in a bunk, and his barn looked like a Home Depot ad: carefully maintained equipment and tools, each stray screw and nail stored in a tiny box or tray. David also kept an online calendar, color coded for both him and Julie. Only lately had his methods started to register on her as smart and utilitarian, but also hollow, devoid of the emotion she craved. The life.

NewLife.com

Julie gave a hard shake of her head. That wasn't right. She'd go online again as soon as she got back, open the bookmarked tab for Opportunity.com—that was its name—then reread the post about the one-room schoolhouse. Both activities might take up enough of the day that sleep could be a reasonable next step, aided by some liquid assistance combined with half of one of the pills Dr. Trask had prescribed. Julie was down to three-quarters of a bottle from her last refill, and carefully conserving. In Wedeskyull and the surrounding towns, meds were no longer dispensed with a free hand. But Julie wasn't going to think about what would happen when her supply ran out, how she would ever sleep more than five minutes at a stretch again. Trask knew she was still relying on pharmaceuticals; maybe he'd have mercy.

Julie scuffed across the driveway, the heels of her flip-flops flapping loosely. Had even her *feet* shrunk, every bit of her diminished now, whittled away?

She started the Ford, its wheel feeling alien in her hands, as if the power steering had failed. Every inch of rotation was arduous, effortful. The road, once she backed out of their drive, didn't look familiar. Had it always been this steep and winding? The SUV seemed poised to topple at the start of a hill, fall nose over tail, like a kid rolling down a lawn.

Julie braked in the middle of the road. One advantage to living on the edge of the wilderness: there was no other car in sight to deliver a beep of protest. She felt around for the gas pedal with her foot and began again to drive.

When had she last been out on her own? After, David was always with her. And before, it would've been Hedley, tiny in age and size, but huge in terms of the space she took up in Julie's life. Since her daughter's birth, Julie hadn't experienced much in the way of aloneness, had even resented that reality, fighting for hard-won fractions of time like every new mother: *Can I just take a shower, finish a cup of tea, or better yet, a nightcap without being interrupted by this sudden, all-consuming presence?*

The space in the rear of the Ford yawned, as dark and empty as a cave. They mostly took David's car now, on the rare occasions that Julie did go out. She'd scarcely been inside this one in over a year. Oh God, Hedley's car seat was still belted in back there, secured as required by law—so many parents got it wrong, but Julie's closest friend was a cop—yet so unspeakably vacant.

Julie hit the brake so hard the Ford jolted, and her chest struck the steering wheel with which she'd just been doing battle.

Only this time there was a car nearby, and it sheered around the SUV with a Doppler's whine of wind and a furious blast of its horn, making Julie throw up one of her hands in a futile, unseen gesture of apology before driving off in halting spurts and stops.

CHAPTER TWO

J ulie decided not to go to the Crescent Diner, the place her uncles
and grandfather used to frequent for a bite between shifts on the
job. On the rare occasions when Julie's father and mother had eaten out,
they'd also been customers at the diner. Nor did Julie choose to go to
the new, upscale café in town, which her mom and dad might've liked,
had they still been alive when it opened. Fancy salads and wraps and
expensive coffee drinks that cost more than most longtime residents'
daily food budgets. "What's wrong with plain black?" Julie could hear
her uncle, the former police chief, asking.

Instead, Julie pulled up in front of a store that barely had a name, at
least not one that anybody remembered. The letters on its aged sign had
faded to the point of invisibility. An old-fashioned general store, or The
Store to the locals, as in, I have to pick up some soap at The Store. Or
pants even. Or berries, sold in season in gleaming rows of jewel-filled
cartons on the front porch. Julie had a different mental name for the
place, almost a term of endearment. The Everything Store. Its wares

had provided distraction for a baby, enabling Julie to get shopping done during the most tender stages of new motherhood.

Her heart thrummed in her chest as she parked. She sat staring through the car window at The Everything Store's facade till her eyes started to tear.

They have sandwiches here, Julie told herself, stabbing the button to turn off the engine. *I can get something to eat.*

The door opened with a welcoming jangle of bells that gave Julie a chill. She looked around before entering to see if the temperature had dropped, leaves showing their underbellies in the type of wind that preceded a thunderstorm, clouds rolling in. But the sun shone warmly in a cornflower-blue sky and the day was still, the kind of weather seen in Wedeskyull only a handful of weeks out of the year.

Julie rubbed her goose-pimply arms and went inside.

The first section to greet her was the easiest: hangers and racks with tees and sweatshirts on display, *Wedeskyull* silk-screened over a row of jagged mountaintops that looked like teeth. Then camouflage gear in adult and youth sizes. After that came camping and outdoors equipment, with portable hunting blinds and crossbows next. Guns were kept behind a glass case to Julie's left, taken for granted enough in her life that their dark, threatening lengths and sleek triggers curving like grins didn't trouble her.

Beyond the guns stood the lunch counter. Julie could swerve right now—stroll past the glassed-in case, or veer in the opposite direction, toward where moccasins sat in boxes on shelves—and avoid the area in front of her entirely.

She had shopped and browsed, hung out and played here, each stage a marker in reverse of the years of her life. Married with enough money to make purchases. A window-shopping single woman, seeing which new goods had come in, but trying to conserve her dollars. A teenager killing time over a soda and candy with friends. A kid at her mother's heels, or a baby in a stroller, as the mysterious tasks required to keep house were taken care of.

Julie could thread her way to the row of stools without looking and not even stumble. Perch on top of a cracked vinyl seat and order a tuna-fish sandwich and iced tea, food as simple and old-fashioned as the want ad she'd read a thousand years ago that morning. Instead, she walked forward as if pulled by a rope. The act had a compulsive, unstoppable feel, a victim returning to the scene of the crime.

These clothes were different from the ones that had faced her when she came in. Tiny onesies and miniature sweaters hand knit by local women, priced at amounts that, even in Julie's near-mesmerized state, seemed shocking, exorbitant. Board books about nature, pairs of fur-lined booties so tiny, both would fit on Julie's palm. Sock animals and corn-husk dolls. Slightly less frivolous items like organic teething biscuits and herbal remedies for nursing moms.

Julie spun around, turning her back, but it was too late. Memories began swarming her like wasps. She tried to bat them away, fight them off, but failed and dropped to her knees.

She couldn't explain the sudden flurry of white; it was as if it had begun snowing right here in The Everything Store. Cloth diapers, Julie saw through blurred eyes, made of fair trade cotton, the packaging somehow torn open, no, *clawed* open, so that the squares fell in a pile on her lap. Julie leaned down, burying her face in the sweet-smelling heap until it grew sodden, plugging her nose and mouth.

"Um, miss? Ma'am?"

Julie looked up, and the woman leaning over her, her pregnant stomach a swell that blocked out sight of anything else, took a sudden, lurching step back.

"I think…we need some help over here!" the woman cried.

Julie bunched up the white drift of cloth in her hands, squeezing it tighter and tighter. It was like a ball, an object that could be thrown.

Thrown at this horrible person with her immense belly, and her innocent, concerned face, just trying to help because she hadn't yet learned that there were some situations that could never, ever be helped.

From the side of The Everything Store where a cordless phone clung to the wall—it had been a modernization not so long ago, replacing the kind of contraption with a curlicued wire—Julie heard a series of bleeps. The store clerk made the call matter-of-factly, her voice bleached of sympathy, allowing Julie a shred of dignity.

Chief.

Not the old chief, thank God, Julie's grandfather, nor the son who came after him.

You mind coming down here?

The next voice Julie heard was husky and deep, echoing in her ear. Julie had known this voice when it was less husky, and not yet deep.

"Come on, Jules," Tim Lurcquer said quietly, squatting beside her.

She blinked.

"Come on," he repeated. "You'll feel better once we leave."

Tim got to his feet—a faint creak from his knees as he rose that surprised her—and extended a hand, strong enough to pull Julie upright. The cloth of his uniform shirt felt crisp despite the summer heat.

She held out a twisted clutch of plastic. "I have to buy these diapers." That was what you did if you broke something accidentally in a store. Or ruined it with malice and fury. Maybe you paid double then. "Also, I think I might've assaulted a woman."

Tim took the packaging from Julie's hand, his touch slow and gentle, as if she were a deer or a sparrow, some sort of wild animal that would shy away from human contact. "No," he said, his voice so kind it caused an ache. "You don't. There's not a person in this town who would take your money."

11

Tim pulled up in front of Julie's house in his police-issue vehicle, a luxury 4×4 that was a relic of another age. A whole other Wedeskyull, a different kind of regime. Subsidized by the wealthy to keep the powerful in charge. Julie's uncle used to drive this Mercury; the model wasn't even made anymore.

Of the Weathers men living here since the town was incorporated, Julie's father had been an outlier. Younger by a fair shake compared to his two brothers, and the only male in the family not to enter law enforcement. He'd chosen logging instead, and had died in a chain-saw accident. Julie sometimes saw her dad's premature death as a near-Grecian tragedy. Scandal and wrongdoing had undone the cops in her family, and although her father had attempted to rebel, find his own way, in the end he had been toppled too.

She unlatched her seat belt, which had imprinted a band of sweat across her shirt. Tim had powered both windows down, and it'd felt cool enough as he drove along at a good clip, but now the air grew swampy and hot.

"It's not the loss that kills you," Tim said.

She looked at him sharply, and he lifted both hands off the steering wheel, flattening his palms. A gesture of retreat, of surrender. But then he went on. "It's the guilt. I see it all the time on the job. Guilt makes it so there are at least two deaths for every one."

Julie's nose plugged solid with tears.

"But I can't imagine less reason for guilt than you have, Jules. There was just nothing you did wrong. Not one goddamned thing."

She pressed two fingers hard against her eyes. "I'm going to leave, Tim." Her throat was raw from crying, and the words came out rusty.

"Take your time." The engine rumbled patiently.

Julie was shocked to feel a small smile lift her lips. At his assumption,

THE SECOND MOTHER

the idea that even a move so small as that would require preparation on her part. Of course, just a couple of hours ago, it had. Then there came a trickle of something Julie hadn't experienced in so long it was all but unrecognizable. Hope. Or at least a dawning awareness that she might be headed toward something. Which was maybe the same thing.

She had grown up here, brought the husband she'd met online back to her hometown, never spent more than a vacation week away. But now there was a newfound sense of movement, a feeling of things tugging and shifting inside her.

"No," she said, turning to face Tim. "I mean that I'm going to leave Wedeskyull."

13

CHAPTER THREE

Certain entries on Opportunity.com—house swaps and anything involving a caretaker, for instance—could be counted on to go fast. But jobs tended to stick around longer, more variables involved on both sides in getting the right fit, and the site prided itself on a high rate of successful matches.

Julie brought up the submission form. Once it was filled out, the original poster could communicate directly with the user, send paperwork to be completed, set up a phone call or even an in-person interview. She clicked on the first box and typed in her last name. Then came first, middle initial, address, marital status. *Married*, Julie entered.

She stumbled over the tiny box into which you could enter your number of children—the drop-down went as high as twelve, good Lord—before leaving it blank and moving on. Choosing "0" seemed an erasure too cruel to bear.

Were you still a mother when you weren't a mother anymore? What became of the role, the identity, once the child was gone?

A series of slots requested background information: where Julie had grown up, gone to college, fields she'd worked in other than teaching. Then came questions about her qualifications for this position, which Julie answered, fingers moving easily across the keys. The consolidated nature of Wedeskyull's school meant that all the students were grouped together in one building, and due to perennial understaffing, teachers got switched around constantly. Julie had classroom experience in each of the grades taught on the place she'd just learned was called Mercy Island.

She opened a tab to Google it after she sent in this application, her hands hovering over the keyboard as she considered one final question.

Why is this opportunity the opportunity for you, and why are you right for it?

That one was going to take a little longer than the rest had. Still, Julie could envision crafting her statement and how it would be received, the seamless slide of a perfect fit. She paused as she considered, staring through the screen on the bedroom window. She was already steps ahead in her mind, having procured the job, making preparations to leave.

Packing would be an ordeal. So many things had been hastily stowed in the wake of Hedley's absence. Swing, highchair, stroller—objects Julie could no longer bear to look at, all boxed away or simply shoved into closets, to be dealt with during a later that never seemed to come.

But other steps would be easier, like slipping out of the pared-down life she was now living. And David could work from anywhere. He was a freelance journalist—one of the few still making a living in an age of vanishing pubs and free content—and even earned enough to rent a room in town where he wrote. He said that getting dressed each morning and leaving the house made him more productive.

Car wheels ground over the gravel in the drive. *Speak of the devil,* Julie thought, with her second partial smile of the day. Or if not a smile, at least some movement of her mouth, her mind, both of which had felt encased in cement for over a year.

David's car engine turned off, leaving only quiet ticking amidst the cricket hum and gentle whoosh of wind through broad, fleshy leaves outside.

Lately David been working longer hours, and it didn't seem like he should be home already; then again, time wavered in and out so unreliably for her these days. Maybe it was later than she thought. But glancing at the computer screen, Julie saw that it was only four o'clock. She looked toward the window again.

David had just opened the back door of his car to let their dog out. Depot jumped down with the resounding bark that signaled reunion.

"She's in town, boy," David called as Depot bounded up the porch steps.

Her car was missing from the driveway, Julie realized. David's off-hand comment didn't take into account how radical the trip had been for her. Her husband missed a lot, although not, thankfully, their nightly ritual, which she was in sore need of right now.

The window already wide open to let in the warm summer air, Julie lifted the screen and leaned out. "I'm home, I'm here!"

Depot gave a satisfied bark, while David craned his head to look up at the second floor. His eyes reflected the sun, making his expression unreadable.

Julie blinked in the bright glare. "The car's in town. I had, um, a problem."

"Yes," David said, voice traveling through the still remainder of the day. "I heard you were in town today."

So he knew. Well, at least that justified his lack of surprise at the fact that she'd gone out. The memory of those crumpled-up diapers returned, and as the sun struck her skin, Julie's cheeks grew hot. But the incident felt somehow distant, a long time ago already, perhaps because of the opportunity she now had to pursue.

David's tread sounded heavy on the porch. Julie went to meet their dog at the top of the second floor staircase, Depot's bulk hitting her, rocking her back on her heels.

"How was your day, Deep?" she murmured.

Back when Julie was still teaching, she couldn't come home in the middle of a school day to give Depot the exercise a big dog needed, and anyhow, David said that having him around for company while he worked made the words flow. But Depot's presence would've been nice during the infinite hours of Julie's days this past year, time no longer blown up like a balloon, expanded by the chores of new motherhood. David had voiced concern that a change in routine might be disturbing to their dog; after all, Depot was grieving Hedley too. He used to lie beside the baby's Moses basket, face between his front paws as he kept his eyes open, taking in the nursery.

Depot was so big that the baby basket couldn't be seen when he lay down in front of it. Long after she'd outgrown it, Hedley still preferred to nap in the basket, and sometimes Julie would come in and startle for a second at the sight of the empty crib, envisioning the terror that would've arisen if Hedley had been snatched by some stranger. One of the things that plagued Julie now was the fear that she'd brought on Hedley's disappearance from their lives by foreseeing it once too often.

Depot twitched in Julie's grasp, a full body shake sufficient to reposition her. Julie felt herself smile; that made three times today. "You trying to wrestle or just get away?" she asked.

If a switch in routine had worried David, what was he going to think about a total change of environment for their dog? On the other hand, David had never fully adjusted to life in Wedeskyull, hadn't come to love it as Julie had hoped he would. He might be perfectly happy to leave.

She bestowed a final pat to their dog, who raced down the stairs in search of food, while Julie herself moved more slowly down the flight of steps. David wasn't in the living room, nor the kitchen either. Poor guy knew there wouldn't be much to eat. Well, she would change that,

Julie resolved. A return to the land of the living—a *different* land of the living—signified life starting up again. She wondered about the food situation on Mercy Island. Did you have to cook every meal—in which case David was going to need to muster some skills—or was there takeout?

She glimpsed him through a screen door that led to an enclosed deck. "David?"

A mere whisper. Her husband didn't look up. She and David had lost the ability to talk in normal tones. Julie coughed, started over.

"How would you feel about moving to an island in Maine?"

CHAPTER FOUR

David twisted to look at her, a cold, beaded bottle of beer in one hand. *That* he had known how to keep the house stocked with. They'd never once run out of beer. To be fair, David always kept a bottle of Julie's brand of scotch around too.

He stood by a screened wall at the back of the deck, looking out over the garden. Tidy rows of regimented flowers. Julie wondered how the perfectly tended beds would fare once she and David left. Depended on the new residents. Should they rent out their place, put someone in charge of Airbnb-ing it maybe, or sell it outright?

The thought prompted a sudden tingle, like the sensation of a foot waking up. Not entirely pleasant, except in how inarguably *there* it was, novel to feel anything again at all. "David? Did you hear what I said?"

"I heard." He took a long swig from his bottle.

The slow, sweet slide of scotch down her throat had made a lot of hours, over the past year and probably others before that, recede into a tolerable haze. Julie had been longing for such a state just a few minutes ago. But suddenly, she wanted to be sharp.

"You okay, honey?" she asked. "Did you have a rough day?"

"Not as rough as yours," he answered. A pause. "Care for a drink?"

From a glass-topped cart, he produced a tumbler and a fifth of scotch, already half-emptied by other cocktails, prior drinking nights. Julie hesitated before taking the generous fingerful David had poured, and her husband closed her hand around the glass.

"Go on," he said. "Looks like you need it."

Neither his words nor the offering conveyed much kindness, but Julie lifted the glass, cool in her hand, and took a sip. The taste, its instant effect, blotted out the quiver of shame that had passed through her upon hearing David's assessment of her day.

"I think things are going to get better now," she said. "*I'm* going to get better."

No reply.

"This island... Can I tell you about it?"

David plunked his bottle down, soldier-straight, not a wobble. "I can't do this anymore."

Julie looked at him. It wasn't as if such incidents transpired regularly for her, although yes, there had been more than one, especially in the initial days, weeks, maybe months. "I know. Me either. But what happened today—I don't mean the thing in town, something else—"

"Thing," David repeated. "Is that the euphemism we're using?"

Julie flinched. How had she missed the anger in his tone, in his whole demeanor? David's body was rigid all over with fury.

She struggled to hit a light note. "Well, whatever you call it, this was the worst one ever. Do you know I actually hit a woman? Not *hit her* hit her. But I threw a wad of diapers definitely in her direction—"

David spoke over her. "This is starting to get humiliating. For you, I mean. I'm not concerned about myself. Having a meltdown in front of a bunch of strangers—"

Julie felt a small charge of her own anger. "These aren't strangers! They're my lifelong friends. Family almost."

"Well, your friend the store clerk didn't exactly see fit to take care of you like family, did she?" David replied bitingly. "She called the police. Yes, that's who I heard from." A pause for an acerbic quip. "Small-town living."

Heat returned to Julie's face on a painful back draft. She swallowed her drink in one gulp, then blotted her lips with her hand. "She was just trying to help."

David's shoulders sank, a sudden softening. He poured Julie a second nip. "You're right. And she was right, too, I suppose. Because I sure haven't been able to do that."

"Oh, David." Julie drew nearer, touching her husband's bare arm. The feel of his skin ignited something long lost. David dressed in button-down shirts to write, but tonight, perhaps on account of the warm weather, he had rolled up his sleeves. The look lent her husband an uncharacteristic vulnerability. "Is that what this is about?"

He didn't respond, though he also didn't step away.

"It isn't you. It isn't anything you've done, or haven't done. I just... I miss Hedley. That's all. I don't mean that's all. What a stupid thing to say. That's everything."

"Everything," David repeated. Venom had returned to his voice.

"Not everything," Julie amended. "There's us. I'm sorry if I've seemed to forget that lately." She'd taken David for granted. He would be there whenever she crawled out of the dark place created by Hedley's loss because he occupied the same cave.

Depot nosed open the screen door, padding up beside Julie. His snout glistened, giving off a meaty odor, the way it always did after a meal. Depot wasn't a neat eater. Julie glanced inside the house. Aside from the Saturn's ring of nuggets scattered around Depot's bowl, the kitchen looked clean to the point of sterility, uninhabited and scentless.

David seemed to follow her thoughts. "It's like I'm married to a shell. It's not even you in there anymore."

"It is me. More than it's been in a long time. Let me tell you what I did today."

He let out a scoff. "Before or after you lost your marbles in town?"

Julie felt her legs sag. Depot moved closer, and his mass served to steady her. "That sucks," she said. "I understand that you're angry—I even think I understand why—but don't you dare make me feel crazy. What happened to me could send anybody—"

"It didn't just happen to you!" David roared. He swept out a hand, grabbing the beer bottle before it could topple off the cart.

With a single step, Depot edged David backward, away from Julie.

It had been an atypical loss of control. David was a careful man who moved in precise, contained ways. He printed articles out in neat stacks to proofread, collated his notes, planted seeds in ruler-straight rows. Made love with slow, steady strokes; grieved with silent tears, one tissue dampened at a time. Even his drinking rarely grew sloppy.

"It happened to us," David said. "You act as if I have no right to be bereft."

"I don't think that at all!" Julie cried. Though, of course, it was she who had been with Hedley at the time, and maybe deep down, Julie did feel that worsened her burden. The shock of checking the stroller and not being sure at first, having to lean over and really look, study the folds of blanket under the hood. "I know you're mourning too."

David scrubbed a hand across his face, smoothing his hair back into place.

Julie took it as a sign of withdrawal. This unusually heated skirmish would pass, become one more part of an amorphous, indistinct mass of sodden days and sullen silences. Her husband let out a breath and Julie did too.

He crouched to give Depot a pat. "It's all right, boy. I'm sorry if I scared you." Then he stood up again. "I think we need a break."

"A break?" she echoed. *But we're going to Maine.* The dazzling prospect, which had yanked Julie out of the darkness, seemed suddenly absurd.

David gave a firm shake of his head. "Not a break."

Thank God. Julie wasn't sure if she'd breathed the words out loud.

"I want a divorce," David said. "I'm sorry. I did talk with my therapist about a trial separation first. But…"

"You have a therapist?"

He gave a nod. "I've been seeing her after I finish up work for the day."

Such a healthy way to process grief and trauma. Julie wondered why she hadn't thought of the same thing herself, or why they hadn't chosen to see someone together. Her law-enforcement family had never been big on therapy; they tended to spurn outside intervention.

"What I realized is that asking for a separation would be for your sake. To spread out the blow, because you've suffered so much already."

"Yes, how good of you that would be," Julie whispered.

"Whereas what I really want is a permanent change," David went on. "I don't want to be married anymore. Did you know that the loss of a child ends marriages in five out of ten cases?"

"Did your therapist tell you that?" Julie asked, snapped really.

David regarded her. "As a matter of fact, she did."

"I wonder if she also explained why you've chosen to fall into the fifty percent that gives up instead of the other half?" Julie asked. The thin skin of shock was peeling away, revealing a cold, blunt pain that she well recognized. Depot twined between her knees and Julie sank to the floor, wrapping her arms around the dog's thick neck.

David stepped over the two of them with soldierly precision.

"It'll be better for us both this way," he told Julie on his way out. "You'll see."

CHAPTER FIVE

Julie stayed on the deck with the dog, listening to David walk around overhead, gathering things from their bedroom. Then the front door snicked shut, David giving one firm tug to latch it, before he got into his car and backed out over the gravel drive.

Julie trudged up the stairs trailed by Depot, and headed over to the computer. Thank God David hadn't taken it. He had his work machine, probably figured he could allow Julie this shared one. In addition to being careful and deliberate, David was a considerate husband, treating Julie thoughtfully—from the steady supply of scotch to his support of her decision not to return to work once Hedley was gone—and Julie didn't know how she was supposed to survive when not one soul on the planet needed her for anything, nor would be there to meet any of her needs. She felt a sob thicken her throat.

Depot wedged himself beneath the desk, lying down heavily on her feet. It wasn't exactly a pleasant sensation—Depot weighed a lot—but

Julie accepted the discomfort as penance. *It's your fault,* said a voice inside her, less accusatory than descriptive, matter-of-fact.

Julie reached down and delivered a sudden, jerky pat to the dog, who squirmed away in protest. She jabbed the laptop to life, and the search she'd already opened appeared. *Mercy Island.* The words blinked like a beacon. Julie clicked and a series of pages appeared: wiki, tourism sites, boat outfitters, restaurants, an invitation to plan a trip at VisitMercy.com.

She spent some time tabbing through the feast of links before finally pulling herself away, recalling the not yet completed form. Beginning to review the information that had been filled in, she skidded to a sudden halt. How was she going to explain being out of work? She would seem like a basket case or, at the very least, less in the run of things than someone merely looking to make a job change versus reenter the field after a year's gap. Unless…what if Julie could use the still unanswered longer form question to demonstrate what she had begun to feel, which was that the loss she'd suffered in some way *qualified* her for this position at a faraway, distant outpost rather than someone who might be gainfully employed, but had never experienced what she had?

Julie's fingers began to move, slowly at first, then faster, lines accruing in the box. Before long, it was as if her brain weren't doing the composing, but instead was taking dictation from some celestial source.

You have 75 words left.

Then *23*

8

Finally, Julie's hands stilled, a last dot of punctuation applied like a final dab of paint. On a whim, she tried to add a comma, but it didn't appear in the box. Her answer had consumed every single character permitted, and not one more.

It felt as if she'd been in a state of hypnosis. Julie began to reread her words, dimly aware that Depot must have gotten bored at some point and wandered off.

During my decade-plus of teaching, I have experienced challenges of a professional sort, which might be typical in this field, but lately personal ones too. Being close to children, the original motivation for my career choice, became the very thing that drove me away from it for a while. During that time, I became isolated in a way I never had before, and it taught me, the teacher, something. In years past, I saw my students struggle to connect, and I struggled to assist them. I would not find it hard now. I am prepared to help a new crop of children forge connections, not only with their peers, but within themselves. I believe this will apply especially to the unusual conditions on Mercy Island with its multi-age learning environment. I know about trying, stumbling, then getting up again, lessons students need to learn to grow into resilient young adults.

Was it too much, being so honest and open on a job application? Opportunity.com claimed to utilize a method that could look past exterior traits to identify people's unspoken needs and desires. It had sounded a little spooky to Julie at first, intrusive anyway, but the preponderance of testimonials and five-star reviews—over seventy percent of the site's users left feedback—changed her thinking. Whatever Opportunity.com was doing worked, resulted in lasting pairings.

Too bad marriages couldn't be driven by the same algorithm.

Julie clicked the button to submit the form, then let her gaze fall from the screen. Her eyes felt hot and dry, as if she'd written the whole thing without blinking. She flexed cramped fingers and stood up, looking around for Depot.

A yawn overtook her. Since losing Hedley, sleep seemed to exist on a distant, unreachable planet, but at least Julie had had the comfort of lying beside someone she loved. As lonely as she felt, she hadn't been truly alone. But if she pulled back the quilt on her and David's bed now, it would give off a whiff of cold vapor, feel as flat and unwelcoming as an Arctic plain.

Julie went downstairs to the kitchen, which emitted an even emptier aura. David had taken two glasses, a plate and bowl, some cutlery. He'd also removed his favorite bottle opener. Where did he intend to stay? Could it be with someone else? Had David cheated on Julie as he planned their demise? She was suddenly convinced that he had, certainly a python constriction around her throat.

The bottle from the deck stood empty. It had been drained; she wasn't sure when.

Julie spun around, already unsteady on her feet, as if anticipating the respite she craved. She faced the row of cupboards on the wall. She pulled one door open, leaving it ajar—a minute lapse David would've quickly remedied—before looking inside the next. This one was over her head, and she had to stand on tiptoes, feeling around on the shelf.

Nudging a vessel forward, taking painstaking care not to let it fall and smash on the floor, Julie finally got hold of a fresh bottle. Amber liquid sloshed as she pulled out the stopper and breathed in the aroma. Filling a water goblet, she took a long, searing pull and went out to the living room to find Depot.

He wasn't there. On the deck? But she'd secured the door; in the wake of David's abandonment, she hadn't wanted to leave the house open to the outdoors.

Julie checked anyway, taking fortifying sips of her drink.

The deck was dark and empty. Night had enveloped everything while she'd been upstairs at the computer. How much time had passed? Enough to allow something to happen to Depot that she wouldn't even have registered?

It came for him too, said the knowing voice. *You* let *it come for him.*

Julie slapped a hand against her chest, where the voice seemed to live, right beneath her beating heart. She sipped from the glass as she squinted into the corners. She refused to flick on a light, cast a vision of herself out into the penetrating night, even though the house faced only forest. Crickets could be heard, a gritty buzz through the screens, but otherwise all was quiet.

No snuffling sound of a sleeping dog's breaths, and Depot was too big to overlook.

With the muffling effect of alcohol serving to stave off panic, Julie took a last swallow, draining the glass, then made her way out to the front hall.

A piece of paper lay on the floor, white in the darkness.

CHAPTER SIX

The source of the note was obvious, written in David's fastidious hand.

Julie, I came to get Depot. I figured you haven't been on your own with him in a while, and I didn't want you to get overwhelmed.

Julie stared at the words till they blurred. She'd been so involved with filling out the application that she'd entirely missed David's arrival, and him absconding with their dog. Julie didn't need any voice haunting her when she had her own husband to demonstrate that she couldn't care for anybody anymore, that no one should be allowed to depend on her ever again.

She pressed two fingers to her eyes so hard that it hurt, then looked down again at the sheet of paper.

Over the next few weeks, we'll have to talk about logistics.

Logistics. What a David word. When she'd met her husband-to-be, his organization and meticulousness had wooed her; they seemed to suggest a man who would never let their lives go awry. But over the years, those traits had lost their appeal.

> *But let's wait on that for now. I hope you have an*
> *okay night.*

We can't wait, Julie retorted in her head. *In a few weeks, I'll have a new job and be living on Mercy Island.*

At least for the purposes of this mental argument with her guilty-of-desertion husband, Julie would declare with absolute certainty that she already had said job, even though in fact she'd only just clicked Send on an application.

Still, it was late July. The start of the school year would vary by district, but couldn't be more than four or five weeks off. Given the substantial move, if she *were* offered the position, Julie would have to get going soon.

But not without her dog.

She let her gaze drift downward.

No sign-off, certainly no *love,* or even a *warmly,* which she supposed would've been worse: fake feeling that somehow connoted its opposite.

Just her husband's meticulously scripted name.

Julie crumpled the piece of paper into a ball. At some point, she'd gone from leaning against the wall to sliding down it, and now she sat, legs splayed, on the floor. She was going to have to get up if she intended to bring Depot home. Which she did. No way was she spending the night alone in this house.

Julie felt around for her glass before recalling that it was empty.

Probably best not to go for a refill when she had to drive.

She patted the pocket of her shorts, which made the series of afternoon events come back to her in a sluggish swirl. Had Tim returned her car?

Julie pulled at the front door, finding that heat and humidity had swelled the wood. When she finally got it open, she stumbled back, coming to a rest on the floor again.

Can't drive from here, she thought, beginning to clamber up, first hands and knees, then onto her feet, wondering what David would say if he were to see her messy maneuvers—

Don't think about David right now. Focus on Depot.

That wasn't any voice besides her own, administering good common sense advice. Julie peered outside, gratified to see the Ford parked in the driveway. Another unseen arrival. Tim must've come while she was working, or looking for Depot, or nose-deep in a glass of scotch. Julie padded out to the lawn, not realizing she'd forgotten shoes until she registered the blades of grass sticking to the soles of her feet.

Probably just as safe as driving in flip-flops.

She walked onto the driveway—bare feet hurting now, the gravel like a bed of broken glass—and crossed to the driver's side door. Inside the car, she set her phone in the well between the seats. There wasn't reliable signal between the house and... Where was she going anyway? Where was David likely to be? Julie figured she would drive into town, at which point her phone would become sentient and she could call him.

She let her back sag against the seat of the Ford. Her fingers fell from the button that ignited the engine, or perhaps Julie lowered her hand herself.

She couldn't drive anywhere tonight, endanger someone on the road, or Depot if she was able to successfully fetch him. She must have filled that glass awfully high; Julie wasn't used to pouring her own drinks. She felt past tipsy and most of the way to drunk.

She would get Depot tomorrow. Determine where David had gone once her mental state was clearer. Then fight her husband for their dog if necessary.

Julie's eyelids grew heavy. Curling onto her side, she reached down to recline the seat. Outside, a cradle of moon hooked the sky. Hedley had never slept in a cradle. Just the basket, then finally her crib for a short while. Stars pierced the sheet of mirrored black. So far away, impossible to touch or reach, that Julie started crying.

She must've continued to cry in her sleep, or started again as morning came on, because her face was wet when she got jolted awake by the buzzing of her phone.

Julie felt her heart clench like a fist inside her.

It was a notification from her Opportunity.com account.

We were pleased to receive your application for the position of teacher on Mercy Island. We intend to schedule calls with potential candidates before holding interviews. Please click the link to select a date and time for an initial phone call that will work for your schedule.

Warmly,
Laura Hutchins

The dreaded *warmly*, Julie noted. It was as distant and chilly coming at the end of this note as she had been thinking of it when she'd read David's missive. Even as she requested the first available slot for a call, Julie knew she couldn't possibly expect to be the candidate chosen, not in her emotionally ravaged state.

She set the phone on the dash, stretching her arms over her head until they hit the padding of the rooftop. The instant she moved, her head began to throb. The sun shone brightly, another beautiful day, and the Ford was starting to heat up.

It wasn't until Julie stepped outside that she became aware of just how bad her headache was, like a clamp screwed into each of her temples. The amount of scotch she'd imbibed—a full glass meant for water, for hydrating oneself, not straight booze—rolled through her gut like a wave, and Julie paused, one hand upon the flank of the car, the other on her stomach. Her mouth felt waxy, and tasted like souring milk.

Julie bent over, throwing up a stream of liquor and bile onto the ground. She hadn't had one bite of solid food yesterday. She wiped her mouth with the back of her hand, then eased the car door closed, wincing at the thud it made.

She needed to take a shower before tracking down David.

Her phone buzzed as she stood under the spray. Julie wiped the haze off the shower door. Unknown number. Spam, or could it already be the hoped-for call, this quickly? Julie slid the door open so fast, it rattled in its frame. Dripping and naked, she got out and grabbed her phone, still buzzing like a trapped fly.

"Hello, yes, hi?" she gasped.

"Ms. Mason?" a voice asked cautiously.

"Yes," she responded. "This is Julie Mason." Now she sounded as somber and sonorous as James Earl Jones. The woman would think she had a split personality. "I'm sorry," she went on in a more natural tone. "I was running for the phone and almost missed your call."

A pause. "How nice that you don't have it on you at all times."

This had to be the pre-interview call. Julie's headache had abated beneath the force of the shower, but her mouth still felt leathery. She turned the faucet on at a volume she hoped would be inaudible, and scooped some water from the sink.

"I have a lot of qualms about how digitally connected we are these days," she said, after swallowing. "Also, I live in a place where cell signal is spotty."

"What a coincidence," the woman said. "We have no cell signal at all on Mercy."

Julie took a moment to parse the confirmation that she wasn't in the hands of a telemarketer, then the piece of information she'd been given, the distance between *intermittent* and *none*.

The woman spoke again. "I'm sorry, I haven't even introduced myself yet. My name is Laura Hutchins, and I'm calling about the position you applied for."

"Of course," Julie said, stooping for a towel on the floor. "Thank you for slotting me in so quickly."

"You're welcome. We're eager to fill the position, as you can imagine, with the school year nigh. At the same time, we want to make sure we find just the right person."

"Is the opening unexpected?" Julie asked.

"Quite. The prior teacher found that life on an island didn't suit her and resigned, giving us very little notice." Her voice tightened with disapproval.

"We experience the same thing in the district where I work," Julie said. "It can be tough to hold on to talent in out-of-the-way locales. But I'm used to out-of-the-way."

"That's what we were thinking when we read your application," Laura said. "The Adirondacks, correct?"

"That's right." Julie felt a tremor of excitement. She opened the bathroom door and walked into the bedroom.

"We're using the phone calls to make sure that candidates are able to commit to at least one year of placement, and have no impediments to leaving home right away."

"Yes to both," Julie said instantly.

Another longish pause. "May I be honest?"

Julie felt a few dots of sweat break out on her skin, a faint sense of strangeness rising up from within. "Please."

"Your application impressed me—us—particularly. I think it

was your little essay that really jumped out. How self-revelatory your response was to the question at the end."

Julie switched hands, her phone slick with perspiration. She recalled the feeling of pieces sliding into place. Exactly what Opportunity.com promised: a unique and ideal fit.

"We appreciated how forthcoming you were," Laura Hutchins continued. "This position—life on Mercy Island—is very special, but comes with some challenges, as you suggested. The right teacher will be able to adapt to those challenges."

Julie bunched the towel around her, and sank down on the smooth, unwrinkled bed. "In my life I've had to approach challenge as a positive thing, not a negative."

"I hope you're as impressive in person as you are on paper."

The calendar icon on Julie's phone beamed up at her, a hopeful grid of tomorrows. "Does that mean…?"

"It means we would like you to come in for an interview."

CHAPTER SEVEN

J ulie needed to procure a new outfit—her professional clothes were all suited to cooler weather, worn during the school year—but first she had to get her dog back. It was daytime now, working hours, which meant David should be in his office.

Julie got dressed and, after a hunt, located her purse, not in her closet but at the foot of the bed beneath a tumble of clean, unfolded laundry. The bag felt overlarge and floppy in her grip; she hadn't carried the thing in over a year, when its size permitted a cram of diapers, wipes, toys, Cheerios in baggies, and teething rings.

Julie stopped momentarily, shutting her eyes. Just one day. For just one day, she needed not to think about Hedley, not be consumed by her baby's absence, her memory.

Is that all right, Lilypad?

Hedley Lillian Mason.

Her daughter's first name had been chosen in honor of her grandmother: it was Julie's mother's maiden name. Her middle name was for the summer flower, which grew in such wild abundance along Wedeskyull's roadsides.

Is that okay?

No voice answered back, ghostly or otherwise. Julie took this as permission.

Depot wouldn't be allowed into stores, and it was too warm out to leave him in the car, so Julie decided to go shopping first. She didn't dare approach The Everything Store again, but a drive on the Thruway where the anonymous big-box options had infiltrated felt doable. At Target, Julie found a striped dress, along with a pair of sandals that looked professional yet beachy. Were there beaches on Mercy Island? Julie had never been to Maine, but her image was of a rockier sea. Oh well. The sandals were cheap, and super cute.

On her way through the automatic doors, hot air hit her like a wall, and she collided with a man who seemed to be studying the shopping carts.

Julie teetered on her feet, and he steadied her with a tentative hand. "Yikes," she exclaimed. She hadn't eaten in a day and a half. No wonder a heat wave, plus a little shopping, had brought her to a state of near collapse.

The man instantly dropped his hand, apologizing even though she had walked into him. He gave her a probing look of concern, and Julie waved him off, embarrassed. She headed past the expanse of stadium-size stores, blacktop tacky beneath her feet, before coming to a Five Guys where she gobbled an entire cheeseburger and downed a shake. The most food she'd eaten in months. Before departing, she bought two Littles for Depot.

David rented a room on the third floor of a building on Water Street that had been threatened with razing before a local arts council amassed the funds to purchase it. They held events—poetry slams and open mics and stand-up comedy—on the first level, while the second had been made into a living gallery of frequently rotating displays. As Julie entered the building and climbed the stairs, she heard the bark Depot reserved just for her.

David's voice also carried clearly. "Hush. We'll go out in a few minutes."

Her husband had never been able to tell the difference between Depot's barks, Julie thought with a mental sniff. He had no right to take custody of their dog.

Depot closed the distance between them when Julie opened the unlocked door.

"Hiya, Deep," she murmured, crouching to ruffle the fur at the dog's neck. She pulled the burgers, just the way he liked them, from the grease-blotched bag. Depot wolfed everything down in a few gulps, administering a slather with his long, red tongue to clean his muzzle or, more likely, scour up the drips.

David hadn't yet said a word, hadn't even greeted her.

She took a look around. A sleeping bag formed a makeshift mattress on the floor, and it looked as if David had spent the night in his clothes. On David, normally so neat and pressed, the sight was shocking, like seeing someone become demented.

Julie didn't feel as angry anymore; she wanted to heal things between her and her husband. Thanks to Laura Hutchins, they just might have a chance at a new start.

"How was your night?" she asked softly.

David straightened a stack of printouts on his desk until their edges were aligned. "It was fine," he answered curtly. "I won't be here long."

"Because you'll be coming home?" Julie asked.

David's expression changed. "No, I'm not coming back. I told you that. In fact, I don't think I'm going to stay in Wedeskyull at all. I'm going to move home."

"To…North Carolina?" The announcement bore proof that there'd be no last-minute reprieve. She and David had met online, and her husband's southern background always felt a bit surreal to Julie, even though she'd made a trip down once to meet his parents.

"Correct," David said. "I can hardly wait. The winters up here are brutal."

Depot let out a whine, curling his body into an enormous hump on the floor.

Julie crossed the room to their dog. "I agree, Deep," she said soothingly. "Snow rocks."

David ignored them, his next words clipped. "We have to come to terms on a few things. Then it doesn't really matter where I go, does it?"

"I found a job listing," Julie said.

David lifted his eyebrows into two precise points.

"I realized something," she went on. For a long time now she had maintained that she could never go back to teaching. "I do want to return to work. I love it, you know I do, and I miss working with kids. I want to teach. I just don't want to do it here."

Her husband folded his arms across his chest.

Julie continued in a rush. "Maybe I feel more like you do than I've let on. Maybe we're both actually feeling the same things. And we just haven't shared them."

David gave a single nod. Terse, but a nod was a sign of agreement, wasn't it?

"That's what my therapist said," he told her.

"She did?" Julie said. Relief began to infuse her.

David stayed silent, though he offered another nod.

"So, there's this position," Julie went on. "On a small island in Maine. Really tiny. It'll be a whole other way of life." When David didn't say anything, she tried a smile. "I don't think it snows much near the sea."

David sat forward in his desk chair, bracing his forearms on his knees. "Julie," he said in a gentler voice. "This isn't about where we live."

"No, of course not," she said. "This move, it means something deeper than that—"

"Our marriage isn't working," David said, still clearly trying to defang his tone. "Hedley—what happened to her made it obvious. But I don't think we were in a very good place even before we lost her. Maybe not even before she was born."

The finality in his voice made the ramifications of his decision come clear to Julie. "But—they're expecting two of us," she said. "I filled in 'married' on the application. I can't look like I'm having a personal crisis, David. Who would want such a person to teach their children?" *That's assuming you get the job.* The voice was back, taunting and cruel, as if it'd just been waiting around for a chance to deliver the perfect, Achilles-slicing slur.

David sat back in his chair, regarding her impassively. After a considered pause, he swiveled around and began striking keys with staccato precision.

"I'd better get back to work," he said. "Deadlines, you know."

Julie's shoulders sagged. She hadn't convinced David to give Maine a try, or their marriage another chance, because she'd never changed his mind about anything once he'd made it up. His move north notwithstanding, it'd been her husband who took control of their lives when they married, and Julie hadn't resisted. In fact, she'd welcomed handing over reins she'd had to take hold of at too young an age. David decided how much they drank, who governed Depot's days, what constituted a reasonable amount of time to mourn.

Depot.

The sound of loud, lapping splashes from the water bowl filled Julie with despair. Leave her dog behind? Move to a new place without him? The very idea was impossible.

The grasshopper clack of typing ceased, and silence filled the room.

Depot even stopped slurping.

"Julie?"

She turned at the door.

David spoke without rotating his seat. "I think Depot might do well on an island."

CHAPTER EIGHT

Three days later, just before the interview was scheduled to take place, Julie's phone rang and woke her while she was tossing and turning in scotch-soaked dreams.

She scrabbled around on the nightstand, checking the number, but the call had already gone to voicemail. She couldn't believe it had been ringing that long, how difficult she must have been to rouse. Scotch. Elixir of the gods, the glum, the guilty.

The number was unknown, and the caller hadn't left a message.

It was just after 2:00 a.m.

Julie lay back, slicking strands of hair away from her face. The room spun as she lay there, and her stomach felt like gelatin. She needed to be clear and on point for the morning, but wasn't confident she could breath-mint away the smell of alcohol, scrub it out of her pores.

The phone rang again, its musical beat sudden and jarring in the still room.

Julie grabbed it blindly.

She just had time to register the number—unknown, and not from an area code she recognized—before swiping her thumb across the screen. "Hello?"

Silence on the other end.

Someone had butt-dialed, or sleep-dialed, rolling over on their phone in bed, or maybe a robo service had gone haywire, making calls in the middle of the night. Julie tapped the screen to end the call.

It rang again, and this time Julie's agitated hello was sufficient to summon Depot. He walked over to her bed, snuffling as if still partially asleep.

No reply from the other end.

Depot stood with his gaze fixed on her, eyes aglow in the dark.

"It's okay, Deep," Julie whispered. "I won't pick up again."

But now she was disturbed. The night felt too quiet. Where were the normal sounds, the buck of the motor as the fridge started up, a summer breeze whispering outside? Julie pushed the covers aside, aware that she had pulled up the quilt for the first time in weeks, then swung her feet out of bed. Depot accompanied her as she walked over to the window and lifted the curtain out of the way. She placed her face against the glass. No car beside hers in the driveway. No imprints in the dewy grass.

The hallway was dim, but from the top of the stairs she could see the front door, snugly shut. Depot stood panting at her hip, and with his bulk beside her, Julie walked down to the first floor, checking the kitchen and the deck. She entered the half bath, Depot squeezing in alongside her. Empty.

She went back upstairs, her hand on Depot's broad back.

As soon as she got back in the bedroom, her phone started to trill.

Julie's heart slammed a gong beat. It was as if someone knew that she'd left the room, and when she returned.

Depot let out a high whine.

Julie stared down at the phone on her bed. Unknown number. The musical beat finally ended, before starting right up again.

Julie snatched for the device. "Hello?" she demanded.

Silence.

Stupidly, not knowing if she was attempting to summon her husband, as if he might still reside in this house, or thinking that it might be him on the other end, using somebody else's phone, she cried, "David?"

No answer. The call remained live for some time, though, for Julie could detect the moment it finally cut out, the whoosh of emptiness like a vortex, a wormhole.

She waited, poised on the edge of her bed, ready to pounce on the phone the first time it sounded, and do something—she didn't know what—to determine the identity of the caller.

But it didn't ring again.

After a long while, Julie set her phone to silent, then threw back the covers so that Depot could jump up and crawl in beside her.

At some point, the two of them slept.

The interview was to be held at an office park on the outskirts of Albany, not far from the Thruway, which made the three-hour ride south convenient for Julie—and signaled that they must be fairly enthusiastic about her, too, unless she was reading things wrong. But someone had come all the way from Maine to another state's capital based on her location. Julie tried to let the arrangement give her a boost of confidence.

It had cooled down substantially overnight, the way it did in the Adirondacks, like a tide being sucked back. Outside, everything looked dreary and gray, the sky one enormous swath of cloud.

The chill in the air served to dispel the final remnants of scotch from Julie's brain, and any lingering eeriness from the series of silent calls. As she left the house, grabbing a jacket to pair with her new dress, she felt a faint flicker of something that could almost be called eagerness.

For the first time in a long while, time was passing too slowly because something seemed to be waiting on the other end of it. The sodden, overcast day did nothing to alter Julie's mood, and the highway drive was calming.

She made sure Depot got in a good long run at a rest area—the sky threatening rain the whole time—before leaving him to curl up in the car in the office park lot with a window rolled down. No one would dare bother Depot.

Julie brushed off the dark hairs that clung to her dress. Depot's coat was a mixture of cream, rust, and black, and somehow the color that stood out most against whatever she was wearing always seemed to shed. Julie turned and headed toward the building, an anonymous, soulless site, all glassy walls and eyeless windows. She had just raised her hand to rap on suite 103 when the door was pulled open from the inside.

Laura Hutchins was a slim woman, her skin lined like tracing paper with the evidence of an outdoor life. She was perhaps ten years older than Julie, in her mid-forties, unless the effects of the sun were misleading. At the last minute, it had occurred to Julie to worry that she had made a poor choice of outfit, demonstrated her lack of fit for life on an island. Maybe the other woman would be clad in different clothes entirely, a slicker and Wellies perhaps. But Laura wore a skirt and low heels, and Julie relaxed a little after the two exchanged greetings, Laura leading her inside.

She gestured Julie to a chair, then sat down herself, arrow straight behind a cheap, flimsy desk. She compressed her hands, interlacing her fingers on the laminate surface, while regarding Julie from the other side of the desk. Julie smiled, blinked, then finally broke eye contact, taking a look around. This office was rent-a-space all the way—Mercy clearly didn't boast some august, private school with a hiring search conducted in hallowed halls—and Julie wondered for a moment about the conditions on the island. Rough and spare, she assumed. Which was fine. Julie's family had lived in the Adirondacks for generations. They were used to a lack of luxuries.

"As I said on the phone," Laura began stiffly, "this is a very special position. It would be hard to overestimate the challenges and rigors of coming to teach on Mercy when compared to modern-day life."

It seemed an abrupt way to open; then again, Julie hadn't had to interview for a job in over a decade. Maybe people cut right to the chase now.

"I feel up for challenges, as I hope my essay made clear." Laura had said she liked that answer; a reminder couldn't hurt. "But can you tell me a little more?" There, Julie thought with satisfaction. Take that, yearlong hiatus.

"Long winters," Laura said, unlocking her fingers and beginning to tick off items, as if from a list. "You'll be used to those. Wi-Fi that often goes out—the year-rounders call it *No-Fi* due to the frequent power outages—which means no cell signal even through a hot spot." Another tick, another glance at Julie. "Ditto in terms of your experience."

The woman must've done some research into Wedeskyull.

Julie offered an unfazed nod. Who needed connectivity? Not she, not anymore.

"Are the children in your district given devices? iPads, Chromebooks, the like?"

Julie shook her head. "We don't have the funds."

Laura looked pleased. "An hour-long ferry ride to the mainland, often over choppy seas." *Tick.* "In bad weather, the ferry stops running and supplies at Perry's—the grocery store—can dwindle alarmingly before someone makes it across to resupply. We stockpile," Laura added. "For slim times." *Tick, tick,* then she switched hands. "No cars."

That one did give Julie pause, which Laura seemed to notice.

"There are basically no motorized vehicles of any sort on-island,"

45

Laura said. "Two pedicabs—driven by the island teens for extra cash—take summer people who require assistance from the dock to points of interest. And by points of interest I mean trailheads, the lighthouse, our resident baker's shop—nothing like a golf course or amusement park." Laura paused. "Construction work and agriculture are achieved almost entirely by hand. Tools are shared; goats, pigs, and chickens are farmed collectively. A few families raise rabbits for eating. Slim times," she reminded.

Julie let the picture take shape in her mind. "You mentioned summer people," she said at last. "Tourism is an industry I know well—it keeps my town alive. But is there anything else the year-round population does?"

Laura refolded her hands. "Tourism is a source of revenue for us certainly. But places like Monhegan and Deer Isle are better known for it. No, Mercy's biggest industry is lobstering. Most of the parents of your students will be lobster fishermen."

Your students, Julie heard. She smiled. "Well, now I believe we have departed from anything I'm familiar with in the mountains." She took a moment, then added, "It sounds like a way of life I would love getting used to."

Laura's face relaxed just a tinge. "If you heard all of that and can say so," she said, "then you may do just fine on Mercy." Laura wheeled her chair back from the desk. "You'll also probably enjoy the next thing I have to share."

She opened a drawer and withdrew a late-model tablet. Tapping a few sleek keys, Laura flipped the screen so Julie could see.

It was a video reel, but nothing created by a slick marketing firm or tourism bureau, instead a montage made by people clearly in love with their unique way of life. First, nature shots scrolled by: a forest of deep green, the inverted cones of fir trees; surf rolling against a dark cliff face, beating its base to rubble; lobster traps stacked in towers, their edges perfectly aligned; a sea captain's mansion, imposing and proud. Then came pictures of people: men in raincoats thick as rhino hide; women with enormous coils of rope on their laps and needles fit for a giant; kids crouched to study tide pools or splashing in the ocean; a circle of teenagers building a bonfire.

"That's an interesting shot," Julie remarked, pointing to the screen.

Laura struck a key, and the reel paused on a photo of a regal woman, striding along a sandy road en route to a glistening curl of ocean surf. Her birch-white hair was smoothed back in a bun, which Julie squinted at for a second. Something about that hair stood out, besides its striking color. The woman walked pied-piper-like in front of a troop of assorted grown-ups and children also making their way to the water. The other people's hair flew about, covering faces, sticking to mouths, as if caught in a wind. But the woman at the helm seemed to inhabit a bubble with its own unique weather system. As Julie kept looking, the feeling persisted, although it had to be an illusion, of course, some trick of the air currents close to the sea.

Laura gazed at the screen as well, her expression rapt. "That's Maryanne Hempstead," she told Julie. "You'll meet her soon enough. A legend really, the lioness at the head of a family that's lived on-island forever. She's wonderful." This last spoken in the tone of voice normally reserved for a star of some sort, or perhaps a prophet or priest.

Julie found it rather charming, especially considering that the person meriting the accolades was, in fact, an elderly woman.

Laura blinked then, as if coming back to herself, and struck a key so that the reel continued to play. While Julie kept watching, a second shot prompted her to take a closer look. She knew that man on the lobster boat, fiddling with the contents of a trap.

CHAPTER NINE

O r she recognized him at least. Had recently seen him? That was the sense she had.

The man's face hovered right at the edges of memory, an impossible specter since Julie had never in her life encountered any lobstermen. She didn't want to ask Laura to pause the reel again. The man's face had been pitched back as he held out a lobster to avoid the clamp of its claws, his chin thrust forward in a way that probably distorted his features, made him look familiar when he was not.

The reel started looping anew, and Laura minimized it on the screen. "Let's move on to your professional background. Have you had experience with special needs?"

Julie didn't hesitate. "I have. In a district like Wedeskyull, the budget is tight, and so we do our best to maintain children in a mainstream setting. There's a contained classroom in the school, and I haven't taught there—I don't have the necessary certification—but the truth is," she concluded on a note of pride, "I never once had to recommend that one of my kids transfer out."

Laura looked as gratified by the statement as Julie had been to deliver it. "We love our children. All folks do, of course, but on a small island, there's a dimension you may not be aware of."

Julie nodded her on.

"Shrinking population," Laura said. "Every year, the school sees a diminished enrollment. During Mercy's heyday, four teachers were employed, and the student body numbered in the triple digits. Now, you'll instruct less than a fifth of that."

The number was miniscule, even by Wedeskyull standards.

"It's difficult to keep folks on an island," Laura explained. "Young people with children are the future of any healthy community, but they're the rarest of our populace. Teenagers leave to attend high school, then college, they find spouses from away, or seek careers and means of employment not available on Mercy."

Julie tilted her head. "We face a similar situation in my town. Although not at the same scale." The other difference in Wedeskyull was that year-round recreation, and a contingent of techies who could work remotely, had brought new people to the area.

"What this means is that every single island child is precious," Laura went on fervently. "Not just in the post-bullying, all-kids-deserve-to-be-valued sense of the term, but because each child is a resource on Mercy Island. One we must at all costs preserve. Without young people, a community can't thrive, go forward into tomorrow."

Children as commodities, as stock options, as futures—almost literally.

"Depression is a condition that more and more children fall prey to nationwide," Laura continued. "The dark days on an island can instill a mental fog as well as a physical one. Suicidality is something we need our teacher to be aware of as a risk."

"One of my best friends in town lost a colleague to suicide, and we teachers all had to attend a weeklong training afterward, focused on identifying copycat signs."

Laura swiveled the tablet back around in her own direction, using a finger to scroll across the screen. Then she looked up and said, "Timothy Lurcquer."

Julie had trouble maintaining her interview-smooth face. "Yes. That's right. How did you know that?"

Laura turned a smile on Julie that plumped up her cheeks, temporarily erasing each one's web of thin lines. "As I mentioned already, we are intent on getting the right fit for this position. Ideally, we'd like the teacher to continue her tenure long past the first year. So we did some research, just as I'm sure you did when you applied."

"Of course," Julie said. "I did, but—"

"We live in a world of waning privacy, don't we?" Laura interjected. "Social media, the worldwide web, cell phones all link us together, whether we want to be connected or not. A place like Mercy allows us to avoid some of that."

Julie swallowed. "How long have you lived there?"

"Oh, I don't live on-island myself," Laura said. "I haven't for a while. But I love Mercy. It will always be home. That's why I took charge of this hiring process."

Julie nodded.

Laura glanced at the tablet again. "On your application, you didn't fill in the box about children."

Julie looked away. "I wasn't sure what to…how to do that exactly." She interrupted herself, trying to come up with a better way in. "What I mean is, something happened that made a clear answer hard to provide—"

Laura broke in gently. "I know what happened."

Of course you do, Julie thought. She wasn't sure whether to feel perturbed or relieved that she was spared having to offer an explanation.

"The news about your daughter was sadly made public. Local human-interest articles, and you also have a fairly popular mommy blogger in your town. Per our discussion, nowadays such things are all too readily found."

Julie stared down at her lap, shielding the sight of budding tears.

"I'm sorry," Laura added. "I should've offered my condolences first."

But she didn't look all that sorry. In fact, in the midst of expressing empathy, Laura's face had twitched with a smile again. It lit her eyes like twin suns.

"All I really need to know in terms of this position is whether you're up for it, despite the tragedy you suffered," Laura went on.

Julie fought to summon a reply, settling on a nod she hoped would signal certainty. Laura didn't even live on Mercy. Who cared if she was a bit dogged in her search, obsessive when it came to finding the right candidate for the job?

"Good," Laura said. "That brings me to one piece of personal information I couldn't procure. I was expecting your husband to accompany you today. As the form you filled out stated, we like to meet the spouses or family members of anyone coming to live on Mercy."

The requirement sounded a bit over-the-top, stringent, stated baldly like that. Still, Julie knew she had better get this over with. One big gulp, like a pill going down.

"We've decided to separate," she told Laura. "It's been a long time coming." True for David, if not Julie. And it wouldn't do to appear blindsided.

"I see." Laura looked down at the keyboard, concealing her face from view. "Typically we find that being part of a family—a couple at least—makes the transition to island living easier. But that isn't always the case."

"I actually think this may work better for me. I can focus on the kids."

Laura nodded thoughtfully. "We're a close and supportive community. You won't lack for company, if you want it."

Julie flashed a quick smile of her own. "I have a dog. A big one."

Laura had woven her fingers tightly together, but freed them then. "I hope he likes to swim," she said, closing the tablet with a decided click. "Well, Ms. Mason—or is there another name I should call you by now?"

Just a second's hesitation before she answered. It slipped back on like an old shoe, an identity that wasn't entirely becoming, but one she'd never fully meant to shed either. "Julie Weathers. But please—make it Julie."

"Well, Julie," Laura began again. "I need to check out the references you supplied, and finish running your background check. But my hunch is that it won't be premature to say..."

She rose and Julie did too.

Laura extended a cool, dry hand. "Welcome to Mercy."

CHAPTER TEN

Over the next three weeks, Julie accomplished more than she had in the whole last year.

In order of difficulty, least to most, she—

- Read everything she could find online about Mercy Island and signed the commitment letter as soon as it arrived, officially offering her the job. She would be given a place to live, and a more than decent salary, given the lack of housing expenses.
- Adapted to the morning and afternoon walks Depot required, which carved a few pounds she couldn't afford to lose from her frame. Previously, she and David had split this task, but since losing their daughter, whole days had gone by, weeks even, when Julie didn't take her share because she never left the house.
- Packed the belongings she'd be bringing, stored the rest in her aunt's basement, while ordering items so alien, they constituted

proof that she was really leaving. Waterproof gear made out of a dense, slick substance, like sealskin, for oversea crossings, rainstorms, and daily life. A pillow whose fill claimed anti-mold properties; islands were damp places. Anti-frizz remedies for her thick, wavy hair (ditto). Dramamine as well as a holistic treatment for seasickness.

- Listed the house for rent. With a divorce pending, it wouldn't do to sell it, which was just as well. Julie didn't want to sever her tie to Wedeskyull so definitively.
- Told the few people who'd remained in her circle despite Julie's best attempts to push them away—some colleagues, her principal, and a couple of sets of parents whose children had graduated—of her decision, thereby ensuring that the news was soon known throughout town.

The last of which explained why, one afternoon, the sun having returned to Wedeskyull after six days of rain, filling the house with light while Julie scrubbed the upstairs bathroom in preparation for a showing, Depot let out a volley of barks.

Depot had two person-approaching barks. One for someone he knew, whose presence might or might not be expected. The other signified a stranger.

Since this was the first kind of bark, Julie gave the dog a reassuring pat, then knee-walked over the swath of suds that had spilled from the tub she'd been scouring, to lift the curtain on the window.

"It's just Vern," she told Depot, getting to her feet and heading for the stairway. She took the steps at a run, Depot thudding behind at her heels.

Julie opened the door.

"Hi, Uncle Vern," she said.

Her father's oldest brother had always been a commanding man, wide in build, with a deep voice that didn't know how to whisper. But the years, and his fall from grace as police chief, had shrunk him. Vern was wizened now, his thick, white hair reduced to wisps on his head. It was strange to see him out of uniform, though he had long since lost the right to wear it. Still, jeans and rolled-up shirtsleeves didn't suit him.

"Hello, sweetheart," Vern said.

Julie stepped aside to allow her uncle entrance. Depot sniffed at him, which Vern tolerated, administering a pat to the dog's big head. Once he would've shoved Depot aside, not meanly, just with the impatience of a man who had too much to do and a small world counting on him to do it.

Vern paused in the hallway, crossing his arms over his chest and taking a look around. His chest was narrower now, the meat on his exposed forearms loose.

"Sometimes the gossip mill gets it right," he said.

Julie turned to take in the taped cartons and draped furniture.

"I was going to call you," she said on a note of apology.

It had been awkward, talking to her uncle over the years. A halo of shame surrounded him once he left the job, the persistent shadow of a downed regime, one that his crooked ways, and his daddy's before him, had been responsible for toppling. In practical terms, her uncle had beat a retreat, leaving Julie's aunt behind in town while he eked out a subsistence level living in a cabin he'd built in the woods. He emerged only for items he couldn't hunt, grow, or make.

Vern lifted sunken shoulders in a shrug. "I made it in time to say goodbye."

"Come in," Julie invited.

He followed her to the kitchen, the room she had left for last to pack up so that she could continue to prepare simple meals. Julie scooped coffee grounds into a filter and added water. She depressed the button to start the machine and got down two mugs.

"Black, right?" she asked.

Depot padded in and Julie refreshed the water in his bowl. All three of them drank for a while, Depot noisily, with splashes, Vern and Julie in silence.

Then her uncle said, "What's this I hear about an island?"

Once Vern would've sounded scoffing, might even have forbidden Julie from going, although her parents would've restored permission; they'd always wanted her to be a teacher. But Vern would've believed he had the right, the jurisdiction over her and everybody else in his fiefdom. What had changed was the frailness of his query.

Julie relayed the details of her new position, keeping information about Mercy itself to a minimum to make her move sound less extreme.

Vern drained the last of his coffee, then shoved his cup aside. It was the first authoritative gesture she'd seen him make.

"I know something about escape," he said. "It don't always work out like you want it to."

Julie looked at him over the rim of her half-full cup. "What do you mean?"

"I'm sure you've heard the saying," Vern replied. "Wherever you go, there you are. Are you looking to get away from Wedeskyull—or what you think happened here?"

"It *did* happen here," Julie said. The coffee sizzled in her stomach, and she set her cup on the table with a *thwack*. "I'm looking to get away from the memories I relive every time I do the same thing in the same place or in the same way that I did it with Hedley. And David now too," she added on an accusatory note, as if Vern might bring his former, misused reach to punish her abandoning husband.

"I heard about that," her uncle said. "Gossip mill's got him in its clutches too. I'm sorry, sweetheart. Marriages can be brittle things. Too much strain and they break."

Julie emptied the coffee pot into Vern's mug, but her uncle ignored the refill.

"We're not a family that talks, never have been," he said. "And the news gets things more wrong than right. You were young when a lot of what happened took place in this town, and I don't know how much my baby brother told you. Then he died, and if he had been going to put his own spin on things one day, give you a legacy you could live with, that day never came."

Julie's vision clouded, and she swiped at her eyes.

"I don't talk about it much myself, living alone as I do," Vern said, "and I've got no intention of changing. This is as much as I'll ever say, and we're gonna call it a going-away present, a one-time-only offer, you hear me?"

Julie bore down on the coffeepot she still held in her hand.

"What happened to your little girl ain't nothing like what I did," Vern said. "You suffered a tragedy nobody could've done anything about. The finest policing, all the integrity in the world, would've had no effect on what happened to Hedley."

Julie couldn't see her uncle before her anymore, detect his mouth moving. She brought her face down on the cool surface of the table and felt it flood.

"The burden I live with every day is because I knew what we were doing was wrong, taking shortcuts for all the right reasons maybe, but still wrong to take 'em. And I went on anyway. It would be like if you had fair warning and still took your daughter out that day, except not even because what happened would've just occurred someplace else in that case. Wherever you happened to be when lightning struck."

Julie shook her head back and forth against the slick surface of the table.

"You look up at me, little girl," Vern said, and for just a moment, her uncle was commander in chief again, at the height of his powers, a man no one would dare disobey.

Julie lifted her head.

"There ain't no similarity between you and me," Vern said. "Except for maybe the Weathers's gene for survival. Wherever that surviving might take place. And if you feel yours has to take place elsewhere, well, you don't need my blessing, sweetheart, but you got it." He withdrew a handkerchief from his pocket and handed it to her. "One last thing."

Julie swabbed her eyes with the hanky. "Yes?"

Her uncle walked over to the pantry. Its door had been left ajar, in anticipation of packing still to come, and Vern reached in unerringly, bringing out two bottles of scotch.

"There's escape and there's escape," he said. "We Weathers have relied on this kind too. Papa Franklin had more scotch in his veins at the end than blood."

Vern strode over to the sink, twisted the caps on both bottles, and poured twin amber streams down the drain. Then he handed her the empties. "Go where you need to. Do what you want to. Just don't do it with this."

Julie stared at her uncle, restored to his deified state, making moves, rearranging pieces on the board, for everything and everybody. She watched the final swirls of scotch at the base of the sink, and pictured the arid, endless nights before her, not lubricated by the syrupy properties of her favorite fix. Then she gave a mental shrug.

She couldn't have gotten those bottles on the plane anyway.

PART II

HAVE MERCY

CHAPTER ELEVEN

The travel promised to be exhausting. Julie had to make the after-noon ferry crossing, which meant that she needed to be at the air-port in Albany, three hours from home, in time for a 7:00 a.m. flight. Staying overnight in a hotel was tricky with Depot. From the airport in Maine, she'd get a Lyft or Uber to Lambert Point, the ferry's port of departure, and a location nearly as removed from civilization as the island itself.

Julie studied the route after deplaning in Portland, then asked the driver if he would mind making a quick detour. The plane had landed a little ahead of schedule, miracle of miracles, and who knew what kinds of options there would be on the island? Even if there was a store with decent wares, it probably kept limited hours. She showed the driver the place she'd found, angling her phone so he could see.

"Not a problem," he said. The *not* came out *nawt* and the *problem* sounded different too. It was as if Maine were a foreign country instead of a neighboring state.

The driver gunned the gas, making miles north.

Julie took Depot with her when they came to the stop, running him around the parking lot a few laps before leaving him outside the store while she dashed in and out. She nested her purchase between layers of clothes in her suitcase in case it got jogged around on the boat, then climbed back into the car.

Another half hour to Lambert Point.

Julie used the phone app to tip the driver as he let her out near the end of a long, sand-strewn road. She glanced down at the colorful, user-friendly icons, so much a part of everyday life, as taken for granted as air. Once Julie got onto the water, all signal would cease, and her phone would become as useful for connecting as a lump of clay.

The driver unearthed her luggage while Julie summoned Depot. The dog staggered a bit as he jumped out of the car, still disoriented from their early wake-up, and his trip in the plane's belly. Julie noted with a glimmer of guilt that the back seat was furred with silky strands.

"Thanks for taking my dog," she said, drawing Depot to her side.

The car made a U-turn, tires gritting on the sandy blacktop, then drove off with a cheerful honk.

Julie and Depot had arrived with twenty minutes to spare.

Wedeskyull and the mountains seemed much farther away than the distance they'd traveled, a life that belonged on a whole other planet.

Julie stood her suitcase in the road, duffel bag balanced on top of it, and took deep breaths of the tangy air. Salt and brine, seaweed and a fish-market odor. Pungent and not altogether pleasant; Julie supposed it would take some getting used to. At home the air smelled like Christmas—a blend of fir trees and cold.

A constant cry could be heard: the tuneless singing of seagulls. Julie looked up to see white slashes of wings against a sky so glaringly blue, it appeared Photoshopped.

For the past year-plus of grief and mourning, Julie had been encased in a rubbery balloon. Kept separate while the rest of the world went on without her. Now, suddenly, it was as if the balloon had popped, releasing her. She was out amongst the living, sounds no longer muted, smells no longer damped. Every sensation left behind a residue.

Taking her luggage in hand, Julie crossed the last section of road to the dock. The blacktop began to deteriorate, until it lay in big shards and fragments, adhering to the roadbed only by gravity. Julie could see why the driver had stopped farther up.

Depot leapt over pieces, kicking up his hind legs and panting. The presence of the sea seemed to excite him, blowing off the doldrums of travel. Julie called the dog back. She crouched before him, ruffling his fur and looking into his eyes. "You like it here, Deep? It's pretty nice, huh? But settle down, okay?"

A breeze lifted strands of Julie's hair. The smells grew stronger, positively dizzying, as the sea struck the footing of the dock, its rhythm so repetitive, unceasing, that it proffered a glimpse of eternity. Depot seemed to sense it, or something equally solemn. He obeyed Julie's command, quieting and staying by her side. Back up the road, cars started to amass, letting passengers out. While before them, appearing as a speck in the distance on the flat plane of the sea, a ferry approached the dock, emitting a long, loud tolling as it neared, an animal bray of its horn.

A rusty sign nailed to a splintery post announced *No open alcohol, music only with headphones, life preservers on children under fourteen, all pets must be leashed.*

Julie paused to dig around in her duffel for Depot's rarely used leash, reassuring the dog as she affixed it to his collar. Passengers began to stream off the boat, and Julie studied them avidly, wondering if she were looking at a parent of one of her students-to-be, a friend she might make, or a neighbor. Most of these people appeared to be tourists, though, walking bikes, loaded down by day packs, some with picnic baskets dangling from their hands.

Depot was overcome by the mix of strangers and scents, jumping at the end of his leash. She had to pull back on the leather strap, using all of her weight while giving her dog a look of apology. People steered clear of him, guiding their bikes in a wide circle out of Depot's reach, although a few sent admiring glances, and one mother crowed to her son, "Even on four legs, he's taller than you are!"

Another man called out, "Gorgeous! Newfie?"

"Probably some," Julie answered. She was a bit overwhelmed herself, wanting to get onto the boat and out to the peace the calm sea promised. "He's a rescue." Sort of.

The boat was finally clear, and the people waiting to board formed a loose line, chattering with each other, raising their voices to be heard above the gulls, moving forward without even having to look, the steps so oft repeated, they'd become unconscious.

Here were the parents of Julie's future students, her friends-to-be, or neighbors, headed to the island in the late afternoon. Although one or two held suitcases, the rest loaded supplies onto the boat that were more easily procured on the mainland: a pallet of rice, oversize packages of paper goods and supersize bottles of cleanser, even a flat-screen TV and a new refrigerator, all ratcheted down with cargo straps. If the purchases hadn't given it away, something else would've done it. These passengers gave off a whiff of the intangible, an invisible aura of fit. The place they were headed belonged to them, and they to it.

The makeshift gangplank, a single board, wasn't wide enough for two, so Julie had to nudge Depot forward, coaxing him to ignore the bustle of people waiting behind, and making sure his broad steps didn't send him off the wobbly piece of wood and into the gray swish of water. She crossed the length swiftly herself—a touch of vertigo quickening her breath—then paused beside Depot to identify a spot to sit. Rows of wooden benches outside on the deck seemed like they would provide the best views.

The salt air was dehydrating, and Julie found Depot's portable bowl in her duffel. She shook it into shape and removed the cap from a bottle of water, taking a gulp before emptying the rest into the bowl. Depot sloshed up the contents, then maneuvered into place, his hind quarters beneath the bench. He laid his head between his paws and fell asleep.

The ferry gave another loud honk and Julie realized they were moving, the water so calm, she'd hardly felt any motion while attending to Depot.

She twisted around on her seat to watch the dock recede into the distance.

Farther and farther away, smaller and smaller, until their last connection to land was gone, as invisible as if it had never existed at all.

It was the loneliest feeling Julie had experienced in a long time. Knee-buckling, nearly bowling her over, except that of course she'd gone through far worse. She suddenly missed her daughter anew, felt every vacancy Hedley had left, and to which Julie had just added immeasurably by abandoning the last places the baby had inhabited. Stinging spray settled on Julie's face, convincing her that she had made the worst mistake since the day her daughter had been lost. And there was not one thing she could do about it now.

The boat headed out to sea.

CHAPTER TWELVE

I n Wedeskyull, the locals had a canard about the weather—that the only thing you could count on was that it never did what you were counting on.

That truth seemed exponentially elevated on the open ocean.

As the ferry churned along, Julie started to shiver, a product of both temperature and the resurgence of grief and doubt. There came a rush of cold air, a panther shriek of wind, and despite his thick coat, Depot stirred on the boat's deck, tucking his paws beneath him in sleep. The bright sky went fleecy and gray, and a chop kicked up on the previously glassy water, forming triangular, shark-fins of waves.

Julie unzipped her duffel and took out a hoodie. No sooner did she have it on, than she realized that she was going to have to exchange it for her new slicker. The sky was ominous now, greenish clouds gathering. Their shade resembled the color in someone's sick face, and with a queasy swallow, Julie registered the rocking of the boat.

The swells it rode kept increasing in height. Depot's body rolled with the movement of the deck, although he didn't wake. Observing the other passengers, Julie zipped up her raincoat and drew its hood down over her face. The locals' timing had been prescient; they beat the sky by seconds. Swollen bellies of clouds gave way, and rain began to spatter the deck, as loud as corn popping.

Julie wrapped both hands around the edge of her bench, and held on. The boat dove into a gully between waves, then leapt back out again, like a bronco. She freed one hand, clutching doubly tight with the other, while pressing the first to her stomach.

A wave appeared that didn't look mountable. Julie watched it approach them—or were they approaching it?—with terror. There was no way such a small craft could take a wave like that and come down on its other side. The boat would pitch over backward, dump all the passengers out into the turbulent sea. The wave loomed higher, like the mountains of home. Julie couldn't stand to watch. She dropped into a crouch, burying her face in Depot's coat. Breathed in the smell of wet dog, spat fur from her mouth.

The boat's angle grew sharper. Julie felt herself start to slide backward. Depot's greater heft and prone position aided him in not moving, but he was awake now, big eyes fixed on Julie. She grasped hanks of his fur in her hands. Then the ferry slapped down hard, sinking deeply enough into the sea that water crested both sides of the deck. Julie leapt to her feet and leaned over the rim, losing every bite she'd eaten along with last night's duo of farewell shots.

Panting, keeping an eye on Depot, Julie wiped off her mouth with the back of one hand. The other passengers sat calmly on the benches, or stood together at the back of the boat, rain sluicing their sleeves and hoods. They studied the sea with mild expressions, as if nothing about it were surprising.

Julie fought to balance herself, but the ferry continued to heave beneath her feet. Its range felt slightly less extreme, the peaks and valleys not as dramatic, but Julie was still scarcely able to keep from falling over. She needed to check on Depot, but taking a step proved impossible.

"Rock your feet," someone said.

Julie straightened up shakily, looking around for the speaker.

A man edged away from the group huddled in the center of the boat. He was dressed in a slicker, boots, and waterproof pants, no exposed part of him so much as damp, while Julie felt soaked to the skin. Rain snaked down the collar of her slicker; the jeans she wore were drenched.

"What?" she asked.

Rain blurred her vision, and she had to squint to watch the man demonstrate, positioning his legs akimbo, and swaying back and forth with the rhythm of the boat. Far from appearing unsteady, he seemed to be in control, as if he were moving the craft rather than the reverse.

Julie copied him, and immediately felt the motion in her stomach still.

The man gave a nod. "If you move with it, things settle down. But if you fight, the sea will always win."

Julie couldn't make out the man's face beneath his hood, and she assumed he couldn't see her that well either, but she gave him a smile of sheer relief. "Thank you," she said. "That's a lot better."

He nodded again. "First time on-island?"

Julie felt her cold, wet cheeks heat. "Is it obvious?"

The man reached toward her, and Julie frowned.

He flicked a label on her slicker. "Leaving the tag on is a sure sign."

His tone was gently teasing—there was a pleasant burr in his voice—but when the man pushed back his hood, no levity softened his features. He was a good-looking guy, black hair that glinted with gray, eyes like the sea or sky when blue, and an expression that Julie suspected often lived on her own face, including just before when the boat had left land. A kind of resignation.

The ferry steamed ahead, suddenly faster, and she realized that the ocean was flattening out. Vapor rose off the deck in tendrils, leaving behind a sparkle of drops.

The clouds parted, glazing the whole world in an apricot hue.

"There she is," the man said, staring out to sea.

Julie turned around on the now level deck to watch a hump appear in the distance, like the back of some enormous, curved beast rising out of the ocean.

"That's Mercy."

The ferry threaded its way through an array of boats competing for space in the water. Working boats; these weren't luxury liners or speedboats for play or sport. Shiny with many coats of paint, lobster traps stacked on their decks, loaded down by coils of rope and blocky tanks. Striped buoys trailed long lines, which tangled amidst strands of kelp, both visible beneath the moving surface of the sea.

As the ferry approached the dock, passengers began to unzip raincoats and shed outerwear. Julie dropped into a crouch to scoop up Depot's leash. The bovine lowing of the boat's horn sounded, and its side bumped gently against the dock, nudging barnacled boards before a wave came up and pushed the vessel seaward again.

The man with whom Julie had been talking leapt out of the boat, a long jump across a jagged stretch of water, before he came down on the wooden dock. Julie started to reach for her suitcase and duffel, preparing to jump just as Depot took his own leap and made Julie lose her footing. The man seized her hand in his. She registered seawater splashing beneath her, for a second was airborne, then landed on the dock.

Apparently, such niceties as planks were confined to the coast.

The man went back for Julie's luggage.

"Thank you," Julie said as he set the two pieces down on land. "Again."

Depot strained at his leash.

"Takes some getting used to," the man said. "Give it time and you'll be fine."

His reassuring words belied the hardness, a quartz-like quality to his eyes. Julie wondered what required time. Disembarking from the ferry? Gaining one's sea legs? Island life?

Depot continued to pull, walking her instead of the reverse. Julie paused to unclasp the hated leash while passengers streamed around them on all sides. Depot remained in place, his demeanor of dignity returning, and Julie took a moment to shed her slicker, shaking off wetness before stuffing it into her duffel.

Straightening up, she searched for the person she had been told to expect. Someone to welcome her to the island, and show Julie her new digs.

The crush of people had cleared, and aside from a shrill of gulls, all was quiet. Back at the dock, the boat rocked up and down, nudging waterlogged padding tacked up to protect the flanks of the ferry. Thorn-sharp barnacles encrusted poles extending into the seabed. A pickling smell, salt and fermentation and rot, emanated from shaggy, kelp-draped rocks. A mouth of beach lay to the left, while the right climbed a steep pitch ending at a structure built of weathered boards. Directly in front of Julie, another trail led upward more gradually, losing itself in a cluster of short, stubby trees.

She looked down at Depot. "You smell," she said aloud. It was the usual stink of wet dog with an overlay of seaweed.

Depot gave an electrified shake of his body, spraying Julie with droplets.

"I suppose I deserved that," she remarked.

The dog settled into a squat at her feet, sugarcoating his haunches with sand that would require a bath, plus a stout brushing, to remove.

"That too," she added. "I'm sorry, Deep. I just want to make a good impression."

There was nobody around to impress, however.

Everyone was gone.

CHAPTER THIRTEEN

Every single person had disappeared from the dock, including the man who had helped Julie disembark. There were no more locals, and how they had all departed that quickly, their heavy burdens of shopping already unloaded, was a puzzle whose solution Julie couldn't imagine. Even the tourists had vanished, no pause to get their bearings or snap a photo of the picturesque scene, as if they had been hurriedly squired away.

Julie hadn't had anything to drink since the night before, and then not enough to have been feeling any effects at this point. Yet the situation had the bleary focus and fuzzy unreality that only scotch imparted.

She looked around, searching out a retreating back, listening for a scuff of footsteps or labored breath as someone disappeared over the hill.

The island had the feel of a place time had forgotten, or left behind. Standing on this slit of a path, barely wide enough for two bikes to ride side by side, Julie looked past the harbor and out to sea, taking in the same view she would've seen a hundred years ago. A thousand.

The scene posed an eerie echo of the loneliness she had felt on the boat.

Sun shone down, dappling the ground beneath the stunted trees up ahead. The silence and solitude were all-encompassing. It didn't seem possible that the presence of a stranger, along with her very large dog, could go undetected this long.

Julie dug out her phone from a pocket on her suitcase. No signal, and although she was used to spotty cell coverage, it felt strange to see her phone as still and glassy as a pond. Not a single voicemail or alert. If nobody appeared—a notion that felt just this side of conceivable, given the quiet that had settled over the land—she would be stuck.

It wasn't as if she could swim back across the sea, and there wasn't anybody left who would come way out here to look for her. Julie felt a stab of self-pity that repulsed her. *Poor me, poor me, pour me another.* A phrase from one of the sobriety blogs she followed, both covetous and admiring of the blogger's clear, purposeful life. Julie could have such a life herself now, but instead she was in what had to be one of the world's most scenic spots, complaining about a little alone time. She clapped her hands together, summoning her dog and scattering the haunted-house feel.

Leaving her luggage at the foot of the path, she decided to head for the wooden building.

Depot made short work of the climb, although Julie's calves ached with every step. New resolve notwithstanding, she felt parched and snappish and tired. She had been awake for so long today already, and assuming she ever reached what was supposed to be her new home, she still had to unpack a few things, find her toothbrush and something to sleep in, plus give Depot a meal.

Julie paused, rubbing her eyes before trudging upward again.

Depot stopped at the steps to the building and started sniffing the ground. Maybe this was a restaurant, remnants of food by its entry, although no sign advertised any such services. Still, Julie felt her hopes spark. It would be nice to find a place to sit down that didn't pitch and fall.

"Ms. Weathers, hello there, wrong direction!"

The call came from behind, and Julie experienced a spike of relief. She hadn't been all the way to scared, of course, but unsettled, yes, that she would admit to. The resurgence of grief and her last-minute doubts about this decision had combined to make the possibility of never seeing another human being again feel realer than it should have.

She turned to see Laura Hutchins standing at the base of the path.

Julie jogged down to meet her, a frown of confusion fighting the smile that arose upon seeing a familiar face. "But you don't... I thought you didn't live here anymore?"

"I don't." Laura waved a hand, gesturing Julie forward. "But my father and stepmother do, and they always reel me in for an end-of-summer bash. Plus I wanted to see you get settled!" She bent over. "Can I take one of these? We have a bit of a walk."

Julie handed off the suitcase with relief, hoisting her duffel. "Come on, Deep."

Laura walked off quickly, hooking a turn onto the sloping path. "You didn't say what a beauty your dog is," she called over her shoulder as they moved along.

The trail let out amidst a cluster of buildings, and Julie exhaled. Here were the missing signs of life. An inn on a manicured plot of land, bordered by a fence of painted white chain links that lent a sailor's feel. And the tourists who had made the ferry crossing, rocking in chairs that adorned a front porch. Laura led the way past a grocery store—Perry's—and a library housed in a building so small, every book in its collection could surely be read in a month. Then came a touristy gift shop, and a restaurant called Harbor House, from which a blend of smells emanated, salt and grease and frying meat.

Depot dug his claws into the ground, coming to a sudden halt.

"We'll come back later for dinner," Julie told the dog, taking hold of his collar and pulling him on.

Laura smiled, though she didn't offer to stop. Perhaps she was in a rush. "Don't worry, you'll find the house well provisioned."

They made their way out of town and toward a crossroads of cottages, each painted a different sea color: sky blue, two shades of green, and a pearly gray-white. They were charming, and Julie found herself wondering if one might be hers. But Laura hurried passed the grouping toward a tunnel of forest.

Depot had been lagging behind, sending yearning looks back at the restaurant whose odors had long since faded for Julie, but as they entered the woods, it was Julie who slowed. These woods were different from those she had grown up surrounded by. The soil was sandy and tree roots were exposed, spreading outward like gnarled bones. They made the soft earth humped and uneven, requiring vigilance at every step. Julie had meant to give Laura the easier burden by taking the duffel bag, but there was no stretch flat enough for the suitcase to make use of its wheels.

They walked on, Julie shifting the duffel from hand to hand, glad she'd had some of her things shipped ahead. After another half mile or so, distance hard to assess in the forest, the trees began to space themselves out, and the ground showed hints of green scrub. Then the woods opened up, revealing a sudden swath of sky, a painterly splash of blue. To the right stood a three-story clapboard house. It had a lacy iron scroll of widow's walk upon its roof and was perched at the rim of a cliff.

Laura's pace finally flagged. "Well. How do you like it?"

Julie walked forward as if something were tugging her. "It's beautiful." It was windy this close to the ocean, her clothes flapping like flags, and she wasn't sure if her voice would carry. It didn't matter. What she'd said had been for her own benefit as much as Laura's. *Yes. I made the right decision. This is the place for me.*

Julie climbed a broad set of porch steps, beckoning Depot forward. She turned the knob on the front door and found it unlocked. Pushing the door open—it creaked on thirsty hinges—she took a step inside. Depot settled down against the porch railing, big head between two posts as he looked out over the yard, his gaze twitching ceaselessly.

The entryway of the house opened onto a combined living and dining room backed by a wall of windows. Here the cliff dropped straight to sea level, sixty feet or more, while upstairs the views were no less spectacular. Three bedrooms and a bath, a bit of a slapdash paint job—Julie could detect color bleeding through the fresh coat of neutral beige—but nothing that couldn't be remedied with rollers or a brush. Maybe the prior residents favored hard-to-cover shades.

Laura came up behind her, and Julie startled. She put one hand out on the wall to steady herself, as if the sea were still surging underfoot.

A smile sparked on Laura's face, then vanished. "I brought your luggage up."

"Thank you," Julie told her. "For that, for showing me here—"

"Quick orientation," Laura broke in, seeming in a rush again.

"Sure," Julie said. "Or I don't mind making my way around by myself."

"I have my instructions." Laura gave such a quick shake of her head that it resembled a shudder; Julie wasn't sure what she was refuting. "Let's see, until last year, the schoolteacher resided in one of the cottages outside of town. They did their best to move everything over, but if anything is missing, you have only to give a holler and it'll be supplied."

"That's terrific. Thanks," Julie said. "Why the change?"

"It's a bit sad really," Laura replied. "A lobsterman passed on last spring, a member of the island's oldest clan. His wife couldn't bear to live here without him."

Julie offered a look of regret.

"Walter had great respect for teachers, so with his house standing empty, the family chose to honor him posthumously." Laura spun around in the hall. "Anyway! You had some bigger items shipped, and they've also been left up here for you. The master bedroom is that first one." Laura led the way back down to the first floor. "Laundry in the basement, keys in the drawer of the breakfront"—she pointed—"Wi-Fi password on the fridge—for when it works, that is. Outdoor lighting can be confusing, but there are floodlights here"—she walked toward a plate of switches—"and this controls the ones in back. Don't forget to turn them on. It gets quite dark once the sun goes down."

Laura pulled open the front door, and a sheet of wind made Julie shiver.

"And now I really must go," Laura told her. "I hope you have a wonderful first night." She flashed her hand in a wave and ran down the porch steps.

Julie called Depot inside, watching as Laura departed across the mix of scrub and sand that served for a yard. She was about to shut the door when she saw someone step out to meet Laura at the edge of the woods. Were they late to the party Laura had mentioned? Did that explain her hurry? Laura's quickened steps and the furtive looks she snatched as she approached the woods didn't exactly seem indicative of festivities, however.

The figure in the trees took on shape and definition as Julie walked out onto the porch. It was the regal woman from the video reel. Hair the color of the froth at the edge of the sea, combed into a severe knot, long legs clad in a pair of seemingly endless silk pants. Laura was looking at her with less idolization now, and more something like alarm. The woman grasped Laura by the wrist, and Laura allowed herself to be led.

The two walked off at a pace that seemed rapid, given the woman's age and stately bearing, their feet churning up soil before the woods consumed them both.

CHAPTER FOURTEEN

Julie's first need was to add a few touches of home. She unpacked the linens she'd had sent on ahead, and made the bed with her own quilt and sheets. No pictures of her and David, of course—not at their wedding, which had taken place at a wildflower farm, nor from the trip they'd taken to Belize, back when they'd both enjoyed brief spurts of travel, nor even a selfie snapped as exhausted new parents. But the last photograph ever taken of Hedley was something Julie couldn't imagine ever living without.

She unzipped her suitcase. Tucked between layers of clothes was a pink china frame. Julie removed it with the care and sanctity reserved for rare jewels, an artifact of antiquity, or perhaps something holy, and set the photo on the bedside table. She pressed her fingers to her lips, then touched them to her daughter's cheek, dimpled and forever flawless behind the pane of glass.

Next, Julie took her laptop out of the suitcase and carried it down to the first floor. The Wi-Fi worked fine—of course, it was a bright sunny day, the specter of a power outage hard to imagine—so she went online to post an update and a few photos on Instagram and Facebook, both of which she'd barely frequented over the last year and doubted she'd visit very often now. Still, she finally had something worth sharing.

a real live island! she captioned one pic. And: me without my sea legs

Then she opened a wordless email from Tim, subject line:

let me know you got there

Julie typed a quick reply, Depot whining and twining around her, rocking her back on her feet. "Okay, okay," she told him. "But it's nice to know the real world still exists, isn't it?" Depot's expression told her that he couldn't have cared less, so Julie turned her attentions to the promised provisions.

She had tucked a few pouches of dog food into her duffel for emergencies, but as she began exploring the kitchen, she found a twenty-five-pound sack of nuggets beneath the sink, and six cans stacked in a cabinet. There were even dog bowls. Julie filled one with water, then served up a mixture of wet and dry in the other. Despite the unfamiliar brands, Depot gobbled two servings, before asking for thirds with his long tongue lolling.

"Okay," Julie said. "But only because we skipped lunch."

She scooped out the contents of a fresh can, watching as Depot downed the additional portion. Hunger assuaged, the dog walked over to the rear of the house, sprawled out beside the sun-warmed glass, and fell asleep.

Julie found the fridge no less generously fitted out. A pitcher of iced tea stood on one shelf, along with a platter of sandwiches. On the counter, a domed cake plate contained something temptingly sweet and multilayered.

The clamor of travel finally began to subside. Julie put a section of sandwich on a plate, then upon a moment's reflection, added a chunk of cake. When was the last time she'd bothered with—allowed herself to have—dessert? She filled a glass with ice cubes, and was about to go for her suitcase, just a drizzle in her tea for a kick, when she realized she was okay for now. Without David there to conceal the accounting of their consumption, a pour seemed more…apparent. Uncle Vern's voice lived in her head. *Do what you need to. Just don't do it with this.* Maybe a nightcap before bed would suffice tonight.

Julie nudged open the front door with her foot and took her food outside. She polished off most of her meal, not quite as hungry as Depot, but appetite definitely stirring to life. Listening to the distant lift and sigh of the sea, Julie leaned sleepily against a porch post. A rocking chair, she thought, as she began to doze. Perhaps a picnic table by the cliff in back of the house. With that pleasant prospect in mind, Julie drifted off.

A change in color woke her: the sun sinking in the sky.

Julie jumped up, brushing crumbs off her hands, then descended the porch steps and ran around the side of the house. She pulled up short, a few feet from the edge of the cliff, gaze fixed on the vista before her. It was as if she stood at the very edge of the world.

Everything had been painted orange and pink. A tremendous orb of sun trembled on the horizon, lighting both the sky and sea.

Julie rotated slowly, as if to make sure the house still stood there. For a moment, at least, it really felt as if it might have disappeared—as if everything might've. Then the rear wall came into sight, with Depot behind the glass, bathed in the citrus glow of the setting sun. Julie lifted one hand; silly, maybe, to signal her presence to a dog, but reassuring in some way nonetheless. Giving a little wave, Julie set off, walking along the rim of cliff while studying the sun's path of descent.

The last line of color dipped below the horizon, and the evening turned gray, dispelling her earlier feeling of anticipation. As the sea sighed and salt air bit her nostrils, Julie grew cloyingly, oppressively homesick. The sense she'd had on the ferry, about making a mistake, came rushing back. All the reminders of Hedley lived in Wedeskyull, every place her baby had been in real life.

Julie missed the mountains, protective interruptions in the night sky. Here the firmament was so broad and empty, it seemed something might come down and pluck up a small creature walking around beneath. She shivered. Even the cold felt different here—a sodden, plastering chill that dampened your skin and weighed down your bones.

Stars began to come out, bits of glass in the darkening sky. Julie turned her back on the sea and started her return journey. The house seemed farther away than it should have, as if she'd traveled a long way without realizing it. Maybe it was the change in her mood: the trip out here swift and light, footsteps propelled by food and drink and a nap, while every step now dragged and it felt as if she would never reach her destination.

Julie had the odd but powerful feeling that the house was moving farther off with each step she took toward it. The vast vista of the sea distorted things. She clearly remembered deciding against opening the bottle of scotch she had purchased, but began to doubt herself now. Surely this must be alcohol-induced, a hallucination of some kind? She licked her lips to see if the telltale taste lingered.

Then Julie caught a glimpse of clapboard, white slashes against the night, and broke into a jog. But the house continued to retreat, dream-like, for every forward move she made. She began to run, a full-on sprint across the open plane of sandy soil. She'd forgotten to turn on the outside lights, and there was no twinkle of a lamp from even a distant neighbor. Julie momentarily lost sight of the house again, hidden in folds of darkness. Smoke-colored clouds had just started to smudge the sky, a mist drifting in from the sea, when Julie came to a halt, breathing fast. Had she swerved somehow, gone off course? Maybe that pitcher of iced tea had been spiked, an extra-special welcome. For whatever reason, her own footsteps didn't feel reliable here. She squinted to make out the shape of walls or a roof.

Then she heard something and swiveled. Depot's resounding bark, his loudest one, unmistakable in the hush. And another, echoing through the night. Julie ran toward the sound, Depot's ongoing series of barks a cannonball fire of noise for her to follow. If they did have any neighbors, this would be some way to make friends.

There was the house, open and unguarded by trees or anything else. It should've been visible long before now; the sea must play tricks on the eyes. Julie mounted the porch steps, each one a small summit, home-sickness at bay for now, simply glad at the thought of a bed.

When she tried the front door, it was locked.

CHAPTER FIFTEEN

J ulie had left the door unlocked. She was even more sure of that than she was about not having cracked open her new bottle.

She walked backward until her shoulders banged the porch pillar, keeping her from spilling down onto the grassless lawn. It was too dark to see anything in the yard. Julie went back and rattled the doorknob, causing Depot's barks to ratchet up again.

"It's okay, Deep," she said resolvedly. "I'll be back in a sec."

She walked the length of the porch, squinting out into the night.

The urge to call out a *Hello, anybody there?* was powerful, but generations of relatives in law enforcement had taught her better. Someone had to have been here to lock the door, and why would anyone do that? Taking another quick peek around, Julie turned her back on the night and approached a window that looked into the front hallway.

Locked. Of course.

This level presented ready access, and the whole house was so removed from any companions. Hadn't Laura said that a widow lived here alone after her husband died? She would've wanted the protection of locks on the first floor.

Julie descended the porch steps as if stepping into a pool of black water. A roof covered the porch below the second story. If she could get up there, she might be able to enter the house through one of the upstairs windows.

She mounted the porch steps again, then climbed onto the railing. She got into a standing position, balancing carefully, fighting the feeling of fingers settling onto her spine. But she couldn't hoist herself from here onto the roof; it was too high.

Walk back to town, find somebody who could help? But Julie didn't have a flashlight, and the thought of that uprooted stretch of forest, like the earth coming loose from its shorings, caused gooseflesh to break out on her skin. Anyway, it wasn't as if there'd be a locksmith available at this hour. Julie was the schoolteacher. She needed to look competent, capable, not like someone who got into YouTube-style predicaments on the very first day.

A shed stood at the back of the house. Julie had seen it during her trip to watch the sunset, which was now starting to seem more and more ill-fated. Jumping down from the railing, she landed on the scrubby lawn and left the protection of the house behind. Inside, Depot's barks picked up again, loud and bracing. Because she hadn't come for him yet or because he was warning her about something? Julie whirled around. She couldn't see a soul.

The sea's reflective surface provided scant illumination, and Julie sped up, power walking toward the shed. She tugged on a metal hasp. The door refused to give, although upon examination, it didn't appear to be sealed by anything. Julie pulled harder and the door screeched open, the sound a scythe through the muted silence of the night.

She was propelled backward by a rotten, mucky stench. It filled her nostrils like paste and coated the inside of her mouth. Clamping one hand over her nose, Julie peered into the little structure. Filled with mounds and clumps of things; she couldn't make out exactly what. Taking a step inside, Julie crouched down and began patting around. She felt tangled ropes, netting; her fingers slid into the slimy holes of a lobster trap. A pair of splintery oars leaned against one wall, while a pile of life preservers were denuded of stuffing. Mice must've been in here, but the smell came from fishy things, the carapaces of sea creatures long gone. Julie fisted her hands, loath to touch anything else.

A cone of white suddenly lit the sky, clouds parting to reveal the moon. It glinted on a stack of crinkly tarps, and wonder of wonders, an extension ladder that weighed down the pile. Dragging the ladder out of the shed, Julie headed back in the direction of the house.

She was stopped by the high, sweet sound of laughter.

The ladder slipped from Julie's grasp, landing on her foot. She sucked in a cry of pain as she yanked herself free. She bent down and felt the injury. She could wiggle her toes, nothing broken, but the metal had delivered a nasty scrape and her hand came away smeared with blood. Whatever noise she'd heard had stopped. All was quiet again.

Julie hefted the ladder and pulled it the rest of the way to the house. From the ground, she looked up at a window, then propped the ladder against the clapboards, making sure to plant its legs securely in the sandy earth. She started to climb. Now a breeze came off the sea; it stirred the hairs on the back of her neck. Julie was on the fourth rung of the ladder when the sound of disembodied laughter started up again.

A snicker, sly and knowing.

The metal sides went slippery in her grasp. She clenched her toes against the rod on which she perched, feeling the wound on her foot smart, then twisted around. Forget not giving away the fact of her presence—it was obviously known—or her location. Mustering all the volume she could, Julie shouted: "Who is that? Who's there?"

Instantly, the laughter lightened, a breathy fading out.

Some kind of bird or animal? Loons could sound as if they were laughing, although they were lake, not shore, birds. Panthers screamed with laughter, but big cats didn't live on islands.

The moon was so bright now there was no way anybody could be lurking around. Angry, both at the source of the sound and herself for getting spooked, Julie stomped up the next two rungs on the ladder, panting with exertion and nerves, then leaned to one side. She could just reach the window from here. Julie placed both hands on the sill and gave a tug. The glass slid upward with gratifying ease.

Now to get herself off the ladder and in through the opening.

"Nobody better laugh," she muttered aloud.

She knew she must look ridiculous, awkwardly placing one knee on the window ledge, then, using the foot still on a rung to give a mighty kick, allowing the ladder to clatter to the ground as she made her way over. For a second her left leg dangled, hanging free before she could swing it over the sill and slide inside.

Julie straightened up, her body bruised and sore in places she couldn't identify yet. Downstairs, Depot let out an escalade of barks. She heard his paws scrabbling as he mounted the stairs. Then he abruptly quit barking. He'd figured out it was her.

Julie patted the wall, feeling around for a light switch. Her hand came down on a piece of furniture. It had a lamp standing upon it, which Julie immediately flicked on. She was in one of the other bedrooms, smaller than the master, and crowded with objects. Cast-off furniture, boxes, crates. The evidence of a seafaring life—it had indeed been a lobsterman who used to reside here—was displayed in the overflow: weatherproof gear laid on top of a bulging carton marked *Walter's clothes*; leather books that upon examination were some kind of log, prices per pound graphed over years in undulating fluctuation; assorted equipment Julie had no hope of identifying, radios or sonar or navigational devices.

She wove through the detritus, feeling sorry for the woman who'd had to store away a lifetime's worth of her husband's leavings. As Julie crossed the room, she realized that at least the woman had a child, a boy from the looks of it, whose outgrown possessions had been tossed with less care into clear plastic bins: a mixed-up jumble of toys buried beneath tangles of clothes. Julie veered around the bins, heading for the door.

A draped and shadowed piece of furniture stood in front of it.

As if it had been dragged there, placed as an obstacle to prevent her getting out, Julie bumped into the slatted side of a crib.

CHAPTER SIXTEEN

J ulie felt the wooden slats through the sheet that covered the crib.
This object she knew even blind, there could be no doubt about
what it was, but just in case, she drew the sheet aside. Her hand began
moving up and down without conscious volition, patting the plasticky
surface of the mattress as if by rote. It was dim here, far away from the
lamp, and the crib was filled with cold, gray air. Julie kept patting, trying
to impart some warmth. The slats of the crib were as hard as bone when
she finally withdrew her hand.

Come back.

A sinister murmur.

Had the laughter Julie heard earlier not been real either? Nor the
optical illusion of the retreating house?

She turned and yanked the door open so hard that her shoulder
rattled in its socket. Depot was waiting for her in the hall, and Julie
sank down, burying her face in his fur. She was never prepared for this
grasping grief, no matter how many times its suffocating shroud was

bestowed, sinking her body without so much as a tug. The hideous paradox of mourning was how utterly, inarguably final it was while at the same time never ending. Julie laid her cheek upon her dog, a trickle of tears worming around her nose and soaking into his coat. At last, she sat up. She got to her feet slowly, breaking the move into parts.

Julie turned on the lights and checked each of the rooms, in case anybody was there, although the mystery of the front door felt less pressing now. Whoever the voice belonged to had probably locked it. That conclusion contained the plausibility of the best drunk reasoning, making Julie realize what her next step should be. She located her suitcase and unzipped it roughly, an angry buzzing in the quiet of the house. The bottle she'd picked up en route to Lambert Point was nestled within a stack of shirts. A full, untouched bottle, golden like the sun.

Depot came padding up beside her.

"Don't judge," Julie told him.

The dog accompanied her to the kitchen. Julie took a tumbler from one of the pristine, well-organized cupboards, and poured herself a drink, draining the glass at one go. Depot stood panting at her side.

"You thirsty too?" Julie asked. She walked over to the sink and filled his bowl. Water sloshed over the rim as she placed the bowl on the floor.

Depot began to lap in fast, flicking splashes.

"I'll join you in another," Julie said. Her fingers felt thick and clumsy as she refilled her glass, once, then twice.

Depot ignored her.

Julie crossed to the wall of windows at the rear of the house, bottle swinging loosely in her grasp. She tilted it to her lips—*Why bother with a glass?*—shielding her eyes at a glint of moonlight. Julie hiccupped, a jarring, painful heave of her chest. At home, David would've paced her, if not slowed her down. But David wasn't here to serve drinks, nor share any other part of her life.

She didn't exactly miss him, even with an endless, empty night laid out before her. In fact, Julie was surprised by how simple it felt to exca-vate herself from the state of marriage. Maybe David was right, and the two of them really had been over for years.

She headed to the couch in a weaving shamble, tripping at one point and completing the voyage on her hands and knees. Curled into a ball, taking up as small a portion of sofa as possible, she let aloneness submerge her. She rolled toward the back of the couch, arms wrapped around her spinning head. Tears began to leak from her eyes, and she used a cushion to blot them.

She might not miss David, but with him out of her life, another of her roles had been stripped away. For a long time, she hadn't been any-one's daughter. Hedley was gone, so the word *mother* no longer applied. Julie had been a mother for such a short time. Barely one at all. Now she wasn't a wife either.

Teacher. In less than a week, she would be a teacher again.

Julie awoke when the wall of glass turned the room into a solarium, her tongue as thick and floppy as a pillow. Not enough moisture to break up the foul-tasting crust on her lips. Depot slept somewhere nearby; Julie could smell his dank odor. He still needed a bath. She looked around, and the motion drove a spike through her head. She snapped just the tips of her fingers, muted and quiet, until the big dog stirred. Julie lifted her hand slowly, the air a mass too dense to move through, then let her palm fall, deadweight, upon Depot's back. Pushing herself off the couch, she leaned against his bulk, and the two of them made their way to the bathroom, where Julie peed, long and scorching.

She attempted to lean over the sink, but was stopped by her throb-bing head and had to make do with turning on the faucet and slapping handfuls of water up toward her mouth. The few drops she managed to imbibe tasted like the nectar of Eden. A hair of the dog had never worked for Julie—in fact, for a few precious hours following one of the binges whose number had steepened sharply over the past year, the idea of her substance of choice prompted nothing but repulsion.

Julie shuffled into the kitchen and located coffee in one of the cabinets. Some sort of upmarket, Maine-roasted brew, strong and bracing. The first cup provided a jolt of clarity; the second cleared the final shreds of last night from her head.

She needed to do this now, while the mere thought of alcohol caused a physical backlash. Holding the bottle as far away from her as she could get it, trying not to inhale, Julie tilted the contents over the sink. It wouldn't be simple to purchase scotch on the island. Everyone knew everything and everybody; the parents of her students would learn she was a drinker and at what rate. Julie watched the last trickle swirl down the drain, then rinsed out the empty and stowed it on the counter till she could figure out recycling.

She turned to look at Depot. "Happy?"

He was tussling with a chew toy she'd unearthed from the duffel, spitting it out before sinking his teeth back in with relish.

"I'll take that as a yes," Julie said. "Let's give you a bath."

She had just toweled Depot off and was mopping the bathroom floor to a Zamboni-like shine when the front door banged open and a voice called out, "Hello?"

Depot let out his sharp, stranger bark; then again, everybody was a stranger on this island. Julie gave him a stern look of warning. "Hey, at least they're announcing themselves this time," she said in an undertone. She started to descend the stairs, peering into the hall.

"I'm sorry!" a woman said. "I knocked, but you must not have heard me."

She looked to be about Julie's age, petite and narrowly built, with a tousled cap of hair. Her skin was lightly freckled, and her eyes a gray so light, they were nearly colorless. A big, open smile made clear the mood you couldn't read in her eyes.

Julie found herself smiling back. "No worries. I was bathing my dog."

Depot had continued his loud barking, attempting to come up beside Julie on the stairs. There wasn't room for the two of them, and from long experience, Julie knew who the loser would be in such a contest. Depot didn't realize no one else was a match for his muscle. She hushed the dog's barks, then gripped the railing so she wouldn't slip, letting Depot squeeze past and proceed her down the steps.

"Oh my," the woman breathed. "What a beaut. Is he friendly?"

"Totally," Julie replied. "He just has to check you out before becoming lifelong pals."

The woman did everything right, staying still, offering Depot her fingers to sniff, waiting for the intangible signs the dog gave once he'd accepted a person: a settling of his huge shoulders, a snuffle and ducking of his head.

Crouching down, the woman ruffled the fur on Depot's throat.

Julie liked her instantly.

The woman rose to her feet. "I'm sorry," she said again. "First I barge in here like the place is mine, then I lay claim to your dog."

Julie laughed. "Not at all. You clearly have a way. You a dog person?"

The woman looked down at Depot. "Isn't everyone?" Her tone was a little off, though, her friendly manner momentarily receding before she reached out to touch Julie on the arm. "Well, come on, we have a lot to do today."

Julie lifted her brows, and the woman frowned. "You were expecting me, right?"

At Julie's blank look, the woman let out a groan. "Oh no. Oh my goodness—I really did barge in! I only opened the door because I was late. We were scheduled to meet at ten, and I was afraid you might've thought I bailed on you."

It was Julie's turn to apologize. "I probably just forgot in the tumult—"

The woman shook her head. "It's us, I'm sure. It was a bit of a thing, finding a new teacher. Let's start over. I'm Ellie Newcomb, and I've been asked to give you a tour of the island."

"How nice! And are you also the one who supplied this house so well—and made that incredible cake?" Julie extended her hand. "Julie Weathers," she added.

Ellie gave Julie's hand a surprisingly firm shake for someone of her size. She was built like a ballet dancer, or maybe a gymnast. "Can't bake worth a damn, I'm afraid."

Julie smiled. "Me either. In which case...would you like a piece?"

An image suddenly reared up, a shot of warning paired against the pleasure of meeting a potential friend. The empty bottle Julie had left on the counter.

Luckily, Ellie refused the offer. "We've got a lot of ground to cover. Besides, I'll treat you to lunch at Harbor House. Their pies will make that cake look so-so, I swear."

"It smelled amazing when we walked past," Julie remarked. Her day felt filled with a pale note of promise for the first time in over a year. "Let me just run up and change. Hey, you don't mind if Depot comes with us, do you?"

Ellie had already turned to open the door. Hearing his name, Depot scrambled to exit first, making Ellie totter a bit and throw one hand out to keep from falling.

"Whoa," she said, though she didn't seem a bit bothered. "Take your time," she called back to Julie. "I have a ball I can throw around while we wait."

CHAPTER SEVENTEEN

When Julie got outside, Depot was sitting quietly at the edge of the sand and scrub, Ellie on her feet beside him. She was so tiny that Depot's head came to her waist.

She turned when she heard Julie approach. "I couldn't find my ball," she said, patting her pockets and making a sad face. "I think I disappointed him."

Julie smiled. It'd been so long since she'd gone on any sort of social outing, let alone made a friend. She found herself asking her daughter for permission in her mind, as she had before her interview. *I think you'd like her, Lilypad.*

Ellie's chatter trailed off, though she continued to regard Julie with an open, friendly expression.

Say something, Julie told herself. *That's what you do to make friends.*

"Depot's never been the biggest fan of fetch," she told Ellie. "Besides, if yesterday was any indication, he's about to go on a great walk." She paused. "And this is a dog who's taken some pretty epic walks." She headed toward the line of trees, turning back when she lost sight of Ellie. "This way, right?"

Ellie ran to catch up. "Right."

Julie and Ellie fell into step side by side, Depot running ahead, then turning back to them, paws scrabbling on the rough earth before he raced forward again.

"So what's surprised you so far?" Ellie asked.

Julie glanced at her, and Ellie inclined her head.

"I read it in this make-deeper-connections thirty-day plan on a blog. Don't just start a relationship with a generic question. Ask the person what surprised them, or tickled them, or even disturbed them."

Julie hesitated. She didn't want to let her new acquaintance know how weirded out she had gotten last night—By what? A crib? Somebody laughing?—but there was maybe one thing about which she could gain some insight. "People cleared off the ferry so fast. I looked around and nobody was there. Or even any of the cargo that came over on the boat."

"Island folk don't know how to talk to newcomers," Ellie answered promptly, and honestly. "They probably had relatives waiting with hand-carts at the dock for their stuff so no one would have to stick around and make small talk." A pause. "Truth."

Julie laughed. "Well, that's one mystery cleared up," she said, although it didn't exactly explain the tourists' scurry.

"Distrust of outsiders," Ellie agreed. "Forget global politics. Tiny Mercy Island's the seat." She steered the two of them into the woods, holding back a flap of branches. "I guess Laura took you along this trail?" She gave a dramatic shiver. "I've always hated it."

"Is there another way you can go?"

"You can come up by the cliff," Ellie replied. "Although it's a little steep, especially if you're carrying things. It's my preferred approach, though, so long as the weather's fair. Maybe I'll show you on our way back."

The woods were as dusky and shadowed as they'd been the day

before, the canopy overhead a mesh through which hardly any light filtered. Despite the tight wall of trees to either side, and braided fronds and ferns underfoot, Julie's feet found the path unerringly; she didn't have to watch Ellie for signs of how to go.

Julie had always been at home in a forest, able to read its crooks and notches like a map. And Depot was the same—she could hear him now, breaking through bramble, snapping twigs, as he stayed true to their course.

"Why do you hate this route?" Julie asked.

Ellie shouldered aside a branch, pausing to hold it back so Julie could pass.

Julie nodded her thanks.

"Trees don't usually get this big or crowded on an island—the wind stunts them, the salt in the air prohibits growth. Something about the unique currents in the patch of sea around Mercy affect the weather. I guess I'm not used to the scale."

"You haven't always lived here then?"

Ellie shook her head. "I'm an island girl, born and bred, but my dad was a fisherman and we followed the catch. Nantucket for a while, then Monhegan, and Isle au Haut. We didn't come to Mercy till I was a teenager."

"Do your parents still live on the island?"

Ellie winced. "They both died actually. Only a couple of years apart."

"I lost mine too," Julie offered, and they traded sympathetic glances.

"We're almost out," Ellie said, picking up her pace. "Where is that dog of yours?"

It occurred to Julie that she hadn't heard Depot in a while.

"Depot?" she called out. "Deep?"

"Great name, by the way," Ellie said.

Julie jogged forward a few steps, calling out to her dog.

But the woods stayed still and silent. Windless, without so much as a bird flushed out of the brush, or a chipmunk scampering across the ground. The differences Julie felt between Mercy and Wedeskyull added up to one factor. There was less life on an island.

"Depot!" she shouted.

It was stupid to feel this flutter of fear in her belly. But the forest was indeed dense, and even though getting lost wasn't an issue—with an ocean for perimeter—other dangers lurked that were unfamiliar to Depot. Such as falling into said ocean.

She turned to Ellie. "How close are we to the—" she began when Depot appeared, huge behind a bowed tree trunk. The dog sat on his haunches, still, not even panting.

Julie clapped a hand to her chest. "Depot! My God, Deep, you scared me."

The dog didn't move.

The trees were starting to thin out, the one that failed to conceal Depot as small and hunched as a crone. Julie closed the distance between herself and the dog.

"He okay?" Ellie called.

She didn't walk into the section of trees Julie and Depot now occupied.

"Fine, I think," Julie said, separating tufts of fur on the dog's coat, looking into his eyes. "I don't see anything wrong."

"Must've been exploring," Ellie offered. "Come on, we're almost to town."

There was a pleasant buzz in town. Tourists—couples walking hand in hand, parents corralling small children—packed the sandy one-lane road, prompting Julie to keep Depot close, walking single file behind Ellie so as to stay out of people's way.

Signs beckoned shoppers into a small handful of stores, their awnings fluttering in the ocean breeze. Seagulls squawked, diving for food that fell from careless hands; and from the dock came the thrum of lobster boats motoring out to sea, the flat *thwack* of traps hitting the water far from shore.

Ellie gave Julie a tour of the inn, then suggested checking out the wares at the general store before visiting a gift shop, all the while making introductions to the people they encountered. Despite Ellie's statements about the natives' standoffishness, most of them trilled happy hellos and even asked a question or two about Julie's arrival—the quality of the ferry crossing apparently roughly equivalent to a discussion in Wedeskyull about how much snow was expected.

The jovial, pleasant mood persisted right up until Ellie brought her to a tiny store that sold sea-themed antiques. The door opened to a tinkle of bells, and the two of them came face-to-face with a customer, an older man with a deceptively thick head of hair and a dignified carriage to his bearing. He was picking up ancient bronze bells from a display case, but when he saw Julie, his face broke into a smile as if he already knew her.

Julie smiled back.

Ellie spun Julie around, closing the door behind them and leading her across the road.

"Who was that?" Julie asked. "You left awfully fast."

Ellie shrugged it off. "He's just not the nicest resident you could meet."

"Really?" Julie replied. "He seemed friendly."

Ellie shrugged again, offering a smile.

"Is he local? I would've thought he was a tourist in a store like that."

Something took hold of Ellie's features, a certain tremble in her mouth, before she recaptured her smile. "He's the localist of locals. And I don't mean to act all weird—the alpha sea captains just don't do it for me. Even when they're old and sick and losing it."

She was clearly going for humor, trying to play things off, but she was upset.

"You know what?" Julie said.

Ellie darted a quick look at her.

"I'm starving."

A hostess led Ellie and Julie to the last unoccupied table looking over the sea. Julie ordered a burger to bring out to Depot, who lay beside the water bowl provided by the restaurant. Depot had already emptied it; he was parched and tired after whatever adventure had made him run off alone in the woods. Julie stooped to pat the dog, then reentered Harbor House, weaving between customers to the sunroom where she and Ellie had been seated.

"Prime spot," Julie remarked, dropping into her chair.

"Of course," Ellie said. "You're our guest."

Julie inclined her head. "What I want is to be the schoolteacher."

"You come from a small town. You must know it can take some doing before you really belong."

Julie opened the menu. "Let's hope my town isn't an accurate measure. Or else I'll fit in here sometime after my students' great-grandchildren have graduated."

Ellie laughed, though Julie noted she offered no contradiction.

"So what do you really think of the island so far?" Ellie asked. "Other than the xenophobic brigade off the ferry?"

Julie smiled briefly, then switched her gaze to the view. She stared out at sparkling water, bobbing buoys, chugging boats, men leaning overboard with ropes and poles. The sea looked as busy and bustling as a construction site.

"It's lovely," she pronounced.

Ellie rolled her eyes. "Obvs. Anything else…?"

Julie hesitated. It had been so long since she'd had real companionship, someone who wanted to know what she thought and felt, instead of just skating over the pleasantries. David and her remaining close friends or family members—Tim, Vern, her aunt—were just glad these days if Julie wasn't falling apart. But Ellie didn't know Julie's past and the result was liberating, even if it also felt like a betrayal of Hedley.

"To tell you the truth, I do find myself surprised by things. Per that deeper connections blog you mentioned."

Ellie raised interested brows.

"Laura Hutchins described this place as pretty lonely. So far out to sea, cut off from the rest of the world. But I feel like it's practically hopping. There's so much life and laughter and light here." Although that laughter could sound sort of creepy up on a ladder in the dark.

Ellie seemed to register her unspoken afterthought. "Right. You'll see."

"That sounds pretty dire." Julie leaned closer. "What will I see?"

Ellie leaned in as well. "Look, Mercy's a wonderful place; I've chosen to make it my home. But the school board chose your arrival date for a reason. Of course you need time to get settled, but there's also something else."

It was Julie's turn to look questioning.

Ellie splayed her hands out on the table. "This is the climax of the tourist season, summer's last and biggest hurrah. You're seeing the place with its best clothes on, all the services set up to cater to the summer people. Everyone's on tip-top behavior—visitors in vacay mode, locals preening for them. But give it another few days and…" She stopped and glanced around.

Julie felt a prickle on her skin; someone had turned on the air-conditioning.

When Ellie looked back, her colorless eyes were fairly crackling, lightning upon orbs of cloud. "Give it another few days and this island will undergo a transformation so great, you'll think you landed on the moon."

CHAPTER EIGHTEEN

Wow," Julie said weakly. "Okay. I stand prepared."

Ellie opened her mouth, as if about to add something—whether in the form of emphasis or retreat, it wasn't clear—but then the waitress appeared. She was clad in an eyelet-trimmed uniform, her name embroidered below the collar of her blouse. Everything about the restaurant screamed midcentury not-so-modern; it was far less a la mode than the Adirondacks with their influx of hipster growers and recreationists. Perhaps people came to Mercy precisely for the feel of bygone days.

Ellie kept her gaze fixed on Julie, the emotion in her eyes waning. "I'd say we deserve a glass of wine. Red or white?"

Julie looked down quickly, pretending to be absorbed by the menu. "Oh, none for me, thanks, but you definitely go ahead."

"Not a drinker?" Ellie asked. "Or just not in the mood?"

She was sharp. Julie suspected that if she and Ellie continued to hang out, she would become the kind of friend who didn't let you get away with much. For now, though, they were still relative strangers, and Julie could brush over things. She shrugged. "I don't drink much." Not as of last night.

"I'll have whatever pinot you've got open," Ellie told the waitress. "With the lobster salad."

"Iced tea for me," Julie said. "And the same thing."

They discussed the lighter details of island life as they ate: how to get the owner of Perry's to open up late if you ran out of something, the typical frequency of Amazon shipments, and number of times a week you could eat lobster without getting sick of it.

Only when Julie asked Ellie what people their age did for fun, did Ellie display a blade of discomfort. "Well, let's see, the guys keep to themselves; fishermen always do. And the women are nice enough, but if you don't have kids and a fisherman husband, it can be hard to find common ground, you know?"

Switch a couple of the fine points, and it sounded a lot like home.

Once they'd finished eating, Julie went outside to retrieve Depot, then Ellie showed the way to the little library, where there was Wi-Fi and phones winked to life even outdoors.

Julie checked hers, before following Ellie through a gate and down a seashell path that turned out to lead to the schoolhouse. The small building sat in a cove, its back to an overhang of black rock face rendered glossy by seeping water. The stone structure appeared to be built out of the cliff itself, although as Julie drew near, she saw the school was in fact freestanding, just with very little space between it and the headland behind. The salt-brined odor of the sea filled Julie's nose as they picked their way across hummocks of seaweed-draped rocks, giving way to a half-moon of shore.

"What an incredible spot," she said.

Ellie nodded. "Past teachers have created some pretty mean marine-biology lessons here."

"I bet," Julie said. She still had curriculum planning to do herself, but right now the only thing she could focus on was having come to teach in the most beautiful place in the world.

Ellie approached a hobbit-like door in the side of the stone structure. "The kids enter through the barn doors at the front of the building, but we'll use this one today."

The door was arched and shrunken. Ellie could walk through at full height, but Julie had to stoop. The interior was chilly, stone walls keeping what heat there was outside from penetrating. Julie wondered what this building would feel like come winter, when the sea winds blew. As if reading her thoughts, Ellie pointed to an immense woodstove occupying a central position. "There are electric radiators for backup, but that baby will keep you plenty comfy."

"I'm familiar," Julie said. "Where I come from, wood is free, and fuel costly."

Depot trotted over and lay down in front of the stove.

Julie took a look around the large space: wood-floored, with a blackboard covering one wall, rows of desks with chairs attached, and a run of empty, unused space behind the teacher's desk. Midcentury not-so-modern again. Even in Wedeskyull, most classrooms used SMART Boards, with slate and chalk only for when the tech got glitchy.

A computer monitor sat on what was to be her desk, with an actual CPU underneath. There were no devices on the student desks, which Julie had expected, although the holes for inkwells did provoke a momentary blink. These pieces of furniture were literal antiques.

Ellie echoed her thoughts. "No Wi-Fi; the school board didn't want the kids who have phones to be on them all day. That old beast you've got to use is connected to an actual cable."

Julie nodded, recalling her own past classrooms. "I bet it does help with focus."

Ellie continued speaking. "Once upon a day, we had twice this many rows of desks, four times even. That was before my time. But now at least you have plenty of room for PE or other activities when it's not possible to go outdoors."

Julie counted in her head. Three rows, eight desks long.

"But wait, there's more," Ellie quipped, circling the stove.

Julie followed her to the back of the schoolroom.

A thick velvet curtain, kingly blue in hue beneath a snowy layer of dust, formed a backdrop to the room. Ellie brushed at the cloth, and they both began coughing, Julie laughing at the same time. "A stage?" she said. "I've got a stage?"

That fact outweighed any meager negative she had felt upon confronting the reality that her phone would be as unconnected as a rock all day.

Ellie finally gave up on her ministrations and tugged the curtain to one side. "Not the biggest one," she said, gesturing to a short flight of wooden steps that climbed to a platform. "Some of the men built this a few decades back during the down season. It hasn't happened lately—too small a class, too little interest—but some pretty neat shows were once put on here."

"How awesome," Julie breathed.

"You a drama nerd?"

It felt like a recollection from a different person. "Totally," Julie admitted. "I once wanted to be an actress. Unfortunately, that was a foreign concept to my logger father. It was as if I said I wanted to be a serial killer."

Ellie sent her a sympathetic glance, then crouched at the base of the stage. "What this is mostly used for now is storage," she said, pulling at a ring set into a recessed panel. The panel swung open and Ellie pointed inside. "Tons of space under there and tons of stuff too. You might want to look through it before school starts."

"Definitely," Julie agreed.

Ellie stood and clapped dust off her hands. She led the way out of the schoolroom, and they emerged into a short hallway. Ellie flicked on a light, pointing to a series of doors.

"Girls' room, boys', and teachers' bathroom," she said, striding past each one.

Julie looked back to check on Depot before catching up.

They came to a fourth door. "Here's your break room—no kids allowed."

It contained a table, a chair, a small fridge, and a counter with a coffeepot on it.

Ellie pulled the door closed behind them, and they wended their way along the hall—by Julie's estimation they now stood behind the stage—until they came to a ladder leaning against a loft.

"You can get above the stage this way, but it's also a neat space in and of itself. Teachers have held poetry circles up there, or discussion groups for the older kids."

"Cool," Julie said. "Mind if I go up?"

"I wouldn't now," Ellie replied. "It's not well lit, and I don't know what all is up there."

"I'll come back, no problem," Julie said.

"I'll ask one of the men to deal with the light situation," Ellie said. "It's always been an issue."

"Thanks," Julie said.

Ellie grinned at her. "I think that's it. Your new home away from your new home away from home."

Julie smiled back.

"Oh!" Ellie said. "They told me to make sure I showed you this."

She ushered Julie past the opening to the loft, stopping before a bank of filing cabinets. Ellie started pulling open drawers, revealing neat rows of folders. Julie bent down, studying the carefully labeled tabs. Eighth-grade science, eighth-grade math, eighth-grade language arts, eighth-grade human studies. Then seventh grade, sixth, with another set of folders in the drawer beneath, and another below that, then another.

"On the one hand, lesson plans aren't computerized, but on the other, you have all this to start from," Ellie explained. "Going back years, but everything's updated routinely. Since the students are educated in the same room, they overhear a lot of the other grades' curricula, and the school board feels this facilitates continuity."

"Makes sense." It would save Julie a ton of work, even sans digital ease of use.

They roused Depot, then left the schoolhouse, pausing at the library so Julie could check her phone again. Still no text or call from David, although sometime in the last half hour, Tim had left a just-checking-in voicemail. Julie answered it with a row of emojis: a smiley, a boat, and a pencil with books. Then she and Ellie reversed their trip through town, Ellie depositing Julie and Depot at the mouth of the woods. She lived in the sky-blue cottage in the grouping that stood at the crossroads, had pointed it out as they'd trooped past earlier.

"Sure you'll be okay?" Ellie asked. "I'd walk you the rest of the way, but I have someone coming over in an hour and nothing besides stale bread for us to eat." A pause. "She can be a bit of a case, or I'd totally invite you."

Julie waved her off. "You've been absolutely wonderful, giving me your whole day. I can't tell you how much I appreciate it."

"It was fun. Please stop by before school starts. Barge into my house next time!"

Julie smiled, nodding agreement as she and Depot struck out for the woods.

When they got back to the house, Julie was surprised at how familiar the place felt already. She fed and watered Depot, then decided to repeat yesterday's alfresco victuals, helping herself to a whole sandwich this time, and going outside with a blanket for a picnic by the cliff. Depot came and joined her, and they stayed to watch the sun drop and the evening sky turn silver. Julie wasn't sure how to put a lid on the night. Normally David would be pouring her a drink by now, and the sudden loss of substance, ritual, and company left a void she didn't know how to fill.

Julie was used to unfillable voids, however.

She had just gone back inside with her dishes when she heard a sound that made dinner lurch in her belly. Depot's stranger bark, a bracing boom. For a supposedly unfriendly island, Julie had received an awful lot of visitors. Or was this the laughing stranger from yesterday who'd refused to show himself, the person who had moved that crib?

She set her plate and glass on the dining room table soundlessly, following the trail of Depot's growls till she came upon him in at the foot of the stairs.

"What is it, Deep?" she whispered. "Someone here?"

A loud bang and the front door shook in its frame.

Depot broke into a volley of barks.

Julie stepped to one side, peering out the window that looked onto the porch.

"It's Ellie," she said, relieved. "It's just Ellie, Deep. Be quiet."

The dog's barks quieted to a low, throaty vibration. He maneuvered his big body in front of Julie, who leaned past him to open the door.

"I'm sorry—" Ellie began. She was breathing hard as if she'd run the whole way. "I happened to mention that we were together all day so she knew the house was empty—"

Julie frowned.

Depot's barks grew so frantic that Julie couldn't hear whatever Ellie said next.

Then a woman came out of the woods, crossing the scrubby front yard in a twisting, weaving dash. Her long legs made fast work of the trip, and in the next instant, she had scaled the porch steps. The sharp cheekbones of her face stood out like blades, her mouth wrenched sideways. As she stared at Julie, her eyes went wide; she appeared to be in a state of true terror.

"Tell me," she pleaded. "Is my son here?"

CHAPTER NINETEEN

don't—" Julie began. "I'm sorry, I have no idea what you—"

Ellie pushed inside, dropping a bag on a table in the hall before stretching out a hand in the direction of the woman. It wasn't clear whether she intended to offer comfort or hold her back. The woman ignored the gesture anyway, whirling around on the front porch and squinting to look through the dark.

Depot's barks increased in volume, so loud and bruising that Julie, who considered herself relatively good with out-of-control parents, couldn't begin to formulate a plan of approach. She leaned down and grasped the dog's collar, then began towing him upstairs. It was slow going, given Depot's resistance; Julie had to stop on each step and knee the dog upward. She'd only had to do this a handful of times before in his life, all of them just after he had come to live with her and David.

Out of breath at the top of the stairs, Julie strained to shove open the bedroom door with one hand, keeping hold of Depot's collar with the other. She dragged the dog into the room, his barks blotting out the sound of her exertions.

"Just for a few minutes," she panted, squeezing herself past Depot's body to reach the door again. "While I figure this out."

Depot turned a look on her that held only one thing. Blame.

Wincing, Julie pulled the door shut.

She ran back downstairs.

The woman had entered the house and was stalking between rooms uninvited. She came to a stop in front of Julie, hands squared on her hips. Julie was by no means short, but this woman topped her by a good half foot, a queen beside a pawn. She had a light-colored froth of curls, past blond to pure white, and long enough to settle on her shoulders. Her hair must have changed color prematurely, for her skin was unlined.

The distress in her features had softened somewhat, though when she spoke to Julie, her tone still sounded imploring. "He isn't here?"

The teacher in Julie rose to the fore, and a sense of command descended. "Your son is missing?"

All the rigid fear in the woman's form seemed to drain. "Yes," she said bleakly.

Julie took the woman by the hand. "Come into the kitchen," she said, leading her.

As soon as they entered the room, Julie spotted her empty. Luckily, the woman remained too distraught to notice, her unfocused gaze flitting about. Julie quickly stowed the bottle in a cupboard, removing a glass to camouflage her action.

Upstairs, Depot still hadn't stopped barking. Either this woman or the move to the island had really thrown him; he hadn't behaved like this in years.

Ellie came in while Julie was filling the glass with water, but the woman waved the offering away.

"Why did you think your son was here?" Julie asked her.

The woman gave a sharp jerk of her shoulders, twin humps beneath her sleeveless silk shirt. "He despised the old teacher. Perhaps he came to see if the new one would be any better."

No pressure, Julie thought.

The woman turned on her accusingly, and to ward her off, Julie resumed her questioning. "Tell me about your son. How old is he? What's his name?"

"Peter's eleven," she said. "But he's tall for his age. He looks older."

Julie nodded again. "I'm afraid I haven't seen anyone here since I got home this afternoon," she said. "And as you can probably guess"—she gestured toward the ceiling—"Depot's a pretty good watchdog. He would've alerted me. So let's think where else Peter may've gone."

The woman lifted the water glass Julie had left on the counter, and sipped. There was a remote elegance to her, which grew more apparent with the departure of emotion.

"He doesn't really have friends, does he?" Ellie, who had been silent till now, posed the question more bluntly than Julie would have. It seemed likely to set the woman off again.

But she seemed unfazed. "Peter's a loner, as you know. And he's not allowed to wander off unattended. He certainly wouldn't be at another child's house right now."

She glared at Julie with a bright-blue gaze. It was unnerving to see such youthful eyes surrounded by all that white glowing hair. The woman's features were disjointed, at odds with each other, and the effect on Julie was to make her feel off-kilter as well, as if she might actually be to blame for something.

"Let's take a look around outside," she suggested. "It's a big piece of land. Maybe my dog missed something."

Upstairs, Depot had finally stopped barking. The woman gave Julie a look as if to say that was all the proof she needed.

The three of them headed out, Julie turning back last and making sure that the front door had been left not just unlocked, but unlatched.

They circled the house, and as they neared the cliff, a pit of fear lodged itself in Julie's stomach. The water lay as flat as a gray flannel blanket, although Julie was learning that even the mildest sea sounded restless, surging against the base of the rocks. The woman and Ellie took out their phones, turning on flashlight apps and shining them along the length of the cliff. The woman's hand flapped like a bird's wing, making the light shoot up and down. Julie reached out to steady it, peering over the edge herself.

"Look!" Ellie cried.

She was facing the house. Aiming her light, Ellie pointed upward. A widow's walk enclosed a section of roof, and in the center stood the outline of an upright form.

"Peter?" the woman shouted. "Peter!"

Although it was hard to be sure in the dark, the person—small enough to be a tall child—looked as if he were leaning against the run of lacy iron fretwork, staring down at the thirty-foot drop to the ground.

Julie sucked in her breath.

In the dark and up so high, all motion looked herky-jerky, like an animated reel flipped by hand. But the person appeared to be lifting his leg. Then his other leg. He now stood on the open border of roof outside the widow's walk.

CHAPTER TWENTY

Ellie turned to the woman, speaking low and under her breath. "What's the best way to get Peter to do what you tell him?"

The woman upturned her palms. "Who can say anymore? It's like he's become a different child since he turned eleven. He'd probably jump just to spite me."

It was the plaintive wail of every parent of a tween, whether the child stood at the lip of a perilous fall literally, or only figuratively. Julie spoke up abruptly. "Go in through the house and ask Peter if you can join him. But say you need his help getting out there."

Rage drove the woman's frame erect. She lunged in Julie's direction, hurling words like spears, while her white curls swung back and forth across her shoulders. "What good will that do? Peter will still be on the roof. Oh my Lord! Do you have any idea what will happen if my mother finds out—"

Julie shot a quick look upward. The boy didn't appear to be making any moves, drawing closer to the edge. There was a bated quality to his position, as if he were waiting for something. "Listen to me. An eleven-year-old needs to feel like he can do adult things. Acting worried about his safety and giving Peter an order will accomplish the exact opposite. We'll have a rooftop standoff—have to send for some volunteers from town with a net or something."

The woman looked as if Julie couldn't have come up with a more outlandish prospect if she'd suggested launching a rocket to get Peter down. Her features knit together with both fear and disbelief.

"Please," Julie said. She looked up again. The child still hadn't budged from his spot. Arms thrust behind him, grasping two finials of fence in his fists, while the rest of his body canted forward. "Trust me. When Peter comes to lead you, or take your hand or whatever, tell him you're scared of heights and ask if he'd mind coming back inside."

The woman looked at Ellie, who nodded. "It's worth a try. She *is* a teacher."

"We'll come with you," Julie offered. "You said Peter might be interested in meeting the new teacher."

"I certainly didn't say he was *interested*." But the woman turned and marched off.

The widow's walk was accessed through a panel in the ceiling of the third bedroom. Julie and Ellie clustered at the foot of a ladder, which could be drawn down or folded up, while the woman started to climb. At the top, she turned back to look at them.

"Say something like 'That's a cool spot,'" Julie whispered. "You'd like to see it, too. Can he show you how he got out there?"

The woman repeated the words in a stilted tone, like an amateur actor, while Julie peered up through the opening. Without apparent regard for his distance from the ground, Peter performed a sideways vault over the fretwork, landing in a crouch inside the fence-rimmed space. Jumping to his feet, he sauntered toward the opening.

Julie and Ellie scurried out of sight.

"You want to go over the fence?" the boy asked.

Julie almost laughed out loud. The skepticism Peter was expressing sounded identical to his mother's tone of voice when she had interrogated Julie.

"Actually," the woman said. "It looks a little frightening."

Peter let out an audible scoff. "Not for me."

Well, you're pretty brave then, Julie mouthed, and the woman gave voice to her words, a tad less woodenly.

Peter shrugged offhandedly, although his mouth lifted in a partial smile.

Pleased with her success, his mother said, "Perhaps you can show me another time? It's quite late. You must be tired." A quick regrouping. "I know I am."

There you go, Julie thought, happy for the woman. *That's how you do it.*

She beckoned Ellie into the hallway so that Peter wouldn't discover he'd had an audience. A set of footsteps could be heard making their careful way down the ladder, then a second, surer pair, quicksilver taps on the rungs.

Julie stepped aside to allow her first student to enter the hall.

Peter stood just over five feet—tall, as his mother had said, and judging from the woman's own stature, coming by his height honestly—with the overlong limbs unique to preadolescence, and a corn-silk flop of hair. The family resemblance was striking, although Peter didn't have curls. His straight hair shone like a sheet of fine fabric. And his blue eyes appeared leaden. He shouldered past Julie as if she weren't even there.

"Peter, say hello to the new teacher," the woman said, following him toward the stairway. "And wait for me. I ran out of Ms. Newcomb's house so fast, I forgot to take the flashlight. It'll be dark in the woods."

"You scared again?" Peter let out a laugh, high and humorless.

Everything inside Julie turned hard, like cement setting. She had heard that laugh before, when she'd climbed in through the window last night. She didn't speak up, though. Peter clearly had some issue causing him to find his way to this house. Part of her job would be to break through the boy's shellac coating and determine what that reason was.

"Hi, Peter," she said. "My name is Ms. Weathers."

Without responding, the boy started down the stairs, taking them two at a time. At that moment, Depot began to mewl in a weepy, undignified way from the bedroom, and Peter halted abruptly, hanging onto the railing as if it were a rope, both feet poised to turn.

Her dog had been shut up for too long. Julie crossed the hall and pulled the door open.

Peter shifted midstep, his mouth parting.

Depot sat on his haunches, filling the doorway from side to side, a giant dog with tricolored patches of fur, oval, liquid eyes, and a lolling tongue.

"That's your… You have a dog?" Peter asked.

"I do," Julie said softly. "His name is Depot."

"Is he nice?" Peter asked.

"Well, he's clearly interested in you," Julie answered. She wasn't opposed to using her dog to her advantage when it came to winning over a student. "He usually reacts to strangers by barking."

"That's true," Ellie put in.

Depot barked then, just once, and both Julie and Ellie laughed. The look they exchanged said they'd take it as agreement.

Peter extended a long, skinny arm. "Can I pet him?"

"It's best not to start right out with petting," Julie counseled, beckoning the boy to the top of the stairs.

Peter mounted them slowly.

"Let him sniff your hand," Julie said. "Depot will show you what to do after that."

Peter followed her instructions, and the dog rested his snout in Peter's palm, looking searchingly up at Julie. *Good boy,* she mouthed.

Peter suppressed a grin. "His breath tickles! I've never seen a dog this big!"

Julie smiled. "I think you can give him a pat or two now," she said, and the boy obeyed, cautiously lowering his hand to Depot's broad back.

Caught up in the magic of the moment, this recalcitrant child coming out of his shell thanks to one very large and noble dog, Julie had nearly forgotten the presence of Peter's mother. But just then the woman thrust her arm past Depot's open mouth, heedless of the dog's teeth, and seized her son's hand in her own.

Anger spiked her body like a lightning rod. "Time to go home."

"Yeah, right," Peter said, his tone so aged and weary, it didn't seem like it could have come from a child. The boy looked suddenly wizened, shrunken from his height, while his eyes bore twin holes into his skull. "Home."

CHAPTER TWENTY-ONE

U m, what was that?" Julie asked once the front door had slammed shut, sealing mother and son from view.

Ellie started down the stairs. "Bet my gift will come in handy right about now."

"Gift?" Julie asked, following.

"For housewarming." Ellie wound her way over to the table in the hall.

Julie stared at the object that stood there. She recalled Ellie setting it down earlier, but hadn't looked closely at the time. A cellophane bag, gathered in a bunch at the top.

Ellie held it out. "Welcome to Mercy!"

Julie gave a faint smile. She slid the gift from its crinkly wrapping—it appeared to be a good cabernet, which held no appeal; Julie had never had a taste for the grape—but oh, the feel of glass in her hand, the bottle's smooth, swanlike neck.

Ellie's good humor faded. "Oh shit. I forgot you're not a wine drinker."

Julie shook her head. "Don't be silly, it's great."

"You sure?" Ellie asked.

Julie nodded. "Let's crack it open."

Ellie's features clenched in a spasm that Julie recognized. A pressing, violent need, beyond hunger to a whole other state, one that didn't go by a single name. Rabid ardor, greed and longing and urgency, combined in a vicious brew. Depot sometimes wore this expression when they'd gone on a long walk and Julie hadn't brought enough treats and then they came upon a small, darting animal.

You're one too, Julie thought. *You're just like me.*

"Let me go look for a corkscrew," she said. "There's got to be one. This house is incredibly well supplied."

"No need, it's a twist top," Ellie answered.

Easy access, Julie thought. She led the way into the kitchen where she put Ellie out of her misery, filling a glass with ruby-colored liquid. She set the bottle on the counter, then leaned back against the lip of tile, although the motion felt more like falling.

"None for you?" Ellie asked, in the midst of raising the glass to her mouth.

The first drink of the night. Julie licked her lips.

"Do you not drink at all?" Ellie asked. "Or just don't like wine?"

While Julie thought about how to answer, Ellie began looking around the kitchen. Julie suddenly saw, as if with X-ray vision, through the cabinet door behind which her empty lurked. The thought planted a skewer in her brain, rendered her mouth dry and gritty as sand.

"Um, I drink occasionally, I guess," she said.

"Me, I couldn't keep from diving into the sea at Hangman's Cove if I didn't have my glass or two every night," Ellie remarked, sipping steadily. "But it's just wine, right? They say it's practically a health food."

Julie tipped the bottle, refilling Ellie's glass. Her hand shook slightly, a hopefully undetectable flutter.

"Great job with Peter, by the way," Ellie said. "Those two can be a tough pair."

Julie watched Ellie lift the glass to her lips, overcome by an envy so great, it left her wobbly. To camouflage her desire—if she recognized the beast inside Ellie, surely Ellie might sense it in Julie too—she said, "More than the usual preteen rebellion?"

Ellie shrugged a little sloppily. "Martha's sort of a friend of mine, I've known her forever. Not a *friend*-friend, but we get together, catch up every now and again. She and Peter are part of the oldest family on Mercy. Which changes things."

"How so?"

Ellie reached for the wine. "Martha Meyers. Née Hempstead. Martha's mother—and wait till you meet her, she makes Martha look like a kitten—and father live in the mansion on Old Bluff, which is now the second-highest point of land on-island since that northern tip sinks a few millimeters every year. This place sits on the first, FYI. It was a wedding gift, restored to full luster by the Hempsteads when the first of their heirs married." She set her glass on the counter, though she didn't let go of its stem.

Julie thought. "Wait—are you telling me that this house used to belong to—"

Ellie nodded, pouring a refill. "Martha and her late husband."

A lobsterman passed on last spring, a member of the island's oldest clan, Laura Hutchins had said. No wonder Peter kept coming back here. It was his childhood home. Had Martha overlooked that fact, or deliberately left it out?

Ellie tilted her glass for a swallow. "The Hempsteads are island royalty, and you need to tread lightly with them. Like, if Peter's having problems, maybe you address them with him in private, you know, during school hours, instead of holding, whaddayacallit, a parent-teacher conference." She drank again, then wiped her lips with the back of her hand. "Things are done differently on Mercy. Especially with that family."

Julie nodded. "Got it." It was, ironically, the same advice a teacher might've been given about Julie's uncle and aunt, if they'd had any children, or her own dad and mom, by dint of their name. Not so long ago *Weathers* signified status in Wedeskyull.

"But none of this came from me." Ellie sloshed more wine into her glass. "Not that I don't trust you. You seem very trustable. Is that a word? You're the teacher."

Julie smiled back weakly. "We teacher types would probably say 'trustworthy.'"

"Trustworthy!" Ellie extended a finger in her direction. "That's it."

Julie knew the lightness now filling Ellie, that feeling of liftoff when all your problems started to recede. A film of sweat slicked her body like fish skin. She couldn't stand to watch Ellie relish her drink. Julie blinked, seeing the tannic hue of scotch in the wood cabinets, the floorboards, her own newly tanned skin.

"Tell me more about the island," she said, grasping for distraction. "How did the Hempsteads come to be royalty?"

Ellie tilted the bottle, taking the measure of its dwindling contents. It didn't seem as if she were going to answer the question, then she said, "Okay, so there are highliners and gangs."

"Highliners?" Julie echoed. "Gangs?"

Ellie laughed, low and slurry. "You didn't read up much about the place you've come to live, did you?"

Julie looked away. "My move might've been a bit of an impulsive decision."

Ellie headed over to the sink, wavering a little on the way. "A gang is what you call a group of lobstermen who fish together. People who control a certain stretch of water, where other gangs won't drop their traps. Lobstering is a territorial industry. People die, or survive, or thrive for that matter, based on where they're allowed to drop."

Julie considered. "It's that tightly regulated?"

"Unofficially. Without any rules or laws or governance from outside."

Like a group of outlaws, Julie thought. "And a highliner?"

"Is a top lobsterman," Ellie replied. "Versus the lowliest, who used to be called dubs. The term's fallen out of use, not PC, I guess. Highliners catch the most lobster, earn the highest wages, get the best women"—this with a waggle of brows over her light-gray eyes—"and are looked up to, gone to for advice. Ours are known as the Men of Mercy."

Julie smiled. "Could be a calendar."

Ellie's laugh sounded giddy. She held her empty glass beneath the tap, then took a gulp of pinkish liquid. Julie recognized the trick. Don't want to miss the watered-down dregs.

"Most of our island men are so hoary and ancient"—Ellie drained the last of the water—"they probably evolved before the calendar was invented. They spend so much time with seawater on them, they practically have scales."

Julie smiled again. "It can't be that bad."

Ellie gave a mock shudder. "Wait till you meet Peter's grandfather."

"Which brings us full circle."

"And me without more wine." Ellie shivered again; this time it looked like it was for real. "But hey, can I ask you something now?"

"Sure," Julie said. "You've certainly let me pepper you with enough questions."

"You're single, right?" Ellie gestured with a floppy wave. "I mean, I would've noticed a husband or boyfriend, or wife for that matter, anyone besides a gigantic dog."

"Speaking of, I'd better go check on him. But to answer your question, I'm single now, yes. My husband and I separated just before I came to Mercy."

Ellie's drink-dulled gaze sparked. "The aforementioned impulsive decision."

"Right," Julie said. "That."

Ellie pushed herself off her slouch against the sink. "Okay. I'm a mess. I'll let you see to Depot while I start making my way home."

"Sure you'll be all right?" Julie asked.

Ellie grinned. "Best part of no cars on the island. No designated drivers."

They hugged goodbye at the door, and Julie twitched the bolt to lock it. She would make sure to remember to do so from now on, at least until she had figured out how to keep Peter off her roof.

Julie went upstairs to the bedroom, where Depot had fallen asleep. He didn't stir even when Julie offered him a belated meal. She left the dog snuffling on the floor beside the bed, and walked over to the dresser, removing a T-shirt from the freshly stowed stack in the drawer. It was an old one of David's, and Julie was again taken aback by how reminders of her husband prompted not the slightest tug of loss or longing.

She bent down and deposited a kiss on Hedley's photo, then changed before crossing to the bathroom on the other side of the hall. As she brushed her teeth, she became aware of something. This was the first night she'd gone without alcohol in over a year. Julie walked back across the hall, consumed by her thoughts. Being cut off—the island store certainly wouldn't be open right now—wasn't having the effect of making her feel trapped, scrabbling to get free of her sober self. Instead she felt something like liberation.

Who had poured their nightly drinks over the past year, and then the second nip, and often a third, before the rest accumulated in an uncountable blur? David. The person Julie had just been aware of hardly missing. Had she been the one to turn bereavement into self-destruction? Or had she been helped along in that?

Suddenly her husband, so capable and exacting, if a little bloodless, began to transform in her head into something truly zombie-like. The already ghoulish process of grief swamped by wave after wave of scotch. Julie staggered—as if drunk again, as if never having sobered up—into the bedroom, seeing only a dark trail of lost days before her. She stooped down, bracing herself against a wall, and delivered a blind stroke to

Depot as he settled more heavily into dreams, smacking the loose flaps of his lips.

Poor guy was probably hungry.

The sight of her dog grounded her, and she was able to rise.

David was out of her life now. Perhaps she could follow her uncle's advice and make sure alcohol was too. Julie threw back the covers on the bed and plumped up her pillows with a couple of brisk, decided pats.

When she went to close the bedroom door, Peter stood in the shadows behind it.

CHAPTER TWENTY-TWO

The first thing Julie did was think, *Thank God I'm not drunk right now.*

The next was to suck in a breath so hard it raked her throat.

Peter looked an unearthly sight, lurking in the dark triangle of space behind the door. Like many tall kids, he was used to slumping, and his back appeared rounded, hunched over like an old man's. His thinness made him seem whittled. And the light locks of his hair, long in front, concealed most of his eyes.

He was the stillest child Julie had ever seen. She would have had to creep closer to make sure he was breathing. From this distance Peter might've been a mannequin, propped up in the juncture between door and wall. A sudden conviction shook Julie by the shoulders—Peter wasn't alive. Like the worst drunk dream, the story took shape, accruing an inexplicable logic. After leaving earlier that night, the boy had been killed by his mother, and his ghost had come back to inhabit the home he once loved.

Not so inexplicable. Julie had known more than one abusive parent in her time as a teacher. And Martha had grabbed Peter at the end of their unscheduled visit with real force: his hand crumpled inside hers as if she were balling up a piece of paper.

Then Peter moved, and Julie screamed.

She clamped down on the scream the second it burst forth. Whatever was happening here, she was the adult and what she did now would set the course of things to come with Peter. Plus, the boy must have been in her bedroom for some time—oh God, she had changed in front of him, she hoped she'd been shielded from sight by the door—and Depot had been sleeping deeply. If her dog wasn't disturbed, then Julie shouldn't be.

"I'm sorry," she said calmly, of her momentary outburst. "You startled me."

Depot had started to rouse when she screamed; now he got onto all fours, positioning himself beside the child watchfully.

No point in asking why Peter had returned, or failed to leave; Julie had a feeling he wouldn't answer. She needed to come at this child sideways.

"Would you like to pet Depot again?"

Peter didn't reply, but interest kindled in his eyes.

"Come on." Julie crouched, making sure that David's T-shirt covered her thighs, and beckoned the boy forward.

Depot lowered his head, and Peter flung his arms around the dog's neck. Depot was a patient, tolerant jumble of breeds and never became agitated, not even when Hedley used to thrash and wail with her chronic stuffed noses. But Peter was a bigger child than Depot had ever gotten the chance to grow accustomed to.

Julie had to return the boy to his family, but Ellie's warning about being careful where the Hempsteads were concerned repeated itself in her head. She got to her feet, giving Depot an assessing glance, which the dog met with a pleading look in return. Peter was clinging to him awfully hard, but that wasn't the reason for the urgency in the dog's eyes.

"Look, Depot needs to go out," Julie said. "How about we take him for a walk?"

Peter lifted his head. "Really? Right now?"

"Just a short one." It would give her time to get to know Peter a little bit better, make sure she wasn't returning him to an unsafe situation.

The boy's face remained expressionless, his eyes blank screens, as they emerged from the house. Depot went scrambling over to a distant tree, farther than he would've chosen if it'd been just him and Julie out there alone, as if he felt modest in front of their guest.

Julie laughed out loud.

Peter stared at her through the night, his face unreadable.

"Dog things, you know?" Julie said. "Sometimes it's like they're almost human."

"They're better than humans," Peter answered, so darkly that she shivered.

"Is that why you climbed up on the roof? To get away from people?"

The sharp knobs of Peter's shoulders settled somewhat, though he didn't answer.

"Hey," Julie remarked. "Depot finished awfully fast tonight. I think he must miss you."

The dog kicked up a cyclone of dirt, then bounded in their direction. Julie stepped neatly to one side, causing Depot to swerve and wind up beside Peter.

Peter set out walking and Depot heeled nicely, as if he'd been walked by the boy for years. The night sky, cliff heads, and sea appeared before them as one seamless sheet, a monochrome gray.

Suddenly, Peter spoke up. "Whose was that picture you kissed?"

Kids could cut to the raw, bleeding heart of a matter without giving any warning. Julie stopped walking, and Depot looked back at her. Exposure prickled Julie's skin; this was worse than if Peter had seen her getting changed. "She's my little girl."

Peter took a look around as if Hedley might be somewhere nearby.

Julie had to stop herself from looking too. She almost never spoke these words aloud, rarely even thought them. Everything inside her recoiled from saying this next part, revealing it to the boy who had laughed at her so eerily and dismissed his mom with adult derision. But she also didn't want Peter to ask. "She died," Julie said at last.

Peter stopped at the rim between cliff and sea. "Your baby? Is dead?"

Depot rubbed his big body against Julie's leg. She reached down and clenched a hank of his fur. She nodded.

Peter nodded back. "That sucks. Really."

Julie's vision clouded. "Yeah. It really does."

Peter's form wavered into shape through her tears, through the darkness.

"I have a picture I kiss sometimes too," he told her.

Then he executed a perfect pirouette at the edge of the cliff—for a second, Julie pictured gravity taking him over—before running forward so that Depot would follow.

He had lost his father and his home in the last year. That could explain the boy's behavior, his attachment to this house, better than anything far-fetched, abuse or worse.

"Peter!" Julie called.

He turned.

"I have to bring you home now. You know that, right?"

After a moment, he nodded again.

According to what Martha had said, their new house lay through the woods, and Peter wasn't sure whether he could direct Julie to it. ("I never get to walk by myself.") So Julie came up with a plan B, recalling Ellie's statement about where Peter's grandparents resided. Given Peter's penchant for escaping his mom, perhaps the grandparents would be a better choice tonight anyway.

The second-highest point of land on the island. Old Bluff.

Julie had been left a map of Mercy, along with some brochures and promotional materials, neatly stacked in one of the kitchen drawers. It would be easy enough to walk to Old Bluff, the northernmost point on the island. Julie served Depot the dinner he'd never eaten, then she and Peter left the house together.

The weather was changing, wind moving through the trees like a live thing, late-summer leaves jangling. Julie glanced down at the map. They had to swerve away from the woods that stood to the west.

She and Peter's grandparents were practically neighbors, which made sense when you considered that the two houses were generational dwellings. The elders' was reached by a lane along the cliff. The grassy path dropped, at first imperceptibly, running in the opposite direction from town, which straddled the southern end of the island.

Clouds began paving over the sky. The lip of the cliff and the sea lay to the east, and once Julie's house receded into the distance, the land she and Peter traversed opened up. Julie checked the map, although they could've been blindfolded and probably still hit Old Bluff. There was nothing between here and it except dark, empty space.

It was quiet on an island in a way Julie had never known before. No trees here, and without the dry clatter of leaves or clack of branches, any noise the rising wind made was snuffed out. The sea lay calmly, any sound of surf inaudible. No birds, not even gulls, who probably preferred the dock, and no other animals either. At home, Julie was surrounded by birds and mammals, some of the latter threatening and dangerous, but each delivering a feeling of kin.

She tasted salt on her tongue. The air had gone opaque, and she lost sight of Peter, who'd been trudging along at her side. Clouds clenched like fists, holding back their load of rain. In the distance, barely visible amongst the emerging tendrils of fog, there appeared a jagged rim of roof. Julie was just able to take in the girth of the house—a mansion really—before fog rolled in, enveloping the whole world in a cocoon.

"Peter?" Julie called out, her voice a whip's lash in the night.

The boy didn't answer. She couldn't see him nearby, and she didn't hear him either. He must've run off, gotten there first. There was a blur of light ahead, and Julie began to make her way forward, extending her hands and walking as if blindfolded. She couldn't discern the tips of her fingers through the wall of mist in front of her.

Julie tried to re-create a mental snapshot of what she'd seen before the fog closed in. Had there been a path, would her feet detect a change from grassy berm to seashell walk? She shuffled along as if elderly, given to falls.

Then the fog parted like curtains. As suddenly as the mist had come in, it cleared. The house stood before her, illuminated by lamplight, and Peter waited outside.

Someone emerged from the house, descending to a walkway made not out of shells, as Julie had imagined, but flat platters of stone that must've cost a fortune to haul in. She was a gargantuan column of a woman, like a stalk in a giant's garden.

It was the person who'd appeared in the video reel, and whom Julie had seen with Laura Hutchins at the very edge of the woods in front of her house. Julie should've recognized the family hair. This woman's version was pulled back so tightly, it could've been bare scalp.

She summoned Peter forward, and he ran to her.

"It's good to see you, child," the woman said, stroking his head as Peter encircled her waist with his arms. "Even at this hour."

Peter screwed his face deeper into his grandmother's side, hiding himself from view.

The woman extricated herself, delivering a pat to Peter's bottom as she sent him inside. "The Captain has hot cocoa on. Just the thing for a foggy night."

The door thudded shut behind the boy, and Julie had just started to call out a hello when the woman strode forward. The regality in her bearing was undermined by a certain contortion to the features of her face, and her mottled, blotchy complexion.

She spoke in a low, discreet tone that somehow managed to carry. "Surely you realize that school hasn't started and your duties are not yet required."

So much for introductions, Julie thought. She offered a nod, shakier than she would've liked. "Of course. But Peter showed up at my house… his old house, I mean—"

The grandmother came to a halt close enough that her skin gave off a whiff of complex, perfumed notes. Redolent of flowers, but with something bodily beneath it, the vigor of emotion. "Please leave. It's quite late."

"I'm sorry," Julie said. "I didn't know where Peter's house was, so I thought this would be the better option."

The explanation sounded perfectly reasonable to her ears, but the woman extended one arm, swordlike.

Julie took a hitching step back.

The grandmother kept coming, driving Julie toward the open lane and sea, while she spoke in a low hiss. "I said to leave my land, Ms. Weathers. We'll look forward to welcoming you another time to our island."

CHAPTER TWENTY-THREE

Julie made her way home, shaken and raw. There was a pervasive drizzle in the air, and her clothes grew damp. She couldn't imagine a much worse start to her new position. She had antagonized the most powerful woman on Mercy Island, someone tightly wrapped Laura Hutchins adulated and even the far more carefree Ellie had warned Julie about.

As she made her way over the open plain that lay between the two houses, Julie couldn't escape the feeling that she wasn't alone. Yet it was precisely the openness of the land, its location next to a sheer drop to the sea, that proved she was. Nobody could hide out here; they'd be visible from any angle. Nonetheless, Julie kept twisting to look behind her, then cursing herself for her nerves. What was she scared of? An old lady?

Her body thrummed with a strange, medicinal hunger, as if it were missing an essential ingredient it needed to run, like insulin. It was all well and good to blame David for her nightly nips, or of late, Big Gulps. But Julie had always enjoyed her nights at the bar with cop friends—Tim and Mandy and a few others—and the rough-and-ready cocktails that the bartender at The Hole mixed. The only difference after she met David was that Julie let him do the serving, and there was less mixing in favor of scotch taken neat.

Julie was shivering by the time she got back to the house. She grabbed a towel from the first-floor bathroom and sponged residual rain from her face as she began to search the rooms, making sure Peter hadn't managed to slip inside—nor anybody else. Depot was asleep, curled into a huge hump by the wall of windows, and Julie didn't disturb him, though she would've appreciated his warm bulk by her side. She turned her check of the house into a hunt for her favorite elixir. Surely Martha's late husband would have followed a hard day at sea with a drop of the hard stuff? But the kitchen cabinets were filled only with the supplies a teetotaling new resident might appreciate, and the twin breakfronts in the living and dining rooms were desert-dry as well.

Julie stomped upstairs, flinging open the bedroom doors. Nothing in her room, and the second one had been cleaned out. She braved the third, which had so unsettled her the night before. In the full light from the overhead fixture, she saw that the crib had been less shifted to present a barrier to exit and more simply stood in her path, given the way Julie had entered through the window. She began to open boxes, pawing through their contents, discarding them in an even less orderly arrangement than Martha had left. It was physical exertion, lifting bins, sliding them over, heaving them up to form stacks.

In the stuffy, closed-in space, perspiration began to slick Julie's body, while dust from crevices and corners stuck to her pasty skin. There was no sign of her substance of choice, no luxuriantly untouched case left behind amid the rest of the boxes, nor even so much as a partial empty hastily stowed in a packed carton.

Julie trudged back to her own room, no longer cold, instead sweating and parched and hurting for her fix. The towel she'd used was a damp, wretched twist in her hand; she dropped it on the floor. Without the muffling cocoon of her nightly ritual, everything was cast into sharp, unflinching relief. No syrupy coating to dull the effects of her failures back home, or how she had brought the same to her first days on this island. Nothing was going to be any different here, and the loss of that hope, her fantasy, however inflated or unrealistic it might've been, pressed Julie down to the floor, buried her beneath a deadly weight.

The sound of a small voice—this one decidedly fantastic; Julie knew no one was here—enabled her to lift her head, then stand up and move toward the bed. She had succeeded at one thing tonight, and it was something that used to infuse her with more strength and sense of purpose than a drink or four ever had.

The first fragile inklings of a bond with a child had begun to take root, send forth tendrils. When Julie told Peter about Hedley, she'd offered the boy a part of herself that she normally kept cloaked, and he had responded in kind. He must've been talking about his father when he mentioned kissing a picture.

The fog and damp had lowered the temperature to even colder depths than August nights descended to in Wedeskyull. Climbing into bed, pulling the covers up over her, Julie reached to pick up Hedley's photo from the bedside stand. She studied her little girl's face in the dark, needing no light to know it. Hedley had been a gorgeous baby, with enormous eyes and petal-blossom skin. Probably every parent thought the same about their child. Still, recalling her baby girl's beauty, all that lost potential, Julie was suddenly seized by a pair of fierce, strangling hands. Everything Hedley could've grown into, who she might've been.

There was something here on Mercy that still could be.

"You don't mind, Lilypad, do you?" Julie whispered to the photo. "I think he might need me."

Behind the glass, Hedley gazed back at her, forever stilled on the cusp of a smile.

CHAPTER TWENTY-FOUR

Julie woke the next morning feeling better than she had in as long as she could remember, with a newfound sense of optimism. It took her a second to figure out why, stretching luxuriously in the clean-smelling sheets.

She had no alcohol in her system, and the difference was profound. No clawing headache, no thick, soupy limbs, no taste in her mouth like the devil's own brew.

This was her payoff for having made it through the night.

No need to clean up, hide the proof of her indulgence; no reason to apologize, if only to Depot. Over the last year with David, he as guilty of excess as she, their gazes would flicker away from each other's like insects every morning. Whole days could pass while each avoided the other's glance.

Julie licked her lips. Why, she hardly even felt the need to brush her teeth. Did the entire sober world live like this, unburdened by a medicine cabinet's worth of toiletries to scour away the evidence? She got out of bed, floorboards comfortably cool under her feet, and lifted a curtain at the window. The island looked as sunny as she felt, no hint of last night's fog. The sea was a sheet of diamonds.

Julie drew on a pair of shorts and a tank top, feeling around beneath the dresser for her flip-flops before running downstairs.

"Depot, come on!" she shouted. "Let's go for a walk."

She and the dog capped off their exertions with a meal while Julie mentally mapped out her day. Best chance of a reboot with the grandmother? Be a great teacher for the children of Mercy. Which was going to take a ton of preparation. She would go into town for supplies and wind up at the schoolhouse. Perhaps stop in at Ellie's house, just quickly, to tell her about Peter's second surprise visit.

Depot showed no inclination to move, so Julie left him behind with water and a bowl for lunch. Her feet made short walk of the forest path—its route familiar already—but when she passed the quadrant of cottages, there was no one home at Ellie's.

A hum grew the closer Julie got to town. Tourists darted like birds in and out of stores, and at the base of the drop that led to the pier, the noise of beachside explorations could be heard. Julie paused at a café with a window open to the road. She got in place in a city-foodie-destination-length line, versus one that belonged on a small island, for what turned out to be elevated sandwiches: lobster rolls with lime-ginger aioli, po'boys adorned with fish roe.

Instead of fighting for a spot at one of the brightly painted picnic tables, Julie decided to take her wax-paper parcel and drink to the schoolhouse, eat as she would be doing for the rest of the year.

She had to twist and shoulder her way through clusters of people who'd come in on the morning ferry. They crowded the sandy street and shelled patches of land to both sides, and Julie experienced a not unwelcome twinge of frustration, a first link of belonging to the island. It was the way she felt when mud season ended and Wedeskyull's nicely trimmed population began to bloat. "Go home," she wanted to say to the folks surging through town or observing the lobster boats from the dock.

Great. Now she was a xenophobe herself.

Julie made up for it by trading smiles with a bedraggled clump of tourists who had waded into the freezing cold sea and were emerging, sandy and shivering.

"They rent towels at the inn," she called.

"Thanks!" one of them called back.

The bustle finally began to abate at the library, and by the time Julie found herself ensconced within the thick stone walls of the schoolhouse, the silence was total. She stood facing the swollen belly of the stove, and rows of desk and chair units. The blackboard was visible peripherally, as well as the dusky curtain cloaking the stage. Fighting the temptation to look for costumes and props, Julie crossed the schoolroom and went out to the short hallway. Dropping her lunch on the table in the teacher's room, she decided to go through the folders in the filing cabinets first. She sank onto a spot on the floor, where she was instantly lost to curriculum creation and lesson planning.

Hunger pangs brought her state of flow to a skidding halt. Julie couldn't recall the last time she'd needed to stop for a meal; in the wake of Hedley's death, eating had come to seem like an optional activity. She walked down the brief length of hall to the teacher's room, where she unwrapped her sandwich.

Back in the schoolroom, the hobbit door slammed shut with a resounding echo.

"Hello?" Julie called out.

She hastily swallowed her bite, crossing the hall.

Nobody stood amongst the rows of desks. The room appeared to be empty.

Julie walked past the stage and called out again, but got no reply. Girding herself, she flung back the heavy length of curtain, inhaling a cloud of dust. She began coughing, her eyes watering madly, unable to see. But when her vision cleared, there was nobody on the platform. She coughed out the last of the grit and went to check the barn doors at the front of the little building. Closed, and no way to tell if either of them had been recently opened.

Maybe the grandmother had stopped by to chastise her. If so, she wasn't still here; no way could such an intimidating presence be missed.

Julie went to finish her lunch. She had just downed the final gulp of iced tea when she heard a door slam shut and jumped to her feet.

"Hello?" she shouted, this time with annoyance.

A voice called out in return. "What's this I hear about some lights?"

Julie walked to the threshold of the teacher's room and came face-to-face with the man she'd met on the ferry. The hallway was cramped, and the new arrival stood close enough that Julie could see a shadow of fuzz on his jaw, smell the scent of seawater on him. His black hair glistened as if he'd just come off a boat again.

"Lights?" Julie said. Then she added, "Were you here a few minutes ago? Did you leave and come back?" Lovely. A xenophobe and an interrogator.

"Somebody else must've stopped by," the man replied. "I just arrived."

Julie gave a nod, though she couldn't imagine why whoever it was would've left without a greeting.

"I'm Callum McCarthy." The man's tone was friendly enough, though the lines carved into his face looked as hard as fissures in rock.

Julie's own face felt stiff and unruly, her mouth unable to form a smile. "Julie Weathers. We met once actually. Not *met*-met, you know, it was just for a second. On the ferry." She was stumbling over her words like a schoolgirl. Oh God, did this man throw her because she found him attractive? Julie hadn't felt such a thing in so long, its prospect was all but unrecognizable.

"I remember," Callum said. "You have your sea legs yet?"

"Getting a little steadier," Julie said, instantly replaying her reply in her head and hearing their whole exchange as one giant innuendo. She sensed her face turn red and looked away.

Callum brought his palms together. He had good hands, knuckles like knots of wood. "Well, let me help with what else needs doing."

Now that really did sound like an innuendo. Julie blushed again before recalling that Ellie had promised to find someone to address the light situation up in the loft. Julie supposed she'd made a good choice, given how ancient and weather-beaten the rest of the options were supposed to be. She led the way down the hall to where the loft opened up beside the bank of filing cabinets.

Callum scaled the ladder, muscles rounding as he mounted it. "What would you like to see here?" he called down.

You. Climbing that ladder again. Julie clapped a hand over her mouth, half-afraid she'd spoken out loud. She was aghast at herself, but also, if she was being honest, a tad delighted. David hadn't incited this much feeling in her since the first days of their relationship; possibly—assuming honesty was still on the table—not even then. He'd slipped out of her life as easily as a stitch from a thread. Which was awful and astounding and exhilarating all at once.

Callum leaned down. In the dimness there was a heavy cast to his expression, a weight, and Julie realized it was this more than anything that spoke to her.

"Lighting for the loft space?" he asked from above. "Or spotlights, say, for the stage?"

Julie felt a catch in her throat. "Oh." Her rummaged thoughts and feelings aside, what if she could do a play? Back in Wedeskyull she'd had to content herself with temporary pallets in the gymnasium whenever a show was put on, and there hadn't been a budget for any sort of production at all over the past three years. "Could you do both? Spotlights would be wonderful."

Callum took a walk around, hunched low beneath the slope of the ceiling. "No reason why not." A final assessing glance, then he backed down the ladder, skipping rungs.

The space was tight at the bottom, and Julie tried to get out of the way, but she and Callum wound up facing each other. They stood close enough to confirm the look of torment on the man's face, or more precisely, in the depths of his eyes. Julie had the most implausible urge to try to ease it. How? She didn't even know this man. Still, she couldn't help but wonder what had gone wrong in his life.

She shrank back against the wall so that he could get by, and felt dampness on his clothes, sufficient to cool her. "Thank you so much for—" she said, just as Callum made a lame crack, something about expanding this narrow hall while he was renovating, and their voices wound up in a tangle together.

Callum ducked his head, acknowledging the misspeak, then twisted to maneuver past Julie. At the moment that their bodies crossed, one of them—or was it both?—shifted, moving by mere inches, but enough that their faces grazed, maybe even their mouths.

And Julie stood there, watching her chest pump hard with her breaths, trying to figure out what had just happened, while Callum, his expression fiercer than ever, left the schoolhouse.

CHAPTER TWENTY-FIVE

After a second drinkless night, and another morning spent reaping the benefits—maybe this would be easy, one part of her thought; maybe you're having a sobriety honeymoon, thought another—Julie spent the next day going over the lesson plans she'd used back in Wedeskyull. Her eyes went bleary, staring at computer files, and she sliced two paper cuts in her skin, riffling through worksheets she'd had sent on ahead.

When her mind frayed from the sheer volume of her task—nine grades in a single classroom; what had she been thinking?—Julie found her thoughts wandering to two things, one pleasant, the other terrifying. Callum first. The intimate if inadvertent contact between them had cast into sharp relief how long it had been since Julie had wanted to be close to anyone. It was a sudden but not unwelcome change.

Then her mind shifted to the more pressing matter—what it was going to be like to be surrounded by children again.

Taking the walk along the cliff with Peter had constituted the most responsibility she'd had for a young person since her daughter had died. Soon twenty charges would be in her care, and the weight of it felt immense, like the whole sea upon her. Yet at the same time—dazzling. A chance to do things right.

After lunch and a walk with Depot, Julie returned to organizing her curricula. The next step would be reconciling it with what the last teacher had left, a challenging task, especially because the requirements differed somewhat by state. Julie had found the teacher's work to be thorough when she'd looked it over at the schoolhouse yesterday. She wondered why the woman had chosen to leave. The quality of life on a small island? Or the demands of the job, multigrade teaching, which Julie had just been ruing herself?

She wandered into the kitchen and poured herself a glass of lemonade, focusing on the intensity of the sweetness, the way she could taste things in a whole new way now. Still, the thought of the empty evening that lay ahead was daunting. Alcohol had the ability to haze out time, strip away many of the features and facets of everyday life in all their uncertain ambiguity and collective messiness. Julie wasn't sure if she could weather the entire lot of them, every single one, unshielded.

Back in the hall, she called for Depot to go on his third walk.

When the two of them got outside, Julie's spirits lifted, seeing a small figure come up from the cliff. Ellie ran around the side of the house, lifting her hand in a wave. She wore linen slacks and a buttercup-colored shirt, a matching headband holding her short hair back. She looked like an advertisement for the yachting life.

"The Hempsteads are throwing a party in your honor," she told Julie. "A combined end-of-summer, back-to-school, and welcome-to-the-island kind of thing."

"Oh, they are not," Julie responded.

Ellie frowned.

Julie clutched her by the arm. "I haven't even gotten a chance to tell you yet, where have you been?" Before Ellie could answer, Julie went on. "I've been buried in work myself. But Peter came back—just appeared in my bedroom, it was the scariest thing—and I had to bring him to his grandparents. Because I didn't know where his own house was. Anyway, they hate me," she concluded. "The grandmother anyhow. She probably wouldn't invite me as one of the guests, let alone host a whole get-together on my behalf."

Ellie had gone silent, taking in Julie's news.

"But on a brighter note, I'm getting the lights done," Julie went on. "Thank you very much for that."

Ellie stared at her. "You have completely lost me. Peter came over again... Did you say he was in your *bedroom*? His grandmother hates you, and thank me for *what*?"

Julie heaved a breath. "I'll catch you up. Want something to drink?"

She instantly regretted the suggestion, but Ellie didn't appear to have brought any wine this time, so Julie poured them both glasses of lemonade, suppressing the thought of how much more refreshing it would taste with a splash of scotch. They took their glasses back out on the lawn so Julie could watch for Depot. She spread a blanket across the scrubby ground, and gave Ellie the full update, ending with her encounter with Callum.

Ellie shook her head. "That's just par for the course for Mrs. Hempstead, she doesn't like surprises. And I didn't have a thing to do with the handiwork, FYI. I think you must have a fairy godmother on this island."

Julie realized that Ellie would've had no idea when Julie would be at the schoolhouse in order to arrange the timing of Callum's visit. She hadn't even been home when Julie passed by. "Maybe you're right," she said. "Because Callum and I did sort of, um"—she broke off, giving Ellie a quick look before going on in a rush—"kiss, in good fairy-tale form."

"What?" Ellie squealed. "Wait a minute, go back! You kissed?"

Julie instantly regretted her pronouncement. "Well, not really. It was more that we were standing kind of close, you know how tight it is below the loft, and then our faces turned, and so we just brushed—"

Ellie had dropped her empty glass and was rolling around on the ground. "I can't believe it. Less than a week on-island, and you're already making out with our men."

"One man!" Julie cried. "And we definitely did not make out." Suddenly, she was stricken by a vision of herself, as if she were floating above, watching as she sat on a blanket with a friend, laughing and sipping straight-people drinks and gossiping about guys. And no voice was even chiding her. *Is that okay, Lilypad?*

"So, this party?" she asked. "It's really happening?"

"Sure is," Ellie replied. "A little last-minute, but the Hempsteads know everyone will come when they beck or call." A pause to deliver a wry grin. "Go in and change. It starts in half an hour."

When Julie got back outside, wearing a sundress she hoped would suit whatever the island dress code decreed, she whistled for Depot. Ellie dashed in for a bathroom break while Julie picked up the blanket from the ground and began folding it, just as Depot emerged from the woods. His snout was smeared with something black; Julie wiped it away with a corner of the blanket.

"You get into something, Deep?" she said. "I hope you don't get sick."

Ellie came back out while Julie was still rubbing at Depot's face. The dog started wrenching in her hold, a battle Julie knew she'd never win.

"Fine," she said, letting go. "But you're still all gooey."

Depot backed away, pawing at the ground and rubbing his snout in the dirt. He looked up, whined, and padded off farther.

"Don't blame me, I tried to help," Julie told him.

"No greeting?" Ellie said. She grinned at Julie as she spoke to the dog. "I get it, don't worry. I come second out of your mama's new best friends now that there's Peter."

Best friend, Julie heard, with a small charge of pleasure as she smiled back at Ellie. "He does seem attached to him already. Peter, I mean, to Depot." She hesitated. "You said you're friendly with Martha. Do you know if Peter's had issues in the past?"

"Well, his dad died, just last spring," Ellie said.

"Right," Julie said. That could certainly account for a lot.

"But no, overall Peter's a pretty impressive kid. He has a lot going for him." Ellie shrugged. "A boy and his dog, I guess. Even when it's not his own."

"I guess." Julie crossed the yard to where Depot hovered at a distance. She leaned down, depositing a kiss on his head. "Time for you to go inside, and us to go party."

CHAPTER TWENTY-SIX

I t didn't occur to Julie until she and Ellie were walking, following the long, grassy lane that lay to the left of the cliffs. If she'd already grown impatient with her unspiked refresher at home, how the hell was she supposed to make it through a whole party?

These islanders probably even favored Julie's drink of choice, at least some of them. It was the preferred nectar in tough climates, bracing and able to beat back the cold. This entire night was going to be awash in scotch.

Before getting to work that morning, rolling over in bed, Julie had spied a calendar pinned to the wall. Beachy shots, coastal living; she'd never noticed it before. The calendar was old, dates a year in the past, but that didn't matter. Julie had flipped to the correct month, and secured the page with a thumbtack. Then, almost idly, not wanting to jinx anything yet, she'd drawn a slash across two of the squares.

How Julie wanted that row to continue! She could already envision the dissection of a third box with a clean, neat line, how it would feel to wield a pen against her opponent of days.

She stopped walking. "Oh shoot. I can't go. I don't have a gift."

Ellie tugged her on. "You're the guest of honor. You don't need to bring a gift. Besides, I didn't bring one either."

"You're a local, it's probably no longer expected," Julie protested. "But I'm trying to correct an impression here."

Ellie bit out a laugh, still pulling her forward. "No one could give anything to the Hempsteads. They have everything. And what they don't have, they just take."

"They don't sound like the nicest neighbors," Julie said, reluctantly allowing herself to be drawn ahead.

"Let's just say you're probably not the only person to have been threatened on the Hempsteads' lawn," Ellie told her. "But not tonight. Tonight is going to be fun."

The sounds of celebration filled the air as the mansion came into view. Music played—from the occasional off note and stutter, it seemed to be live; a second later, Julie spotted the band—and voices could be heard soaring upward, words and laughter dispersing like embers through the early evening sky. People began to turn and point at the horizon. The sun was setting dramatically over the sea, gilding the clouds with gold. After an untold number of such spectacles, nobody seemed inured to the sight.

Julie murmured aloud, and Ellie smiled at her. "Even more incredible than back at your new place, right?"

Julie nodded. "How come?"

Ellie gave a shrug. "My father always talked about topography, how the cliffs are lower here. Crumblier too. This part of the island—it's like the sea wants it back."

Julie felt a slight shiver as night came on. She stared out at the slow, churning mass of water. "That puts the beauty in perspective."

Ellie hesitated. "We're lucky here on Mercy. Did you know there are entire fishing communities whose livelihood is going to be wiped out, probably within our lifetime? Crabbing on Tangiers in the Chesapeake

Bay, for example. Or Ocracoke on the Outer Banks. A hurricane almost did that one in. Whole islands lost, swallowed by encroaching seas."

Julie shook her head. "I don't know anything about it."

"My father used to say 'Go south to fish, but go north to get rich.'"

"He was a highliner," Julie guessed.

"The highliniest." Ellie squeezed her arm. "Hey, that guy standing over there is our constable, Paul Scherer. He's also the superintendent, so kinda your boss. Let me introduce you, then I'll go find Mrs. Hempstead, try and soften your next encounter."

"If you can pull that off, I guess *you're* my fairy godmother," Julie said as Ellie steered the two of them toward a short, stout man with a bristly mustache.

"And what can I bring you to drink?" Ellie asked. "If I don't get my hands on whatever red they're pouring, I won't make it through the night."

Julie laughed feebly. "I'm okay for now, thanks." She smiled at the man Ellie had just led her up to. "Mr. Scherer," she said. "It's so nice to meet you. I hear you know a lot about the school."

Ellie didn't come back right away, but there were dozens of guests in attendance who came over, eager to greet the new teacher, and spared Julie any awkward moments alone. Everyone appeared to have dressed for the occasion, slacks and shirts on the men, sundresses for the women, although the aroma of sea and salt and fish hadn't been entirely scrubbed away. Perhaps it never could be.

Laura Hutchins stopped by to say hello and goodbye; it was her last night on the island. There didn't seem to be any kids at this party, so Julie didn't get to meet her students-to-be, but parents and other more distant relations, the islanders a mesh of family connections, still meant that she practically had people standing in line.

At last the crush began to wane, and Julie was left, mouth dry from all the talking she'd done, a table with a server pouring drinks behind it all too visible in her line of sight. Julie headed over, threading her way between people she'd spoken to, nodding and smiling to acknowledge recent remarks.

"Yes," she said to an elderly woman she had just met. She stifled a cough, in need of a coating on her throat, as if salt from the sea had rid the air of moisture. "It *is* even lovelier when the sun goes down."

The sky was barnacled like a boat, encrusted with stars. Torches had been lit to push back the nighttime chill, and blue and orange fire danced in a mesmerizing swirl.

"No, it never does," Julie agreed, rubbing her arms to ape shivers as a man she'd been talking with a few minutes earlier called out a comment about the summer weather not lasting.

Julie finally reached the bar. Someone stood ahead of her in line, and Julie leaned against the sheet of skirting, pretending to appear casual, as if the need for a drink wasn't a wild creature inside her, triggering a desire to grab the person in front and hurl him over the side of the cliff. She was exhausted from making conversation, the prospect of what school starting the day after tomorrow would bring, plus the simple, impossible task of an unintoxicated life. Only one thing could tamp down her nerves, give her fuel for the fight that a brand-new class of the toughest strangers—young ones—required. It was silly to have chanced quitting now. The binges, maybe. Those could go. But there was no reason not to have a shot or two for relaxation at night.

"Hey, it's the new teacher!" crowed the guy behind the bar.

He looked too young to drink himself. A high schooler maybe, preparing to take his leave. On the walk over here, Ellie had mentioned the exodus that was about to take place, older island kids going off to the mainland for the school year.

"On the house for you tonight," the kid said. He put a hand in front of his mouth and mock-whispered, "Actually it's on the house for everyone."

Julie smiled.

"What can I get you?" he asked.

"Scotch," Julie said easily. "Neat."

The kid poured a generous finger.

"Aw." Julie mock-pouted. "Can't you make it a double?"

No graduate worth the distinction would give a second thought to the teacher of the school he'd aged out of, let alone how she liked her pour.

The boy's hand had stilled, now he dipped it. "Good call."

Fireflies twinkled like stars as Julie walked off with her drink. It had been so long—two days that felt like two centuries—and she wanted to enjoy her first sip without being observed. She swirled the liquid in her cup, raising it while licking her lips in a way that even to her own mental image appeared vaguely animalistic, distasteful.

"There she is!" called a woman with a frothy, light spill of curls.

Peter's mother. With her own mother striding just ahead.

Julie tipped the cup over, letting its contents spill onto the ground.

"Ms. Weathers," the grandmother said. Her voice was comparatively cordial, although its tone sounded inauthentic, like something painted on. "I'm so glad to welcome you to our island. I'd been hoping we'd have an opportunity to chat."

So they were just going to pretend like the other night had never happened. Overall, it was probably a relief. "I'm glad to meet you as well, Mrs. Hempstead."

The grandmother's head of silken white hair inclined. "Before we spend time on pleasantries, perhaps you should see what's happening down there."

She thrust a long, elegant finger into the dark and pointed.

CHAPTER TWENTY-SEVEN

Torchlight flickered, throwing lilting shadows over the night.

Peter's grandmother stalked in the direction of the ocean, her daughter hustling to keep up. Julie followed at a fast clip as well.

The cliffs at this spot on the island, versus those by Julie's house, were low enough to allow descent via a twisting, snaking path. Despite her years, the grandmother took the trail without hesitation, reaching out with a steadying claw to brace herself against rock face, before regaining her footing and starting down again.

Julie had done her share of hiking in her life, yet still was tempted to sit on her butt and slide down the sandy trail. It tended to give way beneath foot, steep as a runaway truck ramp, but a sliver of the width. And sand wasn't like soil. It kept silting away, until Julie feared she'd be left with nothing to stand on besides air.

Dignity kept her on her feet—if a seventy-plus-year-old woman could do this, then so could she—and focused on the two people in front of her. Their white heads glowed in the moonlight. They looked from the rear less like mother and daughter than sisters.

At last the three of them arrived on a curved sickle of beach.

The younger set missing from the party had gathered here, or rather, a short distance out to sea, on a cluster of seaweed-draped rocks. The tide was low enough that reaching the rocks amounted to a splash through calf-high water, no crashing surf or riptide to contend with, so the sight that made Julie stop and stare was not the children's location.

Nor was it Peter's presence amongst them, splayed out across the tallest of the rocks; why wouldn't he be there, given the fact that his family was hosting the party?

It was Peter's demeanor, his mannerisms, everything about him.

He appeared to be a totally different child, perched atop the biggest boulder, legs dangling, princely and cool. Shouts of laughter carried over the water, and though Peter didn't join in, the other kids looked at him each time a joke was made.

Peter's grandmother and mother stood with seawater swirling around their ankles, impervious to the cold. Julie sensed this to be some sort of test, for her to ferret out whatever might be wrong with what looked like a perfectly pleasant kiddie variation of the adult assemblage higher up, with the added bonus of Peter having come into his own, holding court amongst his peers instead of running off to lurk at the teacher's house.

Was it the tide coming in with a vengeance, water now climbing the rocks? But surely these island kids knew how to account for the tides—and swim, if it came to that. The temperature of the ocean, a hypothermia-inducing fifty-five or sixty degrees, despite summer being barely past its peak, didn't appear to faze them.

"I'm sorry," Julie said. "I don't see…"

The grandmother faced her, arms crossed over the broad ledge of her bosom. "From what I heard, your sea legs are woeful." She smiled to remove the sting of her words. "As is your sea vision apparently. The water plays games with the eyes. It can make one miss things."

Julie looked out again.

Martha caught her eye and pointed with a timid, shaking finger. She glanced at her mother, who gave just the slightest twitch of her head, causing Martha to lower her hand.

Julie squinted out to sea, water riding a bright bar of moonlight. At last she spotted a smaller rock, at an angle from the grouping. No, not necessarily smaller. It was just that the tide had already encroached on this more distant rock, swallowing all but the inverted bowl at its top.

Another child sat there.

"That's Eddie Cowry," Martha began to explain. "The other children don't like—"

"I know who it is," the grandmother interrupted. Her voice suggested there was nobody and nothing she didn't know.

"Of course you do, Mother," said Martha. "He's just a bit far away."

"Are you suggesting my eyesight is not what it once was?" her mother said dryly.

"I was just giving our new teacher some context!" Martha replied, causing the grandmother to sweep up her daughter's hand in what appeared to be a tight grip.

"Oh hush," the grandmother said. She looked down at Julie, her blue gaze illuminated by moonlight. "If adults have to intervene, the Cowry boy will never be able to make it in his classmates' midst, poor thing. It's a sad fact of life that children must sort some things out on their own."

The social parameters were becoming clear to Julie. The kids arrayed on the near rocks had prevented the other boy from venturing closer to shore. And the grandmother's snide remark about vision notwithstanding, Julie could make out plenty about Eddie Cowry: how young he appeared to be, hunched over a pair of canted knees, his small body quivering with cold. Had Julie met a Cowry this evening, Eddie's mother or father? The name didn't ring a bell; then again, she'd heard so many names.

Voices drifted down from the top of the cliff. Traded murmurs, calls, and shouted questions, bursts of loose laughter. A group of parents crowded forward, edging past each other to descend the path that led to their children. As the sound of their voices grew louder, the grandmother twisted around in the shallows, sending up a wave of water. The spontaneous socializing the parents had been engaged in ceased as suddenly as a door slamming shut. Everyone stopped talking, laughter cut off, and the parents turned to ascend the path in the opposite direction, scrabbling to get back to the top.

The grandmother chose that moment to make her exit, moving swiftly despite the clutch of the sand, and towing Martha along beside her.

"Wave goodbye to your son," the grandmother ordered.

Puppetlike, Martha lifted her hand.

Julie turned back to face the sea. The grandmother hadn't asked her to go, and despite the woman's dated, if not altogether wrong perspective on peer dynamics, Julie couldn't imagine just leaving the kids to this. Right now, Eddie appeared to be slipping, his fingers digging into rock as the surf threatened to suck his legs out from under him.

"Eddie, Eddie, can't hold steady!" one of the children shouted.

Peter remained impervious as a round of taunts was unleashed, the more vocal children looking to him for approval. He boosted himself higher on his rock, staring silently toward shore.

"Eddie, Eddie, might be dead-y!"

"Eddie, Eddie, I can't rhyme but I still hate you!"

An older-looking boy contributed a mocking "Damn, this water's cold."

The careless cruelty of children never failed to take Julie's breath away. Peter was clearly a leader of sorts in the pack, judging by how the other kids kept glancing at him, but he neither contributed to the goings-on nor made a move to stop them.

"Eddie, Eddie, you're not Freddie!"

"Eddie's smelly!"

"Eddie, Eddie, hit you with a machete!"

A barely perceptible tilt of Peter's fair head seemed to be taken by the kids as a cue, prompting them to point seaward and let out another vicious volley of couplets. Peter kept himself turned away, his distance and remove a tangible force.

Julie needed to interrupt this. The grandmother was right in one respect—if a grown-up had to wade in and tow Eddie out, the child would never regain any sort of stature amongst his fellow students, and it'd be an ongoing problem for the year.

Julie also didn't want to appear stumped in front of her soon-to-be students, and she wouldn't be someone to them who tolerated cruelty. That was most important of all.

Taunts spiraled upward like sparks from a fire.

"Hold steady, Eddie!"

"What did Eddie said-y?"

"Petty Eddie!"

Cruelest of all, as biting as the temperature of the sea: "Hey, Eddie, soon the water's gonna be over your head-y!"

Seawater frothed around the base of the boulders the children perched on, while the one Eddie clung to was nearly covered. Still he didn't jump in and swim for shore. A wordless injunction laid down by a peer could be stronger than prison walls.

The fact of which might form the basis of Eddie's salvation.

These children obviously attended to every detail where Peter was concerned.

"Peter!" Julie called out suddenly, shouting over the noise of the sea and putting a temporary hold on the jeers. "Guess what?"

CHAPTER TWENTY-EIGHT

The boy visored his eyes, then leapt to his feet atop the rock. It was a daring move given the lengths of kelp swishing and swirling in the rising sea, seeking to entwine an ankle or calf. Peter performed a long jump from one rock to another, prompting the other kids to clamber to their feet as well, though none dared a similar move.

A wave hurtled toward shore.

Julie needed to follow up her cry. The only problem was she had no idea what to add. She'd been bluffing, or stalling, and the kids on the rocks seemed to know it. They all faced her now, but at any moment their attention would be lost.

Surf surged.

Julie half turned her back on the children in what she hoped looked like a casual motion. Then, taking a gulp of salt-laced air, she shouted over her shoulder, "Depot's been asking for you! Come back to shore, and you can take him on a walk by yourself!"

She heard more than saw the response.

Splashes of bodies striking the sea, muffled yelps as heads went under, then the sound of water being kicked up by a horde of plowing legs, kids approaching the shore.

And a command tossed off as Peter emerged from the ocean, running his hands through damp blond locks. "Yo, Eddie's gonna drown out there. Somebody call him in."

Julie took the trail leading back to the mansion, her feet and legs gritty, coated with sand. The sight of Peter's slim, upright form ahead of her was disturbing. His feet churned up sandy clods, light, impervious to the distress he had witnessed, if not caused. While Julie, by contrast, felt stooped and bent over. She'd had to contend with bullying before, of course, but she sensed that the remedies she had previously relied on might not transfer directly to this island, with its new set of legacies, nested heritages, and unseen undercurrents.

At the top of the trail, the party had begun emptying out, just parents remaining, waiting for their kids. Julie listened for the name *Eddie*, but didn't see the boy reunite with anyone.

Peter came up to her and asked, "Where's Depot?"

Julie studied the boy. "At home."

His gaze grew hooded. "Huh? You said he was here."

"I didn't say he was here," Julie corrected. "I said he'd been wanting you, and he probably has. I offered to let you take him on a walk." She paused. Julie had found that openness and self-revelation had a way of puncturing even the thickest kid armor. "It doesn't matter. I said whatever would get you back on shore. To make everyone stop being mean to Eddie."

Peter gaped at her. "You mean you lied?"

"You can lie to keep someone from being hurt," Julie told him. "If you get kidnapped and you can convince the kidnapper that you have to go to the bathroom, and then you escape, but you didn't really have to go to the bathroom, was that the wrong thing to do?"

The example sounded convoluted, even to her, but Peter considered it. "I wasn't kidnapping Eddie," he muttered at last.

"Worse," Julie said. "Because he probably thinks of you as a friend."

Peter snorted, shaking his head. "I can't be friends with Eddie."

Julie frowned a question at him. Unless she'd misinterpreted the whole thing, Peter was the most popular kid in school and could do anything he wanted.

"You missed it," he said, disgusted, taking a step away.

Julie held out her palms. She wasn't above admitting total bafflement to a student.

Martha appeared, winding her way through a few late departures. The grandmother stood among a cluster of upturned faces, tending to her final guests while observing her daughter from a point of remove.

Martha snatched a quick peek over her shoulder, and hastened her stride. "You know you're not allowed to leave on your own," she called to her son in a robotic voice.

The grandmother accepted a handshake from someone. "You're most welcome. I'm glad you enjoyed the evening," she said. "And now you must excuse me while I—"

Peter faced Julie, getting his final words out hurriedly. "You stood down there watching, and you still missed the whole thing." Then his bare feet kicked up sand and he turned and ran off, moving so fast it wasn't worth giving chase.

CHAPTER TWENTY-NINE

J ulie had lost track of Ellie, and she didn't want to linger any longer, especially if it meant winding up alone with the grandmother. She walked across the platters of stone that made up the walkway, then located the grassy lane. She didn't have her phone since it wouldn't have worked, and it'd been stupid not to bring a flashlight. In Wedeskyull she almost always had her headlamp on her in case of a breakdown or longer-than-expected hike. But the sea turned out to be as good as illumination. So long as Julie kept it to her left, she would find her way back home.

The murmur of departing guests and clatter of cleanup eroded behind her; no one else seemed to be taking this route. The house the Hempsteads had bequeathed to their daughter and son-in-law was the only dwelling that lay out this way.

Then Julie became aware of footsteps, and she turned around, gladdened. Assuming the grandmother hadn't chosen now for the promised chat, Julie would welcome almost anybody else's accompaniment. Perhaps Ellie had found her.

She peered through the darkness, surprised to see no one on the path. The sounds had been so clear: a faint squishing of grass, then a moist suck as a shoe was drawn out. Last night's rain had made the earth sodden.

"Hello?" she called.

Silence, except for the eternal lift and fall of the sea.

"Peter?" Julie called, so sure of her conclusion that she thought she heard eerie laughter.

But no tall, light-haired boy appeared, and if there had been a laugh, it didn't float her way again. Julie turned and kept walking, using the edge of the cliff as guide. She quickened her pace. The ocean was so immense, it made the mountains of home seem like dwarf structures. Until the house did her the service of appearing, Julie might as well have been walking through outer space, borderless, unending.

A cough sounded behind her, and Julie whirled. That couldn't be Peter with all his youthful provocation and bravado. The cough had sounded rattly, sick.

"Hello?" Julie said. "Are you okay?"

No one appeared. She was alone out here, unless someone were deliberately messing with her, concealing himself. Peter again surely. But Julie's uncles would tell her to trust her instincts, not keep calling out like some unwitting damsel. Mentally agreeing with them, she broke into a run, struggling not to skid on the slippery ground.

The distance to the house was farther than she had remembered. By the time she arrived, her breaths were coming in hard punches, and she lacked the precision to fit the key in the lock. Inside, Depot let out his bark of reunion. The key sliced metal, failing to find its target. Julie tried again, yanking the key out with a grating sound that was almost, but not quite drowned out by the thud of a foot on the bottom porch step.

Julie stabbed the key home, wrenched it sideways, then yanked the front door open. She slammed it shut behind her without taking a look.

For all she knew, whoever it was had been about to grab her. Julie leaned against the door with her full weight, turning the lock while Depot jumped and twined around her, his joyful barks unremitting.

Still panting hard enough that it was difficult to speak, Julie sent him a mistrustful look. "What—happened—to—being—a—watchdog?"

Depot looked back at her just as balefully.

A solid rap sounded against the door. They both turned their heads.

Then the bolt began to turn to the side, unlocking.

Julie took hold of Depot's collar and tried to pull him toward her, though the dog fought her grasp. They could go to the basement, exit through the door down there. If someone had stalked her all the way back from the party, and was brazen enough to enter her house uninvited, that was a person she had best avoid.

It wasn't her house. This had to be a Hempstead.

Since Julie also had no desire to prolong the night with either Martha or the grandmother, the basement still seemed a fine idea. She and her dog could hide out, make like they'd gone for a walk. The only problem was, Depot refused to budge. He was behaving quite calmly, considering the way their domicile was being invaded.

The door slid open an inch or two at a time, and then an old man walked in.

He entered with one hand extended at his waist, as if expecting the greeting he received. Depot didn't bark, just lowered his head and gave the man's palm a long lather.

"Traitor," Julie muttered. "He really scared me."

It struck Julie that if this man had a key, perhaps he'd come over before, made Depot's acquaintance when she wasn't here. The house, so open and exposed, its rear wall laid bare to the sea, suddenly felt intruded upon from within. Julie wrapped her arms around herself and cleared her throat, though the man didn't appear to take any notice.

He rubbed the top of Depot's head, looking around with a smile. Julie recognized him at that moment—the customer who'd been in the antiques shop when Ellie rushed her out. A seaman who had a key and obvious familiarity with the house.

"Mr. Hempstead," Julie said, wondering why she hadn't seen him at the party.

"Captain," he corrected, continuing to look around as if unsure who had spoken. Judging by where he aimed his gaze, it might have been the dog.

"I'm afraid I find myself a bit confused tonight," he said apologetically. "I shouldn't have come." The man took a breath that resulted in a series of feeble coughs.

"The house is let now," Julie said. "I'm the new teacher."

"Of course you are," he replied, bringing one fist to his chest.

Concern traded places with her fright and discomfiture. "Can I get you a glass of water? Would you like to come in and sit down?"

"No, no," the man protested. "I must be getting home. It's late."

Julie reached out to stop him. "I'll walk with you. My dog and I can both go."

But the man turned back toward the door. "I wouldn't hear of it. Please get on with your evening. I hope you enjoyed the festivities at Old Bluff."

He seemed more clearheaded, and his cough had abated. The man poked around in a pocket and withdrew his ring of keys. He separated one from the bunch, then reached for Julie's hand, which he closed over the key before depositing a courtly kiss. "You will be a wonderful teacher for our children, my dear."

"Thank you," Julie began. "I'm really going to try—"

"Please don't let your strength be sapped," the Captain went on, putting a stop to her interruption with one outstretched palm. "This island has a way of doing that."

The Captain's plea was all that allowed Julie to fall asleep that night, licking her lips in what had come to feel like a deplorable tic, the pop-up bar at the party a mirage in her mind. How had she dumped out a full glass of scotch? Not long ago, Julie would've gotten down on her hands and knees, rescued the liquid before it could seep into the ground.

The next morning's slash on the calendar was arduous to draw, the feeling of buoyancy bestowed by new sobriety indeed winding up a honeymoon glow. Still, Julie couldn't quell a feeling of pride when she counted up the number of bisected squares.

A rap on the front door interrupted the dreamy tracings of her finger across the page.

"Who's Eddie Cowry?" Julie asked, opening the door to let in Ellie.

It was a good time for a visit, given their joint penchant for adult beverages. Maybe they could take to hanging out before it was five o'clock anywhere.

Ellie folded small fists on her hips. "You have a way of making me feel like I'm always entering in the middle of a conversation."

Julie offered a quick smile of acknowledgment. "Come in. Would you like some coffee? And then you can tell me about Eddie."

Ellie shook her head, following Julie into the kitchen. "No, you go first, tell me about the party. I'm keeping my expectations low, mind, since your big takeaway involves a child." She paused. "And a social outcast at that."

"Ah," said Julie, shaking grinds into a filter. "We're getting somewhere. There was a terrible bullying incident with Eddie and the other students last night."

Ellie hoisted herself onto the counter, dangling her feet. "It isn't that Eddie himself isn't well liked, although maybe that's true. But really it's about his father."

Julie looked up with interest, sliding milk and sugar toward Ellie. "His dad?"

Ellie doctored a mug. "Mike Cowry. Biggest dub of 'em all."

"You used that term before," Julie said. "When we were talking about highliners."

Ellie held up a finger in a *bingo* gesture. "If a highliner is a top lobsterman, with the biggest catches and consequent wealth—relatively speaking—not to mention being known as an authority, then the guy who used to be called a dub is his polar opposite."

"So Eddie's dad is struggling financially, not respected, and—"

"—lousy at what he does," Ellie concluded.

"And Eddie bears the burden of his father's low status amongst his peers."

Ellie regarded her. "Very good."

"While Peter is high status," Julie went on. Of course—the Hempsteads were island royalty. It explained the children's deference at the party, as if they'd been in the presence of a lord, and also the parents' odd scurrying when they were about to be faced with the grandmother.

"The Hempsteads own half the houses on-island." Ellie drank deeply from her mug, concealing her face. "They collect rent like Monopoly money. I don't think there's a single resident who isn't indebted to them or dependent on them somehow." Her mouth twisted visibly before her expression could lighten. "No, scratch that. There is at least one. And he happens to be a highliner himself. Knows a hell of a lot more than I do, even though I'm the daughter of a fisherman."

"Great," Julie said. "Who is it?"

Ellie jumped down from the counter. "I'll give you a hint," she said. She puckered her lips and performed a dramatic smooch. "Meet you at the schoolhouse around five?"

CHAPTER THIRTY

J ulie fed Depot and took him on a walk before heading out herself. She was curious about the cliff path Ellie used, but decided to go the way through the woods that had become familiar already. She had too much to do today to spend time exploring.

The prospect of confronting a classroom with not enough to say or do was a teacher's equivalent of the going-outside-naked dream. Meager lesson plans that petered out before the allotted time, gaps and silences and trailing sentences when content ran dry and Julie came up empty, corpse dust on her flailing hands. Kids attacked silence as if it were a small, helpless animal, tore out its throat with their teeth. Preparation was essential.

The route to town seemed to take longer than it had before, Julie's drying-out body lagging, and she had to pause in a grove for a drink of water that posed pale contrast to the liquid she really craved. She didn't recognize this spot. Perhaps she had gone the wrong way after all, vision bleary from the lack of alcohol. If she had veered off course, this was an awfully pretty spot to get lost in. The late-summer woods glowed, lit with gold. Yellow leaves jangled like coins on their branches, caught in a sudden, quick breeze.

Those trees weren't birches, as Julie had thought. Stepping closer for a better look, her foot came down on a thick, squishy body. It was a dry-drunk dream, a hallucination, had to be, yet still Julie recoiled, her insides roiling as if she were about to throw up. Picturing some outsized island slug, Julie pulled her shoe free of the pulpy mass. Then things began to clarify, all five senses returning. First, a pungent odor. These were plum trees, so laden with fruit that a purple carpet's worth had fallen to make room for less overripe siblings. The plums on the ground lay cracked and seeping, but the specimens on the branches hung heavily: perfect amethyst globes. There was a sharp tang in the air, a flavor of ferment.

The fruit had camouflaged the path, but Julie could see it now, she knew which way to go. Shaking her head in wonder—in Wedeskyull such a bounty would've been picked clean and sold for princely sums at farm stands—Julie took time to pluck a fat orb and eat it, juice dripping down her wrist as she jogged along the remainder of the path. If she shut her eyes, the snack was vaguely reminiscent of brandy, which might be sufficient to get her through this day.

As Julie neared town, she realized that something had changed, although her mind was still working too sluggishly to catch hold of what it was. She continued running down the sandy road at a good clip, sunshine causing her to squint as she looked left and right at closed shop doors and lowered awnings.

That was it.

She was running down the road, whereas in the days prior she could move only in fits and starts, stepping aside periodically to get out of the way of crowds. Yesterday had been Labor Day, the crowning glory of the season, and now the island had emptied itself out. Summer people gone from their second homes, tourists no longer making the crossing. It was more total a clearing than anything Julie had ever experienced in

Wedeskyull, where the exodus was gradual: summer vacationers giving way to leaf peepers, who made way for skiers and ice climbers, the population only truly reduced to a skeleton crew of locals during mud and black-fly seasons. On Mercy, it was as if a natural disaster had hit, the place apocalypse bare. No more pop-up businesses or kids hawking lemonade, cookies, and handmade art from stands. The island had shed its colorful summer robes, leaving behind a muted landscape.

Just as Ellie had warned.

Julie settled for a plain old deli sandwich from the grocery store. The cart she'd stopped at the other day, worthy of a spot on the Food Network, had been rolled out of sight, gone till the flocks and droves of people that accompanied the high season prompted its return. Munching her lunch, Julie let herself into the schoolhouse and got down to work.

She spit shined the building, leaving not one speck of grit on the desks and beating the stage curtain until it was dust-free. Folders of worksheets and shelves full of textbooks were organized by age group, with activities planned for the inevitable downtime when Julie's attention would be diverted by the other grades and students finished their assigned work early. She had her preferred getting-to-know-you exercise laid out, and a backup in case the kids found her first choice lame. (No one ever argued with a scavenger hunt outdoors.) She'd even gone over to the library where she printed out a discourse on drama and composed a hard-sell speech on the virtues of putting on a play.

She was as ready as could be for tomorrow by the time Ellie came to get her.

They walked along the shore, waves lapping the rocks in a succession of ticks, like a clock that never wound down. Julie hadn't yet been to this part of the island, where the land sat so low, it was all but swallowed by the sea.

"My mother used to say that the ocean was just like the sky," Ellie remarked, pointing. "That they're mirrors of each other—one blue when the other is, or gray, or storm-driven—and that we lived in the best place on earth because top and bottom always matched, up and down, every day the same."

"That's beautiful," Julie said.

Suddenly, she saw the flight from Mercy differently than she had earlier. Instead of the summer people leaving behind an empty shell, a mere husk of island life, they became intruders on an idyll that only the year-rounders knew. Yesterday's population had been engorged, ballooned like a leech, and now, after a summer of being feasted upon, the island could shrink down to its normal state of peace.

Water flicked their sandaled feet as Julie and Ellie walked along the shoreline.

"Fishermen aren't the easiest guys to get to know," Ellie said. "They're a clubby bunch, tend to stick to themselves." She gestured to a hulking building on the right. It was shaped like an airplane hangar, curved roof and walls. "And this is where they do it."

Ellie pulled open the heavy door, gesturing Julie inside. A rotted, fishy odor struck as soon as they entered, and Julie pinched her nose.

Ellie laughed. "Takes some getting used to."

In addition to the smell, there was an overwhelming array of sights and sounds. Rectangular boxes, yellow in color and resembling cages, made up the perimeter of the room, stacked ten high in fifty times that many rows. A few cages sat on long tables, wire shears scattered amongst them. There were smaller tables at the rear of the cavernous space, occupied by men who ran the gamut from just out of high school to impossibly old. Loud, raucous voices seemed to speak a foreign language, its accent requiring translation—*hawba* for *harbor* was one of the more comprehensible substitutions—and the terms also alien. What did sleeves, bugs, and cups mean in this context?

Cups.

The scene contained enough new features that it had taken Julie a second to realize it was just the same as anywhere else. Men laughing, jeering, insulting one another whether for real or in jest, pounding each other's backs, raising their hands in a cheer. The vocabulary might be different, and the workaday details, but these were just guys, gathering after a long day to rehash problems, brainstorm strategies, let off steam.

And like men everywhere, they were doing it with liquid assistance. The fish-market smell had temporarily camouflaged the more familiar odors of beer and liquor.

Tonight Julie couldn't count on an interruption from the grand-mother; there was no chance of a second saving grace. It would be down to her, what happened next.

A roar of voices surged, men noticing her entrance. Julie looked around wildly for Ellie, but they had gotten separated. There she was, standing at a makeshift counter. The man behind it slid bottles around, three-card-monte-style, exchanging their places as if searching for a certain kind. His mouth spread wide in a grin as Ellie looked up at him, flirty, hungry, pleading. These guys weren't wine drinkers, and the one serving in the role of bartender was clearly having a hard time coming up with a pinot or a cabernet.

Scotch though. That would be procured easily enough.

Julie hunched over, sweat pearling at her temples. It was hot in this crowded, sweaty, laughter-filled space. She clenched her hands into fists, muscles quivering in her thighs. She needed to sit down. She needed to get out of here.

Then Ellie was at her side.

"I'm sorry," she said. "Oh, Julie, I'm an idiot, I should've realized."

She clenched a beer stein filled with blood-red liquid in one fist, giving no sign of letting it go. But with her other hand, Ellie steered Julie back outside.

"I'll get him, okay?" she said. "You stay out here, and I'll bring Callum."

CHAPTER THIRTY-ONE

J ulie went to wait by the boulders at the edge of the ocean, leaning against a rock crusted with shards of white barnacles sawn off by the sea. She felt weak with both wanting and the relief of a barely averted catastrophe. The car that almost hit you, the hurricane that struck a neighboring town.

The unceasing rhythm of the waves made time hard to gauge, but Ellie had clearly polished off the contents of her first serving of wine, and possibly a second or third, by the time she emerged from the building, clutching a refill. She walked at a slow, loopy pace, Callum holding her by the elbow.

"Callum, you know Julie," Ellie said, the words sounding slippery in her mouth. "And vice versa."

"The new girl," Callum said, stopping in front of Julie. His tone as affable as always, but his expression discordant with it. Intense, navy-blue eyes searching her face.

Julie felt her cheeks warm under his gaze.

Ellie administered a playful punch. "We go by *woman* now."

Great, Julie thought. *I'm crushing on the guy my friend has a thing for.*

"I'm a throwback," Callum acknowledged, and Ellie sent him a *You so are* glance.

Ellie had cackled when she heard about their not-quite-kiss, but that had obviously been an act of sheer sisterhood and solidarity. Plus, Julie was married, if in name only. Still grieving the loss of her daughter, and if she didn't quite dare call herself in recovery, at least testing its waters. Adding anything on top of that would be absurd. Julie had enough to do here on Mercy in terms of the children. Plenty of challenge for the duration. A new relationship need not apply.

Julie gave Callum the sort of smile someone might deliver upon brief acquaintance. Ignoring the shine of his eyes in the deepening dusk, she clapped her hands together briskly. "Getting chilly out here." The weather. What better topic to lead with when you were emphasizing the platonic nature of your intent?

"Julie has questions," Ellie announced. "About…about…" She broke off, turning around in a circle as if she'd lost sight of where everybody had gone. "What did you have questions about again, Julie?"

Julie forced a smile. "I wanted to learn a little about the kids before school starts."

"Oh right!" Ellie thrust her hand in the air triumphantly. It was the one holding the stein and a splash of red leapt out, sliding down the side of the glass. Ellie bent her head to lick up the drops. "Highliners. Julie wants to know why Peter Hempstead is all set to be a highliner, and wormy Eddie Cowry will never be one."

Julie cringed. If Ellie, who had nothing to do with the boy, so despised him, then Eddie really didn't stand a chance.

Callum regarded them both. "Why?"

Julie hesitated. "I guess I just thought some background would help me—"

"No," Callum interrupted. "I meant, what do you mean by *why*?"

Julie frowned. "Well, neither boy fishes now obviously. Or catches lobsters, if that's how you refer to it. So how do we already know how good they'll be at it? And that's assuming they even choose to do the same thing as their fathers."

A brief smile lit Callum's eyes. "Choose."

"Okay, so maybe it's not really a choice, I get that, believe me. But you still didn't answer the part about their entire worth in the business being predetermined."

Callum's features worked with frustration, the expression of someone charged with explaining a given, the facts of his life. Julie might as well have been asking him to explain why the lungs absorbed oxygen.

From behind came a shriek of glass, and they both turned.

Ellie knelt beside one of the boulders. "Oops," she said, getting to her feet. Wine tinged the patch of sea bloodred before a wave rolled in and dispersed it. "Guess Roy was right about not giving me one to take outside." Another incoming wave tripped her, and Ellie went down in the surf, water fizzing around her hands and knees. She began patting the sandy surface for pieces of the broken stein.

Callum went and pulled Ellie to her feet. "Let the sea take it."

Ellie's shirt had gone see-through, and her shorts were dripping. "Such a gentleman," she said, leaning against Callum so that the wet fabric of her clothes stuck to his. She laughed and sniffled at the same time, resulting in an ungainly snort.

"Let's get you home to dry off and dry out," Callum said.

He raised an eyebrow in Julie's direction, and she nodded, following him onto the road that led through town toward the foursquare of cottages.

"Seems like you've done that before," Julie remarked after they dropped Ellie off, Callum draping a blanket over her as she collapsed on the couch.

He offered a brief shrug. "People on islands tend to be soaked with more than the sea."

"People everywhere," Julie responded, and he gave her another of his sharp looks.

Callum insisted on accompanying her on the last leg of the walk. An ivory horn of moon cleaved the sky as they hurried through the woods, Julie explaining that her dog would be in need of some dinner and exercise.

But when they arrived, Depot wasn't inside.

CHAPTER THIRTY-TWO

Julie's heart clutched as she walked through the house, checking every corner. She left the storage bedroom, with the crib and assorted other detritus of Peter's early childhood, for last. Viewing this room with a guest in the house made her feel vulnerable, exposed. She knew Depot wouldn't be in there anyway; he wasn't a dog who made his presence unknown, and there'd been no bark of reunion when Julie got home.

She pinched her brow, forehead sore with worry. She had been scrupulous about locking the front door. Of course, she now knew that the prior residents had keys.

Callum was in the process of making a loop around the outside of the house; she glimpsed him through a window.

"Does your dog go out on his own?" he asked when Julie arrived at his side.

"Only if I'm home to let him out," she replied. "And he was definitely inside when I left around lunchtime."

She glanced up at the sky—full dark now, moonlight and a splatter of stars—then looked toward the rear of the house, dread building inside her. If Depot had gotten out, if the Captain had come by, say, or Peter—

She started to run for the cliff, but the skid of cleared earth she'd been picturing, proof of a dog's slide over the edge, wasn't there. Julie leaned down, bracing her arms on her thighs, heart pattering as she scoured the base for hints of motion.

Callum grabbed her, holding her back. "Look over there."

Julie had taken off so fast, she hadn't even been sure he'd stuck around. But now Callum pointed at the land that ran parallel to where they were standing, the lane between both Hempstead houses. The scrub and grass lay flat, and when Julie walked closer, she saw the imprint of four very large paws in the earth. She started to follow them.

Callum stayed to her right, helping spot prints and patches of trampled grass.

The old manse loomed up out of the night, its peaks and tower limned with black against the sky, only a single light on in the foyer when Julie climbed the front steps. She hadn't gone inside at the party last night, and up close it was clear that while the house was indeed grand, it had also seen better days. The clapboard was in need of paint—a condition that was probably chronic, given its proximity to the sea—and one of the porch pillars leaned slightly.

Callum came up beside her. He used a knocker, green with patina, to rap on the set of carved front doors, but nobody appeared to be home. Julie ran down the porch steps to the last paw print they'd found, a little ways before the cliff trail began.

She tracked the rest to their terminus, and then she saw Depot.

Someone had either led the dog to the beach at the bottom, or else Depot had scrambled down the path himself. It didn't matter, because he was alone now, and couldn't get back up. When he saw Julie, he let out the bark he reserved just for her, and attempted to come join her at the top. But sand slid out beneath his paws, sending the dog flailing backward. He landed in a splashy pool, whining and yelping as he tried to bound out.

It had been getting on high tide when Julie and Ellie and Callum were together. Depot bunched his paws, front and back, standing on a rapidly shrinking slice of sand.

Callum appeared beside her. "We'll have to lead him up."

"I don't think we can," Julie said, her teeth chattering so hard with cold and fright that she wasn't sure whether Callum would understand what she'd said.

But he'd figured it out. "He's a big 'un," he acknowledged grimly.

Depot's size made many things harder—the cost of feeding, how much time had to be devoted to walks, all the places that tolerated small pets but were biased against large—but at this moment it posed out-and-out danger. Depot's weight would be enough to crumble the already eroded trail, which had seen further damage from the trampling it'd received the night of the party. If Julie tried to help, tugging her dog upward, or pushing him from behind, their combined mass would only destroy their means of egress faster.

And it was the only way out. The dissolving path wound between walls of sheer rock face looming up from the sea. Scaling either side would require either a skilled free climb, or ropes and who knew what, a sling or basket for a dog.

An incoming wave hit Depot, threatening to sweep his legs out from under him, and the dog took a terrified leap onto the trail, which sank instantly, becoming one with the sea. Depot shrank away from the water, barking and snapping at it as if it were a rival dog. Then the tide swept outward, and for the moment Depot was dry.

Julie bit her lip so hard it bled. If she climbed down, she would fur-ther erode the sand, but at least she could offer comfort to her dog. But how would they get back up? She looked around for an answer. Callum had vanished, but she couldn't wait for him. A wave crashed onto shore, making Depot stagger, and sheer instinct drove Julie onto the path. She tried to run fleetly, keep the sand underfoot where they needed it, but particles flew up nonetheless, stinging her legs. At the bottom, she hurled herself against Depot.

"It's okay, Deep, I'm here," she said into his floppy, velvet ear. The dog's quaking body began to calm in her arms. "I'll get you back up. I will."

She was sure he could smell the doubt emanating from her, but he leaned his tired form against hers, causing Julie to sit down on her rear, seawater waist-high around her. Cold seeped into her clothes, then her skin, then deeper yet. Julie was used to swimming in icy waters, but the temperature of the sea rendered a mountain stream Jacuzzi-warm.

A wave surged onto shore, and she and Depot were momentarily afloat before the beach returned beneath them. Julie got to her feet and pulled her dog forward, but ascending the trail by even a few feet had become impossible. The sand collapsed, and they both went sliding back toward the ocean.

Depot's snout quivered with fear. Young Eddie Cowry on that rock last night. So many helpless creatures, and so little Julie could do to help them.

"We'll find some other way," Julie told her dog, putting every ounce of the certainty she lacked into her pledge. Then she looked out to sea, judging the distance of the next wave. Close now. Seconds away. "After this wave. It's going to be a big one, Deep."

Cold hit her as if she'd collided with the wall of a deep freeze. Julie held her breath, clutching her dog's collar with two hands, and they both went under. The sea threatened to pull them apart, but Julie dug her fingers into Depot's fur, slippery fistfuls that nearly escaped her grasp. The wave receded, and Julie surfaced, gasping for air.

She was shivering so hard that she had trouble holding on to Depot.

Julie could stand now, the water up to her chest, but Depot no longer could. He stayed by her side, paws furiously churning the water.

"Settle your dog!"

Disoriented by the blackness of the water and the night, Julie tried to find the source of the shout. Callum was sliding down what remained of the trail, sledding without a toboggan, a coil of rope mounded in his lap. The last of the sand hourglassed away in a trickle, depositing Callum in the sea.

"We'll have to swim!" he yelled. "The Hempsteads have a dock!"

A wave came in, and Callum ducked effortlessly beneath it, grasping Julie by the shoulder to hold her in place. "Quiet your dog," he told her once the water had retreated and he and Julie could both stand. "He's exhausting himself."

Julie bent and slid her arms underneath Depot's belly, the buoyancy of the water allowing her to hold him. Once her own ability to remain on foot was stolen by the tide, she would no longer be able to support his weight.

Callum's hands worked beneath the surface of the water, affixing the rope to Depot's collar. He gave Julie an appraising look. "Swimming will warm you," he said, testing his knot with a stout tug. "It's about a quarter mile. Think you can do it?"

CHAPTER THIRTY-THREE

A wave came in and Julie dipped under as she'd seen Callum do. His motions were expert in the water, and he seemed immune to the cold. When the wave pulled back, Callum could still stand, the water chin-high on him, but Julie was reduced to treading water. Callum cradled Depot in his arms so the dog could rest.

"Where do we—h-h-have to go?" Julie asked, her teeth clacking together. Her voice shook with both apprehension and chill, and she could see Depot react, thrashing with his own display of frenzy when the next wave hit them.

Depot returned to the surface, but Julie had gotten rotated. She turned in the direction she had seen Depot bob up, ducking as another wave crested before spotting Callum, swimming confidently and capably with the rope clenched in his fist.

He stuck his free hand out of the water. "Around that point!" He gestured, though the indication meant little in this featureless seascape.

Julie spit out water, salt toxic on her tongue. At home she'd always been a good swimmer, although the difference between lakes or creeks versus the open ocean was becoming clear with this feat.

"We have to get out beyond those rocks!" Callum said, pointing again and raising his voice to be heard. "Otherwise we'll get banged up pretty good!"

Julie looked in the direction he was indicating, but could see only the vaguest outline, and even that appeared more illusion than physical shape. Callum read the sea as she did the woods, alert to its weapons and traps. While to Julie the entire ocean felt murky and indistinct, not just unknown but unknowable.

They struck out through the lashing waters, Julie trying to mimic Callum's sure crawl, the way he slid smoothly under whenever a wave approached. Depot's paddling looked strong, although Julie kept losing track of him between the hills and bowls of water. If Callum hadn't been holding onto the rope, she didn't know if she would have had the strength to tow Depot. It was hard enough to keep moving forward herself.

The amount of land the Hempsteads must own was staggering; this much ocean frontage indicated a fortune. Julie wished the family could've been a little less wealthy. Her arms were beginning to tire.

Shivering further depleted her strength, and her strokes grew choppy and uneven. Julie fought to make progress in the right direction. At least, she thought it was the right direction—how did you tell which way you were swimming? Everything around her was black, without any landmarks or distinctions. The seawater felt thick and viscous, squirming with life. Julie kicked out, alarmed when something slick knocked against her, and her leg muscles trembled with fear and fatigue.

Callum had gotten some distance ahead. She could no longer see him, or her dog. Julie slowed, treading water while she tried to get her bearings.

A shout came from somewhere in the invisible distance. "There it is!"

Water distorted the way sound traveled; Julie might've been moving toward or away from their destination as she struck out again. "I don't see it!" she yelled. "I don't know where you are!" She was disoriented, bobbing between the twin darknesses of water and sky. "Call out again!" she screamed, on the verge of panic.

A wave got her and Julie fought it, her body tumbling around like a load of laundry. Water entered her nose, a stinging swarm of wasps. She felt the paralyzing vise of the sea. For a second she couldn't tell up from down, and she took in an enormous mouthful of water. Spitting frantically, she began to beat her legs and arms, fighting to follow a stream of bubbles from her mouth. The ocean fought back, pressing on her like a weight, trying to keep her from leaving. She surfaced like a cork popping out. Gasping and coughing, she heard a single clear bark, and hurtled herself in its direction.

Callum appeared in a trough of water, Depot beside him.

"You okay?" Callum asked.

He wasn't even out of breath.

The force of the water prevented Julie from staying in one place. She was swept around as if on a carnival ride, trying to get a good look at Depot. The dog appeared to be paddling gamely, but Julie detected signs of exhaustion in his eyes.

"How much farther?" she gasped.

Callum gestured with one hand, the other clenched around the rope.

Hair had plastered itself over her eyes. Julie shoved back a clump of strands, trying to see whatever he'd pointed to. Wooden poles rising out of the sea. Perhaps they held up a dock. There could've been a boathouse too; Julie thought she caught a glimpse of angular roof. Fifty yards away? More? The water seemed intent on deception, making distance impossible to judge.

They set out again, Julie keeping Callum and Depot in sight. She settled into an easier breaststroke, her forward movement steady. Depot was having a hard time, though. His body lay low in the water, hind and forepaws slowed from their earlier pace. His snout went under, and he had to struggle back to the surface.

How many times had Depot tried and failed to get up that hill before Julie arrived, tiring himself before he even started swimming?

Using the final reserves of her own energy, Julie sped up until she and her dog were apace. "Come on, Depot. You can do it, Deep!"

Callum continued to swim with sharp, clean strokes, the rope taut between him and the dog. Depot didn't turn to look at Julie. He couldn't. His rear half began sinking, hind quarters no longer moving at all. A wave came, and Depot's body rose and fell.

"Depot!" Julie cried. She reached out to grab a section of rope, although holding on to it would do nothing if Depot couldn't stay above the surface. "We're almost there!"

The long line of the dock appeared in a wavery haze, its front portion bowed toward the sea. Maybe a dozen yards in front of them, not much more than that, but it was going to be too far. Depot's front legs had stilled. He was floating, scarcely paddling at all. His gaze met Julie's without a hint of blame or regret, only love.

Then he sank.

Julie didn't see the moment when her dog's body went below; she was staring at the seamless juncture between sea and sky.

Callum dove beneath the patch of water where the dog had gone under. He didn't resurface, both he and Depot vanished from view. After a moment, Depot's big head appeared above water, the level top of his back visible too. It was impossible because no part of the dog appeared to be moving, certainly not fast, yet it looked as if something was causing Depot to skim along the surface of the sea.

Then he was at the dock, propelled upward and onto the boards. Depot collapsed on the wooden slats, his whole body heaving. Callum's head shot out of the sea, plumes of water cascading off him as he gasped for breath. Planting both hands on the edge of the dock, Callum hoisted himself up and sat for a second, raking in breaths.

He had swum underwater the whole way, holding Depot clear of the sea.

Callum got to his feet, calling out to Julie, "You okay?"

She didn't answer. The sea dragged at her limbs like a cape. The water felt almost warm now, or perhaps she had gone numb. It didn't matter. Julie couldn't swim any longer, could barely tread water, as she took in the blank swath of gray above and below. She heard Ellie's far-off, lilting voice. *Top and bottom match.*

All the grayness was a screen on which to watch the events of that terrible day. The sea clenched her in its unyielding grip while Julie squeezed rubber stroller handles, fistfuls of water that were impossible to keep hold of.

There was a splash, and a second later Callum was beside her. "Swim!" he said. "When the tide starts going out, it'll be impossible to get on the dock!"

Julie's legs dangled lifelessly beneath her. Her arms barely stirred in the water.

"Swim!" Callum commanded. "Your dog's waiting! Swim, for Christ's sake!"

He looped an arm around her neck from behind, trying a lifeguard save, but Julie resisted, wanting nothing more than to reach the depths she'd been seeking. The sea was like sodden cloths, a wrap or a shroud, pulling her down.

"Swim, goddamn you!" Callum shouted right in her ear. "You're needed on land!"

It wasn't his anger that did it. She had no idea how Callum knew what to say, but his words snapped Julie free, unlocked her limbs, and she started to swim.

She hauled herself upward, trying to grab hold of the slippery dock as the sea tried just as forcefully to take her back. Julie sucked air into her lungs while digging her nails into softened bits of wood. Depot was on his feet, pawing at the board she reached for. At last, Julie heaved herself onto terra sort-of firma, and Depot shook himself hugely, a waterfall of droplets upon her that felt like tiny icicles.

Callum pulled himself out of the water behind her, then led the way across the boards of the dock, which were slick with seaweed and moisture. It was amazing to walk again, feel something semi-stable beneath her feet. Actually, the dock was solid enough—a bit rotten perhaps, but it was Julie's own body that deprived her of stability. She was shaking so hard, her knees knocked together, and she could hardly stand upright.

Callum came and took her hand, which jangled in his grip.

"Hurry," he said, giving her an assessing glance. "We need to get you warm."

CHAPTER THIRTY-FOUR

C allum ran with Julie down the length of a dirt path that lay per-pendicular to the mansion. Depot galloped alongside, compelled by a deep, instinctual knowledge that they needed to get in from the cold. At last Callum pushed through a tangle of branches, part of a copse of trees that concealed a small cabin.

The front door was locked, if nominally—the mechanism looked easy enough to pick—but Callum slid up a window instead, hoisting himself over the sill, before coming around and opening the door from inside. Depot raced in. By the time Julie entered, Callum had yanked a woolen blanket off a couch and was holding it out.

"Get out of those wet clothes," he instructed, "and wrap this around you."

This time, Julie couldn't project even a hint of innuendo into their interaction; she recognized the danger, and the thrum of urgency in Callum's voice reflected it. Anyone who lived in the Adirondacks was at least on nodding acquaintance with hypothermia, a risk even at the height of summer, if wetness was involved.

Callum crouched before a fireplace, examining a crisscrossed thatch of logs, while Julie stripped off her clothing. She mummified herself in plaid wool as Callum got up and headed for the door.

"I have to go out for some kindling. Wait here."

Julie's body was quaking inside the blanket, her skin ghostly and blue. "You…you…you must be pretty cold yourself. Maybe there…there are some clothes you can change into…"

"No time," Callum said, and strode out of the cabin.

The cabin was seasonal, no central heat, plus the water and electric had been turned off, so neither the sink nor the stove worked. But in the galley kitchen, Julie located a pot and a can opener and some chicken soup. Holding one hand on top of the other to steady it, she managed to dump the contents of the can into the pot. They could heat it over the fire. She found a can of beef barley next and fed it to Depot straight out of the tin.

Callum returned with an armload of sticks and twigs.

Once the fire started to crackle, Julie nestled the pot between the logs. It was bubbling by the time Callum got back from upstairs, dressed in dry clothes that were a size too small. Julie spooned a serving into a bowl for him, and he nodded his thanks.

Julie laid her clothes out to dry in front of the fire, then sat down, hands extended toward the flames. Depot trod over and dropped in a mountainous heap.

"Better?" Callum asked.

"Yes. Thank you." The words were stupidly inadequate. Julie had no idea how to thank Callum for what he had done tonight.

For a while, there was just the clack of spoons against bowls. The fire gained momentum, and Callum put another log on, sending up a spatter of sparks. They had denuded the neat stack on the hearth. Welcome heat spread out into the room.

"Whose cabin is this?" Julie asked.

"It belongs to a painter friend of mine," Callum replied. "Renowned for his summer landscapes, he only comes to the island during the high season. This place has been in his family practically since Mercy was settled." Callum let out something between a rasp and a laugh. "What the Hempsteads would give to have gotten their hands on it, back then or ever. But Andy's famous, their money means nothing to him."

"Why would the Hempsteads want it so badly?"

Callum gestured outside. "This parcel sits adjacent to their land. Splits off a wedge. It's the reason the house they fixed up for their daughter is so far from the old manse. Maryanne would've preferred to be closer neighbors."

"She's controlling," Julie said, leaning toward the heat.

"Only in the sense that her family's in charge of almost everything around here."

Julie wasn't sure whether he was joking or had given her a straight answer.

Callum glanced at her sideways as he spooned up the last of his soup. "You froze out there earlier. Seemed like you couldn't swim. Or wouldn't."

Julie knew she owed him an answer, at the least an explanation for why she couldn't give him one. He'd saved her dog's life, and possibly her own. But talking about Hedley—even just thinking about her sometimes— was still the hardest thing for Julie to do. Clasping her icy hands into a knot, Julie sucked in a breath, surprised at what came out next.

The truth.

The Everything Store had become a second home to Julie as she made the passage into motherhood: a source for the needed paraphernalia of the stage; a way to accomplish all the tasks that had become so difficult to fit into even a good day; and a distraction from all of the above.

185

That warm July day hadn't been one of the good ones.

Hedley was in a rotten mood, ill with her customary cold, or perhaps it was allergies, a possibility the pedi had just started to investigate since who caught colds in summertime? Hedley wasn't even in day care.

There weren't aisles as such in The Everything Store, more like nooks for table displays, and crannies filled with shelves. Julie pushed the stroller into every one of them, examining fun things like room atomizers and throw pillows stuffed with pine, while placing necessities into the basket below the space where Hedley dozed.

The best thing The Everything Store offered was a tasting counter—especially since Julie's days often contained not a moment to eat lunch—but it was always too crowded with shoppers to wheel up a stroller. Julie would tuck the pricey one they'd bought Hedley—thick, shock-absorbent wheels for the forested trails Julie took with the baby and Depot—next to a stand of souvenirs or rack of Wedeskyull wear, then dash back for a sample of locally made jam on homemade crackers or house-smoked sausage.

That day they had coffee as well.

They'd had coffee.

Someone had sliced a blackberry pie—baked with berries currently growing thick on the roadsides—into sliver-sized samples, and next to the stack of boxed pies available for purchase, rows of Dixie cups gave off an intoxicating scent.

It was her first real sustenance of the day. Julie had savored the brew, blowing on it, taking small, discreet sips. Standing a few feet apart from the counter to make room for other customers, the stroller tucked away. How long had she stood there, enjoying that rarest of treats for a new mother, a pause? Not just seconds. Minutes. Maybe as many as three.

When she got back to the stroller, she had looked for Hedley right away to check on her; she remembered doing that.

And for a blissful little while, she still had no idea what had happened.

Flames cast flickering shadows across Callum's face. When he spoke, his voice sounded heavy with sorrow. "Someone took her? Did someone take your child?"

Julie had finally stopped shivering, but her voice still shook when she replied. "No. That isn't what happened."

Callum used a poker to stoke the fire, sending up a hot rush of air.

"It was more horrible than that in a way," Julie told him. "Because then there would've at least been an explanation, something comprehensible. Evil, but comprehensible. Also, then I could picture Hedley out there somewhere, safe." Julie's voice cracked before splitting. "Given or sold to parents who desperately wanted a baby."

"What then?" Callum asked.

Julie stared into the flames till the orbs of her eyes felt heated, deadly. "She was just gone. Not gone like you said. But gone."

Callum gave a slow nod.

"At first I thought she had finally fallen into a nice deep sleep." The softest silence in the world lived in the circumference of a baby's yawn. "After Hedley's rough night—everybody's rough night—I was happy for a moment. Can you believe that?"

Callum lifted helpless shoulders.

"But something made me take another look. Instead of just thanking God for small favors and not doing anything to disturb her." Julie finally blinked, blessed relief she didn't deserve. "She was just so still. Too still. And her skin—it had lost all the redness from her cold. It was this sort of palest blue, like milk. She was beautiful really."

"I bet she was," Callum said softly.

His gaze carried a message that Julie couldn't stand to see, not then anyway, and which Callum visibly tried to suppress, but failed, settling in the end for simply averting his eyes.

"I was a mother for just a second," Julie told him brokenly. "Hedley was so young when she died. And I don't know if you know how it is the first year when you're so tired and overwhelmed and bleary all the time, everything in a fog. I blinked and it was over."

Callum turned his head back toward her.

"The police came. They know me in my town; they're family. But I don't remember much after that." Julie paused. "I could've saved Hedley. If I had been beside her. I would've seen, or heard, or felt when she started to cough or struggle for breath. Teachers in my district have to attend first aid training. I had the skills to revive her."

"Did the police tell you that?" Callum asked. "It was her cold?"

"No," Julie said after a moment. "The police and the medics and the doctor who performed the autopsy thought Hedley being stuffed up was just a coincidence. According to the death certificate, it was SIDS or some variant. But SIDS is just a meaningless term for we-don't-know-what-the-hell-happened. I know, though. I know I could've prevented it if I had been where I should have."

Callum hesitated, then said, "Easier that way, I suppose."

It took a second for his words to penetrate, so lost was Julie to memory. "What?"

Callum reached out, but she recoiled, and his face contorted. "I'm sorry, I don't want to hurt you, but it sounds like you've been carrying around a load of guilt you don't deserve. You said yourself—all the experts disagree with you. And so you've got to be asking, *If I blame myself, then what am I spared?* Maybe the knowledge that life can be a random crapshoot and tragedies happen that no one deserves. You ask me, that's a whole lot harder to swallow than some fantasy of control."

Julie rounded on him, and Callum faced her just as fiercely.

"I'm only trying to help—"

"You should've quit with the swim and the fire." Julie got up from the floor on legs that threatened to give out and snatched up her still-damp clothes. She went into a bedroom to get dressed, leaving the blanket in a heap on the carpet.

On her way back out, she ducked into the kitchen to grab the bottle she'd spotted when she found the soup. Vodka, which she hated, but it would do in a pinch, and this constituted one helluva pinch.

"Come on, Deep," Julie said, voice trembling as badly as it had with the cold.

Depot yawned and staggered to his feet, looking at her with reproach. Julie concealed the bottle by her side as she grasped Depot's collar in one shaking fist.

Callum had staunched the fire as best as could be done so precipitously, logs spread at a distance from each other, ash shoveled over their remains.

He gathered his own wet clothes into a pile in his arms. "At least let me show you the way back—"

Keeping her back turned to him, Julie pulled the door open, nudging Depot outside with one knee. "You don't know the way," she said, and left.

PART III

MERCY ME

CHAPTER THIRTY-FIVE

The woods were a jumble, Julie's feet stumbling and her eyes unseeing, as if she'd already dipped into the pilfered bottle. A yawning opening in the trees let out on a sandy inlet that in a different mood, on a different day, or in a different life would've staggered with its beauty. To Julie now though, the sea was merely a guide, pointing the way back home. She cracked open the bottle as she dragged Depot along.

The first taste of vodka was caustic on her lips, like acid; she'd always hated this stuff. But the second deep pull from the bottle went down easier, a beautiful burn on her brain, searing away the echo of Callum's words.

Not only Callum's.

That same thing had been said to her before. But her frantic and increasingly buzzed mind couldn't compute the other source of the message just then.

Everything had happened so fast tonight. She'd almost lost her dog— then nearly drowned herself—before telling a man she'd just met about a day she never spoke of and could hardly stand to recall.

Julie took another slug from the bottle.

Alcohol had always provided a slowing-down mechanism for her, even before her consumption increased with marriage to David and ultimately Hedley's death. Without scotch, the world tended to rub Julie raw, all sharp points and serrated edges. She hit them, tore against them, acted sometimes, made hasty decisions just to get away.

She and Depot finally reached the house, Julie taking steady sips while she slopped a meal into Depot's bowl. The dog descended on his serving as Julie raised the bottle in a silent toast, both of them refueling themselves after their ordeal.

Tim.

He had been the one to say something similar about guilt and grieving.

Julie made her way over to her laptop on the dining room table. On Facebook she saw that her recent update had drawn a few Likes, although not one from David, and also that her husband had changed his relationship status to *single*. Julie ignored the lash of that, or muffled it rather, with another gulp from the bottle, navigating away from the site before she could post something revenge-stupid for David to see.

I met a new man who saved me from drowning, then drove me to drink!

Julie looked down at the neck of the bottle she clenched in her hand.

Callum drove her to drink. David used to pour her drinks. But it was Julie lifting the bottle and opening her mouth, wasn't it?

After a moment, she set the vodka down with a solid *thunk*, glass against wood.

In Tim's last email he'd quipped that she had obviously found the one place on earth with worse cell signal than Wedeskyull, then added:

I saw the pictures you posted. That island looks like a really nice place. I hope you remember what I said. You deserve a new life out there.

Julie did remember now, despite the clear liquid sloshing around in her gut. How blame caused there to be two deaths for every one.

And Uncle Vern—who knew something about being to blame—had said the same thing.

You suffered a tragedy nobody could've done anything about.

The only thing Callum had done differently was to finally puncture Julie's ability to block out the words. And not even alcohol could enable her to keep doing that forever.

Julie left the partially depleted bottle behind in the kitchen.

She went upstairs and got into bed. Blacked in a square on the calendar to signal an end—no, an interruption—to her slashes, then picked up Hedley's photo and placed it beside her pillow, where it embedded a hard, swollen line in her cheek as she slept.

The next morning, Depot waited for Julie by the foot of the stairs, a look of mournful apology in his eyes. Trailing him into the kitchen, Julie saw that he'd sicked up the soup and the meal she'd served him at home, as well as what looked to be a fair amount of salt water.

"Don't worry," Julie told him as she cleaned up the mess. "I've been there a few times myself as you know. Always good to get the poison out."

She wasn't hungover this morning, however. Hadn't wound up drinking enough for that. In fact, she felt more clearheaded than she had in a long time.

Also filled with faint excitement, of the first-day-of-school variety.

Julie watched Depot lap up three bowls of fresh water, then made her decision. Her dog would accompany her to school today. She wasn't leaving him alone again until she could be sure he would stay put—or more accurately, that nobody would interfere with him staying put. The walk to town would suffice for his morning exercise, and Julie wouldn't have to worry about racing right home after school for his second outing.

They took the trail through the woods; Julie hadn't located the other route yet, and she figured they'd both had enough of cliffs for a while. Although when they reached the cove an hour before school was to start, she was surprised to feel the sea beckoning, and to find that Depot didn't resist. Perhaps they were becoming islanders. Julie walked onto the curved sickle of beach—how calm it was here compared to where they'd entered last night—and Depot lowered himself down beside the rock she sat on. They watched curling edges of lace roll into shore, listened to their quiet sighs.

Julie stared out at the wavering blob of sun coming up over the sea. Sparkles doubled, trebled before her eyes, and when she looked down, tears plashed onto her lap.

"I'm sorry, sweetheart," Julie said aloud. "I am so very sorry."

For what she had done. For what she hadn't done. But really it wasn't either of those things as much anymore. Really it was that Julie was just unimaginably sorry that Hedley wasn't here with her, living her life, experiencing all there was to come.

Depot lifted his head toward the rising sun, and whatever part of a less tamed breed he had inside him let out a wild beast howl of sorrow.

CHAPTER THIRTY-SIX

For a brief section of time, the schoolhouse retained its air of pristine hush, a theater just before the curtain rises. Then promptly at 8:00 a.m., Julie threw open the barn doors at the front of the building and the classroom filled with the scramble of bodies, slapping feet, and an air of expectancy so palpable, it had a sound all its own, composed of breaths and fidgets, mumbles and whispers, new beginnings and fresh starts.

Julie stood in front of the blackboard, surveying the room. She felt like she was home again, in a body and a life of her own. She let the feeling of completeness settle over her, then started to count. Nineteen desks occupied. The children had arrayed themselves largely by age and grade, although one or two looked out of place, a situation that would be Julie's to rectify. She could just imagine the Laura Ingalls–style prank, So-and-So in sixth grade pretending to be in fourth, and chortling over his easy work.

Peter sat in the last row, long legs thrust out to either side. He was as tall as the girl sitting beside him, but according to Julie's roster, she was two grades ahead. As Julie eyed him, Peter's gaze flicked away.

Did you bring my dog to the cliff and leave him to drown? Julie thought. Maybe Peter's motivation had been aboveboard—he was taking Depot on the proposed walk. Or could it have been the Captain in a confused state? A different member of the Hempstead clan?

Children twitched in their seats, glancing at Julie.

"Good morning, class," she said at last, an old-fashioned greeting she never would've dared unironically in Wedeskyull—itself far from a bastion of hipster culture—but that felt right here. "I'm Ms. Weathers."

Another trio of words that would've carried different meaning back home where her uncle had once reigned, then fallen. Her new and tenuous feeling of belonging on Mercy, roots taking hold, made her glad to have the mantle back, even if no one on this speck of land would recognize it.

"I believe I know your names already," Julie went on, peeking at her roster. "So rather than do a boring old attendance sheet, I thought we'd try something different."

She walked back and forth along the rows of desks, laying slips of paper on each surface, before returning to the area in front of the stage.

"As I said," Julie went on, "I think I know each of your names, but that's not a lot to go on when we're going to be learning and hanging out together and doing different things for a whole year. I'd like us to get to know each other better than that."

Collectively, the students' attention shifted; it might've been her reference to the school year, on this very first day when kids were still shell-shocked to be back in class at all. They stirred in their seats, looking over their shoulders at the open barn doors.

Julie strode back and swung the doors shut, talking as she did.

"Plus, I'm new to you too," she said as she passed, aiming a smile at the youngest cluster of students, who smiled back. "So here's what we're going to do."

She had their attention again. Some had taken pencils out and were holding them poised over their scraps of paper.

"Don't write your names," Julie said, and all nineteen heads shot up. In school, telling kids not to write their names on a piece of paper was a genuine shocker. "This is a guessing game. I want you to put down something about yourself. It can be anything you want, but it's in your interest to make it something I can guess because if I'm able to figure out who you are from your hint, then you get to ask me something. I don't *have* to answer, so don't get all crazy—"

Scattered giggles.

"—but unless it's something really, you know"—Julie made woo-woo hands, which earned her more giggles—"then I promise I will. Write the question you want to ask me on the other side of your paper. Everybody understand the rules?"

From the bent heads and hands in play—some scrawling rapidly, others penning careful, painstaking letters, a few frozen in thought— she concluded that they did.

Then the barn door began to open again with a series of slow, halting pushes.

CHAPTER THIRTY-SEVEN

Julie went back to lend a hand with the heavy door, peeking outside to get a jump start on whoever might have arrived. With ducked head and shuffling steps, Eddie Cowry edged around her and entered the schoolhouse.

The other children ignored him. It was as if nothing had changed, nobody new was here, the young boy's presence so meager as to not even disturb the air currents.

Julie leaned down with an encouraging smile. "Eddie?"

He shrank back as if she'd struck him.

Julie felt something pull in her chest. The child's skin was so pale, it didn't seem possible that he lived beside the sea, and his eyelids fluttered when she made eye contact.

"My name is Ms. Weathers," Julie said. "I'm your new teacher, and if you'll take a seat, we're playing a fun game. At least," she added, offering another smile, "I hope it will be fun." She held up an extra scrap of paper. "Can you show me where you sit?"

Eddie looked around as if the question baffled him.

"He doesn't sit anywhere!"

It was a sixth-grade boy, heavyset, packed into a desk in the row in front of Peter. From the sound of his voice, Julie was pretty sure that he had been the author of the meanest taunts on those rocks at the party. And here he was again, twisting to see Peter's reaction, garnering favor.

"Yes, he does," Julie answered firmly. Taking Eddie by the hand, she led him to the empty desk in the sixth grade grouping.

Peter got to his feet, towering over everyone at their desks. "That's mine," he said, as if referring to a sack lunch, or an object in his home, something that he owned.

Julie faced him blandly. "Well, then you should've sat in it," she said, "instead of pretending to be a member of a grade I know perfectly well only has one student."

A few muffled giggles, hands clapped over mouths, guilty looks darted.

Peter looked around at his fellow classmates, who all went quiet. They snatched up their slips of paper and started scribbling again.

"Stay where you were," Julie advised Peter. "You can keep that seat for the rest of the morning, then we'll play a little musical chairs. You're in fifth grade, yes, Eddie?"

The boy lowered his head.

"Eddie?" Julie asked patiently.

A third sixth-grade boy said, "Yes, he's in—"

"Thank you," Julie cut in. "But I was talking to Eddie." She couldn't push this too far—one sure way to incite bullying was to be a teacher's pet—but she wanted to get the message across.

"Yes," Eddie whispered after a moment.

"Good." Julie gave a brisk nod. "In a little while, you'll move over with the other fifth graders, and Peter can have this desk. But first we have a game to play."

The children in kindergarten, first, second, and third grades were a study in guilelessness. Julie guessed every single one of their identities, not from what they'd written down, which would've been a feat of clairvoyance—*my turtle's name is Alexandra; I play Fortnite; I'm a pescatarian; my Instagram name is jamezz:)*—but from each one's tell when Julie read their hints aloud. Giggles, pokes, covered faces. She answered all their innocent questions about herself—where she came from, her favorite show, whether she voted in the last presidential election—while mentally marveling over how aware these Mercy Island little ones were. They might play in tide pools and sell lemonade, but the internet built bridges miles out to sea.

Things got progressively harder as the students aged up, but Julie was able to stumble along until she reached the sixth-grade boys. Five of them, not one girl in the grade. Julie figured these boys would be ready to swim to the mainland by high school, in search of a coed experience. It was less that the sixth graders were difficult to figure out, and more that their clues glared with an in-your-face meaninglessness. *I live in a house; I've been on a boat; I know how to swim; I don't like this game; I don't like this game.*

Julie skimmed the pieces of paper without reading any of them out loud, finally arriving at something workable in one of the questions she'd been asked.

Is it true you have a big fucking dog?

Skipping the curse, Julie faced the class. "I do have a dog. Want to meet him?"

The kids began to murmur under their breaths, not just the sixth graders, but all of the students, their voices swelling into a wave of sound.

"What? When?"

"You mean now?"

"Is he here?"

"Did you bring him?"

Julie nodded. "Let's finish up this game, and then you can all see Depot." She glanced as casually as she could toward Peter.

The boy's face had lost whatever emotion it held when protesting the loss of his seat, and his sun-bronzed skin had gone the color of winter wheat. Refusing to look at Julie, he picked up his scrap of paper and crushed it into a ball in his fist.

Julie read the seventh graders' slips next. The grade consisted of three girls and a boy, all of whom appeared to be tightly bonded, the boy a ringleader of sorts, urging the girls on with nudges and prods and whispered suggestions. They'd clearly collaborated, and the boy kept jabbing his friends and bouncing up and down in his seat, resulting in bursts of hysterical laughter, hugs, and exclamations of mutual love. Julie tolerated the giddiness, even the boy's disruptions, before focusing her attention on the sole eighth grader.

Her slip was blank.

When Julie looked at the girl, she shrugged. "I'm the only person in my grade, I'm out of here by June, and I just want to chill."

I'm sixteen, and I don't need a governess, Julie heard in her head, and had trouble quelling a smile.

The girl—Macy was her name—frowned.

Julie spoke quickly. "I know all of that. But seeing as we have nine months together, maybe we can figure out how to make them at least a little bit fun?"

Macy gave a single-shouldered shrug.

"How about you just ask me a question? Go on. Anything," Julie said.

"Okay," Macy said in the tone her shrug had conveyed. "Why'd you want to come live on this small-as-shit island?"

Macy clearly didn't expect to get a whole lot out of asking the question, but Julie knew it was in truth a make-or-break moment with the class. If she could offer something real, authentic—without crossing over into too-much-information territory—then the tone would be set for the whole year.

"Small," she repeated, lopping off the curse again and hoping it wouldn't render her permanently uncool to the older kids. "You probably can't wait to get out of this place, and here I am choosing to move here. Right?"

Macy gave a reluctant nod. The other students watched her do it, then turned back toward Julie. Even the sixth-grade boys appeared to be waiting.

"Did you ever feel like you needed to get away from something?" Julie asked. "Maybe you don't even know why. But where you are—it just isn't right anymore. You have to find a place that fits you better. Do you know what I mean?"

All over the schoolroom, heads began to turn, kids looking at one another, gazes meeting before being lowered, two or three shared nods.

Peter's transformation was the most acute. His pale face had gone from emotionless to contorted, and he dug two fists brutally into his eyes.

Sixth-grade boys didn't cry. Even unofficially royal ones. If Julie didn't keep the other students from noticing—give Peter time to collect himself—then he would despise her forever for triggering what would be his demise.

"Guess where my dog is right now?" Julie asked brightly.

The whole class, minus one weeping eleven-year-old, swiveled to face her.

They ate lunch in the cove instead of at their desks—Julie explaining that she would join them since it was the first day, and hoping she hadn't just undermined the thirty-five-minute break she intended to take for the rest of the year—so that Depot could accompany everybody outside. He gobbled up two separate servings; no portable bowl could be found that held enough to satisfy Depot's appetite.

The children watched him eat, keeping a safe distance while sneaking glances. The younger ones marveled out loud—*He's so big! Look at his tail! Would he bite my finger if it went in that bowl?*—while the older ones pretended to be unfazed, attempting pats before snatching their hands away.

The tide started coming in, and Depot scuttled backward. He found a part of the rocky cove that the waterline hadn't reached, the kelp dry and brittle, a high-tide mark permanently etched into the stone, and lay down. The children followed, and the dog got obligingly back on his feet, whereby the older students began prompting the younger to touch him, until eventually big were assisting little with rides on Depot's back.

Peter sat at a distance, acting as if he'd never seen the dog before in his life.

The school day was proceeding at a startling clip, and after checking the time, Julie morphed the romp on the rocks into a multigrade science lesson—living studies, earth science, geology—before herding everyone back inside, and telling the kids to take their seats while she led Depot to the teacher's room for a rest.

Back in class, Julie made sure that Eddie and Peter were in their proper seats before going over some housekeeping tasks with each grade, handing out lessons to work on, and explaining her homework policies.

She wrapped up the day with the speech she had planned, directed to all the assembled grades, about the wonders of putting on a play. For a finale, she flung back the newly dust-free curtain to show off the stage and pointed out where the spotlights, due in on the next ferry, were going to go.

"We can decide on a show to do together," she concluded. "Make a list of suggestions and take a vote."

She was pleased to see most of the students listening avidly, appearing to match her enthusiasm. Julie looked around for Peter to get a sense of his response; she needed him in her corner on this, for the other students would follow his lead.

But the boy was no longer seated at his desk.

CHAPTER THIRTY-EIGHT

Julie felt a prick of annoyance. She had explained the bathroom protocol not twenty minutes ago, and there was the wooden pass hanging on its hook on the wall, a flagrant indication that she'd been ignored. Peter seemed to behave as if he could go anywhere or do anything he wanted to, even in school, flouting not just his mother's instructions, but Julie's as well.

"Andrew Beverly," Julie said to one of the sixth grade boys. "Please go find Peter in the boys' room. And I don't want to hear a single joke," she added, seeing the other sixth graders begin to gear up. Bathroom humor was still a favorite at their age.

"Damn, she's psychic," Scott Harness said, getting out of the way so that Andrew could shuffle down the aisle and out into the short hallway.

"He's not there," Andrew said when he returned.

Julie frowned, silently taking roll call as she looked out over the desks. She felt a blip of panic when it seemed that Eddie might be missing too—his body and Depot's conflating in her mind, along with an image of Peter's strong, long-fingered hands pushing both beneath the surface of the sea—before realizing that the boy had merely shrunk low enough in his seat that he couldn't be seen, as if to take up the least possible real estate.

Nineteen children accounted for.

She issued an order for everyone to stay in their seats and begin homework, then hurried as fast as she could without appearing panicked to the teacher's room. Depot lay with half his body wedged under the table, the other half lolling out.

When Julie walked in, he opened one eye, blinking wearily.

"It's okay, Deep," Julie whispered, her heart still pattering. "Go back to sleep."

She returned to the classroom. The children had obeyed her instruction to stay seated, conspicuously and studiously so, in fact. They stared intently at their desks, refusing to meet Julie's eyes, clearly sitting on some knowledge yet unwilling to sell out their leader.

"Ms. W," Macy said, then stopped.

The sixth-grade boys all sent her daggered looks.

The students in the lower grades looked worried, but not even their youthful tendencies to tattle overrode the allegiance to Peter that had been so thoroughly instilled.

Macy's gaze flicked. Just the slightest twitch of her eyes, her face stayed still and forward, but Julie strode in the direction of the barn doors. As she pulled one open, the widening triangle of space revealed Peter, crouched by the tidal pool they'd explored as a class earlier.

Something was floating in it.

"Stay where you are," Julie commanded the rest of the class. Leaving the door partway ajar, she went outside.

She skirted the biggest of the boulders, stepping onto the humped backs of smaller rocks and into dips between them. Peter was intently studying whatever lay in the pool. Not even the squawks and screeches of seagulls, the uneven wheeling of their bodies overhead, disturbed him. Carefully, deliberately, Peter lowered his hand into the tide pool and, in one clean motion, scooped out the object that had been resting on its surface.

A pale-gray bird, a smaller version of the ones aborting dives and shrieking angrily from the sky. Motionless on Peter's palm, as still as a shell.

"Peter!" Julie called. "It isn't safe to touch a dead animal. Come inside and wash your hands—"

He clearly hadn't been aware that she was there, but once the momentary shock of her arrival passed, Peter settled into his customary wordless demeanor. He had the hardest edges of any child Julie had ever met, all Lucite corners and razor rims.

Lifting his hand with the dead bird upon it, Peter sent Julie a look every tween knew how to deliver.

Dare me? it said.

Then he folded his fingers and squeezed.

Peter raced across the hunched bodies of boulders as if they were no trickier terrain than a road, elbowing past Julie, who had gone numb and motionless upon seeing the boy's act of brutality. He ran with the bird still clenched in his fist. He was going to show it to the other students, and the horror of that catapulted Julie into action.

She also began to run, nowhere near so fleet as Peter, straining an ankle as she leapt between rocks. She caught up to the boy just before the barn doors and seized his hand, the one not cupping the bird, in hers.

"No," she told him, pitching her voice low. "Stop."

But Peter twisted and wrenched in her hold, finally breaking free. He gave Julie a shove so hard she stumbled, then slid through the space in the partially opened door. Julie squeezed in after him to see Peter squatting beside the stove. Not showing the other children his fiendish display. Just hunched over, staring at the corpse. Did he mean to put it in the stove? Cremate it?

Julie whirled in the direction of the desks, where the students looked on, unperturbed. They seemed to have zero inclination to question any action taken by their king. And from their angle, they probably couldn't even see the bird anyway; Peter's murderous fingers sheltered it from view.

Then the bird's wing twitched, and both Julie and Peter let out a shout.

She didn't waste any further time considering what might be wrong with Peter. He no longer held a dead bird, but a hurt one, and this Julie knew something about. More than once a bird had been knocked out of a tree whose branch presented too tempting a wrestling partner for Depot, or got trampled accidentally under one of the dog's paws.

Ever so gently, slow as honey trickling, Julie helped Peter slide the bird from his hand to hers, and this time, he didn't fight her.

She turned and faced the hushed classroom.

"Okay, children," Julie said. "Who wants to learn how to rescue a bird?"

School had officially ended, so Julie dismissed everyone, saying she would give extra credit in science to whomever stayed. A few had to leave for the trap house or to help with the day's haul, Eddie included. A chorus of voices jeered at the boy as he fled.

"You couldn't get a bug off the bottom if it crawled into your hand."

"Where you off to so fast, your dad's heap of splinters?"

"Hell, no, his dad drives a boat for someone else! He don't have one of his own."

"Quiet!" Julie commanded.

Peter had remained behind, wordless and watching, and Julie aimed the lesson in his direction since the students all hovered around him anyway.

"Allowing the bird to warm up slowly is key," she explained. She carefully tilted her hand, showing them the gull. "It's in shock. Can anyone tell me what shock is?"

A bouquet of hands shot up, fingers fluttering for attention.

The seventh-grade boy shouted out, and Julie checked him mildly, calling on one of his friends to make the point, and acknowledging the girl's answer with a *very good*. "The first thing we need is a box—there's probably one in those cabinets beneath the stage. Katy, can you take Tessa and go look?" Julie asked, selecting a fifth grader to accompany the little one, and summoning the seventh-grade boy back when he started to go without being told.

Both girls ran off, and the other children crowded around Julie, the seventh-grade boy reaching to stroke the bird as Julie guided his hand away.

Katy and Tessa returned, balancing a carton between them.

The bird's body was starting to thrum in her hand like a miniscule engine. They had to get it to eat something, then leave it tucked away to rest.

"But what do you feed it?" a younger boy called out.

"Hand, please," Julie said. "Then I'll tell you."

The boy raised his hand.

It was lucky she had brought Depot today for the answer to the boy's question was a mash of dog or cat food. Julie led everybody into the teacher's room to put together a convalescent meal, and the class completed the final few steps of creating their schoolhouse rehabilitation center.

Peter hadn't made a move to help.

"Hold on," Julie told him, after she'd let the rest of the class go.

She needed to ask the boy what had happened with Depot, why he would've left her dog at the base of the cliff, but Peter had unraveled at each mention and sight of him today. Julie didn't want to chance a straight-on confrontation, especially right after Peter's second near-fatal encounter with an animal.

The boy faced her, legs in a wide triangle, taking up as much floor space as possible, chin lifted in defiant display, hands jammed to distend his pockets.

"I have your house as being on the road that runs behind the restaurant. Harbor House. Is that correct?" The road didn't seem to have a name; addresses were a funny thing on Mercy Island. Descriptions for students' residences contained notes from the prior teacher like *on the second rise after the post office* and *third up from the high-tide line.*

Peter didn't answer, although his finely wrought features twitched, which Julie took as affirmation.

Hurting animals was one of the most severe warning signs of childhood pathology, plus there was the shove he had given Julie.

First day of school or no, it was time to go visit Peter's mother.

CHAPTER THIRTY-NINE

J ulie stayed at her desk, studying the route to Peter's house, while mulling over what to do about the bird. It would require assessment during the night, and a few more doses of mash, but Julie didn't want to risk taking the creature on the walk home through the woods, especially since she had to make a stop first.

Depot thumped his tail as he lay on the floor beside her.

"I know," Julie said. "I am procrastinating. That woman scares me."

Truthfully, Peter did too. The vacantness in his expression when he'd squeezed the bird had been so disjointed from his potentially deadly action. And the force with which he had tried to stop her—an adult, his teacher—from intervening wasn't normal for a child.

Depot seemed to express agreement, lowering his head and letting his eyes fall shut.

Julie returned to her mental ruminations: the problem of the bird, what she was going to say to Martha, Ellie's warning about involving the family. Then again, Ellie hadn't witnessed Peter committing animal cruelty. Still, it might be best for now just to pay a friendly visit, try to get a sense of the boy's home life.

Depot stood up and let out his someone-has-arrived bark, then made his way over to the side entrance. It took a few moments before the anticipated knock came; Depot was always a few seconds ahead.

The door opened and Callum ducked low to walk inside.

He looked fresh from a day on the boat: waterproof pants with a thin neoprene shirt tucked in, droplets of water lodged in his hair. He kicked one boot against the other, leaving the slime at the door. "I owe you an apology."

Julie stood up behind her desk. "You saved my dog's life."

"Well, maybe that's why you'll accept it."

Julie stared down at the floor. She felt more trepidation now than the prospect of visiting Martha had triggered. She opened and closed her mouth a few times, while Callum studied her, his face scored with lines.

"You were..." Julie started before letting her voice trail off.

Callum waited patiently.

"...right really," she said in a whisper. "I mean, maybe not completely, it's still something I have to wrap my head around. But you weren't wrong to say it."

"Just a little presumptuous," Callum said.

Julie surprised herself by laughing. "It was an intense night. Feelings were running high." She lifted her head to look at him, and the first moments they'd shared in the schoolhouse came back, making her heart pulse a slow beat.

"Would you like"—it was Callum's turn to stop and start—"to go to dinner sometime?"

The flicker in her chest grew more intense. But going out seemed a risky proposition, what with cocktails and after-dinner drinks. "How about I make dinner for you tomorrow night at my house?" she suggested. "As thanks for what you did."

Callum glanced down at Depot, even though the dog was only part of what Julie meant.

"I'd like that," he said after a moment.

"Good," Julie said softly, and he gave her a rough smile before turning to go.

"Hey, can I ask you one more thing?" Julie said.

Callum slid his arm up along the doorway, bracing himself in the jamb.

"Do you know anything about caring for injured birds?"

Back in Wedeskyull, parent-teacher conferences took place at school, requiring a multitude of forms in triplicate, along with a whole bunch of other CYA details. Here on Mercy, things seemed a bit more informal. Julie perused the teacher's manual, but despite reading all the policies and procedures—which covered discipline in class (spanking with a paddle was permitted), lighting the stove, what to do in case of a storm surge, and a host of other topics—she didn't find a single protocol for approaching a student's family.

Julie slid a stack of papers into her bag, grading she would have to finish later, then clapped her hand against her hip to summon Depot.

Peter's new home was located in still another part of the island Julie hadn't yet gotten to know, tucked away and isolated. This was the interior, the core of Mercy, accessed by going around Harbor House and then toward the rear. The restaurant was quiet outside and in, tables visible through a large plate-glass window mostly unoccupied.

A lot in back narrowed into something resembling a road, then, a half mile on, a scattering of bungalows appeared, locked up tight for the season. The prior teacher had made a note when Peter moved, mentioning the last property on the stretch, so Julie kept going in search of a dead end, Depot trotting along beside her.

Once the summer properties had receded into the distance, colorful painted signs began to appear, handmade pennants on rods sticking out of the sandy soil.

The Rainbow Pavilion lies ahead!

Keep going for the Rainbow Pavilion!

You're almost to the Rainbow Pavilion!

You're just steps away from the Rainbow Pavilion!

And finally *Welcome to the Rainbow Pavilion!*

The site of the last sign was a small, grassy yard with a shingled cottage set into a dip in the land. It was a third of the size of the house in which Julie now resided. Brightly colored lanterns had been strung between trees, and garden lighting boasted glass globes in ruby red and topaz yellow, emerald green and sapphire blue.

The bright, friendly lead-up was not what Julie had expected from the alternately angry and remote Martha Meyers. Maybe she only disliked Julie, while this Emerald City treatment was meant for other visitors. Although the Emerald City hadn't exactly presented a paragon of welcome, Julie reminded herself, as she and Depot climbed a set of steps slicked with a fresh coat of paint.

The dog was too big to occupy anything like a discreet corner of the small porch, instead lying down sprawled across most of its surface.

Julie lifted her hand, but the door swung open before she could knock.

———————————

Martha stood in the doorway, towering over Julie, her white cloud of hair adding at least an inch.

Julie looked up as levelly as she could. "Mrs. Meyers, hello. I'm sorry to show up unexpectedly, but I wanted to talk to you about Peter."

Martha's snowy brows drew down. "I bring Peter to school and walk home with him every day. I stayed outside while he did your extra-credit assignment."

"I'm sorry, I didn't know that." Julie offered a weak smile. "Not a fan of the free-range-kid movement? I would've thought island kids tended to roam." But she understood. Peter was pushing away, as tweens do, and his mom was pulling back.

"It's a mother's job to look after her child." Martha sounded like she was parroting a 1950s parenting manual. "I'm sure most of our children do wander... Just look at the Cowry boy. Attending a gathering where he was clearly unwelcome without his parent's supervision! But my mother taught me to keep a closer eye."

Julie jumped at the opening. "That's part of what I've come to talk about."

Martha continued to hold her at bay, outside on the porch.

Julie leaned sideways, peering around Martha's stolid form. "Your house is really quite glorious."

For just a second, Martha's features transformed, escaping their firm confines. Her mouth lifted in the first smile Julie had ever seen her make. She looked like a little girl when she said, "Would you like to come inside and see?"

Julie told Depot to stay, then took a few steps into the house.

Every room visible from the vestibule had been painted a different color. The purple of the hall so bright, it hurt the eyes. The living room to the right was an equally lurid red, while a powder room exposed by an open door had been rendered a bold blue. The kitchen was kelly green. A rainbow array of plastic tumblers had been positioned over the sink, catching the last of the sun's rays in headache-inducing lasers and streaks. Pottery on tables, throw pillows on a couch, picture frames and vases. Anything that could provide a burst of color did. Magenta, eggplant, teal, and coral, all clashing and jangling with one another, exhausting to the eyes.

"Wow," Julie said. "This is... It's really something."

Martha took a look around as well, pleasure lifting her face. "Color is so important, don't you think? It lends a feel to everything. Please, come see the rest."

She turned and led the way up a narrow staircase painted hot pink. The bedroom at the top of the stairs was a yellow so loud it made Julie squint. She took a few steps down the hall, one side fruity orange, the other stoplight red. Only one room had been spared the color treatment. A space at the end of the hallway, its walls and ceiling white, floor carpeted in dull gray, furniture and blinds and bedding a mix of colorless shades.

Peter appeared, a sudden slash in the open doorway.

Julie hadn't been sure the boy was home, although she supposed he'd have to be, given the close watch Martha kept. Peter was so still, self-contained, that his presence could be all but undetectable.

"Hi, Peter," she greeted him. "Nice room."

It was a clear announcement of preteen differentiation, almost a literal black and white to his mom's Technicolor display. Julie was glad Martha had allowed him the independence; imagine if she'd forced an eleven-year-old to follow her decorating scheme. Peter must not have fully settled in yet after their move, however—very few items had made it onto the shelves or desk or walls. The room was so pared down, uncluttered, compared to the accessories and knickknacks elsewhere in the home, that it resembled a cell.

"He wanted something more like the rest of the house," Martha said from behind. "But how could I do that? All the colors had been taken. There were none left for him."

Julie was shocked by how wrong she had gotten it, seeing preadolescent autonomy where there was actually bizarre and flagrant motherly rejection, but there was no time to send Peter so much as a sympathetic glance. Martha suddenly pointed to a window, then grabbed Julie's hand. "Come on! We're going to miss it."

Peter closed his door with a kick so hard, it rattled in its frame.

CHAPTER FORTY

Martha took the stairs at a run, flinging open her front door and going out to the porch. She stepped over Depot's huge form, nimble for such an imposing woman, and dropped down on the splashy floral-print cushion of a rocking chair, gesturing Julie to the plaid surface of another rocker.

The bowl of grass in front of the house was edged by a perimeter of scraggly trees. Julie followed Martha's gaze. The sun was departing from the sky, its peach and violet streaks muted compared to the colors inside.

"I used to watch this display every single night before we moved," Martha said. "Whether it was clear or cloudy. Here the trees conceal things, interrupt the vista. But I trust you are enjoying our view?"

"Yes, it's stunning," Julie responded. She wasn't sure whether to express thanks or remorse for having appropriated it.

Martha smiled, apparently satisfied. "Would you care for a drink as we watch?"

"No," Julie said, meaning *yes*, picturing the drink Martha might've poured, and giving a helpless, unwitting flick of her tongue.

Martha shifted her gaze, just briefly, to send her a curious glance.

Julie licked her lips. "I mean, thank you. But just getting to see this is enough."

"There it goes." Martha let her eyes fall shut.

The final hues were fading from between webbed branches.

"One moment there, the next gone," Martha continued. "It's hard to believe that something so crucial, and bright, and present can be no more, just like that, isn't it?"

She had just put into words exactly what Julie felt like after Hedley had died. If Martha was talking about her late husband, then Julie could imagine feeling a spasm of sympathy for the woman, a first faint tremor of connection.

"It's a loss," she said, hoping her words wouldn't miss the mark. "A small one every day. Maybe it's supposed to help us prepare for the worse ones."

Peter came outside then, shirtless and barefoot, and crouched down beside Depot, stroking his flank as the dog twitched in sleep.

"Doesn't work that way, though," Martha said after a moment. "Nothing can prepare you for all that you lose along the way. Especially those of us who have had everything taken."

The glimmer of connection instantly retracted. *Everything?* The woman still had a son to raise, which was more than some parents wound up with. Martha kept such a close eye on Peter, and yet her rejection of him could be cruel, cold as a splash of seawater. It was an extreme version of the push-pull that exemplified this transitional stage of parenting, and it made Julie hesitate to bring up her concerns, lest she worsen the situation. Unless his mother's periodic spite was causing, somehow incited Peter's own violence and aggression?

As if following her thoughts, Martha said, "What did you come to see me about, Ms. Weathers?"

Julie snatched a quick peek at Peter, who luckily seemed to be focusing on Depot, rather than listening to the adult conversation. "Peter behaved inappropriately with a bird at school today," she said in a low tone. "He was aggressive. It was quite worrisome."

"Is it going to be okay?" Peter asked with interest.

So much for not listening.

If the boy was being deceitful, he was a practiced and adept liar. Of course, someone who could put an innocent pet in jeopardy and try to squeeze the life out of a helpless, injured creature probably would be.

Martha's unfeeling tone cut like a blade. "A bird."

"And my dog was taken to your parents' property yesterday and left at the base of the cliff." Julie snuck a look at Peter, but the boy appeared unperturbed.

Martha positioned her arms across the shelf of her chest. "Is that the reason for what happened to their pathway? My father was terribly distraught."

"Well, yes," Julie replied. It seemed by far the less crucial part of what she'd just said. "I had to go down to get Depot, and I guess that kind of wrecked it."

Martha flapped a large, elegant hand as if bestowing pardon. "That whole place is in desperate need of attention. Sometimes Peter and I spend the night there, and I dream the bed has disintegrated with me in it."

It hadn't looked that bad. The state of grandeur in which Martha had grown up must've been extraordinary. Julie tried to think how to circle back to the topic at hand. "Your family has a lot of history on this island."

No answer.

"That must affect your life here."

Still silence.

"And also Peter's." Julie stole a look at the boy, while Martha remained steadfastly mute. At last Julie said, "I come from a place—and a family—like that."

Martha tilted her head, regarding her with interest. "Another island?"

"Just a very small town," Julie replied. "In the mountains actually. My uncle was the police chief, and my grandfather before him."

"And who's police chief now?" Martha asked. "Do you have a brother? Or are you planning to leave teaching for law enforcement?"

"No brother," Julie replied. "But it doesn't matter. He wouldn't be next in line, and I'm not either, because my uncle lost the position." She wasn't sure what compelled her to go on. "Not quite by choice." The shame of Uncle Vern's fall, shortcuts his department had taken, even crimes committed at his behest, stained her face like the descending sun had colored the sky.

But Martha's response didn't reflect such a state.

"Ah," she said, staring out at the line of trees. "Then you're free."

Her voice so heavy, the words seemed to have physical weight. Peter notched his neck, examining his mother, and even Depot stirred.

"I guess that's one way of looking at it." Julie searched for additional common ground between them, a way to keep the conversation going. "Are you an only child?"

"I had a sister," Martha replied, focused on the darkening sky.

"I'm so sorry," Julie exclaimed. What a lot of loss this woman had suffered.

"She's not dead," Martha said. "She moved off-island."

"Oh," Julie answered.

Martha glanced at her through the twilight. "You're thinking that isn't precisely the same thing. Or not the same thing at all."

It had been exactly what Julie was thinking.

Martha raised her shoulders in a shrug. Her frame was massive, like her mother's, with real heft to it. Peter was built more lightly; Walter Meyers must've been slim.

"But on Mercy it is."

"Is it?" Julie asked, trying to quell her dismay.

"My sister married a man who wasn't a lobsterman," Martha said, as if that should explain things. "He was from away, double whammy. If she'd decided to spend her life with a dragon, that would've shocked and upset my mother less. So long as the dragon came from down east and brought in a decent haul every season."

Martha's face suddenly contracted; it took Julie a moment to recognize the expression as mirth. A little island humor.

"My mother hasn't been the same since," Martha said, rising to her feet. "Family is all important to her. It always has been. So you can understand why I might choose to keep a more watchful eye than some on my son."

"Of course," Julie murmured, getting up as well.

"And now I really must say good night," Martha said. "It's getting near suppertime, and growing boys need to eat."

Julie and Depot had made it to the second Rainbow Pavilion sign when Peter came running up, out of breath and clutching something in his hand.

"Wait!" he panted. "My mom said I could give these to Depot for the walk!"

Martha's tall form loomed on the porch, observing, alert.

Peter opened his fist, revealing a handful of dog treats, which Depot snuffled up, lathering Peter's palm with his tongue. Peter let out a laugh, the demon demeanor that had accompanied his squeezing of the bird vanquished for the moment.

But Julie's insides felt cold, clammy. "Why do you have dog treats?" she asked, fighting to steady her tone. "You don't have a dog." But wouldn't treats be the perfect way to get said animal to follow a relative stranger onto some cliffs?

In her daughter, Julie had seen the kind of untainted sweetness only a child could possess. It had to do with a singularity of emotion, a look that contained one need or feeling or desire, and no other. The plump, unlined skin on a child's face, so little history there to twist or distort it. But Peter was a different creature entirely, lacking all such childlike purity. His eyes were filled with emotion he strived to conceal, layer upon layer, like strata in the earth, each one more difficult to reach than the last.

He stared at her now with intentional blandness. "My mom said I could buy them last time we were at the store. For the walk you and me were going to take."

Depot began sniffing Peter's other hand, then his groin and the rest of his body.

Julie forced a smile. "Well, it looks like you made a good choice. Depot's hoping you might have some more in your socks."

Peter chuckled. "I wish I did! Should I go back and get some?" His hand was nestled deep in the dog's fur, twining strands around his fingers.

"No," Julie replied. "We have to be getting home now, and so do you."

Peter's expression sagged, ridding his face of its carved marble beauty.

Julie turned, but Depot didn't follow. She looked back to assess the delay, and saw Peter still clutching the dog's coat with his fist.

"Come on, Deep," Julie said, hoping the boy would relent without intervention.

Instead, he started to scratch Depot with harsh, rasping fingers, which the dog tolerated, not so much stoically as without apparent disturbance. Depot would've been able to free himself from the slight boy's hold with one heave of his body, so Julie wasn't worried about her dog, but she did wonder at his level of patience, especially when Peter bore down harder.

Julie hunted Martha out on the porch. The woman stood, statue-like herself, not doing a thing to stop her son or even summon him to the promised meal.

"Peter—" Julie began, mustering authority.

But at that moment the boy finally extricated his hand. Depot loped onto the sandy stretch of road, twitching his head, snapping at the place Peter had stroked.

"See you tomorrow, Ms. Weathers," Peter called as they set out.

Tendrils of fur, copper and black and ivory, were looped around each of the boy's fingers as he lifted his hand in a wave.

CHAPTER FORTY-ONE

J ulie walked home with a sick feeling in her gut. She'd witnessed
something ugly in Depot's treatment at Peter's hands, and yet the
boy's behavior hadn't suggested any clear course of action, and her dog
didn't appear at all bothered. He and Julie were almost to the house
when Depot began to bark wildly, leaping forward before circling back
at a run.

"Okay, sure," Julie told him. "You get to eat first."

She had just started fishing around for the key when she saw a slight
shadow sidle around the back of the house.

"Damn," she muttered. How did Peter make it back here before she
did, especially given Martha's oversight? It was as though the boy had
supernatural powers, some sleight of body that allowed him to Tesser
himself or astrally project. "Peter?" Julie called, also beginning to run.

Ellie appeared from the other side of the house.

"Hi there," she said, walking toward them. "I figured you might've
gone out for a walk."

"We had an errand to do first," Julie called back. Ellie drew closer, and Julie felt herself begin to frown. "Are you okay, El?"

The nickname emerged unprompted. Ellie looked so small and vulnerable, distressed somehow, not like her usual devil-may-care, why-does-anyone-care self.

Ellie lifted one shoulder. "Not really."

Julie reached out and took her friend's hand. "Well, come inside." Could this be about Callum? Had Ellie learned of their mutual drama at sea or, worse, tomorrow night's dinner? "You can tell me all about it."

Julie turned back, clicking her fingers so that Depot, who had to be starving, would get off his haunches and close the rest of the distance between himself and the house.

"I'm sorry I don't have any wine," Julie said, once she'd mixed Depot's wet and dry and filled his water bowl. The dog seemed past the point of eating—tired enough that he simply headed over to his spot by the wall of windows and lay down—so Julie brought his meal to him in there. "But I was going to make some sandwiches."

Ellie shrugged again. "That's all right. I'm trying to cut down." She tried to smile, but it was a pale ghost of her usual grin. "On wine, not sandwiches."

"You are?" Julie asked, taking out bread and cheese.

Ellie stared at the counter. "I'm always trying to, but this time I got a wake-up call. Hopefully it will stick." She looked up. "My mom was a drinker."

Julie assembled two sandwiches and put them on plates, sliding one over to Ellie.

Ellie took a bite. "I think it was to cope with my father being out of the picture. You know—all those long days at sea. Seven days a week in the high season. The fish don't take days off, as my dad used to say," she added.

Her mood seemed to be restoring itself as she ate.

"My parents didn't drink; they were sort of rule followers. My own father had one big rebellion, his choice of a job, but other than that he was by the book," Julie said. She swallowed a hunk of cheese and bread, before taking a deep breath. "Everyone in his family had a taste for liquor, though. And my ex loved having a drinking partner about as much as I loved being one."

Julie looked at her friend, and Ellie gazed back.

After a moment, she gave a got-it kind of nod, then said, "Hey, so, just because we're a couple of nondrinkers, does that mean *any* sort of liquid refreshment is off the table? Coke, juice, jeez, what are the kids drinking these days, Gatorade? Red Bull?"

Julie smiled, crossing to the fridge. She felt suddenly happier than she had any right to, with a troubled student, a bullying problem at school, and a dog who'd been placed in peril by person or persons unknown. She filled a glass with iced tea from a pitcher and passed it to Ellie. "I could even make some coffee."

"Well, let's not go crazy," Ellie said, tilting the glass to her lips.

They finished their meal and went into the living room. Depot stirred restlessly in a dream, although at least he'd emptied his bowl and wouldn't wake up famished.

Julie dropped onto the couch, Ellie taking an armchair across from her.

"So what kind of errand did you have to run?" she asked, grimacing when Julie mentioned the Rainbow Pavilion.

Technically, Julie should've kept the visit to herself, but Ellie had given her so much valuable information about the island already. Julie wanted her perspective on this.

"I know it, of course," Ellie said. "All the islanders do. Martha must want them to—posting those signs or flags or whatever. I call her color scheme 'fuck-you orange.'"

Julie let out a sharp laugh. "What?" she asked, even though she sort of knew, felt the rightness of Ellie's pronouncement. "What do you mean?"

Ellie lifted her legs—too short to reach the floor—and folded them beneath her. "Come on, how in your face is that place? It grabs you by the throat and throttles you. Look at me, look at me, you can't miss me!"

"I know," Julie said. "It was positively dazzling. Or dizzying."

Ellie scowled again. "Did you happen to get a peek inside the grande dame's house on the night of the party? The mansion Martha grew up in. It's so lifeless and gray that suddenly all that color begins to make sense."

"That's very insightful," Julie mused. She was learning more about Peter and his family in a few minutes with Ellie than Martha had revealed all evening. Splotches of brightness everywhere, those rabid prints on the walls. That had been a violent boxing match of decor, not anything pleasing to the eye.

Ellie twisted to look through the bank of windows. "Strange family."

It was the perfect segue. "I really shouldn't be talking about this, so please keep it between us"—Ellie turned back, looking curious—"but the reason I went over there tonight is because I'm worried about Peter. He's been involved in a few incidents."

"Incidents like what?"

It would mean telling Ellie about Callum, which Julie decided to chance. If finding out about them, to the extent that there was a *them*, was what Ellie had meant by a wake-up call, then this would allow her and Julie to hash things out.

She told Ellie the story of Depot's unplanned outing, the swim and Callum's rescue, then concluded with what Peter had done to the bird at school that day.

"Huh," Ellie said once she'd finished.

Either the role Callum had played, or Julie's *Bad Seed* description of Peter, had rendered her usually chatty friend speechless.

"Huh?" Julie echoed, prompting Ellie on.

"Well, first of all, can I just say, Oh. My. God?" Ellie grinned, her natural good humor beginning to resurrect itself. "I mean, way to go, Callum, saving that cutie over there."

She arched in her chair, and both she and Julie sent the sleeping dog fond looks.

"So you're not upset?" Julie asked.

Ellie turned back to face her. "About you and Callum?"

Julie nodded. "I thought that might've been what you meant by a wake-up call."

"Oh." Ellie let out a laugh that sounded forced. "That wasn't it. No, look, I'm thrilled if you and Callum are hitting it off. He's always been the distant type, kind of held himself at bay, even back when we were kids. I don't know if anybody's ever really gotten close to him. If they did, it sure wasn't me. But I never even tried. Just no spark there."

"Chemistry's a weird thing," Julie said, relieved beyond measure.

But Ellie's response was a frown. "What do you think is up with Peter?"

Julie sighed. "I don't know. His mother keeps a tight hold on him—I mean, where I come from, kids his age have a lot more freedom—but at the same time, she's strangely distant. I was actually hoping you might be able to shed some light on the situation."

Ellie frowned again. "I know about a lot of things on this island, but the Hempsteads aren't one of them. Beyond the obvious, of course, the no degrees of separation between each islander and someone in that family."

Julie peered at her. "I wouldn't exactly call your color wheel analysis *obvious.*"

"Oh, I beg to differ," Ellie said wryly. "That shade of red definitely qualifies as obvious. Not to mention the orange, green, yellow…"

Julie laughed.

"I would've said Peter was doing pretty okay, considering he just lost his dad," Ellie offered. "Not to mention all the transitions he's been through. New family constellation, new house, new teacher even. Maybe give him a little while to adjust?"

Julie looked at her, and Ellie extended both hands, palms up. "I mean, hey, I don't want to overstep, it's not like I know a lot about kids. But I do know what it's like to come to a new place, especially one as small and insular as this. Maybe charging right in, trying to figure everything out, isn't the best approach—for you *or* Peter."

Julie continued to look at her, nodding slowly. "I think you might be right."

Ellie shifted on the chair, crossing and recrossing her legs. "Man, the nights are long when there's no wine involved."

Julie offered a feeble laugh. "I hear ya, sis. But hey, speaking of no drinking, you'd probably be the single best person I could find to help me with this."

Ellie stood up, stretching her arms and inclining her head in Julie's direction.

Julie asked, "What do I feed a highliner at the end of a long day at sea?"

Julie fell asleep that night, grateful for the arrow-straight slash she'd been able to make across a new square on the calendar, and also feeling good about the decision Ellie had prompted. Not what to cook Callum for dinner, but how to proceed with Peter.

It was the right thing, the fair thing to do. Take her intense focus off the boy for a while, allow it to circulate among the rest of the kids. They were also in need of attention, some more than others, such as Eddie, or the seventh grader, who had such trouble containing himself and almost certainly needed medication and an IEP to get his behavior under control in the classroom. Just because Peter was a Hempstead didn't mean he should command all of her resources. If Julie were being honest, it would also be a relief to distance herself a bit from the child's strange behaviors and the charge of his barely suppressed emotions.

The best teacherly decisions worked in a multitude of directions, serving a whole classroom of children, and those who instructed them as well. Peter's mother seemed intent on depriving her son of space, and by giving the boy some room to wander, Julie might be able to fend off escalating incidents of his behavior. Perhaps they would all be better off.

CHAPTER FORTY-TWO

A s Julie approached the library the next morning, her phone purred in her bag.

It was like a summons from another age; except for her fleeting visits to Facebook and quick email checks, Julie felt as if the ferry had passed through a time warp and she'd been living in a different century.

She fished out her phone, glancing down to scan the notification, then turned to Depot, who stood patiently by her side on the road. "Guess who?"

Depot's tongue lolled and his tail began to wag.

"Yeah, you would say that," Julie told him.

David had texted her. Without any greeting, pleasantries, or sign-off. He hadn't even asked after Depot. Six words made up the total of his communiqué.

We need to start divorce proceedings.

David's texts always read like an email, or even a letter.

Julie swallowed. In some ways her husband's callousness and indifference felt freeing. *Single, are you?* she thought. *Then so am I.*

She texted back:

ill get you the name of a lawyer asap

She reviewed her missed calls and voicemail—Tim had checked in again—then powered down her phone. Maybe everyone in the last century had been better off.

Inside the school, she found the bird tucked into a swaddle of fabric and looking a little more lively, its black eyes bright. Depot gave a bark of greeting, and the bird twitched in response. Beside the box stood a birdcage fashioned from part of a lobster trap, along with a note from Callum.

Had to get on my boat, but Gully made it through the night okay. I made this cage, think he'll be ready for it soon. We still on for supper?

The text from David slipped from her mind like sand down a hill.

Julie gestured for Depot to accompany her into the teacher's room, where she made up a serving of mash that the kids could feed the bird once school started. She smiled hugely down at her dog, who butted up against her leg, almost knocking Julie over before letting out a few joyful barks.

The students were thrilled by the bird's progress, hovering around it to take peeks, big ones pulling little back with reminders not to get too close, before crowding in closer themselves. Julie kept a watchful eye on Peter, using her body as a barricade between him and the bird, then reminded herself that today she would be paying all the students equal mind. The boy's aggression seemed tamped down at present anyway; maybe her new approach was working already. Julie explained to the class that once the bird was ready to stand, it would be transferred to the cage, then returned to the wild as soon as it displayed a range of motion and the ability to flap its wings.

"Till then, I think we should name it," Julie said.

"How do we know if it's a boy or a girl?" the seventh-grade boy called out.

"Hand, please," Julie instructed. "Let's look that up," she suggested, and all the kids trooped over to her desk as Julie Googled the question. "The answer is we don't," she said, opening a link. "Not with a seagull." She studied the screen. "A trained ornithologist would have to rely on seeing the bird in a group, or DNA testing. Now with sexually dimorphic birds—"

Titters, which Julie acknowledged.

"—such as cardinals or ducks, there are easily observable factors like plumage. Let's all try and think of another animal where gender can be determined like that."

Katy raised her hand. "Um, a lion? The mane?"

"Very good. But since this little girl or guy"—she gestured to the increasingly peppy bird—"doesn't have one, how about we decide on a gender-neutral name?"

Callum's designation turned out to be popular.

Julie had the kids get seated, then took attendance—mildly dismayed to mark Eddie Cowry absent—before setting everyone to reading, language arts, or literary arts, depending on their grade, while she walked around, answering questions and checking work. Math came next, followed by global studies, and a walk with Depot that included a multigrade science period focused on marine life. Just before lunch, they moved Gully to his new home, then talked about putting on a play.

Julie held the discussion in the loft, older students helping younger up the ladder, before grouping themselves in a ring.

"The reason to do a play extends beyond fun," Julie told them. "You'll get to know each other in new ways, practicing and performing together, and you'll get to know yourselves better too. Has anybody ever been in a play before?"

Not a single hand went up.

"Well, in that case I think what we should do is learn the whole thing from soup to nuts. Script-writing, lighting, costume and set design, acting, singing, dancing. Each of you will be exposed to it all, and you can find which aspect suits you best."

She was met with an array of blank faces, although one thing she'd said—Julie wasn't sure which—had made the jaded Macy perk up.

"In other words," Julie elaborated, "we write our own original skit, assign parts, and ultimately perform it."

Nods, nascent signals of comprehension.

Then one of the sixth-grade boys said, "Hey, let's do *Star Wars*."

"Or something with a superhero!" said another.

"Spidey!" suggested a third.

For once, the sixth graders hadn't looked to their prince for approbation. Julie didn't want to do anything to quell their enthusiasm so she let the fist bumps, bro hugs, and exclamations of *dude* play out. Then a chorus of other voices began to join in.

"Can't we do something less fighty?" asked Tessa.

"Yeah, like *Hamilton*!" A roar from the seventh-grade boy turned into a hunched-over race around the loft till Julie hauled him back into position in the circle. He really needed an Individualized Education Plan, although this small a student body would impact the usefulness of such an intervention. There was a limit to how far curricula could depart in a grade of four kids.

"Or Disney!" Pushback from a third-grade girl.

"*Frozen!*" A kindergartner's offering, her face wreathed by a smile.

Julie knew it was time to step in. "I have a better idea."

"Better than Spider-Man?" This said with a tone of such disbelief, Julie might as well have suggested that some activity had it over breathing.

She hid a smile. "Well, in that case, the special effects would do us in."

Lowered gazes of acceptance.

Julie looked around the circle. "The script for a play is called the *book*, and it's made available to schools a fair ways after release. Plus it costs money."

The faces fell, expressions of disappointment all around, which Julie knew she couldn't have, especially not right at the start of this process.

"But that doesn't mean we can't do something equally cool," she said hurriedly. "Writing our own play gives us total control. We can make it about anything you want." She emphasized the words, knowing the importance that dominion carried with children.

"But…what do we write about?" someone asked.

"Well, that's the fun part," Julie replied. "Anything. Or"—figuring that creative writing curricula were scant in one-room schoolhouses; she certainly hadn't come across anything formal or written out—"we can base it on something. Like, since some of you love Disney"—a smile for the little ones—"we could use a fairy tale. Only tweak it"—her voice beginning to take off—"to make it unique to you guys. Mercy Island, a life growing up by the sea. Something that not one other person, living in any other place in the world, could say."

Her fervor had ignited something, and all of the children in each of the grades began looking to their friends, smiles building.

Julie gave a satisfied nod. "So here's your lunchtime assignment. Think of a fairy tale—maybe one a movie was based on—or find one in a book at the library or go there and go online, those of you who have devices. And bring your ideas back for the second half of the day."

CHAPTER FORTY-THREE

J ulie didn't know what kind of democratic voodoo had been applied, but when the children clambered back up to the loft after lunch, an idea was proposed that seemed to have the creative fires sizzling without one note of opposition or dissent expressed, and not so much as a single snatched peek to their leader for approval either. Rapunzel.

The seventh graders had assigned themselves the role of spokespeople for this discussion, although the boy did most of the talking, loose and erratic. "We've watched *Tangled*, like a lot, it's really good even if it's for little kids, I love that lizard, once I had a pet lizard, and we figure we can change it around, the story, not the lizard, we don't even need one, or any lanterns, just make it that the character's locked away, except on an island."

One of the seventh-grade girls finally got a word in. "Yeah, 'cause on an island you're kind of trapped anyway. It can be a theme."

"Like a symbol," added her friend. "My mom reads aloud every night—"

"They don't have any TV or internet," interjected the seventh-grade boy.

"—and she talks a lot about symbols."

Julie was struck anew by the blend of innocence these island children retained, as if they inhabited a world that didn't turn at the same rate as everybody else's, combined with admirable levels of sophistication. She looked around at the group of students. "Hey, I like this."

"And we'll have songs, right? We'll sing?" said the boy. "Macy writes music."

"She does?" Julie responded.

Macy opened her mouth and launched into a few bars, her vibrato filling the narrow space of the loft, so soaring and powerful, it seemed to push back the walls, make the solid stone buckle. Her last note wound out, an alto ripple, like the surge of the sea itself. When silence reigned once again, Julie stared at the girl.

Macy looked down. "I mean, we'll come up with different tunes and words. I was just showing you that I can…that I like to sing."

"You sure can," Julie said.

Still looking down, Macy concealed a fierce grin.

It must've been Julie's mention of music that got the girl interested at the start of the lesson. She studied the upturned faces of the class, who all gazed back at her.

"You know what, guys?" Julie said. "I think we have our show."

A resounding hiss of yeses and cheers.

As per her plan, Julie had been deliberately giving Peter some breathing room, not according him any special priority over the rest of the class. But as the chorus turned into shouted suggestions, Julie saw the boy edging over to the side of the loft where a circular window had been cut. Peter faced the glass, staring at a blank swath of clouded-over sky.

The seventh-grade boy demanded, "Who's gonna play Rapunzel, though? We don't have any pretty blonds in here," he added, giving one of his classmates a punch.

His friends tried to fend him off, squealing, while the other kids pushed sideways, backward, away from the scuffling quartet. It wasn't the safest situation given the smallish, high-up space; everyone wriggling and shouting, giddy with ideas. Only Peter held his ground by the window, motionless when a dozen squirming bodies came near. Kids batted his legs with their shoes, hit his waist with flailing arms. The older boys struck with bruising force, but Peter didn't so much as flinch. It was as if he were made out of stone.

"Hey, hey, hold it, quiet down," Julie said, raising her voice. "That's enough!"

As the kids reluctantly settled back into place, she took a look around at the brunette batch of girls who happened to constitute the female portion of Mercy Island's youth.

It was true. Not a fair lock among them.

"Well, there's always washout dye," Julie said. "Or a wig."

Peter finally turned away from the window, lifting his head.

His long-haired, flaxen head.

"I'll be Rapunzel," he said.

If anyone else had suggested it, recrimination in the form of laughter or gibes would've been swift and furious. Or maybe it wouldn't have been, with this Gen Z crew. Maybe it wasn't just Peter's bearing and position that allowed him to pull off such a proposal, but a generational sea change, a true and great shift.

"Like the character is gender fluid?" one of the girls inquired.

"Or trans?" said Macy.

Peter regarded them without responding. The younger students didn't say anything, although even they appeared rapt, awaiting the boy's next contribution.

"It could be a gender normative boy," a fifth-grade girl informed her bestie with a tinge of superiority in her voice.

"Yeah, just one who has super-long hair." This from the seventh-grade boy. "Like that YouTuber with the snakes. I love that guy. I had a snake once. He was dope. Hey, look, my arm's a snake!"

He extended it, wriggling, and Julie stilled his hand.

"Just flip-flop the roles," another boy interjected with a desultory shrug.

A boom of *yeahs* ensued, which Julie seconded.

School was almost over. She decided to allow herself one last quick peek at Peter, and turned her head to catch the boy's eye.

Instantly, Julie wished that she hadn't. Wished that she'd stuck to her original approach, allowing Peter the gift of a little less adult encroachment and oversight, including just that fleeting check at the end of the day. Because then she wouldn't have seen the look on his face.

It was a difficult expression to pinpoint.

The closest Julie could come was one the men back in Wedeskyull wore whenever a deer walked into their blind, at the moment that they determined their prey had been effectively and irreversibly trapped.

CHAPTER FORTY-FOUR

How could a perfectly innocent school play, one inspired by a fairy tale for God's sake, enable Peter to do something malevolent? Yet malevolence had been exactly what she'd seen on his face. Julie felt herself licking her lips, a compulsive scrubbing she'd become aware of lately, as she considered the possibility that she'd unleashed something that was going to end badly in ways she couldn't even predict.

Unless she had misread Peter's expression. Perhaps he was just excited by his proposal, the chance to perform a gender-bending role. Or maybe he was nonbinary, an identity still not accepted on this tiny hump of land, surprising levels of tolerance notwithstanding, and the play would offer him temporary liberation.

Julie had to set these questions aside, at least for now.

She had a date to get ready for.

Before leaving school, Julie researched lawyers, then stopped at the library to text David the name of the first one who had an actual human being answering the phone. Julie felt an inordinate sense of relief upon hitting Send on her text. As if she'd taken a step to setting her life on the course it should've followed years ago.

Except then there would've been no Hedley.

And despite having suffered the nearly insurmountable pain of losing her daughter, Julie didn't regret a single minute that the little girl had lived.

The grocery store was next, dusty even compared to the place Julie went to in Wedeskyull when she lacked the time to make the trip to the chains on the Northway, or the funds to visit one of the organic food markets that had sprung up in town.

Canned vegetables seemed too déclassé for a first date, but the produce bins offered only tattered lettuce and some sad-looking, wrinkly peppers, everything having been plundered for Labor Day bashes. So Julie opened the freezer case to a vaporous blast and grabbed a sack of peas, then paused at the butcher counter, waiting behind two customers. At the cash register, she was gratified to find tea breads made locally, and went back for the one pint of ice cream not covered in stalagmites of freezer burn.

Julie retraced her steps to the school to give Gully a last helping of mash and get Depot. She set one grocery bag on the dog's back, holding it steady with her hand as she hefted the other sack in the crook of her arm. She and the dog made their way home along the road through town, then into the woods and across the scruffy stretch of land leading up to the house. Julie unlocked the front door and walked into the kitchen to get ready.

Callum had clearly cleaned up after his day on the boat. Instead of waterproof gear and boots, he wore laced shoes with a pair of jeans and a button-down shirt, sleeves rolled up to expose his forearms. His hair glistened with the effects of a recent shower. He smelled of menthol, soap, and the sea.

He held out a platter of just-cooked lobster, snowy white wedges of meat, covered with plastic wrap. "I was raised never to show up empty-handed."

Julie started to smile, reaching for the platter.

"Not for tonight—I rarely eat the stuff myself. But I thought you could make a roll for your lunch tomorrow." He paused, looking at her. "I hope this is right."

He hadn't said *all right*; Julie had the feeling he was speaking on a different level. Ellie had brought wine, but Callum hadn't. He seemed to see more about her than anybody else had in years, possibly ever. Then an image of the vodka Julie had taken from his friend's cabin appeared in her mind, and humiliation formed a ripple inside her. No need for clairvoyance—just the discovery of her theft.

"It's great," she said, her voice sounding stilted.

Depot provided welcome distraction, barking a greeting while Callum stooped to rub his ruff. "How did your dog get his name?"

Depot scrabbled at the floor with his paws, and they both smiled.

"Knows he's being talked about," Callum said.

"Yeah, he's super smart," Julie agreed. "We named him for the place we found him—he'd been abandoned at a Home Depot. In the garden center, where he was bounding around, completely frantic, toppling over these enormous planters with his tail. He was just a puppy, and he'd suffered in ways I can't bear to think about. He showed signs of trauma for months after we brought him home."

Callum looked troubled.

"I know," Julie said. "But he's all right now. He's been great ever since."

Callum glanced at her. "Who's *we*?"

For the second time in not many more minutes, Julie was at a loss for what to say.

"I mean—" Callum broke off, scrubbing a fist across his face. "My mistake. You moved here alone. I just assumed you were single."

"I should've mentioned it," Julie said, dismayed. "But I almost am. Single. I officially began divorce proceedings today. And emotionally we've been apart a lot longer."

Callum's hand was still covering the lower portion of his face, while color rose on the rest of it. "I wonder how many times I can overstep with you? Tell me it's none of my business."

Julie didn't actually mind the wrongs, social and otherwise, being on his side for a while. "Anything's your business if you bring me lobster."

"What if you knew I had another eight hundred bugs in my tank right now?"

"Then I'd tell you to overstep again."

Back to innuendo. For a moment, Callum's gaze caught hers, and he lowered his hand from his face. They were standing not quite as close as they'd been in the schoolhouse, but still near enough that a single surge forward on either of their parts would've brought them together. Julie suddenly wanted to do it. Forget the technicality of her marriage, or a sobriety so nascent she didn't need AA to tell her any new relationship would be mistimed, or even her ongoing state of mourning.

Julie admitted to herself what she hadn't yet put into words—that she'd been drawn to this man from the moment he'd helped her on the ferry, that it'd been she who touched his lips with her own the first time they had formally met, and she wanted more than that now.

Then Depot bounded between them, headed for his bowl, and Callum's stomach rumbled as if in echo of the dog's hunger, and both he and Julie burst out laughing.

Julie led the way to the dining room table.

"Thank the Lord," Callum said. "I thought you might be one of those who goes in for little bites before a meal."

Julie served roast chicken, potatoes, gravy, and peas. "Ellie's my go-to obviously, and she recommended comfort food after a day at sea, some-thing hearty."

Callum looked down at the table with a faint frown. "It looks great."

Maybe she had chosen wrong. "I was torn between this and red meat, but the grocery store decided me." Julie began to carve, passing Callum a plate.

"Wares a bit slim today?" he asked, bringing a fork to his mouth.

"Well, only by spoiled, foodie, first-world standards," Julie replied.

Callum grinned. "Is there any other standard?" he asked, before pol-ishing off his serving without another word. His manners were nice—the man even looked sexy while eating—but Julie needn't have worried about making conversation. Callum remarked on the quality of her cooking as he requested seconds, seeming especially to enjoy the crisped chicken skin, which he ate along with helpings of everything else.

Julie had finished her smaller portion first, and she watched as he finally scraped up a last bit of sauce with a forkful of mashed potatoes.

He became aware of her attention, and they both spoke at once.

"That was some—" Callum began.

"Sorry, I just haven't—" Julie said.

He indicated that she should go.

"—seen a man eat like that since my father. He was a logger," Julie added, sensing a connection for the first time between home and the place she'd come to.

Callum confirmed it. "We just do our work at sea instead of in trees."

Julie brought in coffee and dessert, which Callum set to avidly. Then they both settled back in their chairs, staring out at the open expanse of room. The sun sat steadily in its spot in the sky behind the wall of win-dows. There were hours of evening left.

Callum tilted the coffeepot over Julie's cup, giving her the last, and somehow the gentleness, the considerateness of his action caused Julie to speak. The man summoned truth from her like a snake handler. "I have no idea what to do right now if I don't pour drinks."

He stared down at the table, and Julie regretted her impromptu revelation. "It seemed like you kind of figured it out," she said awkwardly. "The lobster instead of wine and..."

She didn't want to bring up the vodka she'd stolen, although she did feel an odd urge to confess to Callum, be open and honest in a way she hadn't in a while. She pushed her chair back, standing and walking over to the wall of glass, where she watched the sea sway far below.

Callum got up and came and stood beside her. "My mam taught me never to bring a bottle as a gift," he said at last. His eyes had gone granite hard and gray, a reflection of the sea. "To the extent that my dad was sober, she kept him that way."

"People everywhere," Julie said quietly.

"You were right about that," Callum replied. Then he said, "Can I overstep again?"

Julie nodded, gesturing him on.

"Is Ellie the right friend for you to be having?"

"Ellie? She's the best friend I've made in a long time."

"Her love of the grape is what I mean," Callum said carefully.

"Oh," Julie said. Did this explain his demeanor when Julie had described Ellie's role in menu planning? "Actually, being around Ellie makes me realize I don't want to be dependent on anything to that degree anymore. Now it's just a question of sticking to it."

Callum gave a slow nod.

"Can I overstep?" Julie asked.

"Seems only fair."

"We both mentioned our parents, but only my soon-to-be ex came up," Julie said. "Have you ever been married?"

Callum shook his head. "The closest I ever came, and it probably wasn't really that close, was a woman in Duck Harbor. We were together for three years."

He's always been the distant type, Ellie had said. "What happened?"

Julie asked, picturing commitment issues, this wasn't a man she should get long-term ideas about—and why should that upset her, the mere thought like a jab, when they'd only just met?

"Her father fished for a rival gang," Callum said.

Julie nearly laughed aloud. The idea that an industry revolving around crustaceans could split a couple apart was so alien—although perhaps it shouldn't have been, given the ski slope wars and farm-stand battles she'd witnessed back home—and also so welcome compared to the deep-seated relationship phobia she'd just been envisioning. "Was he a dub? Your girlfriend's dad?"

"Where'd you come by that archaism?" Callum asked, amused.

Julie glanced at him. "Ellie, of course. She did say it wasn't PC."

Callum frowned at that, lines boring into his face. "He taught me a lot, my girlfriend's father. He just preferred to consolidate income between the generations, rather than divide it. And his daughter deferred to him, which is how these things tend to go."

"This business doesn't make a whole lot of sense to me," Julie said.

"Takes a lifetime to learn it," Callum replied.

"Yes, but I don't have that long," Julie said. "It's the kids' whole world, and I have to teach them, but it feels like I'm driving blind. I tried to reach out to a mom yesterday, but parents never give you the full story. Especially about their own children."

Callum rubbed his chin with one hand. "You know who you should talk to?"

Julie studied his reflection in the glass. She shook her head in question.

"Paul Scherer."

"The constable?"

"Constable, superintendent, general contractor, and all-around good guy. He led the scout troop when we had enough kids for one."

Julie tried to imagine such a time on Mercy. Additional rows of desks in the schoolhouse, children close enough in age to share group activities, sessions that wouldn't be gutted if a few had to leave to go work on their dads' boats. A rousing chorus of youthful voices, bright new faces, promises for the future.

"Fielded a damn good football team back in the day. Soccer, I mean." Callum gave a nod, as if a decision had been reached. "No one knows the children of this island better."

CHAPTER FORTY-FIVE

J ulie awoke early enough the next morning to stop at the town office on her way to school. It wouldn't be open yet, but Julie figured she could check Scherer's office hours. When she got there at 7:00 a.m., however, a secretary already occupied the space behind a counter and explained that while Scherer wasn't at his desk, he was locatable, putting some hours in on a handyman job before the official workday started.

The secretary told Julie how to find the house, and summoning Depot from the spot where she'd left him, Julie set out walking again. She found Scherer at the top of a ladder propped against the wall of a cottage, pounding shingles in.

"Mr. Scherer, hi!" Julie called.

He twisted around to spot her on the ground, then climbed down. "Ms. Weathers," he greeted her. "Call me Paul. Please."

Julie nodded. "And I'm Julie. This is Depot."

Scherer barely glanced at the dog. "He's as big as they say."

Depot trotted off to a stand of trees, offended.

Scherer stuck a hammer into a tool belt slung around his waist. "What can I do for you on such a beautiful morning?"

"I'm sorry to show up uninvited. I know you've got work to do."

Scherer waved her off. "That's always the case. I wear a lot of hats." He looked behind him at the cottage. "This place took a licking with the last renters. Flooded the bathroom so bad, it got into the walls."

"Summer properties are the worst," Julie said.

Scherer offered a pleasant smile. "You said it. Now tell me what I can do for you."

Julie smiled back. "I was hoping you could give me some background about the school. Dynamics between the children, I mean. I'm worried about two in particular."

Scherer squared his hands on his belt. "And who might those be?"

"Well, Peter Meyers," Julie said, watching Scherer's face for a reaction. "And also Eddie Cowry. There are a couple of other older kids who can act pretty mean, but I have a feeling they'll follow Peter's example if I can help with his behavior."

Scherer nodded. "The Cowry boy I'm with you on, Peter not so much. He's about the best cared for child I've ever known. Fretted over sometimes, but always out of love. Not many people have their futures secured like Peter. What's given you cause to worry?"

"Nothing definite," Julie admitted. "He misses his old house, that seems clear. And he tried to hurt a bird, possibly my dog too. Actually, the bird was already hurt, but Peter acted aggressively when he found it."

Scherer hesitated. "I don't want to tell you how to do your job, Julie, but all that sounds pretty normal to me for a boy who recently lost his father. Mightn't that make him harbor some anger? Feelings of longing to be back where his dad used to be?"

"Of course," Julie murmured. She felt almost silly now; then she remembered the other part of what Scherer had said. "But Eddie? Him you have had concerns about?"

Scherer spoke faster now; she'd probably taken too much of his time. "Absenteeism, truancy mostly. But there've been whispers, always are on an island. I haven't actually seen bruises on the boy, but let's just say I've had reason to look."

"Does Eddie live with both parents?"

Scherer shook his head. "No mom in the picture. It's just Eddie and his dad."

If his dad were rough with him, that could explain Eddie's tendency to accept abuse at the hands of his peers. "Thanks for taking the time, Mr. Scherer. Paul, I mean. I can't tell you how helpful it's been." Julie took a look around for Depot.

"Reassuring, I hope. You have a good bunch of apples in that crop. Peter's the apple of a lot of our eyes." He let out a laugh at his word play, although his eyes didn't appear mirthful. "Focus on the Cowry boy. He's vulnerable, I'd say. Wouldn't want something to happen to him on our new teacher's watch."

Julie frowned. Scherer wasn't vocalizing anything she hadn't worried about herself, and yet there was something not quite aboveboard in his injunction. Or was Julie misreading that sheen of manipulation? She'd been given another chance at saving a child; the only problem was she didn't know which one needed saving.

By the time Julie and Depot got to town, the weather had changed with a speed even Wedeskyull would've envied, sun diminished to a bead of mercury in the sky. As they reached the cove, the skies opened up, rain drilling the schoolhouse and driving spikes through the sea. Clapping her bag on top of her head for protection, Julie yanked open the side entrance and ducked inside, pulling the dog in after her. He shook his huge body, spraying droplets as far as the stove.

"Okay, okay," Julie told him. "Don't make a big deal about some rain."

Julie used her jacket to blot damp off her clothes, then paused in the midst of her ministrations. Something felt different about the classroom. She looked down at Depot, but he didn't appear perturbed.

Her desk appeared as she'd left it: monitor dark, an uneven jumble of sharpened pencils, corrected homework waiting to be handed out. The student desks sat empty, their surfaces dusted with eraser crumbs and pencil shavings. The stove stood like a fat-bellied old man, cold and gray and devoid of ashes; today might be the right weather to light it for the first time. The barn doors had been snugly shut; books lined the shelves; kindergarten toys filled baskets.

Julie couldn't spot a thing out of place.

Then she realized, and lifted a hand to her head. She ducked, expecting a gray-winged missile to dive-bomb her, as she approached the cage Callum had made.

It was empty.

The opening Callum had cut in the slats was closed, the hasp he had attached securely hooked. No way could a bird escape, and even if it had, it wouldn't have locked the door behind itself. Julie looked around for stray feathers or droppings, but none were visible. It was as if the bird had disappeared in a *poof* from inside its cage.

Julie headed to the hallway outside the classroom, and when she passed the stage, the curtain shimmied. Just the slightest warble in the fabric, but Julie grabbed a fistful of cloth and yanked it back.

Peter stood on stage, a few sheets of paper in his hand, staring out at the room.

Julie sucked in a small breath.

"I started writing my lines and was practicing them," he said for explanation.

Julie was torn between praising the boy's industry and a need to bring him back in line. "Even so, you can't enter the school before hours," she said. "Besides, don't you think we should hold tryouts for parts? Find out who can sing and dance and act?"

Peter threw her a look of such certainty and confidence, she could see the stamp of his heritage, like a crown and a stole, upon him. This was a child who'd never had cause to doubt he would get what he wanted.

But the play wasn't the most pressing matter right now.

"Peter," Julie said. "Where is the bird? Where's Gully?"

CHAPTER FORTY-SIX

The boy lowered himself into a crouch, straightening the pages of his script.

"Peter?"

He had killed the bird. Julie was suddenly sure of it, and she took several steps away from the stage without realizing she was doing so. She had interrupted the boy's machinations with the creature the first time, so he'd come to school early today to finish the job.

Disgust rippled through her. She forced words out. "Did you hurt Gully, Peter?"

The pages fell from his hand, sliding across the slick surface of the stage. "Why would I do that?" he mumbled, not looking at her.

"I don't know," Julie answered honestly. "But I'd like to. I won't get mad at you, I promise. And if I'm upset, it's just because, well, this is an upsetting situation. But that doesn't mean I won't try to help you. That's all I want to do."

Peter's features set in a stolid frown. "I didn't hurt Gully—"

"Peter," Julie said, feeling her hands form fists. She didn't want to be frustrated with this child who was clearly in need of help, but he incited helplessness in her, confoundment of a sort only outdone in Julie's life by grief. "You can tell me the truth—"

"I released him."

Julie unclenched her hands. "Did you say you released him?"

Peter began sweeping his pages into place. "He needed to be with other gulls." He sent a pleading glance in Julie's direction. "He didn't belong here with us."

Julie stared back at him, sensing there was more to those words than just their surface meaning, but having no idea how to get at it.

Peter had returned to patting his papers into a neat stack, which suddenly he tore at. The pile was surprisingly thick—how much could the boy have written last night?—and he dropped a few of the pages, flinging others down in order to gut the remainder. He began to rip the sheets so violently that the skin on his hands sliced, vicious paper cuts that streaked the white leaves he let fly with bloody slashes.

"Peter!" Julie cried. She crossed the distance she'd put between herself and the stage. "Please stop!"

But the boy kept ripping and tearing, using his teeth as well as his hands, hurling smaller and smaller sections of paper into the air, a blizzard of destruction. His mouth opened in a snarl, his hands formed claws.

"Peter," Julie said helplessly, but her voice was drowned out by his growls, a sound she recognized, frightening and shameful and familiar. The last time she'd witnessed sorrow like this, it had been her own.

Julie reached out, wrapping her arms around Peter's biting, clawing, flailing body from behind, a hug of restraint and shared desperation, until finally he began to still, and the remaining riot of paper settled over the two of them like a shroud.

Peter looked at her as if he hadn't until that minute known she was there, his blue eyes blank. "He didn't belong here," he said.

Then the barn doors opened and a crush of children ran in.

The students surged inside, all thrumming energy in their attempts to get dry, excited for the weekend ahead. Shedding coats, snapping umbrellas shut, but slowing in their efforts when they noticed the goings-on onstage. They stood in silent array, facing Julie and Peter.

Julie extricated herself as unobtrusively as possible, trying not to call attention to Peter's shaking shoulders and bowed form. She got to her feet, sidling in front of the boy to shield him from view as the children looked on.

For a minute words failed her, no reasonable explanation occurring, and as the silence drew itself out, the children began to exchange looks.

"Peter was practicing," Julie blurted out.

A pause, more shared glances.

"We thought there could be a storm." It matched Peter's current emotional state anyway, gave him motivation.

Macy pointed to the bits of paper on stage. "Like with snow you mean?"

Julie felt a jolt of gratitude as all the children turned to the older girl.

"We could make cutout flakes!" a kindergartner said.

"A winter storm would be epic," said the seventh-grade boy, and Macy gave him a kindly nod before he could start cycling on about weather and cold.

"I agree," Julie said.

"This play is going to be so mega," a fifth grader announced, lifting her chin.

"Yeah!" said several more.

"I wanna practice too!" complained one of the younger children. "Is Peter the only one who gets to?"

"Peter, when do we get to rehearse?" asked an older kid.

Julie turned back to the boy onstage. "Gather up that snow," she instructed.

It took Peter a second, then he set to the task. "Snow. Yeah."

Julie hopped off the stage. "Soon," she promised the assembled students. "But first I have some news for you. Gully made an especially fast recovery and this morning was set free!" Julie figured she didn't have to specify who had done the freeing.

"He was?" said a fifth-grade boy, sounding suspicious. "Already?"

Julie held up a restraining hand before the rest of his peers could join him in mutiny. "I wasn't sure how sturdy the cage was. It's a bit makeshift, remember? Besides, Gully is better off in the wild with his friends," she concluded.

And prayed she was right.

Despite her prior plan of being hands off, Julie kept Peter inside at lunch, appraising his mood after the morning's meltdown. She also wanted to ask him about the still-absent Eddie. Peter had made that cryptic comment after the party about not being able to be friends with the younger boy, a statement belied by his position as lord high ruler of the school.

The pronouncement Martha had made when Julie arrived at the Rainbow Pavilion gave her an opening. She waited until Peter had swallowed the last of his sandwich, then said, "Did Eddie come to the party at your grandparents' house alone?"

Peter pulled a granola bar out and proceeded to unwrap it. "No."

"With his parents? His father, I mean?" she amended, recalling Scherer's words.

Peter ate half the bar in one bite. "His dad told Eddie to go *play* with us 'cause he had work to do." He put an ironic emphasis on the word, sixth graders being far too worldly and mature for play.

"So Mr. Cowry suggested his son hang out with you all on those rocks." Did the dad know he was setting Eddie up for a world of trouble, or was he just out of the kiddie social sphere as most parents were? "What do you mean, he had work?"

Peter stood up, crushing his lunch bag into a ball. The boy's hands had been slivered by the script, and his friends had admired the red etchings on his skin all morning, like gang badges or tattoos. "Mr. Cowry does stuff for my grandmother and the Captain. That's how come we can't be friends. Who wants to hang with a kid whose family tells your dad what to do?" He gave a shrug. "Besides, they're dubs."

There was a crushing weight to Peter's words, an understanding, but nowhere near a full one, of the order of things, how it trapped people in cages they could never escape.

Both sides in cages. One of them was just bigger and finer.

The rest of Friday passed quickly, the students working together on the script that Peter had begun, and which turned out to be quite an original take on the tale. Julie explained that she would serve as director and be involved with casting, but other than that, the kids could be in charge of what they had decided to call *Rapunzel Returns*.

Aside from Peter, the sixth-grade boys seemed uninterested in performance, for once not following their king's lead. Although they did react to the idea of sets and carpentry with a series of fist bumps and ideas for how to construct something they described to each other in whispers behind hands, telling Julie that she had put them in charge, so this would be a surprise. The limited number of roles in both the fairy tale and its retelling was turning out to be a boon for the girls who liked costume design, as well as the too-cool-for-school team on hair and makeup. Julie watched the children collaborate, breaking into groups and making plans, with a tidal surge of joy in her heart. They were doing great.

Most of them.

Eddie's second day in a row of absenteeism was a concern, especially given Scherer's stern warning. Since Dad worked for Peter's grandparents, Julie might just get lucky and find him there. For it had struck her that perhaps she'd gone to the wrong mother first.

It wasn't Martha who held the reins over the Hempstead clan, the woman really in command. To find that person, Julie needed to pay a visit to the grandmother's home, the drab, crumbling carapace, which had birthed Martha. Learn more about whatever had driven her and her son from the house Julie now occupied and into the furious burst of color known as the Rainbow Pavilion.

CHAPTER FORTY-SEVEN

Eddie first, though.

The prior teacher had listed an address, but no phone, for the elder Cowry. Landlines were a luxury on Mercy, which meant inquiries about students had to be made not just pre-email or text, but pre–Alexander Graham Bell.

With no lunchtime outing, Depot was in dire need of exercise, bounding along the shoreline and up the road that led to town. The rain had stopped, but a gray pall lay over the island, thick and cottony. Moisture condensed on Julie's clothes and Depot's fur as they walked, the air wet enough to drink.

Eddie and his father lived in a shack on what had to be one of the least scenic patches of land on the island. Julie stood on tiptoes, peering through a cracked window. The house appeared to have once been an outbuilding, now crudely winterized with exposed puffs of fiberglass insulation and divided into a meager pair of rooms. There was nobody home, but Julie left a note asking Mr. Cowry to get ahold of her at school, then set off again, hoping she would find him at her next stop.

When Julie came to the foursquare of cottages, however, she decided to pause, and knocked on Ellie's door. Depot lagged behind, his forepaws poised and snout pointed toward the woods. Julie addressed him over her shoulder. "Not going home yet, sorry."

Ellie greeted them both with her customary smile, and a glass of wine in her hand. Julie must've winced—or startled—some involuntary tell, because Ellie's smile faded.

"Shit," she said. "I told you. I never stick to it."

Is Ellie the right friend for you to be having? Julie heard Callum say. She reached out and grabbed her friend's arm. "Oh God, I've turned into one of those obnoxious, judgy sober saints. I'd rather be a drunk."

Ellie laughed. "No, no, you're totally right. It's just not a good time for me to quit. And to save you having to get all sanctimonious—and then feel guilty about it—yes, I know that's an excuse, and yes, I still want a refill. Can I pour you a Diet Coke?"

"Sure," Julie said, entering the cottage. "Mind if Depot comes in?"

The dog had stayed facing the woods. He chose to lie down on Ellie's front stoop, hind and forelegs dangling off the sides, instead of prolonging the visit cooped up inside.

Julie followed Ellie toward a small kitchen. "This place is so cute."

There were blue and green throw pillows on the couch, embroidered with old-fashioned needlepoint A's and E's, and watercolor seascapes on the walls.

"I feel lucky to have it," Ellie said. "My mom—my parents, I should say, considering who the real wage earner was—paid off the mortgage, so it's just a matter of maintaining it."

Julie sipped her soda. "Hey, mind if I pick your brain about something?"

Ellie lifted her empty glass and examined the red tinge at the bottom.

"Let me just open another bottle. Unless this is going to be a problem for you?"

"Not unless you're planning on a scotch chaser."

Ellie squeezed behind Julie, accessing a tiny space by the back door. She stooped down and opened the flaps on a carton of wine bottles. As she took one out, Julie saw a couple of items in the empty partitions.

She frowned, joining Ellie beside the box. "What's this?"

Ellie crossed to a little bistro table and set the bottle down. "Crackers?" she said, twisting to look while tugging at a corkscrew. "I get my fix and my food from Amazon mostly. Perry's only gets me so far."

Julie shook her head, pawing between grocery items. "This," she said, holding out a package of leashes.

Unexpectedly, Ellie's eyes filled.

Julie jumped to her feet.

Ellie had filled her glass to the rim; now she drained it, swallowing steadily before wiping her mouth with the back of her hand. The skin came away smudged purple.

"El?" Julie said.

Ellie sniffed loudly, and blotted her face. "I never really answered your question about being a dog person, did I?"

Julie thought back to the day they had met. "I'm so sorry!" she exclaimed. "You don't have to tell me anything. I was just being nosy. And weird."

Ellie shook her head, pouring a liberal serving from the freshly uncorked bottle. Ruby-colored liquid sloshed over the side of her glass, spotting the table. "You've seen me quit cold turkey, then fall off the wagon like five seconds later. And I've seen you have sex for the first time since your puritanical husband stopped pleasing you—"

Julie cut in, laughing. "Callum and I have not had sex!"

Ellie flapped a dismissive hand. "Whatevs, you will soon. Anyway, point being, I should be able to tell you this, close as we've become."

Julie felt a smile build that was totally inappropriate, given the story she sensed she was about to hear. She hid her expression, focusing on the spilled wine.

Ellie swiped at it with a cloth. "The dog I had since high school died. Just a few months before you got here actually. We rescued him as a puppy, and he lived longer than anybody had a right to expect. Outlived both my parents. I just can't believe he's gone."

Julie bowed her head. She could imagine the pain Ellie was suffering.

"Sometimes I still buy stuff, just out of habit." Ellie lifted her glass to her lips. "It's dumb, I know. It's almost like…I forget that he's gone."

"That's not dumb," Julie whispered. Her throat felt as if it were wedged with clay. There was so much she still had to share with Ellie. "What was your dog's name?"

A smile briefly lit Ellie's face. "Smarmy."

"*Smarmy?*"

Ellie nodded happily. "Oh, and he so was. Smarmy thought he knew better than anyone else on the planet." She paused. "You know what? He pretty much did."

They both laughed.

Ellie sank down in a chair. "Remember the first day I thought I had a ball for Depot? I buy those sometimes too."

Julie thought back, made an *aha* face when it hit her.

"What was it you wanted to pick my brain about?" Ellie asked.

It took Julie a second to pull herself back to the events of her day. "I'm going to see the Hempsteads after this. Anything more you can tell me about the grandmother?"

Ellie's smile evaporated, and she even seemed to forget her wine, glass dangling from her hand. "I thought we said you were going to be kind of hands off for a while."

"I know, we did, but I don't think I can be. He freaked out in the classroom before school started today."

Ellie bore down on the cloth she'd used to wipe up the wine spill, knotting and balling it with her free hand.

"Stop murdering that dishrag," Julie said. "Look, what's the big deal if I talk to the Hempsteads? You're the second person to try and steer me away from them today. I went to talk to Paul Scherer, and he all but ordered me to focus on Eddie Cowry instead."

Ellie's mouth twisted bitterly.

"What?" Julie asked her.

Ellie didn't respond.

Julie leaned forward, catching her friend's hand in hers. "El, listen, there's a child at risk here, and I don't even know who it is. I'm stumbling around in the dark and it's like there are all these forces amassed and I can't even see what I'm facing—"

Something in her words seemed to jar Ellie, and she burst out, "I bet Scherer was working on a house, right?"

"As a matter of fact, he was," Julie said slowly.

Ellie nodded her head with a vicious jab. "A rental property. And guess who it belongs to? The Hempsteads. I can say so without even hearing which house it was. Ninety percent of Scherer's contracting or handyman jobs are on places owned by the Hempsteads. Another portion of his income comes from his position as superintendent." A deliberate pause. "Know who's head of the school board?"

Julie felt like she was in a room with walls that were being pushed farther and farther out, its perimeter no longer visible. Just how far was the Hempstead reach?

Ellie gave a sharp, jagged lift of her shoulders. "Scherer's also constable, an elected position. And the island election committee is headed by none other than—"

Julie interrupted her friend. "This still doesn't explain why Peter is so troubled."

Ellie shook her head. "Peter's the island golden child, always has been, ever since he was born. You're just seeing the effects of great wealth and unchecked power."

Julie recalled Scherer's assessment of the situation. Could the behaviors she had witnessed come down to the boy's bereavement? It made a certain amount of sense. But some instinct, deep at Julie's core, which had once driven her to double-check the stroller in The Everything Store and was probably shared by the whole constellation of her law-enforcement relatives, told her there was more to this.

She turned back toward Ellie. "Adolescence changes things. Peter's starting to see himself, his family, his whole life in ways he never has before. To question people and places and situations he's always taken for granted."

"Well, he'd better not question the Hempsteads," Ellie said.

They heard a scrabbling at the door, and Julie went to let in Depot.

"I lied to you before," Ellie called out.

Julie turned, her hand on the doorknob.

"Remember?" Ellie said. "I said I'd been asked to give you a tour of the island?"

"Sure." Julie pulled the door open, and Depot greeted her with a boisterous bark. Julie leaned over. "One second, Deep," she whispered into his velvet ear.

"Well, I didn't ask. I volunteered. I really wanted—"

Ellie broke off and Julie walked a few steps back, leaving the door open and Depot waiting outside.

"I really wanted us to become friends, Julie. And I'm afraid..."

Julie frowned. "Afraid of what?"

Ellie's narrow shoulders sloped. "Never mind. I'm drunk. I just told you about the dead dog I never talk about. I don't know what I'm afraid of."

"I just want to help a child who's hurting. What could be wrong with that?"

"Not one single thing," Ellie said, and offered a swift, luminescent smile.

CHAPTER FORTY-EIGHT

Julie asked Ellie if she'd mind walking Depot back; the dog had been wanting to go home ever since leaving school that day. The woods were growing dim when Julie entered them alone, a thin gruel of mist floating in the air. The moon and stars would be blotted out by fog tonight, but for now Julie still had light. She stuck to the path, estimating that her house and the mansion sat at right angles from this spot. Then she struck off, ducking beneath the heavy limbs of trees, skirting saplings.

Tendrils of vapor swirled around her. Julie had to stop to clear her vision, wipe condensation off her face, and the quiet of the woods assailed her. She'd expected to see or hear the ocean by now, and its absence was unsettling. There was so little wildlife on an island, and the lack of birdsong or scampering feet rendered the woods almost silent, with the fog adding its own deadening blanket.

Then Julie heard something.

Coming from a different direction than she'd expected the mansion to lie, but Julie turned and followed the sound. She had gotten disoriented—the tightly packed trees, the muffling mist—and couldn't be sure anymore of the mansion's location. The sound soon resolved into a voice, and from there into singing.

Julie shouldered her way between columns of trees, twigs snapping in her wake. If the sea did lie near, she wouldn't be able to see it for the soupy fog. She paused to listen for surf, but the sound of the voice, high and sweet, subsumed everything else.

Julie muscled past another tree, moving faster now, branches whipping.

Notes climbed to a glass-shattering pitch.

Julie began to run. A final web of branches sought to block her, but she shoved past it, nearly falling over the downed tree that came next. It had the body of a beast, a brontosaurus that had toppled. The trunk jutted out from a massive snarl of roots, four feet off the ground, and angled upward from there. At its crown, another six feet higher, stood Peter, given a little end-of-the-week freedom maybe, and belting out his song.

He looked like an extension of the tree, its tawny leaves interlaced with locks of his hair, his waving arms like the topmost, spindly branches. Peter danced upon the upper reaches, a creature of the forest, a wild child, shirtless and barefoot, notes rising effortlessly from his throat while ghosts of mist swirled on the ground below the trunk.

The song finished on a wailing note of need, and Julie began to clap, loud and ferocious.

As the echo of her applause petered out, silence reigned over the woods once again.

Peter stood, feet planted, toes splayed out in order to keep himself steady on the log, leaning over to peer at Julie as if she were the apparition.

"Ms. *Weathers*?" he said, incredulity in his tone.

Julie took a step forward, mist lapping at her legs, and as the uncertainty evaporated from Peter's expression, his features settled into their customary neutral configuration, giving nothing away.

"What are you doing here?" he asked.

Julie had no idea what her next step should be, but she sensed there was a right and wrong one, a choice that could allow her to get to know Peter better, and another that would drive him away. She fell back on a strategy she knew from her law-enforcement family and teaching both. When trying to get a suspect, or a child, to talk, say nothing.

Sure enough, Peter flinched first. "No one's ever been here besides me. Like, nobody on the whole island, I don't think."

Julie had a direction now. Act impressed. Then try to impress him back. "I can believe it. This place is way hidden. But I'm pretty good at finding things in the woods. I come from a place with a lot of mountains," she added, wagering that mountains would strike an exotic note with an island kid. "Hey, this is an awesome tree."

Peter looked proud. "It's my hideout. For when I can sneak away."

"I wonder when it fell?" Julie asked, though she knew it had to be fairly recently, judging by the amount of decay in the trunk and how much soil clung to its roots.

"Like, forever ago," Peter replied breezily. "Probably before I was born."

Julie concealed a smile.

"I mean, I just found it last year. But it's always been here. You can tell."

She nodded solemnly. "Hey, what was that song you were singing? I can't remember where I've heard it before."

Peter grinned. "You haven't. Macy made it up for me."

"Macy *made it up*?" Julie repeated, disbelieving.

Suddenly, Peter jumped down, disregarding the height, and landing on all fours in a crouch. The kid was a soloist and a Cirque du Soleil acrobat.

He stood up, brushing dirt off his hands. "Where's Depot?"

"I leave him with a dog sitter now."

The boy looked troubled. "Who?"

He probably knew every person on the island, and thus that there were no dog sitters as such. Julie had checked. Depot would be attending school for the foreseeable future. But Julie didn't want the boy to be able to predict her dog's whereabouts.

She offered up a diversion. "How do you get onto the tree?"

It was high enough off the ground that a dead hang and a pull-up would've been required, and Julie didn't think a child as slim and preadolescent as Peter would have the strength.

He took the bait instantly, heading for the enormous carpet of soil at the foot of the fallen tree, then barreling through its Medusa's head of roots, using them like a jungle gym to emerge at the base of the trunk. From there he walked upward, one foot in back of the other, as if he were on a balance beam.

"Cool," Julie called.

Peter jumped down again.

"You must be getting cold out here," she said.

He shrugged. "Nah."

But his bare flesh shone, damp from the fog and prickly with goose bumps, while his lips looked blue in the descending dusk.

"Is it a long way back to your mom's house? Or," she added, striving for a casual note, "your grandmother's?"

Peter stared at her, before letting out a totally spontaneous laugh. "Ms. Weathers," he said, "you are hella awesome to have found this place, but you're also pretty dumb."

Julie decided not to take offense. "Oh yes? Why's that?"

Peter walked beneath the high, sloping ceiling of the trunk, scarcely having to duck. Dancing forward on nimble feet, he parted branches in a stand of trees before them.

On the other side stood the mansion.

CHAPTER FORTY-NINE

Well," Julie told Peter, catching up as the boy ran ahead. "I guess I'm even better at navigation than I thought. Because I was trying to find this place."

He stopped and turned back to look at her, the skin on his forehead wrinkling. "You were? How come?"

"I want to let your grandmother know how talented you are at performing."

"She'll be so glad to hear that," the boy muttered, but he led the way across the platters of stone that made up the walkway to an expanse of front porch. It was as wide as a river, and sank beneath foot a bit just as if it really were water, the wood beginning to soften with the ever-present moisture in the air.

Dutifully wiping dirt from the soles of his feet on a mat in front of a pair of high double doors, Peter twisted a finely etched knob. As soon as he got inside, he sprinted up a flight of stairs that divided at a landing, and vanished.

Damn, Julie thought. There couldn't be a much worse plan of approach for someone as proper as the grandmother. Julie hadn't even knocked.

She took a look around the foyer. Ellie's description had been spot-on. The walls up and down the long hallway were a dull cream, in need of a fresh coat of paint or perhaps just a brighter shade, and the furnishings, a settee and sideboard, were dark and heavy. Probably priceless antiques, but nothing contemporary or quirky or new, not so much as one offbeat knickknack. Framed oils depicted island scenes, heavily skewed toward rainy skies and storm-driven seas.

"Hello?" Julie called. Her voice wavered, and she coughed to clear her throat. "Mrs. Hempstead?"

Slow, shuffling footsteps approached the front hall.

Julie looked up as the grandmother's tall stature would require, wondering at the woman's diminished pace. Instead of the grandmother, the Captain appeared.

"Hello," he said, smoothing back the thick hair on his head. "Who might you be?"

Julie hesitated. "Captain, I'm Ms. Weathers, the new teacher. I'm sorry to have shown up unannounced. Peter let me in."

"Peter," the Captain repeated, an uncertain echo that added years, decades, to his demeanor. "Peter, Peter, of course..."

Julie offered a tentative smile.

"The schoolteacher visiting, that is an occasion," the Captain said, his voice gaining surety. "Martha always does well in school. Melinda, now she's another story."

The name made clear the fact that the man was temporarily residing a generation in the past. Melinda must be the other daughter. *I had a sister,* Julie heard Martha say.

The Captain's gaze had wandered, but he looked back at Julie with the smile that he'd worn upon their first encounter. "Might I offer you a drink?"

"Um, no, thank you though," Julie replied. Making this announcement to someone not in his right mental state felt easier. "I don't drink."

The lines beside the Captain's eyes crinkled. "Not even coffee?"

Julie smiled. "Coffee. Now that I will take you up on—"

A voice called out from the hidden shadows at the top of the broad staircase. "That's not true. You drink, Ms. Weathers."

Julie swiveled slowly.

Peter began descending. "I saw it," he said. "A bottle on the kitchen counter. The night I hid in my old room." He arrived at the bottom of the stairs. "It was empty. So I guess you must've drank it all."

Julie swallowed, an audible click. She had no idea why Peter had chosen to confront her like this. Thank goodness the Captain wasn't exactly sharp and aware at the moment; there was only one response Julie could make if she didn't want to lose the trust she'd begun to build with the boy. "You're right. I used to drink. But I don't anymore."

Peter's eyes, right now the blue of glaciers, held hers.

"Peter!" the Captain said on a note of recognition. "It's good to see you, son."

"You just saw me an hour ago, Cap," Peter replied cheerily. "Hey, is it okay if I take a shower?"

The Captain faced the boy head-on, his gaze boring into his grandson's.

Peter lowered his eyes. "Sorry. May I take a shower, Captain?"

The Captain lifted one hand to grant permission, and Peter walked off, soldier-straight, keeping his hand upon the banister as he mounted the stairs.

Any teacher would covet such rapid obedience. Julie smiled at the Captain.

His voice struck a soaring note of command. "Andrea! We'll have coffee for two in the parlor. And some of those biscuits I asked you to prepare earlier this morning."

There was no reply, nor stirrings of movement from another room.

The Captain let out a sigh. "So difficult to find reliable help, isn't it?"

Julie couldn't think how to respond. Probably it was, in a mansion this size, on an island this small.

"I suppose that means I'll have to attend to our refreshments myself," the Captain said. He stopped for a moment, looking uncertainly down the hall.

Julie tried to imagine where the kitchen would be in a house as vast as this.

The Captain turned back to regard her. "A man can still be the head of the household, can't he, if no longer the captain of his ship? I believe I might enjoy a cup of something warm now and again in the parlor. Even if ailing."

Julie wasn't quite sure what the Captain was asking, but she found that she very much wanted to give the right response. "Yes, I think so—"

"Captain!" A woman's ringing voice. "What are you doing downstairs?"

Julie turned and saw the grandmother.

The ivory hair on her head was raked back so tightly, it could've been bare scalp, and her eyes, like Peter's tonight, were icicle blue. "You know you shouldn't be seen like this. It's one of your bad days, dear."

The Captain shifted on unsteady feet. "Is it?"

"I have your supper waiting in the east wing, as you requested," said his wife.

"I did?" The Captain's cheeks reddened, a quick spark of shame, and he glanced at Julie. "I apologize, my dear—"

"There's no need—" Julie began.

The grandmother glared at her, plucked eyebrows forming a *vee* of displeasure. "Will you be able to make it on your own, Captain, or do you require assistance?"

The Captain's cheeks darkened to a ferocious brick. "No need for help." He turned quickly, off-balance, and put one hand out to steady himself. Then he scuffed off in the direction of the staircase, his goodbye almost too low to hear.

The grandmother turned, striding across the hall. Julie hurried to follow her into a parlor. There were nautical maps on the walls, hair-thin lines against a sickly green background, and a sextant displayed on a mantel. Here too the furniture was old, and valuable: a gray velvet chaise, an oak armoire rich with carving, a low table in front of two uncomfortable, pedigreed chairs.

"And now, Ms. Weathers. Suppose you tell me why you've come."

The grandmother took a seat in one of the chairs, drawing her elegant knees together and crossing her ankles, before offering Julie the other chair with a crook of her graceful, swan's-neck arm.

Julie sat down. "This place is spectacular."

The grandmother gave a gracious nod. "It used to be."

"It's a lot to keep up, I would think."

The grandmother let out a snort that belied her usual dignity. "Oh, Ms. Weathers. You can't begin to imagine." Her gaze swept over Julie in wordless assessment. "Truly."

"I suppose I can't." Julie lifted her eyes to the grandmother's. Her family once held a rarefied position in Wedeskyull, but they'd been cops, not landowners, and had never amassed any wealth. She felt put down, intimidated, then angry at herself for being so.

The grandmother continued to regard her, raptor-sharp, as if sensing her advantage. Then the peaks of her shoulders settled, and she switched to a conversational tone. "How are you enjoying our island?"

"I love it," Julie replied.

The grandmother smiled. "It isn't like other places, is it? Tourists—even the summer people—think of us as behind the times on Mercy. More accurate would be to say that the island is a place out of time. Timeless."

"I can see that," Julie said.

The grandmother didn't appear to hear Julie's response. "Why, some of the men here still use wooden traps! Nobody I'd consider a real, working lobsterman, but still, on Mercy they exist. The old ways persevere."

"Which has its charms, for sure," Julie said.

The grandmother shifted on the hard seat. "But nothing lasts forever, does it?"

"I'm sorry?"

The grandmother leaned a little closer, her blue eyes blazing. "We're the last of a dying empire, the Captain and I. Peter's father is gone. All hopes for our continued survival—no, our resurrection—rest on Peter's young shoulders."

Julie couldn't come up with a reply at first. She wasn't sure if the woman had just given her grandson a bequest, or a threat. She tried silence, it had worked with Peter, but the grandmother was a tougher mark and showed no sign of filling in the gap. At last Julie said, "I'm afraid I don't understand what you mean."

"Of course you don't. How could you?" The grandmother rose and strode out into the front hall, opening both tall paneled wooden doors, right and left, to the night.

After a belated pause, Julie stood up too.

Without turning, the grandmother said, "Why don't you let me show you?"

CHAPTER FIFTY

When the grandmother emerged onto the porch, her regal carriage, her entire bearing, had altered. From elegant, elderly woman to something dragon-like, fierce.

She closed the doors behind her, then rounded on Julie. "You come from a different world. That's why you can't understand. There is no world like ours."

She was beginning to sound a bit melodramatic for Julie's tastes.

"How does the younger set put it these days? You don't get it."

It was full dark now, and the ghostly fog had fled. The grandmother exited the manor to a front lawn—less sandy than the scrub at Julie's house; someone had put a lot of effort into making sure that grass took hold—and pointed toward the roof of the house.

"Do you see that?"

Julie followed the upward thrust of her finger to a web of wrought-iron fencing.

"A widow's walk," the grandmother said. "Telling term, isn't it? Many a wife on this island lost her seafaring husband, my daughter included. My son-in-law's death disrupted the natural order of things and transferred an immutable weight to Peter. He is, quite literally, our last chance."

"To go on in the industry," Julie said. "Lobstering."

It was another explanation for the conflict Peter was experiencing, caught in the vise grip between living up to his family's expectations versus pursuing his own obvious talents.

"To fulfill a dynastic obligation," the grandmother corrected. "Peter has a greater claim to this island than any other resident."

Melodrama again. The woman should try out for the play.

"He's been raised to it by his father, whose family fished nearby waters as my own did the choicest ledges and shoals around Mercy. Tragically, Peter's education ended prematurely—and I don't mean the one you are charged with providing."

The grandmother reached out and caught Julie's hand in her own. Her fingers were like talons, cold, with scant flesh upon them, and Julie fought not to flinch.

"Because it's not an industry, you see—it's a way of life. One that needs to be preserved today more than ever. Children don't care about honoring their roots anymore. But those roots have sustained my family for generations on this island, and I'm not about to let them get pulled up now."

But what if she didn't have a choice? "What happens if Peter doesn't go into the family business?"

"I beg your pardon?"

Oh, you heard me, Julie thought irritably. There was something about the grandmother's stance she found particularly irksome, over and above its obvious narcissism and willingness to handcuff her offspring to a legacy.

"I said, what if Peter chooses another path?" Julie stopped, then decided to forge on. In for a penny and all that. "Acting, for instance. He's shown real talent in class."

The grandmother looked amused. "Well, at least you didn't suggest something impractical, like being a doctor or a lawyer."

This time, when Julie stayed quiet, it worked.

"Yes, I heard you might be putting on a show." The grandmother spoke as if Julie had decided to let the kids play dolls. "Not exactly theater, is it, the selection you chose?"

This time, Julie refused to feel belittled. "My goal is to help the island children discover themselves, who they really are, as they learn. Sometimes it's easiest to engage kids by speaking their language, appealing to updated tastes."

"Fairy stories, not *Antigone*," the grandmother said contemptuously.

"The Brothers Grimm are classics in their own right. Mercy may be as relevant as ever, as you suggest, rather than quaint. But each generation still seeks to put its stamp on things, and this tale has been reinvented enough times that it appeals to the kids."

The grandmother hesitated for an uncharacteristic moment before responding. "You fancy yourself a thespian, Ms. Weathers? A teacher of the dramatic arts?"

"Well, I don't know about the first one—"

But the grandmother cut her off with the swift sharpness of a guillotine, and Julie began to suspect a trap had been laid.

"Why, you don't even deserve the title of failed actress," the grandmother said. She eyed Julie haughtily from above, assessing her response as the full impact, the implications of her words descended. "Acting is a pursuit of chances, of risk taking." One more meticulous pause. "And you never even dared give it a try."

Cold sea air settled over Julie. She felt as if the wind had been knocked out of her; she couldn't muster enough breath for reply. How on earth could the grandmother know such a thing about her? Something so small and secret and unspoken, a nascent wish, practically unborn, its feathers still wet?

The old woman faced her, seemingly satisfied. "There isn't much call for actors on Mercy Island. And I think you will agree as teacher that children should be prepared for more sensible paths."

Julie spoke at last. "Such as lobstering."

"When you're a Hempstead, yes," the grandmother snapped. She gestured out to sea, a broad, black sheet dotted with shark fins of whitecaps. "Do you have any idea how much of that is ours?"

"You can't own the ocean," Julie said, astounded. Were there no limits to this woman's grandiosity? She made Uncle Vern, who'd rewritten the rules to suit his personal law of the land without so much as a check or a balance, seem humble.

"No, but you can own the rights to drop traps in it," the grandmother stated.

Julie wouldn't have said those two were anything like the same thing, but dispute wouldn't have mattered; the grandmother was a cold, hard empress now, informing Julie of the extent of her reign.

"Whether lawfully or by unstated agreement between gangs. And a Hempstead doesn't just belong to the top gang—he runs it. Peter will make a lush living for himself and the family he will one day have. The boy's had his recreational license since he was six years old. Now he's permitted to haul ten traps. By the time he's grown, with a boat of his own, he'll have all this to come home to." The grandmother thrust out her arm. Even in the dark, it was apparent that her face had regained a touch of its youthful glow.

Julie looked in the direction the grandmother was pointing.

"You can hardly imagine this place during a time of abundant hauls," she said. "We've had to put off a new paint job, and restoring our boathouse and dock. Even been forced to sell a few precious heirlooms. Why, we used to employ a staff of seven, now two girls come weekly, and the groundskeeper less frequently than that. But all that can be regained. More even. You're our teacher—picture one of those electronic boards for use in the schoolhouse! Tablets for each student! Why, who knows what will be invented once we are able to purchase it?"

The grandmother's feelings about technology had clearly evolved since the school board's decision not to outfit the schoolhouse with Wi-Fi. The whole tenor of school life could be changed at her discretion. She spoke as if new devices would be introduced to the market just to suit her whims and budget.

The old woman paused to peer at Julie. "Do you hear what I'm saying, Ms. Weathers? All that Peter can do, for himself, and for us, and for future generations on this island? Not just for our family, mind. For all of Mercy."

She thought she was painting a picture of promise, but Julie had never felt so chilled in her life. What a burden Peter carried on his young, thin shoulders.

Seemingly overcome, the grandmother spun around, surprisingly agile for her age as she marched back toward the mansion. She mounted the porch steps, flinging open the twin doors so that she could enter at full stride with both arms spread wide.

She paused to call out from the hall. "I think we've spoken enough for one evening. Thank you for stopping by. I'm grateful Peter has such a dedicated teacher."

And Julie was dismissed.

Julie headed back across the lawn, head clamped by a pain only scotch would touch, brought on by newfound awareness of the grandmother's reach, the bounds—or lack thereof—of the dowager's feverish power. In her interview, Julie had been taken aback by how much Laura Hutchins knew of her background. Now, recalling the younger woman's adoration of the grandmother, she wondered at whose behest that research had been done.

But Laura Hutchins couldn't have known that Julie once dreamed of being an actress. No one knew that besides her parents, both long dead, and David, who probably wouldn't even remember.

Peter caught up to Julie as she reached the lane that spanned the distance between both houses. He held something aloft; in the dark it was impossible to tell what it was.

"My grandmother's helping Cap now," Peter said. "Giving him his medicines. For his heart and blood and head. It takes a real long time. He doesn't like to swallow pills."

Julie offered an empathic nod. "That must be very upsetting for you."

Peter shook his head impatiently. "I just mean that I was able to get this. There are others, but they're super old, like falling apart. I think this one will be the best." He lifted his hands, on which rested a thick bound book.

Julie looked down.

"I need it back, okay?" Peter said. "Leave it at my hideout. My grandmother collects rent on Saturdays. I could maybe say Cap got confused and took it, but she doesn't let him look at them anymore, so that wouldn't be too good."

"Peter," Julie said. The boy had never spoken to her with such elaboration, and she didn't want to rebuff him. But nor did she wish to jeopardize her already tenuous standing with his family. If they shut down on her, she'd never be able to help Peter. "I don't want to do something that could get you in trouble."

"You have to!" Peter shrieked. The sound slit the silence of the night, and the boy lowered his voice. "She's a liar," he hissed. "I hate my mom. She doesn't even act like a real mom. I just want my dad back. I want my dad." Tears wobbled on the blue surface of his eyes.

"Oh, sweetheart," Julie said. "Of course you do—"

A resounding cry carried across the lawn. "Peter Hempstead Meyers! This sort of wandering may be tolerated at your mother's, but it will not be here!"

Peter hurled himself forward, throwing his arms around Julie, and she stooped down, surprised. She thought he was giving her a hug, an indication of their growing bond. But as he turned and raced off, she realized that the boy had in fact left the book in her hold.

CHAPTER FIFTY-ONE

At the house, Depot paced back and forth by his favorite spot in front of the windows, his bowls licked and lapped so clean you couldn't tell they'd been filled. Julie sent mental thanks Ellie's way for the dog-sitting. Another source of worry tonight would've broken her. Depot ran forward at a pace that made Julie back away in self-defense, laughing, which she hadn't expected to do after the events of this night. The dog let out his hungry bark, so Julie served him a second portion. Everybody, even people who knew dogs, underestimated Depot's appetite.

Julie had placed the book Peter had given her on the table when she came in; now she went and retrieved it. Depot walked over, nudging Julie till she sat down on the floor. Then he dropped into the well between her legs as if he were a lapdog, hind haunches and big head overflowing the space. Julie let out an *oof* as she took his weight.

"Yes, okay," she told him distractedly. "But we have work to do, all right?"

She looked down at Peter's offering.

The book was heavy and rectangular and black, a ledger with a hard, pebbly cover and pages printed with rows of horizontal lines. Roughly the first half of the book had been filled in by a sharp, elegant hand: pointy, peaked letters, written in ink that changed from the start of the book to the middle, shiny black liquid evolving to ballpoint.

The content appeared largely numeric, lists of sums owed, paid, and sometimes negotiated or settled by barter. Properties identified by the methods used on Mercy, no street addresses, but lots referred to by location and size, houses described as *stone two story* or *little cedar shake*. These must be rentals owned by the Hempsteads, a record of income earned. The entries extended back years, even decades, the first names an archaeological study of nomenclature, from Mary's and Linda's, William's and Richard's, to Christopher's and Joshua's, Ashley's and Jennifer's.

Peter had said there were older versions too. How old? If Julie had been handed one of those, would she have seen a Cornelius or Hezekiah, an Elspeth or Verity listed on fragile pages of foolscap? And why was Peter so intent on Julie reading such bloodless records?

Perhaps because they weren't as bloodless as they appeared.

She really needed a drink for this. Julie realized she'd been nibbling her lips again, wearing away the skin till she tasted blood, sharp and metallic. She got up and made her way to the kitchen where she put on a pot of coffee. She and Callum hadn't traded numbers yet—on the island, it didn't seem like something you did the same way you would in other places, even ones like Wedeskyull—which was too bad. Julie could've used some advice right now, a little guidance, especially once she spotted the vodka bottle, left in the place where she'd hurriedly stowed it, on a corner of counter, with a few swallows left.

She'd never even put the cap back on.

Julie bit her lip.

The saltiness from the cut she'd opened provoked a desertlike thirst.

A tipple in a cup of coffee? Barely detectable; it'd provide just the slightest smoothing over of whatever she was about to read, find out about the grandmother.

A little balm on her rubbed raw lips.

Julie filled a mug from the coffeepot, then reached for the bottle.

It fell over, knocked by her sweat-slick hand.

She could've rescued it, a sip at least, but instead Julie watched the clear liquid snake its way across the counter, almost invisible, only an acrid odor to give it away.

Julie sponged up the spill, then, for good measure, tossed the sponge in the garbage. She took a deep drink from her mug, a bracing jolt of caffeine and heat. A second later, confusion wrapped a web around her, sticky and opaque. Had she somehow imbibed some vodka after all? For the little red light on the coffee machine had gone suddenly dull, without her even touching it, as if the pot had turned itself off.

As if it were conspiring to get her to take a drink of something besides now rapidly cooling coffee. Julie stamped down on the thought, paranoid and irrational.

The lights in the rest of the house flickered, and then everything went dark.

Julie swallowed her mouthful of coffee, setting the cup on the counter by feel. She made her way into the big, open room, patting her hand against the wall for switches.

None of the lights worked.

This house was so isolated, sitting alone on its hump of cliff, that Julie couldn't tell whether anyone else had lost power, if the outage was island-wide, or limited to this spot.

She began to walk slowly, in what she hoped was the direction of the dining room table, feeling for obstacles before her. She nearly tripped over one of Depot's paws; power losses always sent him into the most restful of slumbers. His outline oriented her, though. She was right near the wall of windows, the table only a few feet away.

When she reached it, shuffling forward, Julie placed both hands upon the wooden surface, situating herself. First things first: a flashlight.

Julie was used to outages. In Wedeskyull, they happened during winter storms and summer ones, or for no reason at all. She knew the cycle they inflicted: at first a not-unwelcome feeling of being cast into an earlier, arguably better age; then a dawning awareness of how spoiled and cosseted everyone had gotten in this one; increasing discomfort and irritability; before relief descended once power was restored seemingly in the last seconds before true madness ensued. But Julie wasn't going to let an inconvenience interfere with the job Peter had begged her to take on—even if deep down it did feel as if something or someone was trying to do exactly that.

Interfere.

Her laptop had plenty of battery charge, although she couldn't get onto the Wi-Fi, feel even as distantly connected to another human being as Facebook allowed. No matter, she didn't need connection right now. Using the light from the computer screen, Julie made her way over to the flight of stairs, then headed up to the second floor to locate a flashlight.

The darkness seemed to have substance, thick and gluey as paste. Oppressive. Although the laptop provided a ghostly glow, the way it cast everything outside its penumbra into shadow wound up making Julie feel more vulnerable, as if a spotlight shone upon her.

She gained the top of the stairs and took a look around, wishing Depot would waken. He'd be up like a shot if anything were to happen—would be barking already if someone were here—but despite that knowledge, Julie couldn't shake off the feeling that someone was right nearby, in a corner or just over her shoulder, taking advantage of the outage to lurk unseen.

Or could he have *caused* the outage?

Somebody might've entered through the basement and accessed the breakers. Maybe he was still down there. If so, depending on which circuit he'd flipped, the lights up here might work. But when Julie flicked the switch, it made a gunshot-loud click in the silence of the hallway, but emitted no illumination.

She kept a flashlight in her bedside table. Once she found it, she would go check the rest of the house, including the basement. Then, after making sure she was alone, she could get started on the task Peter had assigned her, the roles of teacher and student mysteriously reversed.

She moved as quickly as possible into her room and found the flashlight. It was a powerful one, almost as good as if the lights had been turned on, allowing her to make short work of her search. Nobody in any of the rooms. Depot still asleep on the floor. They were alone.

Julie sank down on the couch, aimed the beam of her flashlight, and opened the ledger.

For a while, skimming through the listings, Julie was able to convince herself that there was no more in here than a demonstration of the extent of the Hempsteads' oversight and wealth. Huge sums had been amassed according to this book, were still being accumulated, although the amount had dropped in concert with the island's population.

But as she leafed farther into the ledger, Julie finally came to content that wasn't merely dry and numeric. Jottings and notes and annotations. This part of the book read a little like a journal, although with no obvious personal meaning. Obscure remarks had been penned beside brief accounts of a lunch, a meeting, a social call. Visitors dropping by, outings on a boat, trap house get-togethers. After a few more pages, the lists began to adopt a pared-down quality, extraneous details stripped away, leaving only cryptic notations:

Bouchard, Shaw and Mary
  Gang drops in Tenant's Harbor. (Undercuts co-op rate. Cease.)

Croft, Robert and Violet
  Second son killed two while driving drunk. (Hold in reserve.)

Pelletier, Amanda and "King"
  Rival gang, familial divide. (Offer rights.)

Campbell, Ellen and Lexie
  Artists. Adopting overseas. (Consider donating rental.)

Pratt, Cameron and Alyssa
  Seasonal, seek to reside. Four children. (Winterize property as "gift.")

Sawyer, Max and Anne
  No grounds for eviction. (Turn off water periodically, up rent semiannually.)

Reynolds, Thomas, son of Daniel
Boat in disrepair. (Sell Laura B. at cost.)

Cyr, Gray and Cornelia
Third miscarriage, searching for answers. (Offer to
dig new well.)

Roy, Atticus and Mary
Joint history of depression. (Have Barstow refill
prescription at will.)

Arnold, Scott and Liv
Unclear ethnic background. No children. (Fertility
a question, discourage.)

Julie read the opaque lines a second time, then a third, listening for Depot's snores in the distant darkness while she continued to puzzle over the entries. These carefully recorded assessments and directives concerned tender truths to which no outsider should have any claim, nor any business overseeing. Favors granted, necessities withheld. Issues of fertility, ethnicity, mental health poked and prodded at, to be used how? For business, the running of what the grandmother had deemed an empire? Or as leverage, to establish indebtedness, even blackmail?

Julie stood up creakily, stretched in the penetrating dark. Tried the lights, leaving every switch flipped so that the house would be bathed in an electric glow once the power came back. She paused at the wall of windows, staring into blackness so complete, there seemed to be no delineation, no border, between herself and the night. At last, she made her halting return to the couch to focus again on the need at hand.

On and on Julie read, leaves covered with knife slashes of words and difficult-to-interpret instructions, clearly meant for the writer's eyes only. Hints and reminders about a body of knowledge, or a populace, too great to store in memory.

So much incomprehensible material that Julie began turning more than one page at a time, soon missing a few, and finally skipping whole sheaves. Until a name she recognized flashed by. Julie had gone past the page, had to flip back, and for a moment feared she had lost the one she'd spotted in the tightly penned morass and would have to start over again at the beginning. She ran her finger down the list of entries on the last several pages until she came to the one that had snagged her attention.

Cowry, Mike
Parents of mother threatened custody suit.
(Payment made on his behalf.)

It was the bottommost entry on the page. Julie turned the next leaf over slowly. This one contained names of people she'd met at the party, families of students, and also—

Hutchins, Andrew
In need of wife. (Ask Maddie Pew back to island.)

Scherer, Paul
$1,100.00/month or sister's care facility will discharge. (Up hourly.)

Manning, Chloe
   *Free residence. (Some concerns. Stipend for trial
   year before salary.)*

Then, jumping out at Julie from the ladder of lines—

Newcomb, Elisabeth ("Ellie")
   *Discount in perpetuity. (Gift for services
   rendered.)*

And finally, the last and most recent entry, the ink in which it was written bright, the paper beneath it scarcely touched or turned or handled—

Mason, Julie née Weathers
   *Daughter lost in infancy. Free residence. (Increase
   in salary.)*

CHAPTER FIFTY-TWO

The bank of windows against the rear wall of the house suddenly felt like a series of eyes through which the grandmother could see. Even without light. Suddenly the power outage seemed a factor in Julie's favor; at least she was basically invisible in here.

Still, a thousand pinpricks pierced her skin, and she thumped the floor beside her so that Depot would rouse and come running. When he did, Julie reached up, ringing her dog's neck with her arms. "Jesus, Deep," she muttered. "Who is this woman?"

The dog let out a worried bark.

And what effect was she having on her grandson?

Ellie was in this book. Why? Ellie had said she didn't know much about the Hempsteads, although clearly their background was known to her, as it must be to most of the islanders. What kind of discount could the grandmother be referring to, what gift and which services?

Julie needed to be sharp and on point to figure it all out, and right now she felt anything but, small and exposed and shaking. For a moment she rued letting that vodka spill out, then realized that if she hadn't sobered up already, she wouldn't have stood a chance at protecting herself, let alone Peter, from whatever kind of threat this might be.

No alcohol. But she had something that would at least help her sleep, allow her to wake up with some clarity in the morning.

Shining the flashlight for direction, Julie went to check the lock on the front door. Then, recalling the sight of the bolt turning from the outside, she walked back to find a dining room chair. Clamping the flashlight between her chin and her neck, Julie positioned the chair beneath the doorknob. It would offer an extra layer of privacy, a delaying tactic if a member of the Hempstead clan did try to make use of the darkness to come in.

With Depot at her heels, Julie trudged upstairs and located the amber vial she'd packed when she left Wedeskyull, aiming the flashlight beam in the depths of her suitcase.

No need for power during the night, and so long as this had the intended effect, she could awaken to daylight. Julie bit one of the pills Dr. Trask had prescribed in half and swallowed it dry. Before the cocooning effects of the meds could hit, she tucked herself and Depot into bed.

The electricity came back on just before dawn, flooding the house with caustic light.

Despite the muzzle of the medication in her system, Julie forced herself out of bed. It was Saturday, the day the grandmother collected rent. Peter needed to return the ledger, which meant that Julie had to get it back to him. She wanted it out of her house anyway. Its contents seemed no less sinister with the return of normalcy and power. The log was a dark, sullen presence, squatting on the downstairs couch like an overlarge toad. How many lives had been meddled with thanks to that book, the people living them not even aware that they were being moved around like pieces in a game? Dependent on the grandmother for their homes, their jobs, their livelihoods.

Just as Julie was now.

She looked down at the final entry in the ledger once more.

Free residence. (Increase in salary.)

Her house in Wedeskyull was rented, and Julie had officially terminated the family leave she'd taken from school. Her marriage was ending. If things didn't work out for her here on Mercy, where would she go, what would she do?

But it wasn't only about her own lack of options. Julie wanted to help Peter. She wanted to *teach* Peter, and the other children too. Guide them to figure out the people they were meant to become, the lives they were supposed to live.

First step—keep Peter in his grandmother's good graces, as well as herself if possible.

The easiest way to locate that hideout would be to go through the copse of trees behind the mansion. But Julie didn't want to appear anywhere near the grandmother's dwelling, especially not with the ledger in hand. She would have to retrace the trip she'd made from Ellie's cottage, a tricky task given how she'd gotten turned around in the woods, stumbling upon the downed tree only by accident.

Julie wedged the ledger into a day pack, its edges hard and unforgiving against her back. She was torn between going alone and taking Depot, but the dog was still sleeping, and Julie decided that she needed to be unobtrusive more than she needed protection.

The island was wrapped in a velvet hush of early morning mist as she entered the woods, whatever had caused last night's outage having retreated to an undetectable perimeter. The day pack rode uncomfortably between her shoulders, a reminder of the content she carried. Julie came to the tangle of trees that had barred her yesterday, then broke through a macramé of twigs. No fallen tree lay behind it. She stopped, breathing hard and debating which way to go. Julie took a few steps to the right, then the left. She knew better than to look for the mansion—it had been completely hidden from view until Peter revealed it. But none of this landscape looked familiar.

Julie scoured the ground for signs of disruption. When the tree fell, it had taken a mountain of earth along with it. But the dirt here appeared to be untouched.

Depot would've found it. Smelled Peter's lingering scent, shown her the way. Julie was just considering going back for her dog—except that too much time had passed already, the daytime sun risen in the sky—when she saw a few leaves spinning through the air. It was too early for leaves to be falling unless they were dead, no longer clinging to their branches. Julie walked toward the downward drift and came to Peter's hideout.

It rose up from the ground, trunk slimy with condensation.

Julie stood on tiptoes, patting around for a flat spot where she could leave the ledger, which glared at her like a black, rectangular eye.

From the mansion side of the woods, she heard footsteps, too heavy and deliberate for a young boy. Julie instantly dropped the ledger. She took a fleet second to make sure it was balanced, would stay put in a place dry enough not to damage the cover or leave traces of damp on its pages, before turning and running back the way she had come.

Callum stood leaning against the porch as Julie came walking out of the woods, a plastic cooler at his feet. Julie broke into a jog, crossing the expanse of sand and scrub in front of her house, while Callum lifted his hand in a wave. He looked better than anyone wearing suspenders and oilcloth waders had a right to.

"I thought I could show you better than I could tell you," he called.

"Show me what?" Julie asked, a smile lifting the corners of her mouth. Last night's confrontation with the grandmother's strange might and prowess, the power outage, even this morning's errand, all began melting away.

"Everything you've been asking about. Come on. We're going fishing."

CHAPTER FIFTY-THREE

Julie went inside and found Depot's portable bowls, then ran upstairs to change into warmer clothes. She grabbed her new slicker, taking a moment to smooth some healing gloss over her still sore lips—it would also help balance out the unflattering raincoat—while Callum stayed on the first floor, tussling with Depot who had clobbered him upon greeting.

The three of them headed through town toward the dock. The remnants of mist had cleared from the air, giving way to a light-filled, cloudless sky, the kind of day that whether in the mountains or on an island, defied the death throes of summer.

Julie got herself into Callum's dinghy, while Callum helped with Depot, cradling the dog's hind quarters as Julie snapped her fingers to encourage the dog. The little skiff lowered, accepting Depot's weight, but quickly rose back up again to the calm surface of the sea. Callum climbed in and started to row out to his boat.

It was called the *Mary Martin*, scrolling letters painted across its rear.

Or was it the stern? Julie realized how little she knew of this man's world, the world she'd come to live in. The *Mary Martin* was smaller than Julie would've expected—a lobster boat, not a ferry or pleasure craft, she reminded herself—but freshly painted and immaculately kept.

Depot ran in excited circles around the tight space, eventually settling down beside a tank with a spout that spit and spurted froth. Callum walked to the front of the boat and started the engine, a mild rumble underfoot. One arm draped comfortably across the wheel, he turned to Julie and said, "Want to get a few bugs off the bottom?"

They motored out to sea, the surface a sheet of blue denim, then Callum took the boat in a curve, sending up a glassy curl of water. Depot had fallen asleep in a patch of sunlight, soothed by the vibration of the engine. A whole poppy field of brightly striped buoys dipped beneath the surface as the boat chugged by.

"Lobsters like to tuck in around ledges," Callum said, gesturing overboard to something Julie couldn't see. "Right here's one of the best."

"How do you know it's there?" Julie asked, mystified. "Do you use equipment?"

"Well, there are depth finders," Callum replied, rolling the chrome wheel with one hand. "But the more experience a fisherman has, the less he relies on technology."

He lowered a pole over the side and hooked a rope beneath a yellow-and-red-striped buoy. "This is called a gaffer," he said, tugging a handle beside the wheel.

A winch started turning, then a trap broke the surface, raining seawater into the boat. Cold droplets struck Julie. Callum opened the trap, tossing out clumps of sea muck and flipping lobsters over to expose their bellies. He used a tool to cut a notch in the tail of one before throwing it overboard, measured another with a quick spread of fingers, and dumped two in a bucket, each move made with the swiftness and precision of a machinist.

"Wow," Julie said when he was done attending to the contents of the trap.

He looked at her.

"How…" She broke off, feeling stupid. "How'd you learn to do all that?"

Callum leaned back against the wheel. "I came to this island when I was a lad of just thirteen. My mam had emigrated to the States and kept moving us farther and farther north. This was the first place that reminded her of home."

A lilt in his voice had grown apparent. "Ireland?"

Callum gave a nod, staring out to sea. "My da was killed in the Troubles, and my mam had a brother in New York. But she died here on Mercy, only a few years later."

Was this what Julie had recognized in Callum that day on the ferry, the shaky, untethered quality of being an orphan? It didn't matter how old you were when you lost your parents. Nothing rooted you to the ground the same way once they were gone.

Callum braced his hands against the side of the boat, his body moving with the rise and fall of the water. "My boat is named for them both. The *Mary Martin*."

"That's lovely," Julie murmured. "You're an only child?" Callum didn't respond, lost to memory, so she went on. "Did you start fishing here on Mercy?"

"I have what the locals call a nose for fish," Callum said after a moment. "A couple of the fishermen took a liking to me—Walt Meyers and Frank, whose daughter I dated. Frank made me sternman and later sold me my first boat. I joined a gang on Mercy. It was where my mam brought us. I didn't want to leave."

Ellie had used the term, and the grandmother too. "Do you have to join a gang?"

Callum lifted the lid of a box built into the boat, releasing a fish market stink and revealing a slippery, silvery mass. He slid a couple of small bodies into a mesh sleeve, baiting the trap he had emptied, then dropped it overboard.

Crossing to the wheel, he pulled back on the throttle.

"It's everything, the gang you're part of," he said over the grumble of the engine. "It's what gives you the right to drop traps in certain places. And where those places are can spell the difference between living and dying, starvation and wealth."

Maybe the grandmother hadn't been so melodramatic after all.

"What happens if another lobsterman, you know, not in your gang, puts his trap down in your spot, say he finds it with the depth-finder thingy? I mean, it's the ocean." Julie gestured beyond the boat. "It's not like there are police."

Callum steered toward another buoy and lowered the gaffer. "Well, there are. But that's not how such a thing would be settled."

"Settled," Julie repeated.

Callum started the winch. "Dumping in the wrong spot is a sure way to find yourself hurting the next day. Some of the novices do what you say, follow a more experienced guy around, drop their traps on top of his. They find themselves with a string of cut lines, perfectly good traps sunk, and not too many can afford that kind of loss." Callum flipped open a second trap. "The nicer guys might try to fool the novice, lower a series of concrete blocks into an area no self-respecting lobster would burrow. And the nastier ones? They use their fists to prove their point. Or worse."

"That sounds pretty cutthroat. For seafood."

Callum began sorting the contents of his new trap. "Seafood can be a fifty-thousand-dollar tuna in Japan. And the stakes are no lower here. It's people's bread and butter. How they survive."

Julie thought about the kids leaving school to help out at the trap house or on their dads' boats. "Are people entering the field in good numbers? Young people, I mean."

"Fewer and fewer," Callum told her, tossing clumps of seaweed over the side. "There's a long apprenticeship program now, it's pricey to set yourself up with equipment, especially the new stuff, bait prices keep rising, and the cost of buying a house near the coast is astronomical. I know men who live six hours from where they tie up." Callum examined the underside of a lobster, then threw it back to sea. "Climate change means lobsters live farther out—more time on the water. And unless you have a relative to show you the ropes, it's tough to gain experience, which is paramount to success, as my story shows. Way more than the equipment you use or boat you drive."

What Callum had basically done was confirm the grandmother's whole diatribe. Thanks to his highliner dad, Peter was uniquely set up for success in a business that was in peril. Fewer young people entering meant a dying industry—or rather, one ripe for corporate takeover, the oceanic equivalent of big agribusiness. But lobstering could still accord a luxe, rich living to those lucky enough to be at its pinnacle. All that the grandmother had lived and built and loved could topple or rise in a single generation.

"All this space out here," Julie mused, watching the water lift and sway. "It's bigger than land, and there are scary enough things on land. You guys are brave who do this."

Callum let out a bellow so loud that Depot leapt to his feet.

Julie tried to walk forward, stabilizing herself against the side of the boat. The lobster that had been lying across Callum's palm had gotten a piece of his skin between its pincers. Callum gave a furious tug and flung the creature overboard.

He'd torn his hand, a bead of blood welling up.

Julie went to look for a first aid kit, but Callum's stark, dead tone stopped her.

"I'm a goddamned coward," he said.

CHAPTER FIFTY-FOUR

I 've been a fraud ever since I met you. Since the night we saved Depot anyway."

We was overly generous. "What are you talking about?" Julie said.

Callum swung the boat around a little too fast, and a plume of water struck her. Julie gasped, and Callum turned to face her, steering with one hand behind his back.

"What haven't you told me?" Julie asked, squeezing water from her shirt.

Water lapped the sides of the boat as it rose and sank with the swells, a cradle gently rocking. Callum turned the engine off with an abrupt twist of his injured hand. Blood had worked its way to his wrist.

"I'm not an only child," Callum said.

Julie might've told him that wasn't the biggest oversight, except she sensed the depths beneath his statement.

Callum wiped dampness from his face; he had gotten wet during his reckless spin as well. "And I know what it is to feel responsible for a tragedy even when you're not."

Julie's eyes stung with salt and sudden tears. "Oh."

Callum faced the sea. "My brother and I learned to fish together. He was better at it than I was, but not by much, and he was two years older. We had a rivalry—who could drive the boat faster, drop more traps, whose lobsters were legal, who used less bait, threw less crap back—we could compete over anything. Girls, our mam, losing our accents, Gaelic."

Julie smiled sadly. "Sounds like brothers."

"Yeah, well, one day it came to blows. I got a good slug in, and Declan went over the side. That wasn't so unusual, Dec was always throwing me overboard. As I got bigger, I took him with me when he had me in a good hold." Callum placed his hurt hand against his mouth. "Only this time, Dec didn't come back up."

Julie ducked her head. She well remembered the only reaction she could tolerate after Hedley had died. A near-invisible nod of acknowledgment, no surprise or dismay or sympathy conveyed because the lesser degree of that person's emotions just served to emphasize the fact that Julie's own were all-encompassing. Swamping her, pulling her down, while the other person would at least be left standing.

"I dove for hours, searching for Dec," Callum said. "Dove until it was dark, till I got so far away from the boat, it was a miracle it didn't smash on rocks and strand me. Wouldn't matter if it had—I didn't drive it home. Another lobsterman came and fished me out of the water." Planes in Callum's face shifted like tectonic plates.

Julie had grown chilly, the sun sliding behind a wall of clouds. Depot came and rubbed his body against hers, but even that wasn't sufficient to warm her.

"My mam died less than a year after Dec," Callum went on. "She died swearing it wasn't my fault. Trying to tell me how easily it could've gone another way, and Dec would've swum back up to the surface, laughing and taunting me for not being able to haul him into the boat. If the rock he hit his head on had been one inch deeper, or to the left, or the right. If the line he got snagged on were frayed and he could've pulled free. Or some scenario we never considered."

Julie wrapped her arms around her shivering frame. The meaning Callum was trying to impart felt crucial—for them both—yet cold had sapped her ability to follow.

"It was the last lesson me ma ever taught me," Callum said, voice deepening into an echo of the place he had come from. "How if me da had been standing next to a car that didn't explode. If he'd fallen off the wagon and stopped for a pint, or been sober and didn't stop for one, or didn't go to work at all that day. The whole endless stack of events we can't control or change—or maybe it's the opposite, that even if we did alter them, it wouldn't matter, because the thing we wish we could take back would just happen some other way. And to think otherwise is ruinous, and maybe arrogant too."

Julie was shaking too hard to nod. Her chin jabbed her chest and she flinched.

Callum suddenly saw. "Christ, sweetheart, you're cold."

The word momentarily stilled her shivers. Julie's parents used to call her that. Papa Franklin and Uncle Vern. No one else. David had never been one for endearments.

Callum strode over to a lidded bench. "Here," he said, returning with a pair of waterproof waders. "Perhaps it's fitting, as these were Dec's. He died before he stopped growing, so they should do well enough."

"Wh-wh-why am I putting on waders?" Julie asked, stepping into the thick rubber legs of the pants.

Callum took her by the elbow. "You'll see."

He led her over to a fifty-gallon barrel, the top third or so of which had been sawn off. Callum kicked a crate toward the side of the drum. "Use this as a step," he told her. "Get in."

Julie looked at the barrel, then back at him, her teeth clattering.

Callum gave her a nod.

Awkward in the waders, Julie lifted one leg over the rough lip of the barrel. Her foot touched a pool of water. The sensation was instantaneous, the liquid somewhere between bathtub hot and boiling. Balancing on the edge, Julie got her other leg over and lowered herself down. She moaned with sheer relief. "Oh my God. Why do you have a Jacuzzi on a lobster boat?"

Callum laughed. "You might not call it that if you knew what it's used for."

"I don't care if you use it for skinning mermaids," Julie replied, letting her hands skim the surface of the heated water. A pause. "Um, what do you use it for?"

He laughed again. "It's a dip barrel. Feel that coil you're standing on? It heats the water to kill the sludge on the ropes. Also handy for heating up a can of soup."

"Callum?"

"Ayuh?"

"How am I going to get out of this thing? I used the box to step in."

Callum slipped both hands beneath Julie's arms and helped her out, the rubber waders catching momentarily on the edge. Their faces drew near, and for a brief, searing moment, Julie anticipated a replay of their kiss, only less accidental this time. She felt her wet skin cling to his, their clothes a sheer layer between them, and a surge of longing seized her.

Callum placed one rough palm on her cheek. "No," he said, voice thick with sorrow, or desire, or both. "Not now, on a day that's been touched by memory." He took his hand away, but held it cupped, as if her imprint were still upon him.

Julie felt his on her face as well.

"The next time we kiss," Callum said, "it will be for real."

They emerged from the dock and walked through town.

"Thanks for the orientation," Julie said. "And the day, and the wisdom."

Callum gave an it-was-nothing sort of shrug.

"Seriously," Julie said. "Everything you told me. So helpful. Ellie's given me some background, but it's from her father, which is nothing like getting it right from the source or seeing things up close."

Callum stopped and faced her on the road. "What's from her father?"

Julie had kept walking, she paused a few feet away. "What Ellie has told me about lobstering. It all comes from her father."

Callum scrubbed his chin with one hand. "Ellie doesn't have a father."

"Well, I know that, he died—"

"No," Callum told her. "Ellie never had a dad at all."

Julie questioned Callum, then questioned him again, before they parted, but his certainty was unswerving. Ellie had come to live on Mercy around the age of thirteen, in the care of a single mother who never married, although she might've dated someone for a brief period, which still negated the possibility of a stepfather. In fact, Ellie's mother and Callum's had once tried to start a singles club, which Callum's mother used to jokingly and heteronormatively refer to as Mums without Men.

There was nobody home at Ellie's when Julie and Depot reached the cluster of cottages. They walked the rest of the way back, Julie swaying a bit as she made her way through the woods along its humped and knotted trail. She felt as if she were still on the boat, not yet fully returned to land, but the wobbliness really resulted from Callum's revelation. Why would her friend have invented a fictional father?

Depot's pace lagged as they crossed the scrubland. Julie had expected her dog to pick up speed when the house came into view, eager for food, but instead he slowed down, a rumble starting in his throat. Julie's thoughts shot to Peter and she felt a shard of fear. What if the missing ledger had been discovered?

She edged forward, taking a look around. Depot stuck to her side as if mortared there. Then he halted abruptly, his muscular bulk causing Julie to lurch. She stepped away from him, and his growls grew louder, crescendoing into a bark just as she reached the front porch.

Peter didn't stand in front of the door. No one did.

But on the mat lay the crushed and mangled body of a bird.

PART IV

NO MERCY

CHAPTER FIFTY-FIVE

G ully.
   Julie stared down at the desecration on her doormat, swallowing back the bitter taste of bile, her hands curled into fists of rage.

Gully would benefit from no last-minute resurrection this time, Julie observed with another surge of bile, no sirree. Its wings were bent and crumpled; its whole body had been pounded. The bird's gray form wasn't intact enough to be certain of its identity, but whether it was actually Gully or one of its brethren, the message was clear.

In her years as a dog owner, Julie had witnessed many a small, lurid death: creatures whose skeletons Depot chewed clean before Julie and David became habituated to the full extent of his appetite, and before the wilder parts of Depot's nature had been habituated to civilization, accidental tramplings beneath a puppy paw that didn't yet know its own force.

This wasn't that.

No inadvertent demise here. Something or someone had deliberately beaten the bird into a pulpy mass, its species indicated only by color, and a single, beetle-like eye. A note written in a loose, childish scrawl served to emphasize the purposeful nature of the kill.

the bird should've stayed in school and
so should you

Julie swung around on the porch, the flesh on the back of her neck prickling. The dying thrum in Depot's throat presented proof that they were alone. The scrubby yard sat empty, the distant woods still.

Julie was a country girl, born and raised, and country girls knew how to clean up messes. And they didn't shrink away from redness in nature's tooth or claw.

They also knew when to call the police—and when not to. Small town, small island, it made no difference. Inhabitants of such places didn't handle exigencies and emergencies like everybody else. The interconnections formed a web of closeness and protection, and also ties that shackled and bound. Although for a brief, painful second Julie wished for Tim or even one of her flawed, demoted family members, she didn't have that option here. This would've been approached a certain way in Wedeskyull, by the locals at any rate, and Julie was betting that island folk would handle it without due process as well.

She brought Depot a safe distance away from the bird—worried he would eat the poor thing, not get hurt himself—and told him to stay. Then she marched to the shed at the back of the house. There she found a shovel, and walked a few yards to dig a hole in a spot where the cliff plunged to the sea. It was as close as she could get the bird to the skies in which it once had soared. Julie returned to the front of the house and scooped the corpse up from the porch floor, keeping as many of its parts intact as she could. Making the trip for a third time, she lowered the bird into the ground and poured in a shovelful of earth.

Depot came and stood beside her.

Julie glanced at him. "Want to say a few words?"

The dog barked, foghorn deep.

"Perfect," Julie said, and scooped the remaining dirt into the grave.

She sat on the top step of the porch, knees drawn up to her chest and arms wrapped around her quaking calves, unwilling to go inside. Depot waited, tail extended, snout thrust forward. He would let her know if anyone approached.

Could Peter be responsible for something as gruesome as this? If he had succeeded in crushing Gully in his fist at school that day, the bird might've wound up in such a condition. And she mustn't forget Depot's near miss. If Julie and Callum hadn't arrived, then the sea would've swallowed her dog without sign or mention.

Committing either act had to be a cry for help, just as giving Julie the ledger had been. The only problem was, she had no idea what kind of help Peter needed.

Today had been an emotional rodeo ride, from the rush of togetherness with Callum to the shock of the murdered bird. There were times only a best friend—even a new one, even one who had lied—could restore a person to sanity and strength.

Ellie was drunker than Julie had ever seen her when she opened the front door.

No way could Julie ask about her place in the ledger now.

Ellie let out a laugh that turned into a gurgle, tugging Julie urgently inside before falling against the door to close it. Julie didn't wish for a drink herself precisely, but she envied the absolution her friend had been granted. Alcohol banished things so nicely, pressing them down beneath fathomless depths. If only they didn't tend to rise back up to the surface. And then act really angry that they'd almost been drowned.

Ellie peered closely at Julie, leaning in until the two of them touched.

"What is it? What's wrong?" Ellie said, all the S's a slurry in her mouth.

"I don't even know where to start," Julie said. "My dog's starving, we were with Callum on his boat—it was great but we didn't take time for lunch—and then when I got home, there was a warning, I guess, or a threat—"

"Hold on," Ellie said.

"—on my doormat—it was a bird, a dead bird, but not just dead—"

"Hold on!" Ellie said again, her voice teetering dangerously. "Holy shit, your life is like a movie. You've brought more excitement to this island than it's ever seen."

"Excitement—" Julie cried.

Ellie flapped a hand. "Sorry, sorry." More slurring. "Tell me about Callum."

"The bird part didn't stand out?"

"Callum sounds way more interesting." She snorted. "Come on, let's give Depot something to eat. Let me finish off this bottle, and you can get a jump start on some coffee." She twitched her butt, leaving the room. "Don't judge by a number," she trilled.

Two empty bottles stood on the small table, while a third had been given the old college try. Julie felt a pang of fear. Ellie was so tiny, and she'd consumed the equivalent of a dozen glasses of wine.

"How about we share that coffee?" Julie suggested casually. "There's something I'd like to talk to you about. Other than my filmic life." Asking Ellie about her pretend father would probably sober her up pretty quick.

Ellie clapped her hands over her ears. "Not the Hempsteads again," she pleaded, discarding both empties with disgust before taking a swig from the bottle that hadn't been drained. "I've had enough of them to last a lifetime."

"No, not the Hempsteads," Julie agreed. "Your father."

Ellie met Julie's eyes with the bottle still clamped to her lips. She lowered it, then went and dumped some dry nuggets out, overfilling a bowl. Depot set to them hungrily while Ellie took Julie by the hand and led her out to the living room. Attempting to sit on the couch, Ellie missed and came to a rest on the floor. Julie sank down a few feet away.

After a moment, Ellie said, "Damn pillow talk."

Julie winced. "We still haven't had sex. And if it helps, I didn't tell Callum much of what you've told me, as soon as I figured things out."

Ellie blinked blearily. "Unreal. I lie to you, and you try to make me feel better about it." She crawled forward to give Julie a hug, squeezing her with strength her small size belied. "You are the best friend I've ever had."

Julie extricated herself as delicately as she could.

"I'm sorry I lied," Ellie said, sniffling in sloppily. "Mercy is so small, you know? Everyone knows everything and everybody. When you came, totally new to the place, and I had the chance to give you the island's story, I guess it was just too tempting not to make up the place I always wished I had here."

"So your mother was never married to a fisherman?"

Ellie sponged at her eyes with a fist. "Just slept with a lot of them. That's how we came to Mercy. She followed a man she had hopes for, but he turned out to be a dub. Couldn't pull up a legal lobster if it'd been in a tank. My mother set her sights high, she didn't want just any fisherman. For all I know, my biological dad really was a highliner."

"Why did you guys stay? It had to be a tough life for both of you."

Ellie looked so furious that Julie instinctively scooted back.

Ellie registered it, and forced her face to relax. "Sorry. I just knew we'd end up talking about them. I can't get away from the Hempsteads no matter what I fucking do."

"What do you mean?" Julie asked. Had there been a reference to a Newcomb from the older generation in that ledger? If so, it hadn't stood out from the army's worth of entries. But the grandmother seemed to have most everyone on the island in her sights. She must have done something for Ellie's mother—or to her.

The look Ellie gave Julie was wounded, unfocused. It hurt, almost physically, to gaze back, yet Julie felt she owed at least that much to her friend.

"Why did we stay?" Ellie said. "Because my mother got tired of chasing and moving and fucking and failing. And she had a good placement with the Hempsteads."

CHAPTER FIFTY-SIX

R ememeber how I said I hated the trail that goes to your house from here?"

On the first walk the two of them had taken. Julie nodded.

Ellie bit her bottom lip. "The Hempsteads rented us this cottage. I'm sorry, I don't really own it, and in fact, I get a break on the rent or I'd never be able to afford a place here at all. Anyway, that path is the quickest way to the mansion. And my mother was always late. Mrs. Hempstead was such a demanding witch. She didn't care if my mom was a single mother, no source of support or way to share the work of raising a child. She had to be at the mansion to start work by dawn, before any of the residents woke up."

A staff of seven, the grandmother had said.

Ellie raced on, as if having started she wasn't able to stop. "My mother towed me along that trail, barely awake, with those trees, those nasty trees—" She broke off with a shudder. "Maybe I was still sleeping sometimes, dreaming, because it felt like the trees were reaching for me, they came alive. We'd turn at the lane, and when we got to the mansion, my mother would hide me in the basement. Mrs. Hempstead knew I was there, she must have, she knows everything. But she wouldn't let a servant's kid make an appearance. That huge, awful basement, the air so thick with cobwebs, I'd choke on them." Ellie swallowed arduously, as if her throat were cotton-packed now. "My mother would make it so she had errands to do for the mistress and master in town before the first bell rang, then walk me to school. We took the cliff trail so long as the weather was clear. That was better. I was free of the basement, for that day at least."

Julie frowned, holding up a hand. "I don't get it. Weren't you thirteen when you came here? Why didn't you stay home in the morning and go to school by yourself?"

But words and memories were continuing to pour out of Ellie, too fast to control. "Sometimes my mom would arrange things so she could come get me at school by the end of the day. Finish all the chores she had to get done, and there were always so many, acres of floor to sweep, every grain of sand picked from between the floorboards, the table laid, the beds turned down, these special butter biscuits that the Captain liked—"

Andrea! Julie heard the old man call, as if the past were the present, Ellie a teenager, and her mother still alive and there to do his bidding. The Captain seemed nice enough, courtly, inclined to be kind, and yet the way he had lived, the demands he'd made, inflicted suffering whose effects lasted to this day. Julie wondered if it was possible to be the holder of such riches and authority and not do the same. Peter, in years to come, for example.

And still Ellie's recounting went on, hurled out like something sicked up.

"—linens washed and hung to dry every damn day, curtains beat, fixtures shined, this intricate carving dusted with cotton twine wrapped around the tips of toothpicks. So much work that sometimes Mrs.

Hempstead wouldn't let my mom go, for hours and hours and hours, and I'd have to wait till after the teacher went home, all alone in the cove, scurrying away from the tide if it came in." Ellie took a gulp of air. "I was scared of the tide, and the woods, and that ghastly basement, but nothing scared me as much as—" She finally skidded to a halt, clutching fistfuls of her shirt to subdue her shaking hands and staring at Julie.

"As what?" Julie asked. She felt as if she were supposed to know.

Ellie continued to look at her bleakly. "Being alone in this house."

Julie drew back, taking a paranoid glimpse around as if whatever had so terrorized Ellie might be here right now.

"I've had to drink every day since my mom died," Ellie went on, "just to get through the night on my own. For me, being alone in a house is like drowning. You know that sensation when there's about to be no more air, and you know you've taken your last clear breath?"

Julie looked at her. She knew. She and Depot both did now.

Ellie's small form began to rock with sobs then, and Julie gathered her friend into her arms. She shrank from the smell of alcohol rising from Ellie's pores, but didn't let go. How had she missed this? Ellie was so wry and in-your-face funny. But she had the saddest soul of anyone Julie had ever known. She was even sadder than Julie herself.

Ellie continued to cry, using her shirt to stem the tide of tears.

Julie wouldn't tell Ellie to hush, or that she got it, or that it was okay. She wouldn't even pose the interruption of going in search of tissues. She just held Ellie, and murmured soft sounds, as if crooning to a new baby.

"She's a demon," Ellie sobbed. "That woman put me in hell every day. She puts everyone on this island exactly where she wants them."

All the names and lives and listings compacted in the grandmother's ledger. Tiny figures moved around at a whim on the playing board that was Mercy Island.

They hung out the rest of the day, Ellie sobering up with cup after cup of coffee. Then she and Julie took Depot on a long walk, avoiding the woods, while the dog kept a vigilant lookout, growling low in his throat as nighttime arrived to take over the island.

"Who would you seek out, if you needed to go above the grandmother's head?" Julie asked as they strolled. They were coming to the road that led to the Rainbow Pavilion and, by unspoken agreement, veered away. "I mean, you said she's involved with the school board and police and town government, which doesn't leave a whole lot."

"It sure doesn't," Ellie agreed, pointing the way to a lane that wound down to the sea.

Julie followed. "Say I was worried about a case of abuse. Paul Scherer said he's had reason to keep an eye on Eddie Cowry. How are social services handled on Mercy?"

Ellie stopped on a small rise of sand. "They're not."

Depot had continued loping forward, scenting the sea. Now Julie called him back.

"Actually, that's not true," Ellie went on. "I remember hearing about a call someone once made. A teenage girl was involved. It was an anonymous report, and a social worker got sent all the way out here. I think they talked about foster care, but that didn't seem ideal—move a kid off-island, and in the winter months when the ferry doesn't run, there couldn't even be supervised visits or whatever."

Julie nodded, keeping an eye out for Depot.

Ellie's face turned grim and shadowed. "So you know what happened?"

Julie shook her head.

"The Hempsteads volunteered to let the kid stay with them. No official foster parent certification through the state, wealth and resources speed paperwork along every time. The girl stayed at the mansion for a few months, then went back home, where everything started up again only worse because she'd talked." Ellie started backing away. "And *that* is what happens when you try to get outside help on Mercy Island."

Depot came bounding up from the beach, and Julie tugged him forward, shaking her head. "It's like the grandmother's a queen."

"She is," Ellie replied tartly. "This is a small fiefdom, but the Hempsteads rule over it like feudal lords, and Mrs. Hempstead holds the real power of the clan. They're the wealthiest family on-island, and they've kept those riches here on Mercy. Peasants never realize how short their end of the stick is, do they?"

"Well, not until there's a revolution," Julie replied. She was glad to see Ellie smile. "Did the grandmother hurt Peter's father? Did she kill him, or have him killed?"

"Whoa. Where did that come from?" Ellie's mirth faded, a light winking out. "You really do think your life is a movie."

It was Ellie who'd proposed the idea, but Julie merely said, "Is that a yes or no?"

Ellie spoke in a lilting manner. "Murder's a bit crude for Grandmama. She doesn't need to resort to such unpleasantries. Why would she stoop to dirty business, break any laws, when she can drive everyone to do what she wants of their own accord?"

"She drove Peter's father to his death? How?"

Ellie came to a stop in the dark. "Look, all I know is that during the last several seasons, Walter Meyers was bringing in less lobster. Then for a while, the market turned ugly—there was a collective on the mainland artificially deflating the price. Walter began having trouble keeping him and Martha and Peter afloat—pun intended—let alone carrying the grandmother and the Captain and their estate."

The sold-off heirlooms the grandmother had mentioned.

"A couple of times, when I was with Martha, I overheard the old woman hounding her son-in-law," Ellie went on. "Like, hard. What was wrong with him, was he going dotty like the Captain, he'd be a dub before long." Ellie's tone turned shrill and commanding. "Get on the water, spend longer days out, don't take any time off."

Julie cringed.

Ellie's voice returned to normal. "There're only so many traps a fisherman's allowed to drop, of course, but Walter had a great nose and the thought that he was losing it—even though there are always good years and bad, the sea is an uneven giver—made him susceptible to his mother-in-law's demands. Old Lady Hempstead knows where a person is weakest—and that's where she presses. She'll do it till you crack."

A person's weak spots. All compiled in a ledger.

"Walter wanted his streak back," Ellie went on. "He started going out, day and night in all sorts of weather. That much time at sea—a man is bound to get unlucky."

Nothing had actually been done. Nothing had to be done. The people did it to themselves. Because everyone had a weakness, a failing, a life loss, a need—or even just a moment when they were down. And with her ever-watchful eye, the grandmother ferreted each one out to make use of at the perfect, soul-digging, appropriate time.

Ellie watched as Julie accepted the truth, the weight of what she'd said.

"Come on," she told her. "Let's go home. It's getting cold." Ellie extended a hand toward Depot, who trotted over to Julie as they all walked back to the cottage.

Julie decided to spend the night at Ellie's. She didn't know how she'd ever let her friend stay alone again. Maybe they should become roommates. Live at the cottage together, let Peter return to his childhood home with his mother.

They fell into Ellie's bed, and as sleep surged toward both of them, Ellie mumbled that it was the first night she hadn't ended with wine since her mother had died. Julie offered up sleepy congratulations, mentally notching another square on her own calendar. She woke in the middle of the night, disturbed by Depot, whose throat thrummed as if it had a motor in it. He pulled Julie's shirt with his teeth, tugging her out of bed.

"What's the matter, Deep?" Julie asked, sleep-soft and slurry, trying not to wake Ellie. She had the feeling that Depot had been trying to rouse her for some time. The emotional upheavals of the day had knocked her out better than Trask's prescription.

A bulbous moon had risen in the sky, visible through the windows. But though Julie looked in every room of the cozy cottage, and around outside besides, she found nobody there, certainly not a tall, slight boy, putting together the pieces of another diabolical plan. Julie slid back into the bed as quietly as possible while Depot wedged his big body into the last slice of space in the room.

Ellie rolled over and began to mutter, gibberish at first, that slowly got clearer. "He molested me, you know."

"Who did?" Julie whispered.

"Donald. The dub." Ellie spoke in staccato stops and starts. "Guy my mother followed here. That isn't why she ended it, though." A short, sharp laugh that caused Depot to whine from the floor. "I think she would've stayed with Donald. Let him hang around this house forever, even when she was at work. If only he brought in a good haul."

Ellie fell asleep then as if she'd been pushed, and didn't utter another word all night, while Julie lay awake beside her for a long, long time.

CHAPTER FIFTY-SEVEN

I t was you, right?" Julie asked when glaring sunlight finally bestirred both her and Ellie the next day and they meandered into the kitchen. "Who called social services?"

Ellie busied herself with the coffee pot. "Mrs. Hempstead worked me harder while I was living there than she ever did my mom. Fucking Cinderella, that was me. Mrs. Hempstead came off better than Donald and his wandering hands, but only just."

Gift for services rendered, it had said in the ledger. But the grandmother had bills she couldn't possibly pay. She'd traumatized a young girl, all but enslaved her.

"And the Captain was worse than useless," Ellie added, getting down two mugs and taking out milk from the fridge. "He's supposed to have been a bro, a hero, a driver of ships?" She dumped sugar into one of the mugs. "He turned a blind eye to everything except his traps, and getting his damn biscuits at night."

She slid a cup across the table toward Julie, and silence fell. Everything seemed to have been said. They hugged goodbye at the door and Julie headed home with Depot.

Her gaze went to the doormat—a traumatic recapitulation—as soon as they emerged from the woods. Julie could see something lying on it all the way from here.

"Damn." She spoke out loud. "What is it this time, Peter?" She glanced down at Depot, but the dog trudged along beside her, tired but apparently unbothered.

Julie climbed the porch steps, leaning down and squinting at a bundle of sea oats and grasses, stems tied with a rough strip of twine. A note tucked under the twine read:

> Hope you're not sick of lobster yet. Meet me
> after lunch for another dip in the barrel? Cal

It was almost lunchtime already; she and Ellie had slept late. Julie had trouble taking the time to put together a sandwich, shower, change, and open a can of food for Depot, all the ordinary, mundane tasks that stood between now and the utterly not mundane get-together with Callum. She hurried Depot out of the house again without offering him a second serving. By the time they left the woods, the dog was exhausted, shambling along, his tail hanging so low, it glittered with sand. It came back to Julie, dreamlike and wavery, how much of last night Depot must have spent awake, standing guard by her side.

He could sleep on Callum's boat.

But as they neared the library, Julie's phone blew up with texts and voicemails and calls. The person trying to get in touch with her was Tim.

In his final message, Tim had said that he'd wanted to tell her in person, or at least its digital equivalent, rather than leave it on voicemail, but in case they didn't get a chance to connect, he thought she should know.

David was coming in on the next ferry.

Nearly dropping the phone, Julie scrolled frantically through the call log.

When had that message been left? What did Tim mean by the next ferry? This morning's? Was David on Mercy already?

Standing on the patch of road where her phone had come to life, Julie hit the receiver symbol to call Tim back. "Come on, come on," she muttered as the burr of a ringtone sounded in her ear. "Pick up."

"Jules!" Tim said. "It's good to hear your voice."

Till then, Julie hadn't realized how much she had missed him. "Yours too. But Tim, what's this about David?"

For a chief of police, Tim was woefully spare on details. All he knew was that David had remained in town after Julie had left, camping out in his office. And according to the postal worker, a packet of information had been sent to him about Mercy Island. When Tim asked David about it, he'd said he had ferry tickets reserved.

For this afternoon's crossing.

"What the what," Julie said on a breathy rush of surprise.

She could not imagine why David would be making a personal trip. Divorce papers could be mailed. All communication was going through their lawyers now anyway. Julie glanced at the time on her phone. She needed to find Callum, tell him their outing would have to be postponed.

"How is it out there?" Tim asked. "Everything you hoped?"

"Better," Julie replied. "And, well, worse too," she added honestly.

"Oh yeah? How's that?"

Julie would lose signal if she went to the dock to look for Callum. But the answer to Tim's question was complicated. "Mercy is kind of like Wedeskyull, back when the old guard was still in power. Uncle Vern and his father before him."

"Really?" Tim said. "I remember those days. That doesn't sound good."

"It's good and it's bad," Julie responded. "People trying to keep things as they were."

Until that moment, Julie hadn't been able to find a mote of empathy for the grandmother's position, but she suddenly understood it. Resisted her stance, knew it wasn't fair or just, and would never work ultimately, but now got a glimmer of the reasoning behind it.

How people who had survived tough conditions bred of a tough land couldn't be expected to greet with unalloyed joy an influx that was going to cast Eve out of Eden, introduce new creatures to a roiling, tumultuous stew of the unknown, painting the old, whitewashed sameness with a rainbow of change. It was a brutish, battle-filled process, the tug-of-war between old and new. Julie suddenly missed her hometown, and felt proud of it with a sharp, fierce pang. The locals might frequent the diner, the expats the pricey café, but at least both existed side by side. The pristine homogeneity on Mercy had yet to be complicated by the humps and fissures and crenulations Wedeskyull had tolerated, summoned, welcomed to its fore.

"I'm having trouble following you," Tim said. "Are you all right out there?"

All the way from the mountains of her homeland to the tiny, seaswept island that had become her home for now, a swell of doubt quested, then fell. "I'm better than all right," Julie told him. "I'm needed again for the first time since Hedley died."

"I haven't heard you say her name like that in over a year. Just right out loud."

How sad that was, Julie thought. For Hedley, and for her too.

"What do you mean about being needed?" Tim asked.

Julie started to walk, hoping the connection would hold. "I have this student I'm trying to help. He seems to be in trouble." She hadn't expected it, but suddenly she was pouring out the whole story, Peter's behavior, his history, the entrenched forces at work on the island. In addition to being her oldest friend, Tim was also a cop, and a damn good one, so any perspective he might have on the situation would be valuable.

"Have you been in touch with the old teacher?" Tim asked once Julie had finished. "I bet she'd have some information to offer."

The idea was so good, and so obvious, Julie wondered why she hadn't thought of it herself. It was as if the island had become not just her whole world but *the* whole world, nothing and nobody existing beyond it.

"Should I be worried, Jules?" Tim asked. "You're all alone out there."

"Nobody's tried to hurt me," Julie assured him. "I think Peter actually likes me. His actions have been limited to a bird that, I'm sorry, isn't exactly an endangered species around here, I can hear about a zillion squawking overhead right now, and—"

"—your dog?"

"I'll watch out for Depot," Julie said firmly.

The signal was getting spotty; it took a moment before Tim's reply came through.

"Do you want me to come out there? Because I will. I don't have any authority or jurisdiction obviously, but I'm owed some vacation time, and I could be there as a friend."

The quiet hush of home, from what seemed a million miles away, brought tears to Julie's throat. Luckily, the connection was probably poor enough by now that thickness in her voice wasn't audible. "I'll call you if I need to, I promise." No response from Tim, hopefully he could still hear her. "Anyway, at the moment, I'm not even here by myself. I've got a date to delay and a soon-to-be ex-husband to contend with."

Before Tim could say anything about the date part, the call dropped.

Julie couldn't find Callum on the dock, and squinting between sunspots toward the sea where the lobster boats were moored, Julie didn't see the *Mary Martin*. Hoping Callum would think to come get her at the schoolhouse, Julie led Depot in that direction.

It was time to track down last year's teacher.

CHAPTER FIFTY-EIGHT

When they reached the school, Depot yawned hugely, refusing Julie's offer of food and staggering around in a circle before dropping onto the floor in the cramped space of the teacher's room, where he promptly fell asleep.

Julie searched the filing cabinets, the drawers of the teacher's desk, and even the supplies stowed under the stage, but she couldn't find anything that identified the prior teacher by name. Then she realized she already knew it. The teacher had to be the person listed in the grandmother's ledger above the entry for Julie. She too had been given a free residence, and there'd been details about her compensation begging an explanation that Julie still couldn't supply. A stipend. Whereas Julie had been given a salary jump.

The grandmother preferred Julie as teacher for some reason, which after reading the ledger, was the opposite of gratifying. Instead, the fact seemed to present a strangling hand.

Julie closed her eyes and tried to picture that spider's scrawl, those vicious, life-invading letters. Zoë Manning. That was it. She booted up the computer, but any Zoë Manning who was a teacher either had an extremely limited online life, or else all her social media accounts were set to *private*. There was a Zoë Manning hand model, and one who had a lifestyle blog.

Julie finally stooped to LinkedIn, figuring that if Zoë had just left a position, she was probably networking hard. There she found a Chloe Manning who listed educator for her profession. Upon further thought, *Chloe* did seem like the name she'd seen in the ledger. Julie sent a message explaining who she was and sharing a little of her experience on Mercy, before asking if the woman had any relevant details she could add. Then Julie went to check on Depot, still wedged into a spot on the floor, the high arch of his side rising and falling in sleep.

Walking back to her desk, Julie decided to take care of some grading and student assessments, and was soon lost to a pile of papers. The work-induced stupor didn't shatter until a reply from Chloe popped up on the screen.

> r u in a place where yr phone works? id rather not
> put this in writing

She had sent Julie her number.

Julie stood up slowly behind the desk. On the one hand, it was a more receptive response than she had anticipated; the most she'd been hoping for was that Chloe might send along a few thoughts, maybe agree to trade email addresses. On the other hand, Chloe's note was almost sinister in its terseness, and implication of scrutiny.

Depot was still sound asleep. Julie stooped to drop a kiss on his head, setting out food and water for when he woke up. Then she left the school, heading toward the part of the winding path by the library where Wi-Fi would kick in.

Chloe Manning answered the call the instant it went through, her greeting lighter than Julie's initial impression had suggested.

"So you're the new victim," she said.

"Yikes," Julie replied. Then, "Thanks for agreeing to talk to me."

Chloe let out a laugh. "I don't mean to alarm you. Mercy Island is just a weird place." A pause. "Isn't it?"

Julie took a look around the tiny patch of library lawn as she thought about how to answer. It's a place I've fallen in love with. It's a place that scares me. It's a place where I've found people to tether me to the earth once again. And that comes at the cost of worrying about those people, caring about them so much it may hurt. In the end she settled on, "It definitely offers challenges for a teacher."

Chloe snorted. "Understatement."

"What were those challenges like for you? If you don't mind sharing."

"Not at all," Chloe said breezily. "That's why I wanted you to call." She took a breath. "So, at first I was all loving on the island, just like you are right now. I'm a person who has a lot of get up and go, and I like putting my own stamp on things."

Julie was just picturing how well that would go over on Mercy when a pair of women she thought she recognized—perhaps they had older children in the school—came walking up the path, pushing toddlers in strollers.

Julie smiled as she stepped aside to let them pass, and they gave terse nods in return.

"Are you there?" asked Chloe.

Julie wasn't sure whether she imagined the look one of the women gave her as she turned back in the midst of wrestling her stroller up a stack of stone steps to the door. Questioning, maybe even disapproving. As if Julie didn't have the right to be talking on the phone, were doing something wrong, or unseemly. Probably she was just being paranoid. Still, the encounter made her take a few steps away from the populated library path—story hour was about to begin—and conceal herself in a grove of trees.

"Yes," she said hurriedly. "I'm here."

"Anyways, then I started to get some pushback," Chloe said. "You know, not our way, do it more like this, no, like that, kind of thing. Which was fine. I'm the sort of person where if I get kicked, I just get right back up again, you know?"

"Uh-huh," Julie said. In her experience, the kind of person who tended to get right back up after being kicked had never been kicked very hard.

Chloe pitched her voice low. "At least I used to be."

"What do you mean?" Julie asked.

"Well, none of that is the reason they fired me," Chloe said.

"Fired you?" Julie echoed, thinking back. "I thought you resigned."

"Is that what you were told?" Her tone darkened further.

"Um…" Julie wasn't sure why she was protecting Laura Hutchins, or the grandmother. "Maybe it was more like implied."

Chloe went on as if Julie hadn't spoken. "Because my compensation package was all these soft things, housing and a stipend, I can't even collect unemployment. Not to mention the lack of references. I asked Maryanne Hempstead for one, and you know what she did? She laughed in my face. That awful, queenly laugh she has… Have you heard it?"

Julie wasn't sure that she had. The grandmother was such an ice pillar of control. Restrained amusement was as far as Julie could recall her going in terms of humor.

"That place ruined me, Julie… That's your name, right?" Chloe spoke in a hiss. "It ruined my life. You should really watch out, Julie. And I should probably go."

Chloe's account, albeit dramatic—this island seemed to pull for that—had stirred the hairs on the back of Julie's neck. A breeze coming in off the ocean peppered her skin with goose bumps. She peeked between a screen of leaves, making sure she was alone.

"Wait," Julie said, almost pleaded. "What was the reason they fired you?"

"What?"

"You said none of the new stuff you tried was why they fired you."

Chloe's response, though disturbing, didn't surprise Julie; it was almost like having something confirmed.

"They fired me because one of the students liked me too much. And how fucked up is that? I was doing *too* good a job. A kid was talking more than usual in class, asking if he could stay after school, and I let him. He was dealing with some shit at the time, a death in the family. They let me go because I tried to help. Try explaining *that* as a résumé gap!"

The library door opened, noise spilling out from within, a barrage of young voices and clapping and laughter. Story hour was still going on obviously, but the mother who'd passed Julie before appeared on the stone stoop, without her child in tow.

Chloe's voice splintered, high-pitched, almost hysterical. "And why do you think they didn't want me to get close to this kid? What do you think they were trying to keep me from finding out? I don't know, Julie, but I bet it's big. I bet it's really, really—"

Chloe broke off. There was a fearful quality to the sudden stop; it was as if she were trying to bring herself into line because wherever she had gone after fleeing Mercy didn't matter, couldn't get her far enough away from the person who was listening, watching, observing with a hawkish eye.

The mom on the library stoop took the stone steps as one, an acrobatic leap.

Julie stepped deeper into the trees. She couldn't tell if the mom had seen her here or not.

"Peter Meyers isn't who you think he is," Chloe went on at a whisper, as if the mere act of saying his name might bring down retribution. "One thing I can tell you is that whatever he's up to, it's not what you think."

"What is it then?" Julie whispered back.

This was ridiculous. She was hiding in the trees like a little kid her-self—or a criminal—and why? Because she was on the phone? She walked back onto the path.

The mom headed down it at a fast clip, almost as if getting a running start.

"I don't know, but Peter's not just a grieving, loss-stricken boy. And not a diagnosable, oppositional defiant one either. I mean, cruelty to ani-mals, is that what you said in your note? How textbook is that? Peter wasn't that bad when I had him; he's obviously getting worse. Or *acting* worse." Chloe let her emphasis settle in the air. "He's playing you, Julie, just like he played me. Every single thing that boy does is false. Peter Meyers is always putting on a show."

The mother rushed past then, bumping into Julie so hard that her shoulder rattled and the phone flew out of her hand.

And Julie stood there, listening to the echo of Chloe's words in her ear. That last statement had been said with such dire derision that it momentarily blotted out the question of whether the woman's attack had been heedless, or premeditated and deliberately staged.

CHAPTER FIFTY-NINE

J ulie heard the grandmother's phantom order in her head, like a line from a movie, as she rubbed her sore arm and stared after the mother, aghast. *You must end that phone call at all costs.*

Impossible. Even if the grandmother did somehow know that Julie was on her phone—had eyes and ears all over Mercy—how could she possibly have learned who Julie was talking to? Unless any call was off-limits, constricted, the island a world unto itself not only because Julie needed such a place, but also because it needed to be so for its inhabitants.

The mother turned around on the path, still in a hurry, jogging backward, hand clapped to her mouth. "I am *so* sorry, Ms. Weathers! Diaper emergency during story time!"

Also impossible. There were other moms in there with diaper bags.

Although the mothers of Mercy did seem less loaded down with detritus, the accoutrements of early childhood, than parents were in other locales. Their strollers not supersized, a morning's activity not cause to pack as if for an around-the-world cruise.

"It's okay," Julie called back. She went and retrieved her phone.

The call had ended, so Julie texted Chloe a quick explanation, before saving her as a contact and beginning to walk away from the library. At least any told-you-so text from Chloe wouldn't come through for a while.

A few seconds later, the mournful wail of a foghorn announced the ferry's arrival.

Julie walked toward the dock, watching for David to disembark. The sight of him struck her like a club to the knees. Not with memories, or still extant love. Instead what nearly bowled her over was how hard it was to believe that she had married this man, had a baby with him.

He looked like a stranger.

She worked up a smile as David stepped off the ferry, placing one hand on the looped rope of the railing to steady himself once he was back on dry land.

"Rough crossing?" she asked, reaching to take the backpack he wore.

David shrugged the pack off gratefully. "I didn't think you'd know to come."

Julie slipped the straps over her shoulders. She recognized this backpack; they'd taken it on many a hike. "You were clearly aiming for the element of surprise."

"Not really," David said. "You're just a difficult person to get hold of these days. And I didn't want to say this in a message or email."

Julie acknowledged the point. "Say what? What made you come?"

David's face was starting to look less sallow. "Is there somewhere we could go and get a—"

Julie girded herself in case David suggested a drink.

"—little quiet? I have something I'd like to discuss."

He looked serious, and although the effects of a rough boat ride could mimic those of a hangover, Julie was pretty sure that David was sober.

"I'll take you to see the island's best view."

They stopped in town to buy coffee, then carried it to the cliff trail, whose location Ellie had described the night Julie slept over. The trail crept up from the schoolhouse cove, and after a few yards, Julie and David came to a flat ledge overlooking the sea. Both it and the sky were the color of blue jeans, no apparent weather coming in. Perhaps the crossing hadn't been that hard, and David was just a clumsy seaman. The idea gave Julie an uncharitable nip of pleasure. She sat down, patting the rock beside her.

"How's Depot?" David asked, taking a seat.

Julie blew on her coffee. "Good overall. Some adventures. I can take you to see him; he's right down there in the—"

David cut her off. "Probably not the best idea. I took Depot on so many drunk walks, I think he might be a trigger for me."

"A trigger?" Julie repeated, trying to wrap her head around the fact that David didn't want to see their dog.

He looked out to sea. "This is quite a spot. You were right."

Julie accepted the diversion, studying sparkles on the water. "Calendar worthy."

"I meant the whole island," David said. "I thought you might be doing a geographical, as we say in group, but it looks like you were right to come."

The statement felt presumptuous. "Why are you here, David?"

He set his coffee down on the ledge. It wobbled a bit, and Julie reached out to steady the cardboard cup, nestling it in a pocket of stone.

"I'm in recovery," he told her.

"That's great," she replied. "So am I."

David laced his fingers together and looked at her. "AA?"

"No," Julie replied. "The population is pretty small on-island—I don't even know if there's a group. And I wouldn't necessarily want to announce my problem to all the parents who would find out. But twelve-step isn't the only way to get sober."

"It's not," David acknowledged. "But it's been instrumental for me. And I'm trying to work the ninth step, which is really the one that hangs over my head. Owning up to things you did that hurt the people you love. Trying to make amends."

"What do you have to own up to with me?" Julie asked.

David shook his head. "You always did have a way of cutting to the chase." He picked up his cup and took a sizzling gulp, then rubbed his brow, the way he used to do to ease a hangover headache. "You know how Hedley was sick the night before?"

No need to ascertain which night before. There could only be one such night for the two of them, now and forever. Julie tasted coffee, bitter and undigested, in the back of her throat. She had a feeling that what David was about to say would call for a drink stronger than this, maybe stronger than any that existed in a bottle.

He drank down the rest of his coffee. When he set the cup back on the ledge, his hand was shaking so badly that the cup overturned and rolled off the edge.

They watched it vanish beneath a foaming wave.

"David," Julie said quietly. "Talk to me."

Neither of them was used to communicating without the lubricating effects of booze. But David responded at last. "I gave Hedley her Benadryl that night. Remember?"

Something in his tone shot an icicle spear through Julie. "Yes."

"Well, I gave her too much." David whispered it, but the statement was as loud as shattered glass. "I was pretty drunk, and some spilled out of the cap, and when I added more, I lost track of how much. I might've given her a dose and a half. Maybe even two."

The sun burned Julie's eyes, causing spots to bob in her vision.

David turned to her, and his face looked like it had been ravaged, as if an animal had attacked him, were attacking him still. "Do you understand, Julie? You've carried all this guilt around. You thought you were responsible because you happened to be out with Hedley that day. But it was me all this time. I killed our little girl."

David's mouth wrenched with fear, venal and ugly. "They could charge me with something. Endangerment of a child. Accidental homicide. Maybe even manslaughter. If you tell Tim about this—for all I know, they will."

Julie was seized by a spasm of rage so strong it left her trembling. She felt as if she could've shifted the rock ledge they sat on, hurled it into the sea. She hated David for keeping this from her, for letting her bear the blame, although he believed it to have been shared, or even his alone, all along.

David took both her hands, his flesh lizard-like, dry against hers, and she had to work not to pull free. "Can you forgive me? You know the state I was in. The state we both were in. Our marriage was over—should've ended years before—but drinking glazed that over, kept us from admitting it." He looked at her with the zeal of the convert.

Julie didn't speak. She couldn't.

David dropped her hands. "Well," he said with a rasp in his throat. He got to his feet on the ledge, wiping his mouth with the back of one hand. "I leave it in your hands, what to do next. Whatever you decide, I will make my peace with."

Julie stared out to sea.

"Can you just tell me one thing?"

Julie shifted to look at him.

"When does the return ferry depart?"

She almost laughed. No repeat request for forgiveness, nor a question about whether she thought his self-flagellation was warranted. Well, she sure wasn't inviting David to stay over. She wouldn't mind if she never saw him again in her life. "Not till the morning. But there are always men hanging around by the dock. You can charter a boat."

She sat for a long time after David disappeared down the trail, and what prompted her to move was a change that had nothing to do with the guilt she had carried, or her view of her husband, their marriage, and their daughter's last hours alive.

It was the weather.

Grayed-out vista, opaque clouds blotting the ocean from view. Julie shivered, her clothes gone damp and speckled with moisture. She stood up on the ledge, surprised at how slippery the rock felt underfoot. She hadn't brought David very far along this trail, but she could no longer see the cove.

She needed to get back to Depot. He would be wanting company.

A sudden stiff breeze was sufficient to sway her, and she dropped onto her hands and knees to keep from going over the edge. Tears stung her eyes. Why hadn't anybody warned Julie that the wind by the sea could mimic the high, shrill sound of a baby crying? Hedley crying anyway. With her stuffed noses, she'd often had an especially pained cry. Julie used to cringe at its sound, use a pillow to block her ears when there was nothing she could provide in the way of comfort. She missed that cry now, would do anything to hear it. She wondered if David would too. Julie rose shakily to her feet, touching strands on mossy rock, and feeling soft, sweet hair.

She tried to mentally re-create her steps back to the schoolhouse. Less than a quarter mile, but she was beginning to understand why Ellie had deemed this trail usable only in good weather. Though it was simple to maintain her bearings—the direction from which the mist blew in off the ocean, the fact that she was descending—a single misstep and Julie would slip off the edge just like David's coffee cup had. There was not one thing to hold onto. And while the cliffs weren't terribly high at this point, there were rocks beneath the surface of the water, and an under-tow that would be hard to fight.

Julie felt for the path, patting around with her palms. A hairpin line of sand and gritty dirt. Amazing how simple taking this trail was when you could see it, and how daunting it was to do blind. Rising to her feet, Julie began to shuffle forward, testing each step to make sure there was solid ground beneath. She couldn't see her shoes. The incline steepened—indicative of a plummet over the side, or just the path dropping to the cove?

By the time Julie tripped over the first seaweed-slicked rock and stag-gered onto the beach, she was filled with an electric hum of paranoia. Even the weather seemed to be conspiring against her, as if the grand-mother had the power to control that too. The fog distorted the shape of things two inches in front of her. Julie didn't feel sure of what was real in her life, and what had been orchestrated by invisible hands. David's revelation prompted other thoughts to crowd into her mind. Why had Julie's salary been upped after Chloe was fired? Had she met Callum by chance or design? Was Peter hiding something, or was something being hidden from him?

Cold seawater swirled around her ankles; she was back on level ground. Sucking in a breath of relief, Julie began to feel for boulders, taking their dimensions so that she could climb over humped backs or weave between stone walls toward the schoolhouse.

Lifting one leg over a large, bulbous rock, Julie slid down its other side, then began to pat the air before her, trying to determine where the next obstacle stood.

Instead of kelp or stone, she touched the solid chest of a man.

CHAPTER SIXTY

Depot gave a bark of reunion, and launched himself at her out of the fog.

"Christ," Callum swore when they'd each confirmed the other's identity. "What were you doing up there in fog as dense as this?"

Seawater lapped Depot's paws, and he bounded away to get clear of it.

"I won't again, I promise," Julie said, the ebb of adrenaline leaving her weak and wobbly on the rocks. "How did Depot get here?"

"He was barking up a storm in the schoolhouse when I came to do the lights. I let him out," Callum said. "You must be part mountain goat to have gotten down that trail."

"There are five-thousand-foot peaks where I come from," she reminded him. "And snow and ice and whiteouts and—"

Callum grabbed her hands, cradling them between his salt-roughened ones.

Depot had been racing above the high-tide line amongst gummy masses of kelp, nipping at them, then growling in displeasure at their taste. He paused, a tubular length dangling from his teeth as he observed them.

"Just thank God you're okay," Callum said, still holding onto her hands.

And Julie thought, this is real. No matter who or what the grandmother might be controlling behind the scenes on Mercy Island, it wasn't, couldn't, be any part of this.

Back home that night, Julie put in an emergency call to Dr. Trask's service, knowing the physician would call her back. He listened to her description of the situation, then gave her the assessment she had been pretty sure would come.

Next, Julie opened her computer and composed a brief email.

> Dear David: As we both know, they did an autopsy on Hedley and no traces of medication were found in her system. She died more than sixteen hours after receiving her last dose, whether it was the right amount or not. The ME, the pedi, the cops all agreed.

Julie knew David would take her words as deliverance. He didn't yet know that absolution came with its own breed of burden.

She typed a few final lines.

> I don't think it was anything you or I did. In a way, I wish that it were, that one or both of us could've prevented what happened to our daughter. Because one day it might hit you—the fact that nothing and nobody could is even worse than what you've been living with. Julie

---

Monday morning dawned gray beneath a cotton-batting sky. Inside the schoolhouse, Julie started a fire, spreading her raincoat over the ornate metal door of the stove to dry. She fed Depot a second breakfast, then let him play a solo game, scrabbling between the legs of the student desks while she organized the day's lessons.

Somebody pulled at one of the barn doors, drawing it open effortfully, and Julie frowned, checking the time on the clock on the wall. School didn't begin for another forty minutes. She walked to the front of the schoolhouse and heaved the door the rest of the way ajar.

Outside stood a man encased in oilcloth waders and a raincoat. As he edged into the classroom and tugged off his hood, his identity became clear. It was the man from the video reel Laura Hutchins had shown her, and Julie now remembered the reason she'd recognized him in that still shot, had thought that she knew him.

She'd also seen him in her own hometown Target.

This was the man who had steadied her, looking at her in a strange, probing way when she'd bumped into him coming out of the store.

Depot came and stood beside her, though he didn't bark or growl.

The man glanced down at the dog nervously, taking a few steps to one side. "Name's Mike Cowry. I'm Eddie's dad."

"Mr. Cowry," Julie said. "It's nice to see you again."

"Don't believe we've met," he replied. "It's hard for me to get time off the boat. The owner's been working me hard. Why I took so long to respond to your note."

Julie faced him headlong, and the man withdrew a few more steps.

"No, we haven't met," she agreed. "I meant that it's nice to see you on-island."

"Shit," Mike Cowry said, drawing the word out. "You recognize me?"

Julie hooked her fingers around Depot's collar and walked him into the teacher's room. Then she went over to the fire, rearranging the crocodile hides of burning logs with a metal poker. "Why don't you tell me how you came to be so near my little town?"

Mike Cowry averted his gaze. He didn't seem like a man who, once confronted, would be inclined to put up much of a fight, and his next words confirmed that.

"Mrs. Hempstead paid me to go. Never earned that much all at once in my life."

"And why did Mrs. Hempstead pay you?" Julie asked.

He still didn't make eye contact. "I was supposed to keep tabs on you for a few days. She likes to do that if they bring in somebody from away. The doc, our pastor."

Those mute calls and hang-ups, Julie's feeling of being watched. Back when she was still drinking, and spending the night in her car, and driving around while grieving with such force, it'd nearly broken her.

Mike Cowry seemed to follow her thoughts. "Don't worry, nothing you did surprised no one. I had to report back, and the old lady liked what she heard."

Julie felt as if she'd been seen in the bathroom naked—which, for all she knew, she had. "What are you talking about?" Her gaze shot to the front of the schoolroom to make sure no early comers had arrived and could overhear the hysterical tenor of her tone.

Depot trotted in from the hallway, hailed by her cry, but halted when Julie held out a hand.

Mike Cowry shrugged beneath the heavy folds of his raincoat. "You were someone who'd had the shit kicked out of her by life, right? I seen that and Old Lady Hempstead said we could help. You know, let the island sort of nurse you back to health."

Yeah, right, Julie thought. That's what the grandmother wanted for her.

Mike Cowry's gaze flicked to take in the distant recesses of the room. "The old lady also asked me to give you a message today."

"She knew you were coming." Not a question, a statement.

She knows everything, Ellie had said.

Mike Cowry dug a balled-up piece of notepaper out of his raincoat and uncrumpled it. "'I believe we have enough,'" he read aloud, the imperious words sounding strange on his tongue, "'not just to remove you from this post, but to cast doubt as to your fitness for the teaching profession in general.'" A note of apology snuck into his tone. "That's probably 'cause of me. I took pictures when I was in New York. Of you outside. And your recycling."

Julie flinched with a near-physical humiliation. She and David had always gone to the dump themselves. Ostensibly a money saver, it was really because they wouldn't have wanted anyone—not even the privatized collection service used by the town—to see the number of bottles that piled up in their bins.

Mike Cowry jammed the piece of paper back into his pocket.

Back bowed with defeat, Julie went to add another log to the fire. She stared into the shower of sparks that shot up, heat searing her face, soldering the tears that stung her eyes. At last she brushed wood dust off her hands with a couple of claps, and turned.

"I think it would be best if we spoke about your son," she told Mike Cowry. "I'm his teacher, and if Mrs. Hempstead tries to say otherwise, then I will fight her, go to the school board even if she does sit on it, because I *want* to be Eddie's teacher, and the other children's too."

Mike Cowry finally met her eyes.

"So let's get a couple of things cleared up," Julie went on. "Eddie needs to be in school regularly. That's the law, and he'll fall behind if he isn't. We have a very full year in store for us. Is that going to be a problem?"

Mike Cowry hesitated a moment, then said, "I'll make sure he's here."

"Thank you," Julie replied. "Finally, one point that's a bit awkward to bring up, but I have to. Do you discipline your son physically?"

Mike Cowry's face turned the color of the embers Julie had just been prodding. "Hit him, you mean? Do I hit Eddie?"

Julie gave a nod.

"Never!" Mike Cowry said. "My son's all I got. I would never hurt that boy."

It wasn't unfettered proof, but Julie would've bet a decent sum on the truth of the man's declaration. "Nonetheless, it was implied that you did." A pause. "The slander-blackmail game goes two ways on this island, Mr. Cowry." Dozens of ways actually. Hundreds over the years.

Mike Cowry's brow knit. "Someone told you that?"

Julie went to the doors to let him out. "Thank you for coming by. I look forward to seeing Eddie a little later this morning."

CHAPTER SIXTY-ONE

By the time school started, sunshine had blotted out the rain and burned off the last shreds of fog. Julie flung both barn doors open and the students streamed inside, laughing and chattering over their shoulders. They greeted Depot with hugs and pats, then assembled themselves in their seats in record time.

Hands shot up, and Julie called on each child as quickly as she could.

"We have a surprise, Ms. Weathers!"

"We have a surprise for you!"

"There's a prize!"

Julie leaned down to smile at the kindergartner. "A prize?" she repeated, walking to the blackboard and writing down the word. "How wonderful!"

Though Peter didn't add his voice to the chorus, even he looked pleased, all hints of brutality vanished for now, in addition to the strange, manipulative qualities Chloe Manning had described. Peter's blue eyes were bright, eagerness openly written on his face.

"What a coincidence," Julie said, spelling out that word on the board as well. "Because I also have a surprise for you." *S-u-r-p-r-i-s-e*. She turned back to the class. "Can I get a volunteer to climb up to the loft?"

Waving hands filled the air, and the boy in seventh grade began to go. Julie guided him back to his desk, explaining the classroom rules about being called on again, then selected one of the fourth graders instead, the girl's face glinting with pride at her assignment. Once she was up there, Julie ducked behind the velvet curtain and called out directions. "See that lever?"

"Yes!" the fourth grader shouted down.

"Lift it!" Julie said, and threw back the curtain so the class could see.

Light from twin spotlights crisscrossed the stage, dust twinkling like stars in their beams. Callum had finished installing them after their reunion in the fog.

The children oohed and aahed, getting out of their seats to clamber up onstage and dance in the glow. The seventh-grade boy began doing something that couldn't quite be called dancing—more like a cross between *American Ninja Warrior* and gymnastics—but Macy started slapping out a rhythm with one hand on her leg, and the other on the wall, until by the end she was keeping his beat.

"Okay, okay," Julie said at last. But she was unable to suppress a smile. "Come on down, class, return to your desks."

A pause for the inevitable stragglers, till there was only one, whom she led.

"It's a double coincidence, yo," Macy said, taking her seat and calling out without raising her hand. "Because our surprise is about the play."

The kids had practiced all weekend at the lobster pound, stealing time between helping with trap repair and sleeve knitting. They had finished writing a scene and set it to music.

"Don't forget to tell her about the you-know-what!" Scott said.

Julie had never seen a jaded sixth-grade male so enthusiastic.

"Oh yeah," Macy said, clearly enjoying her role as assistant director. "The boys have been working on the set. It's in pieces at Scott's house."

Julie stood regarding the class. An idea had begun to build in her mind that might tick a few boxes. "Do you think you guys could let me see that part you have down?"

Desks squeaked and chairs slid back as the students trooped back onstage. And while Julie clapped loudly, watching the seventh-grade boy take exaggerated bows and his classmates mimic him, following an enactment of lines that almost all made sense and flowed, delivered with something approaching spontaneity, she decided something.

If the grandmother and her coterie weren't so big on a play, wouldn't it be a good idea to let the parents see what their kids had been up to? Social skills, memorization, exercise, and critical thinking were all selling points that came from the theater world. Julie could shine a literal light on the students' growth and development while demonstrating her competence as a teacher in the process.

"How come you wanted to see us act it out, Ms. Weathers?" asked a third grader, bent over and out of breath.

"Because you guys are amazing," Julie replied.

The students let out a cheer, fist-bumping each other, older students leaning down to make sure they didn't miss the younger. Even Eddie Cowry got a thump, causing him to smile so hard, as he kept turning back to offer his hand for another, that he tripped coming off the stage.

"So amazing," Julie continued, "that I think we should let your parents have a sneak peek. This Wednesday afternoon say. Just what you showed me right now, and maybe a song"—a quick look at Macy, who nodded—"to get them excited for when you perform the whole thing. What do you guys think?"

The roars were loud enough that they could only have signaled assent.

Julie finished the morning lessons, then let the students continue rehearsing during lunch, while she took Depot on a walk to the library. She mocked up an invitation and printed out two dozen copies, which she handed to the students to give to their parents. Toward the end of the day, she gathered everyone in the loft for a circle talk about acting.

"We all sort of know what acting is," Julie began. "I mean, we watch movies and TV." There was no movie theater on Mercy Island, and at least a few homes didn't have televisions; it was possible some of these island kids had never seen a film at all. "But how would you describe acting to an alien, say one who doesn't have access to any media?"

Pauses for everyone to exclaim over how unbearable such a life would be, and for the seventh-grade boy to inform Julie that his granny didn't have a TV, or his step-aunt and uncle, but his older cousin did, and did she since she'd just moved here? Which was a step in the right direction, Julie noted—at least that question stayed on topic.

Lara Milton, the shy third grader Julie hadn't heard much from until she'd gone up onstage that morning, raised her hand. "My mom says that acting is lying."

Julie wove her fingers together, studying the circle of upturned faces. Even Macy, old enough to look Julie straight in the eye, appeared to be awaiting her teacher's response.

"I know what your mom means," Julie said at last. "You're not being yourself in a play. You're playing a role, acting like somebody else."

The children remained hushed and quiet, not stirring from the positions they all occupied in the loft. Peter lay recumbent, like the young prince he was, taking up more than his fair share of space. But nobody asked him to move, even when his arms and legs twitched, perhaps in response to Julie's statement. The kids that he accidentally bumped against seemed to take it as an expression of favor, smiling, edging closer to the wayward limb.

"And you can look at that in different ways," Julie went on. "First of all, aren't we all, always, playing a role, even in real life? Are we ever truly ourselves?"

Eddie stared down at his cramped patch of floor.

"Assuming we even know who those true selves are. When I was your ages, acting was the only thing I did that made me feel real," Julie said. "Acting isn't lying. It's the opposite. It's about finding the part inside you that lets you reveal your truth."

"Like what's the truth in *Rapunzel Returns*?" someone asked.

Julie answered slowly. "You have a child stolen away from his home, his family, right? In the scene you worked on, Rapunzel is growing up, not allowed to know where he really comes from. And you wrote those lines about the pain his parents felt after losing their child." Julie looked down at the ring of earnest faces encircling her. An array of ages Hedley would never reach. "That was one of the truest things I've ever seen on a stage. When you described, what did you call them, dry tears—well, you nailed it. Because you cry forever after a loss like that. There's nothing else like the pain. There's just nothing else that horrible in the whole world."

Vaguely, as if from far away, she heard the sounds of small feet descending the ladder, then climbing back up again. But Julie didn't realize she was crying until Eddie Cowry handed her a bunch of clumped-up tissues, damp from the sweat on his hand.

The children sat with quiet gathering around them while Julie dabbed her face.

"Wow," Macy said after some time had passed. "You should put that in a play. You could give one of those, you know, one-woman shows."

Julie worked up a smile for the eighth grader, quelled slightly when she noted Peter's blank, unseeing eyes. He hadn't reacted, either to her speech or her breakdown.

"Understand?" she said once she could speak again. "Acting is about things so deep that sometimes we don't even know what they are until we perform them." Julie brought her hands together. "Now. I think you should all get going for chores and homework. I'm hoping you might be able to get in a little extra practice on your own before bedtime. And maybe the sixth graders can work some more on their creation?"

Voices soared with plans. School was officially dismissed, and the children scrambled to their feet, taking turns down the ladder from the loft. There came the sounds of backpacks being swept up, the barn doors were heaved open and banged shut again, and then all was hushed and quiet in the schoolhouse.

Julie made a trip back up the ladder, ducking for headroom in the low space as she hunch-walked over to a shadowy, hidden corner.

"Not ready to go?" she asked the boy who lurked there.

Peter wasn't as good at concealing his actions anymore, or else Julie was getting better at detecting them.

"—believe what you said?" Peter asked, barely audible.

The boy had never appeared so bleak and desperate. A few moments ago, he'd lain in resplendent repose across the floor of the loft, but now his knees were drawn up to his chin, his back curled over them, and his face buried.

"—acting getting at the real…" He went on, mumbling. "…you can't say?"

Julie pieced his words together, thinking of all the roles she had played, as a Weathers, as David's wife, even as Hedley's mom. "I believe acting lets us say things we otherwise couldn't. And realize things about ourselves that we otherwise never would."

Silently, with no change in expression, Peter began to cry. His hands seemed to move of their own volition, not a part of the rest of him, as he felt around for the tissues Eddie had brought up. Peter pressed a fresh batch to his face.

"It won't matter," he said dully. "They'll never let me go."

"Go where?" Julie asked. Hollywood. New York. Anywhere besides Mercy.

But Peter just lifted his shoulders helplessly.

"Sometimes," Julie began, feeling for words. How much harder it was when there wasn't any script. "A stage is the only place we can say what's true. To an auditorium full of strangers whose faces we can't even see." A pause. "But sometimes we start by saying it to someone who's really there first. A person we think might tell us the truth back."

Peter raised his chin, and doubled down on his fists.

Then, with the force of a cork exploding, a volcano erupting, he told her the secret he'd been harboring for so long.

CHAPTER SIXTY-TWO

Peter had been in his hideout, a placement that provided perfect access for overhearing a conversation. Especially on the kind of unblemished sunny day so rare on a northeastern island, windows raised to let in the balmy air, grown-ups going outside to sit on a porch, voices carrying from rooms opened to air out, or along the tendrils of a breeze.

The Captain began to talk first, and maybe because he sounded so lucid—Peter struggled to identify the concept for Julie—so much like his old self, the grandmother seemed to be in a listening mood.

For a while.

Then the Captain mentioned a place called Duck Harbor.

"Duck Harbor?" Julie repeated. "Is it here? On the island?"

Peter's fine features squeezed together in concentration. "I don't think so. I've never heard of any place like that. It must be on the mainland."

Julie nodded.

The grandmother had answered in a low tone; Peter had to scramble out along the branch that poked nearest the mansion in order to hear her. She said she never should've let them stay in Duck Harbor.

"Let who stay?" Julie asked.

"Bobby Croft?"

The name nudged a nodule in Julie's brain. "You don't know who that is?"

Peter shook his head. "And then Cap started to argue. And he never argues with my grandmother. He was all, he wanted to see her, he didn't want to have to travel so far away he'd never have a chance to get there, and Duck Harbor was a really good spot."

"Her?" Julie said. "I thought you said it was a man named Bobby."

"I think Cap just got...you know, like he sometimes gets now..." Peter's voice trailed off.

"Confused," Julie supplied. "He gets a little mixed up."

Peter nodded gratefully. "Just sometimes."

"Peter," Julie said. "I'm not getting why this conversation upset you so much."

It was warm in the loft, hot air from the stove rising, and Peter's skin had gone slick; it looked almost gelatinous with sweat. "Because of what they said about Bobby."

The grandmother had told the Captain that she should've made him do what she wanted to Bobby all those years ago. "And I think what she wanted him to do—" Peter broke off, his blue eyes glassy and frightened. "I think it was something bad, Ms. Weathers. Like really bad because Cap said he would've wound up in jail. Prison. Even though my grandmother told him that was stupid, a Hempstead would never go to jail."

Julie strained to put the pieces into some cohesive form. There was a man named Bobby Croft. He lived in Duck Harbor, which the grandmother now felt was too close. To Mercy obviously. And a long time ago, the grandmother had wanted her husband to do something bad to him, something that might've been criminal.

Peter began to rock back and forth, arms around his knees. "And then my grandmother—she got really mean. She started saying all this bad stuff, like did that really matter, if he had gone to jail, look how he'd ended up anyway, and Cap said he should've supposed her a long time ago"—Peter was caught in a maelstrom of memory now, trying to recapture words—"and then Cap started crying—he was *crying*, Ms. Weathers, *the Captain*." Peter said it as if he couldn't have witnessed a less likely scenario if the sea had drained of water. "And my grandmother told him if I ever found out—they were talking about me, Ms. Weathers, *me*, and then—" Peter closed his mouth, tears flying off his face as he shook his head in mute refusal.

"Then what?" Julie crawled toward him across the loft.

"Then she said something about arithmetic," Peter whispered.

"Arithmetic," Julie repeated blankly.

Peter gave a nod. "'It's simple arithmetic.' Something like that."

Julie frowned, uncomprehending.

And Peter hurled himself into her arms, his tall, skinny body heaving and jolting like a live wire. "Grandmother said it would be one more damn fool lady and one less little boy."

———

Peter went into the boys' room to wash his face, then trudged outside to meet Martha, who was waiting by the edge of the sea. She gave Peter no greeting, just took his hand dutifully, and led him out of the cove. Julie waved goodbye to them before heading off along the library path, up the road through town, and into the woods with Depot.

Interpretations of what the boy had told her played out in Julie's mind.

The Captain should have opposed his wife—assuming that was the word Peter misheard as *supposed*—in some important way. Maybe he'd been in love with another woman, which was why he'd slipped and referred to a *her*. The damn fool lady. But who was Bobby Croft? The woman's husband? And how did any of it subtract Peter from the equation? Not allowing adultery to bloom could well be yet another weapon in the grandmother's arsenal, even love subject to her denial or granting of permission. After all, an affair would besmirch the image of a united pair at the helm of a powerful family.

Depot started jumping as soon as they neared the house. Julie unlocked the front door, letting the dog enter first. He raced inside, headed for the kitchen.

"Okay, yes, I'm going to feed you right away," Julie said. She walked over to the cabinet, dragging out the big bag of dry food, then pulled open a drawer for the can opener. The dog was still jumping and panting.

Julie set his water bowl on the floor so he could get started, but Depot didn't lower his head to drink. Julie frowned, looking down at him. Then, slowly, she lifted her head back up.

She must have already seen it when she turned on the tap to fill Depot's bowl, but the sight was so impossible, so at odds with any expectation of what should have been in the kitchen, that it hadn't registered.

Depot wasn't eager for dinner. He wanted her to know that someone had been here.

Julie turned to face the counter beside the sink.

A bottle of scotch stood on it, amber liquid catching the sinking rays of the sun.

Julie backed away as if she had spotted a detonator. If there had been a countdown, one of those digital timers in movies showing mere seconds left, she couldn't have left the house any faster. She didn't bother closing the front door.

What was even worse—far worse, in fact—than the temptation

with which she'd been presented was the fact that someone loathed her enough to want to do this, was that hell-bent on trying to bring about her downfall.

Julie was focused only on getting away from the whiskey, but when she made it across the porch, legs shaking, mouth as dry as sand, a whip-like flash of black caught her eye, and she swung around. The figure started to run toward the lane that separated this house from the mansion.

Peter.

He knew Julie drank, had referred to it the other night at his grand-parents' house. Had the boy gotten away from his mother after school, somehow nabbed a bottle of scotch, or maybe had it in his backpack all day, and raced Julie back here? Depot knew Peter's scent. He would've run eagerly into the kitchen in the hopes of seeing the boy.

The hopes. Depot had no room in his nature for how diabolical Peter could be.

A brand-new fifth of scotch was as much of a threat as the mutilated bird.

Julie took the porch steps at a jump, then gave chase.

Peter was dressed in dark jeans and a black oilcloth raincoat with the hood drawn over his head. A tall, skinny boy with long legs who knew this path better than Julie, had been venturing down the lane between the two houses his whole life.

Julie fought to match his pace, but he was outrunning her.

"Peter!" she cried. "It's okay! I'm not mad! I just want to talk to you!"

The boy picked up speed, and Julie's breath was stolen as she tried to keep up. She didn't have the wind to call out again. The sea to their right moved frenetically, tide rising up the base of the cliffs. Depot appeared, big as a pony beside her. Forelegs and hind carried him along the grassy lane, his glorious coat of fur blurring with the speed he attained. Depot began to growl in a way Julie hadn't heard him do since he was a trauma-tized puppy, lips pulled back to bare his fangs.

"Deep!" Julie panted. "It's okay! It's just Peter!"

Peter's pace faltered ever so slightly upon hearing the dog's snarl.

Just enough for Julie to catch up and plant her hand on the boy's shoulder. Peter twisted and wrenched, trying to get out of her hold, and Depot skidded to a halt, clumps of grass and dirt torn up beneath his paws as he let out another menacing growl.

"Depot, cut it out!" A tone of voice she hadn't had to use with him in years.

Julie turned Peter around, and his hood fell back.

The face beneath the slick fabric wasn't Peter's.

It was Ellie's.

CHAPTER SIXTY-THREE

A tall, skinny eleven-year-old boy in a dark, hooded raincoat could be mistaken for a small, slight woman, especially running, and especially since Julie had already made the assumption that the deliverer of the threats and all the bad things that had assailed her and Depot since they'd come to Mercy Island was the same person as the child who'd reached out to his new teacher in such desperate need.

Julie backed away so swiftly, at such a stumble, that Ellie thrust out her arm, snagging Julie's. Julie twisted partway around and saw how close to the edge of the cliff she had come. She took off at a run, and then it was Ellie chasing her, back up the lane.

"Julie! Please, wait!"

But Julie didn't stop running till she reached her house.

Depot held Ellie at bay on the porch, jumping and nipping.

Ellie's eyes pleaded with Julie, and finally Julie relented. "Okay, Deep, quit it."

The dog quieted, although he continued to stand guard before the front door.

Words crowded Julie's throat, a leaden, choking mass. Questions, accusations, demands that in the end boiled down to one word. "Why?"

Ellie's narrow shoulders slumped. "I'm sorry, Julie. I really am. I didn't want to."

"The grandmother made you do this? Threaten my weeklong sobriety?" Betrayal slithered over Julie's whole body. "Hurt an innocent bird?"

Ellie slapped her hands over her ears. "Stop it! Don't you think I know how disgusting I am already?"

Julie's tone was so scathing, it burned her throat. "Are you asking me for *pity*?"

Ellie's pale eyes went lightless. "Do you have any idea how low my rent is? I couldn't stay on Mercy if it weren't for Mrs. Hempstead. And I could never live anywhere else. I don't know how to live anywhere else. This island has a way of doing that to you once you've been here a while. It institutionalizes you, just like a prison, or a psychiatric hospital. Mercy ruins a person for life on the outside."

Julie shook her head back and forth.

"Fine!" Ellie bit out. "Maybe that's an excuse, I have a way of making them. You want to hear the truth, Julie? You want to know the real, ugly truth about Mercy Island and Mrs. Hempstead?"

Julie hesitated, and Ellie barged on.

"No, really. You kept asking and needling and wanting to know. All sorts of things that are none of your business. That's the reason Mrs. Hempstead insisted I do what I did. To ensure you learned your place. To take you down a peg or two. To make you easier to control because that woman is all about control."

The grandmother's practices made a rotted sort of sense. She'd cut the same kinds of corners Julie's uncles and grandfather had when they'd been in charge of Wedeskyull. A corrupt police department, a lawless aristocracy. Why deal with annoying resistance, pushback from people who had competing needs and desires, when you could bend them all to your will, make everyone do your bidding via favors, gifts, leverage, blackmail, threats, and in Julie's family's case and perhaps here on Mercy, too, crime?

"Mercy has always been ruled by an iron fist in a velvet glove." Ellie's mouth recomposed itself in a sneer. "So here it is. The real reason I did what Mrs. Hempstead said to is because she knows the smallest, ugliest parts of me—the smallest, ugliest parts of us all—and she uses them to convince us we're not fit for any other sort of life. How can I live with the fact that my own mother let that man come to me every night he spent with us?" Ellie held her arms thrust outward, away from herself, as if she couldn't stand to touch her own body. "I'm lucky to have this place. It's the only one that would have somebody like me."

Julie tried to shake her head in protest, but Ellie put up a hand.

"Oh, stop. You have your own shame, Julie. The grandmother used it against you too." Ellie's face and neck and hands, all her exposed skin, had gone ruddy and blotched. "But I was trying to resist her this time. Just this once. No way was she going to mess with our friendship. That was the reason behind my latest attempt at quitting. I figured I would need to be sober if I was going to stand a chance. Obviously I didn't succeed. At either." Ellie's slim form turned and walked off, shielding itself in descending shadows.

Julie called out, her throat still raw with hurt and anger and unshed tears. "You kidnapped my dog! You could've gotten him killed!"

Ellie whirled around. "No," she said. "I promise. Mrs. Hempstead wanted Depot to get used to listening to me, in case we ever needed him as leverage. So I had treats and food and I might've cowed him a bit, that first day we met, yelled at him a little. I gave him some cough medicine in the middle of the night when you slept over because he was so agitated. He's so big, he probably didn't even feel the dose. But I swear, I would never hurt your dog, and I didn't lead him onto those cliffs."

Depot's long nap the other day in the schoolhouse. He'd felt the dose all right, although worry over Julie must have somehow delayed its effects. Tears sprang to her eyes. Ellie had lied about so many things—a stack whose height Julie couldn't even begin to assess right now—that she had no idea whether to believe her about this. She turned and stepped past Depot, leaning around his big form to open the front door.

Ellie followed her. "Maybe no one took him there," she said, appearing to think. "Mike Cowry has been keeping an eye on things here at the house—how you were settling in, if you were drinking—so maybe he came over that day and didn't close the door all the way. Or maybe Depot ran him out. And then Depot could've followed your scent…you had just been on those cliffs at the party. I don't think anyone wanted your dog to get hurt."

The cold recitation of the facts of her stalking undid any relief Julie might've felt upon hearing this claim. "Were you at the schoolhouse that day before school started?" she demanded. "Did you come by and not answer when I called out?"

Ellie dropped her gaze. "Yes, that was me. But if it helps, I was just making sure you were there so I could send Callum over. I wanted you guys to meet."

"Great. You massacred a bird on my doorstep *and* helped make a match with the first man I've ever really found—" Julie clapped a hand over her mouth. She wasn't even sure what she'd been about to say, but she had no intention of saying it to Ellie. Not then anyway. Still, when Ellie looked at her and asked, "Really?" Julie whispered back, "I think so."

Ellie gave her a small smile.

Julie turned and walked into the kitchen to finish serving Depot his missed meal. He looked from Ellie to his bowl and back again, torn between vigilance and hunger.

"It's okay, Deep," Julie told him. "Eat."

Depot gulped down a mouthful. Ellie gave the dog his space, her hands held up in a gesture of surrender. "Mind if I use your bathroom?"

"All that running and chasing makes a girl have to pee, huh? Sure. Go ahead."

Julie listened to Ellie trudge up the stairs, close the door, run the water. When she came back down again, Ellie sidled into the kitchen, stretching to lean past Depot. A thrum started low in the dog's throat.

"I just—" Ellie's voice faltered. "I was going to take that away for you." She pointed to the bottle still standing on the counter. The scotch emitted a haloed, golden glow.

Julie shook her head. "You've done enough."

Ellie's pale skin flushed.

Julie walked by her and opened the front door. After a moment, Ellie went outside, and all sight of her was soon lost to the gloom of the oncoming night.

In the kitchen, standing some distance from the counter, Julie leaned forward on legs that already felt drunk and unsteady. She reached one arm out so far that the bottle nearly dropped when she snatched it up. Might as well do this outside, in a place that had come to mean something to her.

She walked toward the edge of the cliff, hearing the approach and retreat of the surf, the soft sough of the waves. Her fist choked the neck of the bottle, which dangled from her hand. She licked her lips, realizing that the skin on them was healing. Felt the slosh of liquid behind glass and imagined the gurgling sound that would accompany a long, deep draft.

Julie drew her arm back and gave a giant heave, a Frisbee throw that sent the scotch hurtling end over end where it landed invisibly out to sea.

Then she went back inside. Depot had gone to sleep by the wall of windows. Her dog had never been comfortable with Ellie, Julie realized, had been trying to caution her about her new friend's dual nature since the very first day when they'd all met and Depot had sat so silently at the edge of the yard, then ran off alone in the woods.

That black goop on Depot's nose after Julie left him alone with Ellie to go change for the Hempsteads' party. Just a treat of some kind, or had it been something to make the dog sick, render him unable to go with them? Depot tended to pose a distraction, perhaps the grandmother wanted to observe Julie in her pure, unvarnished state. Julie thought of the times she had asked Ellie to watch Depot, or walk him home, with a queasy sense of treason. Depot hadn't been trying to protect Julie from some outside threat that night at Ellie's house. He'd been guarding her from the danger lying right beside her in the bed.

And Julie had thought Peter was the one she and her dog had to watch out for.

Did the boy really exhibit the twisted behaviors Chloe had described? Or had both she and Julie missed the fact that Peter himself was in jeopardy?

Try as she might, Julie couldn't imagine a source for that potential peril, though. Everybody kowtowed to Peter. He was at the helm of the ship, or would be one day soon.

Julie trudged across the first floor. She felt as if the surface beneath her feet, whatever kept Mercy Island from simply drifting out to sea, had shifted. The extent of the grandmother's intrusiveness and willingness to do harm was a difference in degree. As soon as Julie read that ledger, she'd been made aware of how the grandmother tampered with lives. But Ellie's betrayal was a change in kind. In quality not quantity.

Julie sighed, giving her sleeping dog a last look as she started to mount the steps. Without Depot beside her, it was going to be a long, lonely night. Perhaps she would take the other half of her pill. Leave the bottle with a round number in it.

She went down the hall to the bathroom, but couldn't find the vial in the medicine cabinet. Had she left it somewhere after taking her dose the other night? Julie walked into her room, checking beside Hedley's photo and elsewhere on the night table. She looked at the dresser top, then in each drawer, and even flung back the covers on her bed.

Peter could've gotten his hands on these pills when he'd hidden in the house. Anybody could have; Julie had been a fool to leave them unsecured.

Then she figured out what must've happened, and she started to run.

CHAPTER SIXTY-FOUR

Julie was scarcely aware that Depot had woken up and followed her. The sounds of his anguished yelps and skidding paws were muted by the roar in her head. Like the sea, endless, unbroken. Julie ran along the trail through the woods, heedless of roots and knolls that threatened to trip her. Her hands broke her fall when it happened, fingers scraped and knuckles bruised in the dirt, before she got to her feet and raced onward, breath coming in gasps that tore her throat.

The foursquare of cottages came into view, an aging gray sky for backdrop.

Julie fell against Ellie's door, barging inside unannounced.

Ellie was slumped over, her head on the table, one hand on an empty bottle of wine.

Just one tonight. That was all Ellie had needed, given the pills.

Julie knew her friend was dead even before she touched her fingertips to her motionless body, felt the lack of a flutter in her throat and the white marble quality of her skin. As soon as she saw the expression Ellie had never worn in real life, the glazed look of peace in her eyes.

Julie called Paul Scherer, using Ellie's landline, and trying to blind herself to the sight of the wine, the table, her friend. The constable didn't pick up—it was after hours—but there was a machine on which emergency messages could be left, and Julie delivered the news in a sodden monotone of grief.

She knew what would happen next, and what her role should be. Julie retraced her steps to the front door, making sure not to touch anything on her way. Then she waited outside, no measure to the passing time, as long as this was going to take.

Depot wandered off into the trees, sniffing the ground, while Julie stood on the patch of sand and soil outside the cottage until the constable came walking along the road through town, the grandmother by his side, matching his stride.

She swept past Julie, entering the cottage to assess the scene. Scherer and Julie trailed her in, and the grandmother turned, confronting them both with her piercing gaze.

"How terribly, terribly sad," she said. "Ellie Newcomb has been a tortured soul, ever since she was a child. Do you know, I once took her in?"

Depot came running back and Julie grabbed him, clenching his collar so fiercely that the leather dug a well in her hand. "Yes," she said faintly. "I think I did hear that."

"Ah," the grandmother said. "The famous dog I keep hearing about."

A rumble began low in Depot's throat, building to an explosive bark. "Depot, no!" Julie cried. That made twice in one day she'd used that tone with her dog.

Depot's head drooped so low that his snout grazed the floor. Shame was the emotion Depot had shown most often after being rescued, and a fuzzy haze of it enclosed him again now.

Julie despised this woman with a hatred she'd never felt toward anyone before. But she couldn't reveal it—had, in fact, to display the opposite. If the grandmother knew that Julie suspected she'd played a role in all this, then she would make good on the warning she had sent with Mike Cowry this morning. She'd already done it to Chloe.

And then Julie would never find out what the grandmother was intent on hiding from Peter, or why the boy might be suffering so.

They were talking about me, Ms. Weathers.

Julie's body quaked with anger, causing Depot to whine and edge closer. Finding out the truth would mean playing the part of the woman Mike Cowry had spied on back in Wedeskyull. Meek, crushed by life, accepting.

The old woman offered Julie a condescending nod. "Word of largesse tends to spread. Or was it Ellie herself who told you of my efforts? I did so wish to help her. But some situations can't be rectified, no matter how good one's intentions or how much force is applied." A deliberated pause. "Now, I believe you must speak to our constable?"

Julie gave a statement to Scherer, aware of the components it needed to contain—and all that it shouldn't. Ellie had overdosed on prescription sleeping pills and wine. The meds she had taken belonged to Julie. Julie hadn't realized they were gone.

She asked the constable if she would be needed for anything else that night.

"We'll take it from here," he told her, not unkindly.

The grandmother stood in the center of the room, legs spread wide, hands planted upon Ellie's couch as if she owned not only the cottage, but everything in it, including the people, its history, the lives it used to and ever would contain.

"You may go, Ms. Weathers," she said, with a curve of her outstretched arm. "On Mercy we know how to take care of our dead."

In the middle of the night, guilt crept up on Julie like an old friend.

She'd known how hard it was for Ellie to be alone at night. And she had let her go without even saying she forgave her, that there was nothing to forgive. Ellie was one cog in a wheel she had no chance of turning. And now Julie was another.

Depot stirred beside her, disturbed by her fractured shards of dreams, or his own. Julie dozed in brief snatches so as not to be clobbered by recollection as soon as she returned to consciousness. She had already experienced that once in her life, the forgetting that only sleep afforded, what it felt like when the gift was stolen back.

A knock shook the front door as Julie lay awake in the predawn dullness, a new tree ring of grief forming around her heart. She got out of bed on feet that felt like blocks of wood, and went down to open the door. Callum stood on the porch.

"You already heard," Julie said, peering around him to the lightless, gray morning.

"Scherer," Callum said. "He's a friend of mine."

"Oh," Julie replied. "Right." A tear drizzled down her face. Mercy Island felt less alive without Ellie on it, as if more lives than one had been snuffed out.

"I'm sorry," Callum said. "I know how close you two had gotten."

Julie looked at him. "Did Ellie have a dog as a child?"

But she could already anticipate Callum's answer, given how effortlessly Ellie breathed life into a pretend father. Smarmy wasn't real either. The lies she had told, everything she had done, had been at the grandmother's behest. Ellie had never been free, not since her mother instructed her to don the same shackles she herself wore every day.

"No," Callum said. "No dog and no da. Must have been a lonely life."

Julie stepped forward, placing her cheek against Callum's, bristly with a growth of beard. The tears she'd been crying mingled with a coating of salt on his face.

"I think it was lonelier than anybody knew," she told him.

Over coffee, Julie asked Callum where Duck Harbor was.

Callum crossed to the wall of windows, stepping over Depot, who was breakfasting in his usual spot. "There," he said, pointing. "With a telescope, you might even be able to see it. A promontory that sticks out to sea from the mainland."

"The ferry would get me there?" Julie asked.

"The ferry doesn't go there. It's an out-of-the-way port. But you could get a cab."

But Julie couldn't be on the ferry anyway. Though part of her was inclined to cancel school for the day, tack up a sign that read *Closed due to death on the island*, Julie didn't want to leave Peter unattended—or worse, in his mother's care—all day. And taking the afternoon boat would mean getting stuck for the night on the mainland. Her absence might be noted. For all she knew, the grandmother would hear about it as soon as Julie left. Paranoia prickled her skin. For the first time, it occurred to her how few ways there were off this island, how little ability she had to leave. Mercy could close on its people like a fanged trap.

"Could you take me?" Julie asked. "On your boat? Today after school?"

Callum raised his steamy cup for a sip. "Sure."

Julie felt her face flush with thanks. "There's just one thing."

Callum refilled Julie's cup, nodding her on.

"I need you to tie up the *Mary Martin* near the schoolhouse cove instead of by the dock. And row your dinghy over to pick me up there."

She hoped it would seem as if she were going for efficiency—spare her the walk to the pier—but Callum was too smart for the dodge.

"Trying to sneak off the island?" he asked.

Julie kept quiet.

He took the cup from her suddenly shaky hand. "What's in Duck Harbor?"

Julie raised her gaze to his. "That's what I have to find out."

CHAPTER SIXTY-FIVE

C allum offered to keep Depot with him till he came to get Julie. The school day progressed as if encased in cement. Every assignment, each question, seemed to take ten times as long as normal to administer or answer, and Julie had to remind herself that the students' boisterous chatter wasn't insensitive. Most of them probably didn't even know Ellie was gone.

Only Peter seemed somberly aware, unless it was yesterday's revelation in the loft that explained his mood. On stage for the run-through of tomorrow's sneak peek, Peter didn't speak above a rasp when he delivered his lines, and his moves looked gluey, lacking the untethered lift the boy had shown when he'd danced in his hideout.

Macy came up to Julie when the day had finally ground to a sluggish end, speaking in an undertone. "Should we assign an understudy for Rapunzel, Ms. W?"

Julie gazed out over the schoolroom. The children were closing the lids on their desks, stuffing belongings into backpacks. "I don't think so. I'll talk to Peter."

Macy nodded soberly. "Okay. And I'm sorry, Ms. W."

Julie gave her a little frown, not understanding.

"Something bad happened, didn't it?" Macy said. "My mom was upset this morning, but she wouldn't tell me why. And you look like you did when you were talking about finding the truth in a play. Anyway, I just wanted to say sorry."

In a small community, news traveled like electrical impulses amongst a web of nerves. But the desire to protect one's children from tragedy was universal, unconstrained by geography.

"Thank you," Julie replied, feeling tears swell her throat. "And Macy?"

The girl turned on her way toward the doors.

"You're going to do an amazing job as Rapunzel's mother tomorrow," Julie told her. "You put the truth in Peter's song, and found it for yourself as well."

A grin took hold of Macy's face, then vanished, like water running off a plane. "Our play is about being who you are, getting what you want. No matter what it takes, or how high the price. Right?" she asked, and Julie nodded. Macy gave a nod in return, then said, "I realized that can be a good thing, or a bad, depending. And that's the truth."

Julie summoned Peter back at the barn doors. He had to be able to perform tomorrow—it was the one thing in his life that truly seemed to imbue him with joy—and he also needed to know that Ellie's death hadn't deterred Julie from trying to help him. If anything, it had strengthened her resolve.

"Remember how on the first day of school I brought Depot? You seemed surprised. And upset. You looked like you'd just learned"—Julie tried to think of something that might totally throw a preadolescent boy—"that girls were actually cool."

Peter made a *blech* face, and Julie felt an unexpected smile rise. "Exactly. Can you tell me why you felt that way?"

Peter glowered as though the same thing were happening right now.

"I thought Depot was my special dog! I didn't think you would share him with just everybody!"

Julie had come to suspect as much, although it hadn't appeared that way then. "And Gully, Peter? Were you trying to hurt the bird when you squeezed it in your hand?"

The boy shook his head wildly. "I wasn't squeezing him, I was warming him up! I knew he might get alive again if I could just make him warm!"

As indeed the bird had. Julie had misjudged Peter from the start, attributed malice to actions that could be interpreted as plaintive pleas, if not heroics.

She pulled at the barn door, and Peter started to edge his way through.

"I need you to do a good job in the scene we put on tomorrow," Julie told him. "Really show them what you've got inside. Can you do that?"

Peter nodded.

"Nobody can ever take away what you do on stage," Julie said. "It's yours no matter what happens."

Peter nodded again. Then he said, "Is something going to happen?"

Julie held his blistering blue gaze. "It will if I have anything to do about it."

The shock of reaching the mainland was like an electric jolt. Even before the *Mary Martin* had docked, the noise of engines, a crush of people that despite numbering only in the dozens was still a great horde by Mercy Island standards, and the sight of clustered buildings posed a stark contrast to Julie's last few weeks. A car looked like an alien being, a parking lot full of them seemed like an invasion.

There was an ocean adventures outfitter, an old factory that had been converted to luxury lofts, and the pier that was huge in contrast to the one on Mercy. Callum was able to tie up his boat alongside, no dinghy required. He offered Julie a hand as she jumped out, then leaned over and helped with Depot.

"How long do you think you'll need?" Callum asked.

"I'm honestly not sure," Julie replied. "Do you have things you can do?"

Callum gave a nod. "Never any shortage of that on the mainland. And you should have signal. Text me when it's time to meet."

They entered each other's number in their phones for the first time.

"Thanks," Julie said, hearing the meagerness of the word. "Would you mind—"

"Keeping Depot? Not at all. Be nice to have company on my errands." He gave her a wave. "I'd wish you luck, but I don't know if that's what's called for."

"It can't hurt," Julie said.

She crouched to deliver a smooch to Depot on his glistening snout, then watched as Callum walked to the road, where he stuck out his thumb. Depot sat down on his haunches, camouflaging his size. The two snagged a ride in a pickup, and then the only companions Julie had left in the world drove away.

Julie entered the ferry station, figuring she would ask if anyone knew the local she was looking for. As it turned out, she didn't have to. A group of men stood around, chuffing and gabbing, slouched against a long counter. Much of Duck Harbor's business seemed to be conducted behind this counter—mail, money orders, notarizing, and general gossip. One person was in charge, and his nameplate read *Robert Croft Jr.*

The name had been in the ledger. Julie couldn't remember the details the grandmother had included in the entry, but that was why it had rung a bell when Peter said it. It had been one of the older entries, dating years in the past, so this must be the son.

"Mr. Croft?" Julie said.

He was tall and skinny with a reddish mustache and an open, friendly gaze.

The other men regarded Julie with that age-old look insiders reserved for everyone else. It was the one true equalizer, shared across color barriers and gender lines and socioeconomic strata. Cavemen and members of primitive tribes probably wore the same expression that blue bloods gave to immigrants, that residents of small villages offered the stranger who came to town. Back home, Julie was part of the clan that delivered this look. Here, she was its recipient.

"Bobby'd be fine," the man said.

Julie ventured a smile. "Would you mind if I asked you something in private?"

To their credit, his buddies suppressed any jeers.

She and Bobby Croft walked out to the dock, wooden boards under foot, seawater sloshing against posts, gulls observing with interested, beady gazes.

"What's this all about?" Bobby asked.

Julie hesitated. "This may come a little out of left field. But do you happen to know a family named Hempstead? Two grandparents, Martha, and the boy is Peter?"

Julie had thought she might get a head shake, a look of confusion. Or possibly a small-town *Sure, I know them*, and then not be able to determine a good place to go from there. What she didn't expect was the total rigidifying of this man's body, the way his hand shot up to his face to tug at his mustache, while his eyes briefly closed.

A particularly large wave broke, spattering the dock with glassy green droplets and froth, making the seagulls skitter from their perches.

Bobby Croft said, "I think you'd better talk to my wife."

CHAPTER SIXTY-SIX

Bobby Croft clacked a metal door down from the ceiling, sealing off the counter behind which he worked. He turned a key in a stubby lock and tacked up a *Sorry, we're closed* sign. His friends had dispersed to the rear of the station where there was a self-serve coffee stand, presumably so they could observe Julie without being as obvious.

Bobby opened the passenger side door of an old hatchback, waiting until Julie had buckled her seat belt before driving off. They didn't speak during the ride. Bobby looked nervous, tugging on the hair above his lip, and he didn't seem the talkative type anyway. Julie stared out the window, watching the streets of Duck Harbor go by.

The house Bobby drove to sat at the end of a line of spare two-story structures. Bobby got the car door again for Julie and let her go first up the walk.

He opened the front door, gesturing Julie inside to a low-ceilinged hallway with small, neatly kept rooms visible off to each side. Not many decorative touches, but pleasant in their unassumingness and lack of pretense.

A woman came out from the rear of the house, twisting a dishrag around her hands. She had silky black hair, cropped short, and wore jeans and what looked to be a hand-knit sweater. "You're home early, hon—" she began on a pleased note, then stopped when she saw Julie, although she continued to smile. "Oh, hello."

Bobby Croft spoke up. "Mellie, why don't you go and put the kettle on? This lady has come to talk about the Hempsteads."

His wife's face shed all color, though her smile remained shakily in place.

The sudden paleness of her skin revealed it. The woman's razored locks of hair were striking enough to pose a distraction—they contained purple hues, like crow wings—but hair could be dyed. What the woman hadn't chosen to change was the color of her eyes, an all-too-recognizable sunny sky blue.

Julie realized she hadn't responded to the woman's greeting. "Hi, Melinda."

———

Peter's aunt's face didn't change, but the way her hand tightened its grip on a side table told Julie she had guessed correctly.

Bobby spoke gruffly. "Let's go in the kitchen."

Melinda went ahead down the hallway. Her hand shook as she tried to light the stove, and the burner clicked, a mad, insectile sound, until Bobby walked over to place his own hand gently on top of his wife's, and a blue flame burst to life.

Melinda began to busy herself, taking out tea bags and mugs, slicing a packaged cake, laying plates on a small table with woven place mats.

"Please," she told Julie. "Sit."

Bobby went back out to the dining room and returned with an extra chair.

Melinda took a seat next to her husband, then poured the water for tea. She sipped while the liquid was still piping hot and winced, giving Julie a flicker of a smile. "I'm sorry. I'm not usually such a mess."

Julie shook her head, contradicting the charge. She liked Melinda— liked both of them—quite a lot actually, even just upon first meeting. Bobby sat, straddling a chair from behind, with his arm hooked around his wife's waist. The gesture didn't appear showy or possessive; he hadn't draped his arm visibly across Melinda's shoulders. This display of affection seemed to be for her benefit only, an extension of support.

"Who are you?" Melinda asked after a moment.

Julie flushed. "I guess it's my turn to apologize. My name is Julie Weathers. I'm your nephew's new teacher."

Melinda and Bobby exchanged looks.

"You've accepted the post on Mercy?" Bobby said.

Julie nodded.

"How's Peter doing?" Melinda asked. "How does he do in school?"

"Quite well actually," Julie replied, looking at her across the table. The Hempstead resemblance was remarkable—the tall stature, and those shining blue eyes, elfin facial bones under a glassine complexion. All she was missing were her sister's curls. "And he's a talented performer— dancing and singing both."

A smile lifted Melinda's lips, and she looked at her husband again.

"But that isn't why I came to see you," Julie went on.

"No," Melinda replied softly. She slid the platter of cake across the table, gesturing at Julie to take a piece. "I wouldn't think so."

"Peter's been troubled," Julie said. "Ever since I met him. The other day he told me that he'd overheard a conversation between your parents that upset him very much."

"What did they say?" Melinda asked.

"I'm not 100 percent sure," Julie told her. "Peter's account was a bit... Well, he's eleven. I don't think he understood everything he'd heard. But your father mentioned Bobby"—Julie turned to look at the man—"and what sounded like some conflict between them."

Melinda's features twisted; the expression didn't look at home on her pleasant face. "Yes, well, my parents didn't like Bobby very much, or want us to get married."

"Oh," Julie said.

"Bobby's from away," she explained. "Vermont. An inland state—can you imagine the horror?" She tried to work up a smile. "And obviously, he doesn't know anything about lobstering, the work I was supposed to be born to—or my husband was."

Bobby spoke up, somewhat shamefacedly. "When you think about it, it's a pretty classic story. Controlling parents. Uptown girl. Boy from the wrong side of everywhere."

Melinda laid her hand on top of her husband's.

"Your mother hasn't made amends, tried to heal your relationship?" Julie asked.

Melinda laughed, a harsh sound devoid of mirth. "My mother's never made amends to anyone. And in this case, she wouldn't believe I was owed any. She still hasn't forgiven me for defying her." She paused. "I upended the entire family order when I fell in love with Bobby. I haven't seen my mother in more than eleven years."

Bobby overturned his wife's hand and gave it a tight squeeze. Empathic, loving, but the gesture also looked strong enough to serve as a warning.

The mood in the room had shifted. Bobby pushed back his chair and stood up.

Melinda followed his lead. "I appreciate your coming out here to try and help Peter. The island can be a lonely place to live."

But this house seemed lonely too. A couple deprived of family support—mother, father, sister, a brother-in-law until recently, not to mention their nephew. Peter had been robbed as well. He could've benefited, especially in the wake of his father's death, from having an aunt and uncle who truly seemed to care about him.

Julie rose from her own chair. "Peter has friends," she told them. Sort of. "And I think he's really coming into his own with this play we're doing. You both should come see the performance when it goes up. I think it'll be a holiday production."

"Oh." Melinda's voice caught. "I would love that."

But in her eyes Julie read the fact that it would never happen.

There was an awkward pause, a moment of unfilled silence. Julie realized she didn't have much else to say. Melinda had pressed her hands to her face, and her husband was consoling her.

"Mind if I use your bathroom before I go?" Julie asked.

Scotch was easier on the bladder than all the coffee and tea she'd been imbibing, and this would also allow Melinda and Bobby a minute alone to ease the pain stirred up by discussing the familial rift. Julie looked around for where the bathroom might be. Not finding one on the first floor, she started upstairs. Suddenly, Bobby came running up behind her, taking the steps two at a time. But the door to the room at the top of the stairs stood open and Julie had already seen.

The walls were covered with photo after photo of Peter.

How exposed Julie had often felt behind the bank of windows in her house. These pictures she was seeing would've been taken with a telephoto lens, assuming a clear line of sight, say from a boat anchored not far offshore. Peter grew up in stages in the array, vantage point always roughly the same, shots of the dining room through glass, or outside on the lane, or in the part of the scrubby yard that could be seen from sea. At first a baby in somebody's arms, then a toddler, supervised by Martha or the grandmother or the Captain. Soon Peter began to play without somebody hovering right at hand, and the pictures chronicled this evolution, the final one capturing the boy's long-legged flight out of the frame.

This must explain Martha's move to a cloistered house, tucked away in the interior of the island. She had learned that Peter was being photographed.

By a doting aunt and uncle? Such loving attention, not to mention this kind of display, seemed to bespeak a closer relationship than that. Julie's thoughts shot to her own album of Hedley's first year, the tabletop photos she and David had arranged all over their house, including the one framed in pink china.

Melinda had chosen to marry a man who knew nothing of the life Peter had been born to. Or hadn't been born to.

Gooseflesh crept along Julie's skin, the result of a chill from the less well-insulated second floor, and a slow, dawning horror at what the grandmother had done.

She turned around slowly at the top of the stairs.

Bobby and Melinda both stood there.

"He's your son," said Julie.

CHAPTER SIXTY-SEVEN

I took those pictures," Bobby told her. "I may not know how to sink a lobster trap, but once it came clear we had to stay in Maine, I figured I should learn to drive a boat."

"We were going to move to Vermont to be near Bobby's family," Melinda explained. "Ironically, my mother got me to stay close to home, even though once she did what she did, she wouldn't have cared if I moved to China."

"Come on down," Bobby said gruffly. "We'll tell you the rest."

This time they sat in the living room, Melinda on the couch with her feet curled beneath her, Bobby beside his wife, and Julie in an armchair across from them.

Melinda began talking first. "My older sister was already married. To a man my mother had worked hard and long to lure away from home so they could live on Mercy. And they were having trouble conceiving."

Martha and Walter Meyers. The perfect highliner couple.

Except for their inability to produce an heir.

"I was lucky," Melinda continued. "Or unlucky, depending on how you look at it. I got pregnant right away. Before Bobby and I were even married."

"Although not before we'd decided to wed," Bobby put in.

The two traded looks that recalled the giddy, lovestruck twentysome-things, or possibly teenagers, they must have been.

Melinda blushed a schoolgirl pink as she turned back to Julie. "That kind of thing wouldn't matter these days, or even twelve years ago, if it had happened elsewhere, but it's still a big deal on Mercy. The island is in a time warp. My father wanted to kill Bobby—literally. My mother settled for banishing me. While solving my sister's fertility problems and the family's need for a next-generation lobsterman, all in one fell swoop."

Julie was still trying to take the full measure of the deception. "You and Bobby wanted to keep Peter? It wasn't that you thought you were too young or not ready yet?"

Melinda faced her with fervent eyes. "Oh, how we wanted to keep him. I don't know if you can imagine—I hope you can't—what it was like to let him go."

Bobby crushed a cushion in his fist, brows drawn down with fury.

Melinda leaned over and touched her lips to her husband's cheek, withdrawing the throw pillow from his hands. "I know what you're thinking," she said, looking at Julie. "You think that I'm weak. You think I failed to fight for my child."

"We both did," Bobby interjected. "We were kids, and we were scared, and we were stupid. Mrs. Hempstead manipulated us into signing away our parental rights when we hardly even knew what that meant. Mellie had a real tough time in childbirth, and I was half out of my mind with worry even after we knew that she'd make it."

But Melinda spoke over him bleakly. "And you know what? You're right. I've always been weak when it comes to my mother. I've never had any idea how to fight her. I don't even know if such a thing is possible."

"Couldn't Peter have learned the business from his uncle?" Julie asked. A relative to show you the ropes, Callum had said. "Then you and Bobby could've stayed and Walter—"

Melinda cut Julie off, and for a second, a touch of her mother's imperiousness rose to the fore. "My mother didn't want me there once I met Bobby. She would never have given my brother-in-law a nephew to train up." A quiver in her voice grew audible. "I don't know if you quite understand the place you've come to live in. It's taken Bobby years to get it. As our son, Peter would've been…" Melinda's face crinkled with shame. "There used to be a term for it, a disgusting one. No one uses it anymore, or shouldn't. A half-dub."

Julie spoke on impulse, wanting only to help rid this woman of her guilt and humiliation and pain. "Peter's not happy at home. I mean with Martha."

Melinda looked up so quickly, her neck jerked. "My sister was always forced to live such a rote, colorless life. Every step of it planned out for her from birth. Don't leave Mercy except to board for high school. Marry a highliner. Become a lobsterman's wife. Deliver an heir, possibly a spare; life on the sea is a dangerous business." She shook her head, another hard, brutal twist. "Martha didn't want any of it. She had all these dreams—she wanted to be an artist. I actually thought she was kind of good, growing up. And there I was, with the life she dreamt of. Bobby and I met in a traveling production of *Les Miz*. I got true love, and to act to boot. My mother wouldn't have it. Wouldn't let Martha live as she liked, nor me either."

"Peter senses there's another place for him," Julie told her. "That he doesn't belong on Mercy." *They'll never let me go*, she heard the boy say.

Melinda got off the couch and knelt in front of Julie, hands laced together. "Don't say that," she said, though her words were belied by the posture of prayer. "Please don't say that. You'll never get Peter off that island."

"Don't you think we tried?" Bobby asked, coming over to help his wife to her feet.

"One time—" Melinda's voice cracked. "One time I convinced my father to fake a bout of appendicitis. Peter was a toddler. I had my father feed him a ton of candy so the cramps would be convincing. My father was just loading Peter into his boat when my mother pointed out to sea. She'd paid for a surgeon to come, a *surgeon*, not just a doctor, from the mainland, in the middle of the night. A good one too—it wasn't like she took chances with Peter's health."

"There were other attempts like that," Bobby said dully. "Some stupider, some smarter. It didn't matter. Mrs. Hempstead won't be fooled or bested."

"Do you understand what we're saying?" asked Melinda. "If my mother could've gotten the baby out without me being there, or made it so I died in childbirth, I think she would've. I came close, and the last thing I remember seeing before they knocked me out was my mother handing Bobby a piece of paper to sign."

Bobby's glower deepened as he studied Julie. "There's something else."

Melinda looked at him, alarmed. "No, hon, you don't have to—"

But her husband spoke over her; it was the first time he hadn't been solicitous and gentle with his wife. "My little brother did something back when we were young and he had come to visit me," he said. "It was bad, but it was an accident, kids getting up to no good." He gave a harsh scrub to his face with one hand. "I had met Mellie so I was settling down some, but my brother could still act a little wild. Anyway, he managed not to get caught, but a very powerful family here on the mainland was involved. My brother might've spent the rest of his life in prison. Which maybe would've been right, Lord if I know, I've lost a lot of sleepless nights over it. Years really. Only, the thing is, he was my brother. And he shaped up afterward like you wouldn't believe. He stayed in Vermont and he's a pastor now."

Julie frowned, then smiled, then offered a nod. There was too much in the recounting to really parse, yet something in it tugged at her, a kernel of memory.

"Mrs. Hempstead heard the news," Bobby went on. "Powerful families being what they are. She pieced it together, knew my brother had been visiting the area, then left all of a sudden. But she never said a thing. Until the night Peter was born."

Silent tears had begun slipping down Melinda's face.

"It was a devil's choice," Bobby said. "Give up our son—but to people who loved him, could maybe even offer him a better life than we could—or let my brother rot in prison."

It appeared like a flash before Julie's eyes, the entry in the ledger.

Second son killed two while driving drunk. (Hold in reserve.)

Melinda looked at Julie, her eyes webbed with red. "Be careful," she said. "You know what you're up against now."

Julie rose from the chair. It had gotten dark, and she needed to meet Callum.

"I'll be careful," she promised. "And I'll be back. With Peter."

———————

Bobby returned Julie to the dock, driving off with a brief beep of his horn.

There was no one around at this hour; no lights shone from the ferry station. The sea on both sides glimmered darkly. Neither Callum nor Depot waited nearby.

Julie checked her phone.

Callum hadn't answered her text, saying she was on her way.

And the *Mary Martin* was no longer tied up at the pier.

Julie walked up and down the full length of the dock, the receding tide quietly lapping both sides as she made sure she hadn't missed a lobster boat in the darkness. She read each name painted in elegant, looping letters across the sterns of the boats.

The *Mary Martin* wasn't among them.

Julie checked her phone again, fighting a fizzy feeling of panic. No way could Callum be one of the grandmother's minions. Nobody could fake the connection, the desire, perhaps even more, that had begun to grow between them.

But Julie of all people knew that wasn't true.

Acting was about finding the truth inside a part.

She bit back a bleat of fear. Callum had her dog.

CHAPTER SIXTY-EIGHT

Running now, Julie veered toward the unlit ferry station, twisting the knob on its door. There was nobody in there, but Julie pounded on the door anyway. Walking over to the window, she leaned her face against the glass and strained to get a look inside.

Empty.

She stopped to check her phone, fired off another text to Callum, all caps screaming CALL ME NOW. Realized she could make a call herself, dialed, got voicemail, ended the call only to try again, and again, the messages she left increasing in intensity, in urgency, the last one all but hysterical.

Ellie had been driven to suicide. Peter's real parents had been forced to give up their son. Anything could happen on Mercy Island. Even, or especially, to the teacher who had sought to interfere. Or to her dog.

Callum's ex-girlfriend. Hadn't she come from Duck Harbor?

Julie spun around on the pier, then sprinted to the road, turning first left, then right.

A car whizzed by, blasting her with a cold rush of wind, and a furious honk as it swung wide to avoid a collision. Julie stepped back, but another car came, this one also not so much as slowing down, before there were no more cars on the road, no red trace of taillights in the distance. Julie leaned over, hands on her thighs, trying to control her breathing.

Her phone lit up, a laser beam in the night. A split second later, it buzzed like a wasp in her hand. Julie slapped the screen to her ear. "Hello? Callum? Hello?"

In the background, Depot delivered a cheerful bark of greeting.

Julie hadn't realized how hard her heart had been knocking in her chest till it started to slow. "Callum? Is that you?"

He answered, his voice pitched low. "Sweetheart, it's me, be quiet."

A pause, some barely audible sounds that could've been mumbles, then Callum said, "Listen to me. Everything's okay. But you have to stop talking and listen."

Julie obeyed instantly.

"I can't come back for you now," Callum told her, still speaking quietly. "I'll tell you why later. There's a motel, maybe half a mile south on the road. Go and get a room for the night. I'll pick you up at first light tomorrow. You'll be back in time for school."

"Callum—" Julie found herself whispering too.

Explanations arrowed through her head. The grandmother had gotten to Callum. He was setting her up; one of the Hempsteads would be waiting at the motel. But when Callum spoke again, his voice laden with emotion, that sort of traitorousness felt outside the realm of possibility. Callum was protecting Julie from something.

"Sweetheart," he said. "Don't answer your phone tonight, okay? Even if it's me."

Julie didn't expect to get any rest, far away from her dog, on an uncomfortable motel bed, sheets coarse with laundering. But after a hot shower and dinner from a vending machine, grief over Ellie, last night's missed sleep, and the events of the day assailed her, and Julie could no longer fend off fatigue.

What if the grandmother knew where she was and sent someone to come get her, or vanquish her farther away, in the night? A yawn cracked Julie's jaw as she leaned back against the headboard. The grandmother might have total dominion over Mercy, but Julie had a feeling that her reach didn't extend off-island. She should be safe here for the night. Julie collapsed onto the paper-thin pillow, and didn't stir until the alarm on her phone woke her just before dawn. She got up to trudge the half mile back to the ferry landing.

Callum stood on the dock, Depot trotting in an anxious circle around him.

Julie started to run, but her dog covered the distance faster, nearly knocking her down with his heft. "Deep," Julie murmured, kneeling to bury her face in his fur. "You okay? Did you have a good night?" The dog licked her face, a long, rough swipe of his tongue that seemed to signal assent.

Callum stood above them, arms crossed over his chest. He smiled at the dog's rejoicing, but his face wore the hardened expression it had when he and Julie first met.

Julie rose. "What happened? Are you all right?"

For her dog was clearly fine. His breath smelled like meat; he must have eaten a kingly repast. Callum wouldn't have had any dog food. Perhaps he and Depot had shared a steak.

"We'd better get on the boat if I'm to get you back to school on time," Callum said. Something had changed in his voice.

She followed Callum, assisting Depot on board. The dog paced back and forth a few times before positioning his body in a mound on a dry section of floor.

Julie walked over to the bow, noting that she didn't require a hand for balance, even though the water was choppy, white-tipped triangles of waves all around. The *Mary Martin* started chugging out to sea. Callum eased the throttle forward, then turned to face Julie.

"I hung around on the mainland for as long as I could and still count on getting back to the island before dark," he said. "After nightfall, a boat coming to Mercy is like a beacon, no way to hide its passage. Especially not from anyone on the cliff side of the island."

Julie wiped a slick of spray off her face. "You knew who I was hiding from?"

"I took a guess," Callum responded. "You're the teacher, and that woman's always had a strange thing where your star pupil is concerned. I assume she knows we've been spending time together, and I figured it'd be better if she didn't have any reason to wonder why you'd made a trip off-island."

Julie sent him a look of silent thanks.

"But I would've come back for you," Callum continued. "First of all, I could've been wrong in what I guessed, and second, the Hempsteads don't intimidate me. Walt was a good man, but the rest have always kept their distance, which is what we all seem to prefer." He paused. "I would've suggested you get a little tough with the family if need be. You're allowed to leave if you want to, and if you insisted on keeping the trip a secret, well, then you and I both could've spent the night in the motel."

"So why didn't you?" Julie asked, suppressing a flutter of longing as she imagined the night if Callum had been there beside her. "Come back?"

"Because Mrs. Hempstead sent someone to my house."

"What?" Julie said. She recalled her paranoia in the motel room. "Who?"

"His name is Mike Cowry. Do you know him?"

Julie sent him a do-I-ever sort of look.

"Cowry said Mrs. Hempstead needed to see you. He was to bring you to the estate. He'd checked your house, knew you weren't there. Or out to dinner or maybe seeing to something at Ellie's. Which was a little too much knowing for my taste. Then Cowry heard my phone blowing up, and it seemed like"—Callum broke off with that same troubled air—"he'd guessed you were the one who was calling, which would've given the lie to me telling him you were upstairs in my room."

A bright streak of scarlet appeared to line the horizon.

Julie blinked. "You told him I was there?"

Callum gave a nod. "Indisposed. Sick. I might've suggested we both had a little too much to drink. I had to convince him that you were on-island but unable to make it to the Hempsteads. Having your dog helped with the story. Cowry seemed to buy it."

"I guess I'm lucky it was him," Julie said. That pallid, stumpy man, willing to do everything from rifle through her recycling to abduct her for the grandmother's purposes. "I have a feeling the grandmother might not have been so readily fooled."

The streak in the sky began to paint the underbellies of clouds with coral.

"That doesn't look good," Callum said, tracking her gaze.

"Is it true?" Julie asked. "Red sky at morning, sailors take warning?"

Callum looked at her levelly. "What does the old lady want with you? As I say, that family has never been my favorite group of people. But this went beyond that."

Julie splayed both hands on the side of the boat, pushing down as if bracing herself. Spray coated her skin and the floor rolled underfoot.

"All right." She took in a salty breath. "I'll tell you."

"That's not possible," Callum said, once Julie had woven the incidents involving Peter, her own heightened suspicions, and what she'd just learned from the Crofts into as coherent a narrative as possible. "I remember when Martha Hempstead got pregnant. Doug Meetz over at Perry's is a pal of mine, and he joked about all the supplies he had to order—early pregnancy tests, vitamins, this special pillow, things he didn't usually stock."

Julie opened her mouth, but Callum went on.

"The whole island was talking about it. They felt about Martha and Walter's coming baby the way folks do on the other side of the pond"— Callum gestured out to sea, then spun the wheel on the *Mary Martin*— "when one of the royals is expecting."

"They were *trying* to get pregnant," Julie corrected. "But they wouldn't have succeeded in having a child apparently. Not a biological one."

At which point, the grandmother banished Melinda, never to be seen on Mercy Island again, while sequestering her firstborn daughter somewhere for the remainder of the gestation, or maybe helping her fake a pregnancy for the benefit of the islanders.

"I felt the same way," Julie said, watching the look of horror in Callum's eyes rise like water as the implications came clear. A stolen child, imposed adoption, duplicitous parenthood achieved—or inflicted. She licked her lips, tasted a lacing of salt upon them.

"Okay," Callum said, squinting as the western shore of Mercy penciled a thin line across the horizon. "So what do we do about it?"

We, Julie heard. How could she have suspected Callum of being another trick in the grandmother's dark book of spells, one more soldier in her lair?

"I want Peter and his biological parents to see each other," Julie said. "At least once. Then the family—families, I mean—can take it from there."

"Makes sense. I guess we don't know what they'll decide to do."

"But teachers are supposed to act in loco parentis," Julie went on. "Not kidnap their students. Which this would basically be."

Julie could never inflict the pain of losing a child. Even though Martha didn't really seem to want to be a mother. She'd said as much, and the caretaking attempts Julie had witnessed all looked wooden, rote, often driven by the grandmother. If Peter had a chance to meet his biological parents, then the playing field that had been tilted so steeply in Martha's favor would be leveled a bit. Martha could still choose to fight for the boy if she wished. Melinda and Bobby had lost a baby, an agony Julie knew all too well. Only they had a chance to get theirs back.

Callum rubbed his scruff of beard. "It isn't kidnapping. It's island justice."

"Island justice," Julie echoed. She didn't need Callum to explain what he meant. Her uncle and grandfather had dispensed mountain justice, often not using the most moral of means. But perhaps Julie could do better.

"If Cowry's visit last night is any indication," Callum said, "it isn't going to be easy to get Peter off-island."

Julie moved to stand beside him at the wheel. "No, it won't be. I'm never alone with Peter when I'm not in charge of all the other children as well." A pause to run through something in her mind. "But I have an idea. If you can get to the cove again with your boat." Julie computed quickly. "This afternoon at 3:20, maybe a bit earlier. Don't be late."

If the students could be in their places, do their parts as directed, and everything went as scripted, then this just might work.

Callum gave a slow nod.

"First," Julie told him, "I have to put on a show."

PART V

ANGEL OF MERCY

CHAPTER SIXTY-NINE

J ulie ran around the building a few times to give Depot some exercise, then opened up the schoolhouse. Still early enough to arrange things before the children arrived. She brought Depot to the teacher's room, fed him, drank a cup of coffee herself, then climbed up to the loft to make sure the spotlights were aimed correctly. From this angle, it would be impossible for the audience to see the wings of the stage. The kids were only performing one scene today; the lights could stay fixed in position.

Island justice, Callum had called it, and Julie for the most part bought that as an explanation. Or justification. Unless that was just excuse making on her part? If anything went wrong today, she would be at best a loose cannon, at worst a felon, and no ends-justifying-the-means-style rationalization could save her. She would never teach again. Ruin the life she'd only just begun to piece back together.

But far worse than that was the possibility that she might ruin Peter's.

Julie climbed down the ladder, lost to her thoughts, her mental ping-pong, should she or shouldn't she, as she felt with her feet for each rung. When she reached the bottom and turned around in the narrow space, the grandmother stood there.

Julie clapped a hand to her chest, letting out a muffled swear beneath her breath.

The grandmother's mouth lifted in a partial smile. "Language unbecoming to one charged with the care and keeping of our youth."

"I'm sorry," Julie said. "You took me by surprise."

"I imagine I did," the grandmother replied.

"Would you like to come have a seat in the schoolroom?" Julie suggested. "I just made coffee and there's extra."

"No need for that," the grandmother replied.

She turned and led the way out from backstage, behaving for all the world as if the place belonged to her, were just one more part of her domain.

When they got to the classroom, Julie sat down in the chair behind her desk before the grandmother could appropriate it, too, take it for her throne.

But the woman seemed content to remain standing, looking down at Julie. "I'm sorry to hear you were taken ill last night."

Julie nodded shortly. "Thank you. I feel much better now."

Uncharacteristically, the grandmother hesitated. "Have you ever had a child who disappointed you, Ms. Weathers?"

Julie felt something twist inside her. "Now, Mrs. Hempstead. You did your research. You already know I've never had the privilege of experiencing that."

The grandmother threaded her long, elegant fingers together. "Well, I have," she said. "One who did something so incorrigible, such a betrayal of all who loved and raised her, that she fled, never to be heard from again." The grandmother's face tightened in a pinch of contempt. "Martha knew better. She married a man from a family with all the shine and staying power of our own. She and Walter gave us an heir, and if not a spare, that was all right, because Peter holds the potential of any two children."

It wasn't quite a statement of love. Need perhaps. Regard for who Peter could be. But not for who he was.

The grandmother's gaze hooked Julie's, offering no dispute. She was fine with Peter's role in their dynasty, his reason for being. She'd stolen him to meet it. "Peter is not an actor, and never will be. And he won't be in your little show."

Was the grandmother faking her out, pretending that the only problem was Peter's desire to act? Or did she know that Julie had learned the truth about his lineage, and Julie's plan for today as well? The former was just this side of possible, but the latter would've required mind-reading. Still, as the grandmother's eyes went glacier-blue, Julie was convinced that via whatever dark magic means, she had somehow ascertained everything. It didn't really matter. Julie couldn't allow her to ban her grandson from performance; Peter needed to be in the mini-production this afternoon. Period. Julie's thoughts scrambled, trying to come up with a way to convince the grandmother of something when the old woman was always the one to do the convincing, employing any strategy necessary.

She couldn't change the grandmother's character. But she could use it against her.

"We're only putting on one scene this afternoon," Julie said. "A run-through of sorts, like a trial session. But all the parents will be here. I don't know if it would do for the Hempsteads not to be front and center at an island-wide event. That might suggest a certain downturn, a step away from a previously prominent position."

She met the grandmother's blue iron gaze, steely, unblinking.

"You were good enough to approve my last-minute budgetary request for the spotlights. I think it would be appropriate for this to be known as the Hempstead Theater." Julie pointed behind them to the stage. "I have a thank-you all prepared to share with the crowd."

A gleam sparked in the old woman's eyes, desire for what was on offer perhaps, but also respect for Julie. *Well played, Ms. Weathers,* her expression seemed to say.

The grandmother answered with stately dignity. "As we do wish to support young Peter, we will make the effort to be here today for your special project."

Julie bowed her head a respectful distance.

"But after that, Peter will be removed from this classroom and home-schooled. His mother has been at loose ends since her husband died, and this will be a productive form of endeavor for her." A studied pause. "We'll ask for your removal as well, Ms. Weathers. Laura Hutchins is already in the process of finding an interim replacement."

Julie's whole body buckled. She felt the announcement like a physical stab.

The grandmother's expression contained an uncustomary softness. "Go home, Julie. Return to where you came from. You have family there, people who care about you. I hear that your husband came to visit you the other day. It's not too late to reconcile, try to save your marriage. Go back where you belong."

For a fragment of a second, Julie's perception of the grandmother shifted, finding a certain benevolence in her rule. For the first time, she understood why people chose to listen to this woman, believe that while autocratic and in control, she had their best interests at heart.

It hadn't been a request, but still Julie murmured, "Perhaps you're right."

The grandmother didn't have to resort to breaking laws, Ellie had told her. She possessed other means. She would find your fault lines, push till they cracked. The grandmother ferreted out a person's true nature, the sore and wanting spots, yes, but also people's deepest desires, needs, and urges, which made them susceptible to her command.

Julie glanced through the schoolhouse windows to the cove. As the gray swath of sea lifted and fell, she thought of the mountains back home. She missed them; they'd always been steadfast friends to her, life-long presences and hulking protectors she never took for granted. They would be a kaleidoscope of color before too long, a living, dying, impressionist tableau.

Julie pushed back her chair from the desk and stood up.

She extended her hand to the grandmother, who took it between the lacy skin of her palms, the wrinkles of old age on hands that had known both hard work and cosseting.

"I believe we are in agreement?" the grandmother said, and Julie nodded.

The grandmother wanted her to leave the island, and Julie would obey that order.

But she was taking Peter with her.

CHAPTER SEVENTY

J ulie opened the barn doors and the students trooped in.

She watched as all but one of them got settled at their desks, nudged the seventh-grade boy into his, while ticking off names for attendance. Everyone was here for the big day, except the sixth-grade boys, who were missing. Julie's eyes found Macy in her seat. She didn't even have to pose a question; something was clearly up.

Macy fought, but failed, to repress a grin. "It's surprise time again, Ms. W. Go over to the other door and look."

Julie crossed to the side entrance, and drew it open.

Outside stood the sixth-grade boys, minus Peter. They were balancing structures covered with sheets, three, four feet high, one steeply peaked, and each with the circumference of a gargantuan tree, a Sequoia or Redwood. A flatter one had the shape of a round banquet tabletop. The boys held the objects upright, breathing hard with effort. Scott Harness gripped the handles of a wheelbarrow, which looked to be filled with a heap of blocks, ranging in size from a brick to a microwave, their outlines apparent beneath another drape of cloth.

"What on earth?" Julie said, fighting a smile herself.

"Hey, can I get some help over here?" Scott asked, the demand concealing his obvious excitement. "It's not like you can just push a wheelbarrow across sand."

The students formed a conga line between the side door and the stage so that the wheelbarrow could be unloaded. Then the larger objects were tipped on end, rolled, maneuvered, or lugged into the school, before being hoisted up to the waiting arms of the biggest children who pushed and heaved and dragged them onto stage and behind the thick velvet curtain.

Martha appeared at the end of the library path. Without a word of farewell, she sent Peter on his way, and the boy came skidding into the schoolhouse.

Huffing and panting, he called out, "Am I too late? I want to help!"

It was like a camera angle changing, revealing the image that had been distorted before. Of course Peter was Melinda's son and not Martha's. That silky flop of hair, its texture identical to his mother's feathery strands versus his aunt's spiral curls. Sometimes Peter's eyes appeared gray-blue, and that was all Martha, but whenever azure light returned, while performing, or in his hideout, or with Depot, he became Melinda's again.

Peter ran and joined the throng of students. And as he extended his arms to accept one of the draped pieces and pass it to the next child in line, another transformation occurred. Peter didn't blend into the group so much as become one more distinct part of it, an additive factor no greater nor lesser than any of the other children around him.

In deed and comportment, he emerged, essential and unique, as one of them.

Lara Milton gave Julie a shy smile, then yanked the curtains shut. A thud of hammers followed, objects falling, hissed commands telling the seventh-grade boy to watch out, older students cautioning younger to be careful, until Julie cried, "What are you all doing back there?" She thought they might need adult supervision, although island kids were capable, roaming free, assisting their parents, keeping themselves from drowning.

Eddie Cowry pulled the curtains apart just far enough to form an oval opening around his face. "Shh! You'll see in a little while." His voice contained a ringing note of authority, and Julie felt a flicker of happiness for the boy.

Knocks and banging continued to come from behind the curtain. Then the grating sound of wood against wood. At last, a dusk of quiet fell, and all was still onstage.

"Ready, Ms. Weathers?" someone asked.

"Close your eyes!" another child shouted.

"Put your hands over your face, okay?"

Hurried exchanges of last-minute thoughts, ideas, decisions.

"Fasten that piece tighter."

"Macy, is this good?"

"Yes. Oliver, can you stop it, just stand over here."

"Not there, here."

"Hey, quit it, Oliver!"

"She said over there, Ollie!"

"Now?"

"Okay, ready!"

The curtain was hurled back, and Julie uncovered her eyes.

On the stage stood a lighthouse.

The children had written their script so that instead of a tower, Rapunzel was locked away in a lighthouse, the beam forever aimed toward ships at sea, never able to reach land. This served as a metaphor for their play, and now, a physical backdrop to it.

Julie had been in dozens of shows in her life: school productions, then community theater, even summer stock for one glorious July before her parents finally reeled her in, chastising her for how impulsive she'd always been, while claiming this was the worst example yet, a whole month squandered when she could've been earning money for her education, until Julie, aflush with shame and guilt and selfish regret over what she was about to give up, abdicated her part to an understudy who went on to achieve minor fame off-Broadway.

Never had the sets equaled the sight before her now.

Julie boosted herself onto stage, not bothering to use the stairs.

The lighthouse rose eight feet in the air, stabilized from behind by long planks of wood nailed to brackets on the floor. The structure had been fashioned out of plywood, its surface painted to look like stone, with blocks affixed here and there in patches across the exterior, which gave the whole thing a dimensionality worthy of the pros.

In the uppermost, narrower portion, a circle had been cut out through which a light could be aimed to simulate the beam. Crude but sturdy steps had been nailed to the interior wall in a spiral, leading to a platform at the top with a hole for entrance and exit. The front wall swung open on metal hinges so the audience could watch the actors perform.

The rear of the lighthouse had a wide slit, allowing for hidden access and departure.

"Do you like it, Ms. Weathers?"

"What do you think of the lighthouse?"

"Ms. W? Are you okay?"

"How?" Julie could scarcely speak. "How on earth did you do this? You told me none of you had ever been in a play. You couldn't have any familiarity with set design."

She walked in a circle around the structure, trailing her hand across the stones. They felt craggy, practically real. The children had used glue to adhere sand and loops of kelp at the base, and painted cresting waves.

The sixth-grade boys all began to talk at once.

"We may've never built a set before but—"

"—we've built chicken coops and boat slips and—"

"—chimneys!"

"Dude, you've never built a chimney."

"That needs a flue. And to, like, vent properly—"

"Have so—"

"No way—"

"All right." Julie intervened with a smile. "The fact that you know why a chimney would be hard to construct tells me how you were able to do this."

She had been planning to stack crates, maybe do a team mural at lunch. But this would be like a magic trick. Make the eleven-year-old boy disappear.

"Our dads helped," Scott Harness said on a confessional note.

"Only a little," another put in.

"Mine didn't haul traps all day. He said rain was coming, but it never rained."

"My dad made the slots that let us put it together so easy."

It was a marvel of engineering, both in construction and assembly, and Julie told the boys so. They ducked their heads, hiding red-flushed cheeks. Their level of pride went beyond fist bumps or high fives, rendered them still and contained. Only the boy in seventh grade broke the spell, racing up to the top of the structure, whereupon all the children began taking turns testing the staircase and pushing open the front wall.

"Careful!" Julie called. "No more than three at a time up there."

The students climbed down and assembled onstage without being told—even, for once, the seventh-grade boy. The degree of excitement present in the schoolhouse felt physical, unseen, like wind or heat.

"Everyone have the scene we're going to perform down? We'll run through it one more time, dress rehearsal at lunch today. But first we have to do our usual lessons—"

Groans and complaints, which Julie quickly shushed.

"Don't worry, we'll devote the afternoon to getting ready. The song Macy wrote for Peter with the rest of the cast a-cappella-ing the beat—"

Peter beamed, accepting fist bumps, exclamations of *You got this* from his friends.

"—after which Rapunzel leaves the lighthouse for the first time in her life, just like we practiced, and her mother—"

"That's me," Macy burst out.

"—who's just barely been trilling her song, bursts into a wail, longing, terror, rage, then the curtain comes down, you all take your bows, go home to celebrate, and tomorrow afternoon we start getting ready for the full shebang, which goes up in just a few months."

At lunchtime, Julie called Peter aside. The other kids would figure she was giving the lead a few last-minute directions. "Peter? If I asked you to go somewhere with me, would that be scary for you? Would you be frightened?"

Peter's eyes looked like placid blue pools. "You know some awesome places on this island already, those tide pools, the walks you take Depot on. If you wanted me to go someplace, I'd probably just think you found something else to show me."

"Well," Julie told him, "you'd be right."

CHAPTER SEVENTY-ONE

The only change that needed to take place in the schoolhouse in order for Julie's scheme to work was for the curtain to be extended so that a section could hang in front of the side door. Julie took Depot on a walk, going over details in her head. A bit different from the usual setup, but it should seem like a reasonable part of turning a classroom into a theater for any parents who noticed.

Come tomorrow, Mercy Island would close over Peter like a lid. He'd either be removed from Julie's circle of influence, or she from his. If she didn't do this today, then Peter might never get the opportunity to learn that he had a whole other set of parents who loved him, a chance at another life. The grandmother clearly intended to let her grandson live out his days never knowing of Melinda's and Bobby's existence.

Julie found a bolt of fabric in the compartment beneath the stage. While the performers practiced, she asked the sewing-whiz/costume-design girls to turn a section of flannel into a drape. Attached by a row of

Velcro tabs, it would cloak the exit stage right, anyone behind it invisible to those in the audience.

"Ms. W?" Macy called out from the lighthouse.

Overseeing the curtain process, Julie glanced up and nodded.

"We're ready to run through the first song for you now."

Peter wore a silken shirt of glistening lilac and a pair of brown trousers. His blond locks appeared freshly combed, the work of one of the girls on hair and makeup who had an impossible-to-hide crush and had made Peter's head shine like a cap of gold.

At the top of the lighthouse, he pushed open the front wall.

Down on stage, a hush fell. The other performers crouched, hands on their knees, only the seventh-grade boy starting a jittery tap prematurely. For just a moment everyone else was frozen, holding their positions as they aimed their gazes up at Peter. Then the kids deepened into squats, before straightening up again and dropping, up and down, up and down, human bellows giving life to the beat Macy had composed.

Peter broke into a hard-hitting volley of words, each syllable punctuated by the rhythm being stomped out onstage.

"This tower's—a bower—it don't have the power—to hold me—"

His voice gathered force and speed, as on stage the chorus made instruments of their bodies, crooned a wordless melody with their mouths.

"—a prison, a fortress, that saves all the ships lost at sea—"

Peter's song continued to pound, while his moves took him around the lighthouse so fast his body blurred. He gazed outward at the audience, although from his desperate expression, it seemed he might actually be seeing the ocean, vast and endless, searching for something that never appeared. Peter moved fast and faster, a human whirlpool, and yet he never missed a step, and his notes were delivered not one bit out of breath.

"—grants protection—course correction—to captains and merchants and sailors—"

The sounds from the chorus waned to a simultaneous patter-clap of hands and a butterfly tremble of voices. Continuous yet quiet, even the seventh-grade boy momentarily subdued in his antics, so that Peter's final line seemed to shatter the stage.

"—so why can't it give—the safety that's promised—to me?"

Julie wondered if a gathering of boisterous children had ever in history been so silent. If she didn't start clapping soon, it might be that no one ever would, captured and stilled for all time in this moment of utter pleasure over what they had done, combined with awed appreciation for greatness in one of their own.

The parents arrived right on time at three o'clock.

Come Christmas, if she was still here, Julie hoped to have adult-sized chairs, even just folding ones, but today she had settled for the children angling the seats away from their desks and orienting each one toward the stage. The awkward act of fitting into the undersized accommodations would create delay if the grown-ups tried to get up. Every extra second Julie could get before her ruse was discovered would help.

Macy was almost as much of a scene stealer as Peter. When she appeared in the lighthouse, howling out her rage and betrayal and loss, the audience would be transfixed.

No one would be thinking of Rapunzel at that moment. They would've just seen him perform. Have no reason to think he had gone anywhere except backstage to await taking his bow. Or so Julie hoped.

She checked one last time that the cast had taken their places. Peeking out from behind the curtain, she saw every seat filled. The children doing sets and costumes and hair and makeup sat on the floor beside their parents to watch.

Mike Cowry had come.

The fathers of the sixth-grade boys had shown up along with the mothers, and Julie knew by now what such a thing meant, how hard it was to get time off a boat.

Only Martha was missing from the audience.

You're free, Julie heard her say.

The schoolroom vibrated with chatter and exchanges of news, people gathered who hadn't seen each other beyond a quick hello in passing for a while, who might never have been together in this large a group before, not even at the Hempsteads' party.

Julie stepped out from behind the curtain, and the chatting decreased in volume to murmurs before dying out altogether. Before coming here, Julie had envisioned the islanders as a hard and flinty people, steeped in the salt of the sea, connections as difficult to till as island soil. But the faces that turned to her were rapt, expectant, even friendly.

"Hello!" Julie cried.

She hoped the tremor in her voice would be attributed to nerves over the performance rather than the discreet looks she kept snatching at the wall clock, checking how much time they had before Callum could hopefully muffle the sound of his engine sufficiently to conceal his boat's arrival in the cove. She felt a pinch of panic, no way could this be pulled off as planned. The grandmother saw and heard everything, and anything she didn't, she had found out for her.

But Julie had no choice. Because Peter had no choice. It was up to her to give him one. The children's voices would drown out any noise from outside, hints or signs of the escape.

"I'm so happy to see you all here today for our first-ever performance at the Hempstead Theater!" Julie continued.

After a second's delay, the assembled crowd began to clap, finding the grandmother and the Captain in the audience and leaning over or twisting back to smile and congratulate them in whispers, delivering handshakes or touches on the arm, if they could reach.

Looking out over the seats, Julie aimed a smile whose wobble she hoped wouldn't be detectable at this distance. "First, I would like to introduce you all to someone I know there's been some gossip about, my big, friendly dog, Depot."

Julie walked Depot back and forth in front of the stage, mocking the motions made at a dog show, and feeling relieved when the audience members laughed convivially. Then she led Depot behind the newly strung-up portion of curtain, getting the parents accustomed to seeing it used. Julie told Depot to stay before slipping back through a gap in the fabric.

"Next, I want to thank Mrs. Hempstead and the entire school board for our brand-new spotlights. I think you will all agree in just a few moments that we are already putting them to great use. And now, without further ado, I present to you your children!"

The velvet curtain was drawn back, and the students launched into their act.

There were gasps of admiration and even fright from the audience when Peter skidded to a stop at the open lighthouse wall, belting out the final line of his rap. Each word was delivered like a blow, a punch; the audience rocked in their seats, mouths open in wonder at this Peter who had never appeared to them before, at least not in this form. His performance had been so magnificent that Julie feared it would be cruel, if not impossible, to drag him away before curtain call. Peter might forget their plan entirely, caught in the throes of the theater high.

But when Julie ducked behind the newly attached length of curtain, using the pounding of applause to shield any sound of her motion, she found Peter standing there, his hand on Depot's collar. Their gazes darted back and forth as they waited for her to appear.

"Oh good," Julie said, breathless with relief. She tugged open the side entrance, and nudged both boy and dog through.

She was just about to follow when a woman came up and blocked her exit.

Julie knew who she was, could identify her now, although she hadn't been able to put a name to a face the other day on the library path. Perhaps because this mother had been in the company of a toddler then, instead of here on behalf of a seventh-grade boy.

The side door swung shut, casting Julie and her companion into darkness.

On the other side of the curtain, a hushed silence hovered, the moments before a new performer was set to take her place, and a new act could begin.

During Julie's conversation with Chloe Manning, this woman had straddled the line between harried, slightly out-of-control mother and menacing threat. Today the side she inhabited was clear. The woman barred Julie's way, though she didn't quite face her or look at her, instead staring somewhere just past with a cold, dead blankness in her eyes.

"You're not going anywhere, Ms. Weathers," she said.

Julie might almost have laughed at the idea that the warrior who'd been sent to prevent her passage was a stay-at-home mom, last seen attending story hour, except that when Julie made a move to get by, the woman reached into her purse and took out a knife.

CHAPTER SEVENTY-TWO

The woman seemed utterly ready to use her weapon; in fact, her leaden expression had changed, suggesting more than preparedness. Relish, delight, as if the bounds of normalcy had been loosened, and something dreadful inside her had been unleashed. She bounced on her toes, just daring Julie to oppose her; the skin on her face glowed with a manic coat of perspiration.

From the stage came the slap of Macy's footsteps up the lighthouse steps.

Julie didn't have much time before the performance ended, the children took their bows, and everyone cleared out of the schoolhouse. She wasn't even sure where Peter and Depot were right now; when Julie hadn't come out, would they have just stayed put?

The woman kept the hand not holding the knife on her hip, in a posture that looked for all the world like a disciplining mom, which Julie supposed she was. The blade she wielded belonged to a kitchen set, although that didn't make it any less lethal, especially given the fact that it was held between steady, unshaking fingers, angled right at neck height.

Julie heard the first words of the solo Macy had written, which she'd titled "I've Already Lost You." The song would end two minutes from now, give or take, on a single, wailing note of rage. Macy could keep such a note suspended for a staggering, dazzling amount of time, and Julie had instructed her to hold it as long as possible.

"Mrs. Pratt," she said, the name coming to her just in time, one she had recently circled on the roster as requiring outreach. "This is... Well, it's nuts."

She was hoping plain speech would jar the woman out of whatever surely temporary state of insanity had allowed her to transform from island mom to knife-flaunting lunatic, but Mrs. Pratt didn't shift or stir from her position, nor did her grip on the blade falter.

"Maryanne has done so much for me and my family," she told Julie, eyes alight with a by-now-familiar fervor. "The least I can do is make sure today goes without a hitch."

"Even if it's illegal?" Julie said. "Threatening bodily harm? Assault?"

Mrs. Pratt appeared to consider the question. "Or worse."

Julie recoiled, retreating backward just a step toward the roar of Macy's song.

"You still don't seem to understand our island," Mrs. Pratt said distantly. "Maryanne Hempstead protects us. She gives us life. And in return we do whatever she asks. In this case, making sure you don't leave the schoolhouse before she does."

Julie wasn't sure which was worse—the madness of the woman's statement, or the fact that she didn't appear to know it was mad. She fought to find words, anything that could combat such ferocious but misplaced loyalty.

"In less than two years," Julie said at last, "your son is going to leave for the high school on the mainland, where he will either be medicated into a stupor, placed in a self-contained classroom hundreds of miles away, or both." Julie brought the woman's face into focus. "You will need a teacher who knows Oliver well to be an effective advocate so that a better plan can be put in place. Now"—she looked down at the knife—"I suggest you get out of my way."

Briefly, the woman's eyes flickered with the awareness of someplace bigger than Mercy Island, and in that moment, Julie gave her a shove so hard she stumbled.

When Julie got outside, the day was both sunny and gray, a strange, two-faced dichotomy, as if the weather couldn't decide who to be. Peter stood in the little plot of kelpy grass, holding onto Depot. When he spotted Julie, he met her eyes with a look of certainty and heightened expectation, as if he'd known all along that things were going to go this way. Julie grabbed Peter by the hand, and they started to run toward the cove, Depot racing along at their side.

Assuming Callum had brought the *Mary Martin* to the closest possible point next to shore, they would still have some distance to cover in the dinghy. And a dinghy could only be rowed so fast; it wasn't a craft built for speed.

The tide was coming in, up to the boulders that stood between Julie, Peter, Depot and the beach. Suddenly, a shadow, long and sloping, was thrown in front of them, cast by the sun and a dark cloud. Julie lifted her head to see the grandmother looming beside one of the rocks, water swirling around her ankles in a furious froth.

"You must think yourself very clever," she said to Julie. "Such a perfect choice of play. Why, this move of yours feels almost…scripted." The grandmother's thin, sculpted brows drew together in a frown. "But what did you intend to do with Peter? Do you imagine taking him to that backwoods village you call home and raising him yourself? As a substitute perhaps for the child you let die?"

As blindingly cruel as the words were, Julie was glad to hear them. They meant the grandmother did not in fact know that Julie had learned the truth about Peter's birth. And thus had no clue where Julie planned to bring him.

The grandmother raised her voice to be heard over the roiling surf. "Don't you think others have tried to best me? That awful, impoverished man who thought himself good enough for my secondborn. My own husband even. No one has ever succeeded in battling me. I can muster a bigger army." Her gaze scoured Julie. "You should have remembered whom you're opposing. All of this"—she thrust out a hand, and it wasn't clear whether she meant the school, or the island, or the whole of the ocean—"is mine. It's been my family's since this slab of rock was settled. And now I'm the ruler of—"

"—a speck of land that sits eight miles out to sea," Julie broke in.

The grandmother eyed her as if from a great height. "How naive you are. The size of what comes below doesn't matter. All that matters is who's at the top." A pause. "Now come, Peter. It's time to go home." Turning her back on Julie, the grandmother stretched out an arm behind her, so confident it would be taken, she didn't even look.

Peter glanced at Julie before beginning to walk toward his grand-mother, hand obediently extended. But he darted back to deliver one final pat to Depot's head.

Julie had just described Depot as big and friendly, and he was.

But he could become dragon-fierce when someone he loved was threatened.

Depot pulled back his lips in a tremble of fury, then took a leap for-ward, knocking the grandmother onto the sand. She struggled into a sitting position, trying to get to her feet, but Depot staved her off against one of the seaweed-slick rocks.

Julie snatched up Peter's hand and ran with him toward shore.

Depot kept growling, not so much as a pause in his threatening rumble until Julie and Peter had reached the sea. When they got to the curl of surf at the water's edge, it became clear how rough the seas had grown since Julie and Callum had made the crossing that morning. A few yards to their left, Callum held the skiff in place, arms straining, muscles bulging, as he prevented the craft from being driven seaward by incoming waves. He rowed toward Julie and Peter as soon as he spotted them, and they splashed through the water and climbed into the dinghy. From behind, at a galloping run, only a second's hesitation at water's edge, Depot entered the sea. Julie and Peter heaved and hauled, pulling the dog into the little boat. His weight forced the skiff down before it popped back up into a well between waves.

Callum sank the oars into the water, pulling back on them fiercely, and grunting with the effort it took to battle the crests. For a second, gray skies obliterated fair, but the sun fought back, throwing out shafts of light so bright they were blinding.

Julie searched the water for the *Mary Martin*. Fifty yards or so out, and once onboard, they would have the power of an engine. But the peaks and valleys of the sea opposed them. The skiff dropped and climbed, steep angles that Callum had to work to navigate. Which was probably why he didn't realize it first, get the chance to warn them. There was too much weight in the skiff.

The floor of the small craft sat low in the water, waves coming halfway up its sides. The farther they got from shore, the higher the water rose; it was now at the rim of the dinghy. Seawater trickled over in streams, then the largest crest yet towered. When it broke, it would pour into the dinghy, a waterfall, not a trickle.

Julie grabbed Depot's collar, holding onto her dog with one hand, while keeping Peter close beside her with the other. Callum lifted the oars free of the water; no way to row in the face of a wave that size. They all braced themselves as it plumed, drenching them, water pooling at their feet. Another wave like that one would submerge the small craft.

Callum's eyes met Julie's.

"You'll have to row!" he yelled. "I'll take Depot and swim with him to my boat!"

Julie's gaze shot to her dog. He was trying to get free of a puddle of seawater—ever since their swim by the cliffs, he hated being soaked by the ocean—which only made the dinghy pitch up and down more steeply, like a cradle rocked by a demon hand.

A wave loomed in front of them, and Callum fought to hold the skiff steady. The force of the water jolted the craft.

As soon as it bobbed back up, Julie found Callum's gaze, and nodded.

He crawled over the seat, approaching Depot, but the dog backed away, eyes liquid with panic. His paws scrabbled for purchase on the slippery floor. Then his big body hit the bottom of the dinghy with a thud. Depot dropped to his belly, flattening himself out while emitting small, terrified yips.

The dinghy climbed the peak of an oncoming wave, before dropping into a trough and taking on a great gush of water. Callum reached for Depot, who got onto all fours and tried to scuttle away. But there was nowhere for him to go in the tiny, sinking craft. Julie pushed past Peter and knelt before her dog. A wave came up and splashed them both as Julie laid her wet hands on Depot's dripping fur and lowered her face to his.

"It's okay, Deep. You hear me? You're going to be okay." She paused, tears trembling in her eyes, mixing with the wetness already on her face. "But you've got to do this. *We've* got to. For Peter."

Callum edged forward then, keeping himself upright by bracing his hands on both sides of the skiff. He bent down and placed one arm underneath Depot's rump.

The sea let out a mighty roar, and the dog looked at Julie with terror. Then he let Callum lift him, settling into the crook of his arm.

With one immense heave, the two of them went over the side of the skiff and into the mouth of the next huge wave.

CHAPTER SEVENTY-THREE

With its lightened load, the dinghy stayed on top of the water, sliding across the pitched crest of the wave that had taken Depot and Callum. Julie drove the oars like spears through the sea, rowing them in the direction of the *Mary Martin*. The skiff bucked like a rodeo bull in her grasp.

"Sit down!" she told Peter, who was leaning over to try to spot Depot. The boy obeyed instantly, dropping onto the plank seat.

Julie fought to pull the skiff forward, but it felt like trying to move through cement. A great roll of water began to curl, propelling them upward as if they were riding the back of some beast. Julie twisted around, trying to find Callum's boat in the churn. She blinked stinging seawater out of her eyes just in time to see a wave loom up.

"Peter!" Julie shouted. "Peter, duck—"

The wave broke, driving the skiff downward.

"Ms. Weathers!" Peter coughed, spat out a mouthful of liquid. "Look!"

Sputtering and gasping, Julie swiped water from her face, scouring the sea for whatever Peter had seen.

Another lobster boat appeared out of the strange shimmering light, and as soon as Julie read the name painted across its stern, she knew that if their escape hadn't been defeated already, it would be now. *Island Family.* There could be only one family with sufficient belief in its claim to the title to thus designate their boat.

As the *Island Family* chugged closer, taking on form and dimension, Julie slid the oars into their rings, letting the skiff be shunted along by the force of the sea. Thrashing around, trying to row, would only draw attention to them. Perhaps the grandmother would lose sight of the dinghy in the bow and dip of the waves. Julie drew Peter to her across the plank seat, while searching the water for signs of Depot and Callum. She tried to get a bead on the *Mary Martin.* Maybe her dog was already in the boat.

The *Island Family* was upon them now, lifted and dropped by the swells of surf.

Fear, worry, and their near capsize had distorted her thinking, but the realization crept up on Julie now. There was no way the grandmother could have made it to the pier, onto her boat, and out to the cove already. She had been on shore, forced by Depot to stand down, mere minutes ago. Unless the woman were more sorceress than human being, able to defy the laws of time and weather and physics to get to her grandson?

"Come!" came a ringing command, and someone leaned overboard, holding out a hand.

It was the Captain.

———

"Hurry, son," he said, reaching for Peter and swinging the boy up with a show of strength that belied his years and ailments. Then the Captain leaned down again. "You too, my dear," he said, and took Julie by the hand.

When they were both onboard, he confronted her without his customary smile.

Julie tried to dry off her face, but her hands were shaking too hard.

"And now," the Captain said to Julie. "Shall we get our boy where he belongs?"

Peter walked across the boat, legs wobbly, but mostly upright, and lifted a hinged lid on a seat. He pulled out a life jacket and buckled the straps across his narrow chest, passing another one to Julie. The boy enacted the moves automatically, as if being onboard his grandfather's boat called forth training long since impressed.

The *Island Family* was bigger than the *Mary Martin*, and the ease with which it passed over churn that had nearly capsized the dinghy was startling. Waves flattened underneath the boat like hummocks of soil pressed beneath the tread of boots. Julie didn't see the *Mary Martin* anywhere.

With obvious effort, the Captain began to turn the wheel, pointing them toward the mainland. It was only then that Julie noticed how pale and gray the man looked. On Julie it might've been seasickness, but not on a lifelong lobsterman.

"Where are we going?" the Captain asked, speaking over his shoulder while he squinted out toward the horizon. He seemed to have forgotten the last words he had just said. "For our fine day at sea."

Julie swallowed. "Um, Duck Harbor?" She mustered more force in her voice, and repeated it. "Duck Harbor."

"Ah," the Captain said, rubbing one shoulder. "A fine destination indeed. One of my favorites."

"Yes." Julie swallowed again. Her mouth was so dry, salt-parched. "Only could you…can you please go a little faster?"

Peter came up and stood beside her.

The Captain adjusted the wheel in minute increments, turning it arduously, hand over hand. He looked back at them, wearing an expression of affection that shone a light across Peter's face, and even seemed to encompass Julie.

"You girls always did like to go fast," the Captain said. "I used to say, what do you think this is, a motorboat?" He was trying to smile, but his face was beaded with sweat that the sea breeze couldn't evaporate.

The boat bounced gently up and down on the waves, a gymnast on a trampoline, preparing. The Captain held onto the wheel as if it were trying to buck him off, although the sea seemed calm enough now. Suddenly, he removed one hand and clapped it to his arm. Rotating his body in a slow circle, he peered around until his gaze landed on Peter.

"Get to the stern!" he commanded. "Sit down and stay aft until we dock. Do you hear?"

"Yes, Captain," Peter said.

The Captain squeezed his upper arm, fingers trembling with the force he applied.

"Captain?" Peter said, his voice wobbling. "Grandpa? Are you all—"

"I said get going, son. Now!"

Peter ran down the slippery length of the boat, and threw himself down.

The Captain faced Julie. "Take the wheel." Despite his bleary, rheumy vision, there was an unyielding quality to his voice that brooked no protest or delay.

Julie took a step forward, and the Captain let go of the wheel as if it had finally thrown him free. Julie wrapped her hands around the cold metal disk, feeling an instantaneous tug from the boat, a racehorse whose reins she now held.

The Captain gave her a nod. "I knew you'd be the one," he said, and it was the clearest and most certain statement Julie had ever heard him make.

The earthquake tremor of his fall could be felt underfoot, surely all the way back to Peter, perhaps even as a ripple along the ocean floor. The

Captain's eyes were open and staring, fixed on the turbulent sky above, gray and blue still fighting for dominion.

Julie dropped into a crouch, one hand above her on the wheel, and placed two fingers against the Captain's neck. No pulse. Not even a thin thread of breath when she placed her hand an inch or two over his mouth. The Captain's chest was sunken and still. But that ghastly gray tinge had left his face, and he looked almost happy.

Julie rose swiftly and faced the sea.

She couldn't see any sign of land, but the sun had finally beaten its way out of the clouds, and it was possible to tell that they were headed west.

The task seemed doable—certainly the Captain had trusted her with it, even though she had his grandson in her care, not that he'd had much choice—yet boats got lost at sea all the time. The radio system looked complicated. Julie couldn't imagine trying to figure it out and driving at the same time. Who were you even supposed to call for a Mayday?

Briefly, she considered summoning Peter to the front of the boat, but Julie didn't want to frighten the boy more than he already was, nor give him reason to doubt Julie's ability to protect him. Plus, the Captain's wishes had been clear. Peter had already experienced one death this year. He didn't need to see his grandfather, so meager and reduced, lying on the floor of his boat.

They were on course; the Captain had made sure of that. And by this point, Julie could pick out features at sea as she had spied landmarks all her life in the woods. Up ahead bobbed one of those green oversize buoy-type things she'd seen when Callum took her out on his boat. It meant that an obstruction lay underwater, the marker telling you which side to steer clear of.

With a mighty wrench of her hands, Julie sent the *Island Family* past it.

Duck Harbor was a promontory. They should reach it before coming to any other land. And if Julie somehow missed it, the town from which the ferry departed would be next. With the sun having revealed itself and beginning its afternoon descent, so long as Julie kept the boat going straight, the worst that could happen was they would run aground at some spot on the mainland that didn't have a pier.

One damaged lobster boat—but Peter would still be free.

Focused on the horizon, squinting so as to be able to detect the first thin splinter of land, Julie pushed the throttle forward, lurching a bit as the boat picked up speed.

CHAPTER SEVENTY-FOUR

Driving a lobster boat was both easier and harder than Julie had expected. The sea kept wanting to shift it; Julie had to put up a fight with the wheel due to all but invisible, infinitesimal changes in the slug and sway of the water. At the same time, the sheer blankness of a seascape, its total lack of interruption, made whatever you were looking for relatively simple to find.

Duck Harbor was a finger of land poking out into the Atlantic. Julie recognized the ferry station by its size and shape, and turned the wheel abruptly, steering toward the dock in a zigzag line, and coming to a hard stop that pitched her against the wheel. She had no idea how to tie up the boat, but Peter took care of that, jumping out and fiddling with a stout rope.

The ferry station was where she should find Bobby. Julie would bring Peter over and let his father decide how to introduce himself, whether he wanted to call his wife, take Peter to the house, or some other scenario entirely.

But before any of that could happen, someone came running down the pier, a slimly built woman in jeans and a thick sweater, the lowering sun catching purple lights in her hair.

"You came," Melinda said.

"So did you," Julie replied.

Melinda snatched a quick peek around, her gaze darting out to sea. She didn't spy Peter crouched beside the two-pronged hook, nor did he notice her.

"I don't think I've left the dock since you did," Melinda said. "Bobby and I slept in the station last night. Do you have an update for us?"

Peter stood up then. "Ms. Weathers, I got it. It's good."

Julie hadn't been able to hazard a guess about the way in which Peter would be told the truth, although she had considered different possibilities, all filled with confusion, upset, and fear. To learn that the life you'd lived so far was in many ways a falsehood. To feel the ground beneath your feet disintegrate, discover you'd been standing on water and lies.

But when his mother's gaze found him, Julie realized she'd gotten it wrong.

There was no choice to be made, about where or when or how.

And there didn't seem to be much confusion or fear either.

Peter studied Melinda for a moment, his eyes widening. His nostrils did a strange, fluttery thing, as if he'd detected a scent.

Then the boy walked forward, and when Melinda saw him take the first step, she started to move, too, until they were standing in front of each other, two strangers with feathery wisps of hair and matching blue gazes, who were suddenly strangers no more.

They all turned as a colossal thud shook the dock. A second lobster boat was coming clumsily into harbor—his arrival making Julie's look a bit better.

Back in the cove, the grandmother had implied that she could have summoned a whole fleet, a battalion, with one snap of her elegantly gnarled fingers. But all she really needed was a single loyal henchman to reinforce and transport her. She'd found it in Mike Cowry, driving the largest lobster boat yet, newly painted and snazzily fitted out.

The grandmother got off the boat before it came to a full stop, taking an ungainly, lurching step onto the dock, yet somehow giving the impression that she had disembarked with a dockhand at her service, holding her elbow to steady her.

The grandmother's gaze flicked to Melinda, scant notice before she uttered a command. "Get away from that child. Do you want to terrorize him? Alter his entire world? Of course you do. You've never had a care for anybody on earth besides yourself." A mere twitch of her eyes. "And yet you dared to think you could be a mother."

Melinda moved as if she'd been yanked by a rope, a set of reins, or a chain. She sent Peter a quick, halting smile before taking several steps away. Her shoulders flattened into a sunken plane, her head turned, and she stood gazing out to sea, unblinking despite the now-blinding orb of the sun, with tears rolling soundlessly down her cheeks.

Satisfied and sure, the grandmother switched focus. The old woman transferred her attention to Julie, who stood at the edge of the dock.

"You," she intoned. Then her voice erupted in a scream so ragged and hysterical, it seemed to come from a different person entirely. "You were supposed to be broken! Laura Hutchins called you a mound of wretched, guilt-plagued ash!"

Now that hurt. Julie had actually thought she'd done pretty well in that interview.

She faced the grandmother. "Broken people like things to be fixed, Mrs. Hempstead. And I've never seen a life—not even my own sorry one—that needed more fixing than yours."

For just a second, the corners of Melinda's mouth lifted. Then she whispered to Peter, "Let's take a little walk while they talk things out, okay? There are hot drinks in the station. Do you like cocoa?"

Peter shrugged. "Sure." He broke into a jog, heading straight for the building, before turning back and waiting for Melinda. "Are you coming?"

His mother quickened her step, giving a joyful nod. "Oh yes, I am!"

Seeing them walk off, the grandmother let out a wordless shriek, charging at Julie, who stood so close to the edge of the dock that spray sprinkled her. If the grandmother pushed her into the water, she would have time to put a halt to Melinda's new and tenuous attempts at care-taking. To take Peter for her own again before Julie could even make it back to land and lend Melinda a hand in battle. Julie had just seen the woman cow her daughter; she understood now how her mad manipu-lations worked.

As the grandmother came at her, Julie grabbed hold of her wrist.

And they both went into the sea.

The grandmother's wet dress slapped Julie, a weighty, drenching shroud. Her fingers clawed at Julie's skin. Julie struggled to loosen the woman's hold on her so that she could make it back to shore first. Kicking free of the cloth, she started to swim.

One strong hand settled around her leg.

Then the grandmother was upon her, an eel-like length of muscle on top of Julie's back, driving her down beneath the surface.

Julie bucked, throwing the grandmother off, but the woman hurled herself forward, swimming and lurching beside her until she got her hands around Julie's throat. It was shallow enough to stand here, but the grandmother had Julie in her grasp, and she pulled her back toward deeper water, dragging her by the neck.

The grandmother's fingers were weakening; she couldn't maintain such a choking grip for long. With air restored, feet madly treading water beneath her, Julie thrashed back and forth, attempting to push the grandmother away.

The grandmother's hands moved lower, settling onto Julie's shoulders, then suddenly, she drew Julie close in the water. Julie blinked her vision clear of burning droplets. For the oddest moment, it seemed the grandmother intended to embrace her.

Julie had time to stare into the woman's lightless blue eyes, read not just hatred, but outraged disbelief in her gaze. She twisted around just in time to see the submerged rock below the skin of the sea. The grandmother pulled Julie toward her. She was going to use her force, the full weight of her body, to dash them both against the rock.

But Julie was beneath and would hit first.

She curled her legs underneath her, relying on the grandmother's furious grip to keep the two of them afloat. The grandmother used the last vestiges of her strength to draw Julie another inch or two forward, so near that Julie could smell the brine and age on her breath. Then the grandmother gave a vicious shove, driving Julie onto the rock.

Julie's tucked feet scraped first, a long, sandpaper razoring that sent a vaporous cloud of blood into the sea. Kicking off the stone surface, Julie hurtled her body sideways, letting the grandmother fall on top of it instead.

The sound of the impact was muffled by the water. It wasn't possible to tell how hard the grandmother had landed until she floated to the surface, facedown in the sea.

CHAPTER SEVENTY-FIVE

Fighting to catch her breath, Julie treaded water some distance away from the inflating balloon of the grandmother's dress.

Pounding boots along the dock, then somebody leaned over the side. Bobby Croft.

He got his hands underneath the grandmother's arms and heaved her out of the water. He flipped the woman's body over and pressed hard on her chest.

Mike Cowry staggered off the lobster boat, shambling over to study the grandmother's prone form. He'd been there the whole time Julie and the grandmother had been struggling in the water.

Melinda and Peter appeared halfway down the dock; from behind, Bobby seemed to sense their presence and threw one arm out.

"Take the child back to the station!" he commanded, and Melinda turned, grasping Peter's hand in hers and weaving with him between the people just starting to assemble.

Bobby knelt down, did two chest compressions, then started rescue breaths. A plume of water erupted from the grandmother's mouth. Bobby leaned back on his heels while the woman coughed and gasped. When her sputtering had ceased, and her chest rose up and down in something like a steady motion, Bobby got to his feet and bent over her.

"Bob Croft? Is that you?" Even recovering from a near drowning, flat on her back on a dock, the grandmother managed to adopt an imperious expression. "What do you think you're doing, standing over me?" Her hair lay plastered in strings to her scalp; loose flesh on her arms and legs was exposed, fishy and pale.

"I'm arresting you, Maryanne. For assault. Possibly attempted murder."

Maryanne Hempstead let out a hawking laugh, but started coughing again, her breath stolen for another few moments. Finally she quieted and just lay there, eyes open and blinking, as she stared up at the sky.

"I work in various capacities for the port of Duck Harbor. And recently, I was deputized." Bobby's hand moved to his waist, where he unclasped a pair of handcuffs. Easing the grandmother into a sitting position, he pulled her wrists behind her back. "You have the right to remain silent. You have the right to an attorney. If you cannot afford an attorney—" And here Bobby broke off, delivering the last line a second time with dignity and just a lick of relish before continuing on to the rest. Then, hauling the grandmother to her feet, Bobby took a quick look behind him. "Michael Cowry?"

The man darted a quick look at Bobby.

"That fancy boat you just gaffed at my dock was reported stolen by its owner an hour ago," Bobby told him. "You'd better come with me too."

Julie sat on the edge of the dock, dangling her feet over the side. The salt water lit her scrapes on fire, although she hardly registered the pain. She was soaked and shivering, but couldn't imagine going indoors, or anywhere else, to try to do something about it. She couldn't imagine ever being warm again. Julie had experienced enough grief and loss in her lifetime to sense when it was coming and be able to ward off—if not the dread reality, then at least the slamming unexpectedness of its blow.

Callum hadn't come back. It had been too long. He was on Mercy, either searching fruitlessly for Depot in the sea, or else trying to figure out how to face Julie and tell her that this time, he hadn't been able to save her dog from drowning.

A police car arrived. Julie glimpsed a whirl of lights before she heard the car drive onto the uneven boards of the dock, tires thumping across its surface. She would have to give a statement for the second time in as many days. If only speech wasn't another thing Julie couldn't imagine ever taking part in again.

Going back to Mercy was about the only thing she could foresee doing. Now more than ever, Julie wanted to stay in the last place where Depot had roamed and wandered. Wanted to continue teaching the children who'd also loved him. Maybe things would be different with both Hempstead women widows, the elder having seen the view from below at least once, while the younger no longer had to live out a lie.

"Ms. Weathers?" said a voice behind her.

Peter stood between his parents.

Julie worked up a smile. For Peter, she could do it. Encourage him. Nod the boy on. It had been worth it, hadn't it? She and Depot had risked it all, given everything they possessed, so that Peter could have a chance to live the life he was meant to.

"Mr. Croft—" Peter snuck a look to one side. "I mean, Robert— Bobby—" Another snatched peek.

Bobby gave the boy a crooked smile. "Whatever you want to call us. That will be just fine. And it can change, too, you know. Things can change over time."

Peter looked down at Julie, then took a breath. "Um, my other dad told me what you did. How you figured it all out. I just wanted to say thank you, Ms. Weathers. That was a really cool thing for you to do. That was even cooler than the play."

Tears burned twin trails down Julie's cheeks. She sniffled in, wiping her face with one hand, holding the other out to the boy.

"Ms. Weathers?" Peter said, squeezing her fingers between his own. Julie tried to nod.

He wasn't looking at her anymore. His gaze was fixed on the sea.

"How come you're letting Depot swim by himself? I don't mean to be mean, but your dog's really not that great a swimmer."

Julie's head turned so fast, she felt it in her neck, still sore from Maryanne Hempstead's choking grip. Depot paddled alongside the dock, paws gamely churning the water. He let out his bark of reunion and staggered onto shore.

It was impossible. A dog couldn't swim such a distance, not in the amount of time Depot had had, especially not given his fear of the water.

Julie raced along the dock, lowering herself over the side the instant she could manage the drop, and crouched at the seam where sea met land. Her dog barreled into her, knocking her over in the sand, his wet fur slopping her face.

"Deep, oh my God, Depot, you're here, what happened, are you okay?"

Depot gave her inflamed feet a deliberate, doctorly slather, as if treating the wounds, then added a shower spray across her whole body as he shook himself madly.

Julie heard the drumbeat of feet running across the dock.

"He jumped," Callum shouted. "Right out of my boat as soon as he knew you were here." He swung his legs over the dock and took his own leap, venturing to Julie across the sand.

438

Julie held out her hands, lifted her face, though she didn't take a step away from her dog. Callum lowered his mouth to hers, and when they kissed, she tasted the salt of her tears and his ocean on their lips and their tongues.

Julie felt herself sag in Callum's arms, terror and relief both draining from her in a heady, tingly mix, while Callum kept her upright, pulling just a few inches away to look at her, to check.

"It was," she gasped.

He shook his head, not understanding.

She was too breathless to utter more than a word or two at a time. "Real."

He bent and spoke against her lips. "I don't know if *real* is enough for what that was."

"Gross!" came a voice, and they broke apart.

Peter dangled by his hands, dropping from the dock at a height that drew sharp inhalations of breath from his parents, who stood above him with their hands interlaced. The boy danced across the shore toward Depot and began unknotting hanks of the dog's fur, coaxing strands loose between his fingers. "She was just waiting," he said.

Julie wasn't sure who Peter meant. She thought he might be talking about her, awaiting her dog's safe return.

"My whole life for me." Peter looked up at Julie then, his blond lashes like shafts of sun around his shining blue eyes. "I had another mother. I had a second mother the whole time."

READ ON FOR AN EXCERPT FROM

WICKED RIVER

BY JENNY MILCHMAN

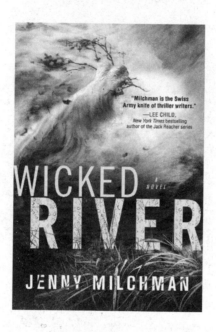

AVAILABLE NOW FROM

SOURCEBOOKS LANDMARK

ONE YEAR BEFORE

Twigs and branches tore at her arms like razor wire, so fast was she running. Breath coming in bull puffs, stinging her nose, drying out her throat and mouth. Her feet churned the soil into clouds of dust. It hadn't rained in weeks, the driest August on record.

If rain had been predicted, Terry wouldn't be here right now, caught in this mad race to a nonexistent finish line. She always checked the Weather Channel assiduously before a hike. Five-day forecasts were relatively accurate, and Terry didn't backpack for more than three. That way, she only had to take two days off, brackets around a weekend, including time for travel. As with everything else, Terry was practical in her outdoor pursuits. She didn't push herself to cover long distances, nor deal with things like bad weather. Trying to get a stove lit under a drumbeat of rain, slick outer gear humidifying the inside of your tent. Who needed that?

What she wouldn't give right now for the annoyances of a drowned-out expedition.

He was right behind her.

Huh, huh, huh came the breaths she fought to drag in. She could feel their pulse in her eardrums. She couldn't keep going at this pace much longer. She'd had a head start, but the man was taller and fleeter than she, made strong by all the work entailed in the shelter he was starting to build.

He had asked Terry if she wanted to see the shelter, and for a moment, she'd been tempted. With horrified regret, she recalled the keen insight and interest the man had exhibited in her approach to hiking and equipment preferences. His attention had been compelling. But coming to her senses—just go off with a strange man in the woods?—Terry had declined, and then he had gotten angry.

That was when she ran.

Woods surrounded her on all sides, both cape and canopy. She broke through another pincushion of sticks, shutting her eyes to protect them, hoping the ground would stay level before her. Fat, fleshy leaves slapped at her face; then, she realized that the leaves were actually flying through the air like missiles.

Terry twisted, shooting a look over her shoulder as she raced on.

The man was hacking at trees with a machete, reducing their protruding branches to stubs. Whereas Terry had only her body to use as a blade, which was taking its toll on her. Bubbles of blood dotted her arms; welts stood up on the exposed part of her chest. Her shoes relentlessly beat the clods of earth, stirring up that crematorium wake of ashy dirt behind her.

She had told the man her name. That was the thing Terry couldn't let go of now—how susceptible she had been to his charms. "Terry," he had echoed. "A solid, capable name." If he had said her name was beautiful, or even pretty, the connection would've been lost. Terry herself was neither of those things, and she knew that her name wasn't either. Its full version—Theresa—felt too fancy and she'd adopted the diminutive in girlhood. Terry lived alone, cooked herself solid, nutritious meals, and assisted a pool of doctors during the week, while hiking solo on the weekends. The man seemed to recognize all of this about her, and be drawn to her despite it.

Or because of it.

A meaty stick caught her in the back, thrown like a javelin by the man. Terry nearly went down, but stumbled and regained her footing. She was close to giving up, just stopping like a kid in a game of tag. *Okay, you got me.* He would in the end anyway, wouldn't he? But no, she couldn't die out here in her beloved Adirondacks. The man was close enough now that she could hear the hissing slash of the machete blade, feel a rainfall of slender pine needles when he sliced through the air with the weapon's steel edge. She drilled down and found a final spurt of speed, not daring to take another look behind her.

But the woods were opening up at last, giving way to some other sort of terrain. What was it? Her brain was too oxygen deprived, too terror fueled, to process the change in landscape.

The man hurled his machete in a great, soaring arc of rage, its silver spear turning end over end, headed right for her.

They were at a gully. That was what explained all the sudden space.

Terry dove just before the blade hit the rim of earth and plunged into the ground.

He would expect her to roll all the way to the base of the ravine, use the creek that rushed there to make her escape. Instead, Terry threw both hands out, clawing her nails into dirt, stones, and grit, arresting her fall halfway down the hill. Scrabbling on her belly in panic, praying that her movements were invisible from above, Terry made her way to an overhang of rock and slid beneath it. The stone ceiling protected her

JENNY MILCHMAN

from sight. Terry tasted soil, felt some creature of the earth—a worm, or maybe a small snake—squiggle away, its sinuous body cool against her bare cheek.

The man bushwhacked past the new, wobbly trees that clung to the ravine, maneuvering downhill through brittle, rain-deprived brush, and coming within a few feet of Terry. Upon reaching the bottom, he entered the water and went splashing downriver. After a while, she could no longer hear his churning feet.

Enough time passed that Terry began to picture her getaway. She'd only be half a day later than expected, and who was there to expect her, really? Just the doctor who worked Mondays. Terry pictured signing the Turtle Ridge trail register, her hand shaking so hard that her entry would be nearly illegible, although she would still follow protocol, do the right thing; that was Terry's way. She could actually feel the wooden lid on the box that protected the log, too heavy to hold, given her compromised state. It would fall, catching her bruised and scraped fingers, and she would bite back a bleat of pain.

But at least she'd be safe.

She had saved herself. Calm, capable Terry, far too prepared and competent to wind up in trouble in the woods, would be out of this mess soon.

Then a pair of arms as strong as winches slid beneath the rock and pulled her out.

READING GROUP GUIDE

1. Describe the community of Wedeskyull. Why can't Julie bear to live there anymore?

2. How would you characterize Julie and David's marriage? Do you think it was ever a healthy relationship?

3. Despite the job post sounding a little strange—no Wi-Fi in town, very poor phone service, and an incredibly tight-knit community— Julie wants the teaching job very badly. Would a position like this appeal to you? Why or why not?

4. How did you feel about Ellie when she first meets Julie? Did you trust her?

5. Put yourself in Julie's shoes. How would you feel moving to such a remote place? Would you find it intimidating, or would it feel like a fresh start?

6. Julie feels that there is something off about Martha's relationship with her son, Peter. Why do you think that is?

7. Compare David and Callum. In what ways are the two men different? Are they similar in any way?

8. Describe the Hempsteads' power over the island of Mercy. Are there any characters above the family's influence?

9. At the end of the story, we realize that Peter's odd behavior is a result of a troubled family life. How did Julie misperceive his actions? Do you think her negative impression of him was justified?

10. Think about Melinda, Peter's biological mother. Do you think it's possible for her to make up for the lost time with her son?

11. David visits Mercy and admits to feeling guilty for Hedley's death, and Julie forgives him. What do you think this says about her?

12. Discuss the ways that Julie changes throughout the book. How has she grown?

A CONVERSATION
WITH THE AUTHOR

This novel is deeply rooted in its setting, a remote island off the coast of Maine. Why did you choose Mercy as the main location for your story?

Mercy is a fictional place, but it feels very real to me. My family didn't have a lot of extra money when I was growing up, but one thing my parents saved for every year was a summer vacation in Maine. We stayed in rental cabins, and my mom cooked just like we were at home (except she added some of the regional foods as described in the book!), and these were some of the happiest times of my childhood. After I met my husband during our senior year of college and we were deciding What To Do Next, I had the fantasy of applying for a job in a one-room schoolhouse on Monhegan Island. I have no doubt if we had, it would've gone a lot more smoothly than the plot of *The Second Mother*! I'm drawn to the location because it feels like a part of me...and the dark side and secrets and terror crept in for reasons I can't quite explain, but which seem to happen whenever I write a book.

What does your writing process look like?

I write in the mornings in a tiny backyard studio that has electricity and heat, and that's about it. It doesn't need more than that—it has the stories. Writing a book is one of the purest joys I have, right after being with my family. Not to get all mystical, but it doesn't feel like I'm doing the writing. I don't know where these people and their stories come from really. The process is like being hurled into a whitewater river and tumbled and carried along on a wild, exhilarating, sometimes terrifying but always joyous ride. And if it sounds strange that I write psychological suspense novels—where some pretty scary stuff happens—yet still feel joyful, I think that's because the potential for triumph is so strong. When I'm writing, I am waiting to find out, along with the reader, if my heroine clambers out, dripping and stronger and victorious at the end.

***The Second Mother* delves into one of the greatest fears of motherhood—losing one's children. How did exploring this theme affect you?**

It was so hard to write about that even responding to this question is difficult. I give thanks for my children every single day. What Julie suffered was grief of an unimaginable sort—unless someone has been through it. And what I found, when she was the heroine I was living with during the nearly two years of writing and polishing this novel, was that her grief wasn't limited to what happened to her baby girl, but extended to all the parts of life the two of them never got to share. My hope is that as Julie climbs back out of an existence that had become intolerable to her, it might give readers who are experiencing or have experienced their own losses a little bit of light as well.

When you're not writing, what kinds of books do you like to read?

I am a huge reader of my own genre, psychological or literary suspense. I find that sometimes my tastes align with what other people love—I am a big fan of books by, say, Liane Moriarty and Ruth Ware,

Gregg Hurwitz and Lee Child—but some of the authors I find the most talented are less discovered than I think they deserve to be. Big shout-out to Koren Zailckas: no one does suspense and fractured family relationships like she does. I love wilderness thrillers; Tim Johnston's are gems. And also books about the great divide in this country, of which David Joy's work is a terrific example. I was weaned on the horror of the 1970s and still go back to Stephen King, Frank De Felitta, Ira Levin, and others when I need comfort (as crazy as that sounds).

Julie works hard to make connections with the children of Mercy's insular community. Can you talk a little bit about her role as a teacher?

First of all, may I say that teachers are the unsung heroes of this country, and if I could give every single one of them a raise—and an even longer vacation—I would. I mean, seriously, we put some of our most precious, beloved relationships in their hands, five days out of the week and ten months out of the year, and they in turn educate, nurture, and inspire our kids. No salary or benefit package can repay that. So when I was writing Julie's role as schoolteacher, it was really important to me to convey how challenging and all-encompassing the position can be. I think that what Julie does well, and what the best teachers all seem to do, judging by my own kids, is to be honest with the students. Teachers don't have to know everything, their roles as purveyors of knowledge notwithstanding. It's sometimes hardest to say what you don't know.

This book is full of flawed, dynamic characters. Which was the most challenging to write?

Callum. Hands-down. He is the opposite of me: a man's man, used to working with his hands not his thoughts, and emotionally, the way he reacts is by holding things in. I am much more the spill-it-out type. It took me at least four drafts before I got (I hope) his voice and how he would behave when intensely drawn to someone in a way that meant all those blocked-off feelings would begin to rise to the surface. Watching him start to fall in love with Julie without once coming out and saying so was tricky to translate as an author. Callum is all subtext; he didn't let me put anything directly onto the page.

Are you working on anything new?

I just started my latest Wedeskyull novel! It's a big change for me because the antagonist is in some ways also the heroine of the story—at least she thinks she is—while the real heroine's entire life is held together with pins and air. (The latter may not be such a departure, come to think of it.) The story is about a woman whose son has been diagnosed with a spectrum disorder, so she seeks help from a controversial and dynamic practitioner, known for treatments that are way, way outside the box.

What do you think Julie's journey teaches us about grief?

My guess is that this answer will be different for everybody. For me, it was a privilege to get to write about the resiliency many people have at their core—a thrust toward life, no matter how beaten down their circumstances may have made them. In *Jurassic Park* by Michael Crichton, Ian Malcolm says, "Life will find a way." This can be a good thing—or a total horror show, at least where dinosaurs are concerned. But I believe that Julie exemplifies this truism in the most positive of ways.

Why did you choose to center this story so heavily on motherhood?

Motherhood is at the center of so much, isn't it? We all have mothers—even when two fathers raise a child, there was an egg involved, and that egg lived inside a woman. Even when a mother is not present, the shadow of her is. Motherhood is at the core of religions, myths, and philosophies. And as you say, it's the raw, beating heart of this novel, right down to its title. I wanted to write a book about the many facets of motherhood, how it can be the most precious of roles to one woman, and not even wanted by another. You can be the first mother, or the second, or never a mother at all, and each of these is an equally valid approach to life.

What do you ultimately want readers to take away from this story?

That hope, even when it has flagged to a tiny, dim spark, is worth holding on to. One day, it might burst again into flame.

ACKNOWLEDGMENTS

Some readers know that I am not the most, um, adept when it comes to research. In fact, I have a saying that goes "If I can make it up, I will." Actually, I just came up with that saying this second, so I don't know if it can be called a saying yet—but I suspect it will still hold true if I am lucky enough to be writing to you fifty books from now.

However, there's a limit to how well a writer from the land-locked Catskill Mountains who grew up in suburban New Jersey can write about life on an island and the lobster industry of Maine without doing any research. I can only hope that I did justice to this fierce, beautiful, and ever-changing way of life. To the extent that I did, I am indebted first and foremost to the work of James M. Acheson and his scholarly books, especially *The Lobster Gangs of Maine*. Mr. Acheson coined a term that I made use of in this novel and was kind enough to provide updates per the changing times of the industry by being in close personal communication, answering questions only a complete neophyte could ask. And with whom did Mr. Acheson communicate? That would be my son, Caleb, whose tireless, exacting, and just plain intelligent efforts in the research department allow me to skate by. I also read *The Lobster Chronicles: Life on a Very Small Island* by Linda Greenlaw (of *The Perfect Storm* fame). Thanks to the miracle of YouTube, Capt. John's Bar showed me what a day on a real, live lobster boat is like. Any errors, mistakes, or misconceptions are entirely mine, and please chalk them up to flights of imagination—versus the aforementioned deficits in the research department.

Over two years ago, I was lucky enough to find a home at one of the most venerable yet cutting-edge publishers on the literary landscape. My deep thanks go to Dominique Raccah for demonstrating every day that one can have both an abiding and lifelong passion for books *and* the ability to steer a ship through the tumultuous seas of major media. One part of that is hiring some of the most talented editors I've been lucky enough to work with. Thank you, Shana Drehs, for the depth of your vision, and for never letting me stop at the easier or lesser stages of a book; thanks to Margaret Johnston, for your eagle eye and ability to fine-tune a scene to a needle-sharp point; and thanks to Diane Dannenfeldt for myriad catches—and more than one great suggestion as well. Thanks to Heather Hall and the entire production team.

The independent publicists of JKS Communications have launched many a literary career—including my own—but what is really wonderful about this particular firm is the way they are in it for the long haul, playing the long game that is required to build a writing career, a marathon, never a sprint, with passion, wisdom, and one heckuva Rolodex. My thanks go to Julie Schoerke and Marissa DeCuir, publicists, booklovers, and friends extraordinaire.

After one's spouse and one's family, a literary agent is probably the next closest thing to a relationship that needs to be there through thick and thin, and—for a very lucky writer—has a degree of click and connection as well. My thanks to Julia Kenny, whose vision, doggedness, and belief have guided my career since my debut novel—and for quite a few years before that. Thanks to everyone at Dunow, Carlson & Lerner for all the work that goes into being one of the top boutique agencies in the country, and one I am proud to be represented by.

To the booksellers who welcome me and my books into their stores—thank you for providing a warm, beating epicenter of face-to-face exchanges, stories in which to get lost, and sometimes just a simple place to sit down. Bookstores are like *The Giving Tree*! These pleasures are all too often shunted aside in today's virtual, (dis)connected world; their value is all too easy to underestimate. But you, keepers of bookstores, never do.

The librarians and libraries that are the great equalizers of this country, making books and information and intellect available to all who seek them—thank you for offering safe harbor to me since I was a very little girl. Seeing my books in one of those cellophane jackets on one of your shelves was always a bucket-list item for me.

To the reviewers who have supported me through each book, from Denver, Colorado, out west to Washington State and San Francisco, back east to Rhode Island and New York City, plus many places in between—my thanks. I hope this one takes you away, and that I have done you proud.

To the book bloggers who make word of mouth virtual—you are the online tastemakers and I am grateful to you every day. I hope you love what you do half as much as we authors love you for doing it. Thanks, Suzy Approved, for the awesome party—and Tamara and Kristin, so great to see you there!

Thank you, International Thriller Writers, Sisters in Crime, and Mystery Writers of America—writing organizations that offer support, resources, and more than a little bit of fun.

To the readers and book club leaders who say that a Jenny Milchman novel leaves you feeling just a little bit stronger—thank you. You are the ones I write for.

Thanks to James and Viv, boots on the ground in Portland, Oregon.

Finally, last but really first, to Josh and Sophie and Caleb, my very first readers, first in my heart.

ABOUT THE AUTHOR

Jenny Milchman is the author of four other psychological thrillers. She speaks and teaches nationally and has traveled to nearly one thousand bookstores across the country—and beyond. Jenny lives in the Catskill Mountains with her family.

Photo © Franco Vogt Photography